Puffin Books

DEADLY!

Sprocket's lost his memory.
Amy's lost her dad. So now
the two of them are on a quest
that will take them to the weirdest
nudist colony in the world.

Uncovering deadly secret after deadly
secret, Amy and Sprocket are lured deeper into
a mystery that gets more exciting with every turn
of the page.

The best-selling, spine-tingling tale.
Two wicked authors.
One DEADLY volume.

You could die laughing!

OTHER BOOKS BY

ALSO AVAILABLE BY MORRIS AND PAUL

DEADLY!

All six books in one

MORRIS GLEITZMAN & PAUL JENNINGS

Puffin Books

PUFFIN BOOKS

Published by the Penguin Group
Penguin Group (Australia)
250 Camberwell Road, Camberwell, Victoria 3124, Australia
(a division of Pearson Australia Group Pty Ltd)
Penguin Group (USA) Inc.
375 Hudson Street, New York, New York 10014, USA
Penguin Group (Canada)
90 Eglinton Avenue East, Suite 700, Toronto ON M4P 2Y3, Canada
(a division of Pearson Penguin Canada Inc.)
Penguin Books Ltd
80 Strand, London WC2R 0RL, England
Penguin Ireland
25 St Stephen's Green, Dublin 2, Ireland
(a division of Penguin Books Ltd)
Penguin Books India Pvt Ltd
11, Community Centre, Panchsheel Park, New Delhi-110 017, India
Penguin Group (NZ)
67 Apollo Drive, Rosedale, North Shore 0632, New Zealand
(a division of Pearson New Zealand Ltd)
Penguin Books (South Africa) (Pty) Ltd
24 Sturdee Avenue, Rosebank, Johannesburg 2196, South Africa

Penguin Books Ltd, Registered Offices: 80 Strand, London WC2R 0RL, England

First published in six volumes by Penguin Books Australia, 2001
This edition first published by Penguin Books Australia, 2002

18 17 16 15 14 13 12 11 10 9

Text copyright © Lockley Lodge Pty Ltd and Creative Input Pty Ltd, 2001

The moral right of the authors has been asserted.

Designed by George Dale, Penguin Design Studio
Cover and text illustrations by Dean Gorissen
Typeset in Sabon 10.5 pt by Midland Typesetters, Maryborough, Victoria
Printed in Australia by McPherson's Printing Group, Maryborough, Victoria

National Library of Australia
Cataloguing-in-Publication data:
Gleitzman, Morris, 1953- .
Deadly! all six books in one.

ISBN 978 0 14 330024 3.

1. Adventure - Juvenile fiction. I. Jennings, Paul, 1943- .
II. Gleitzman, Morris, 1953- Hunt. III. Jennings, Paul,
1943- Hunt. IV. Gleitzman, Morris, 1953- Brats. V.
Jennings, Paul, 1943- Brats. VI. Gleitzman, Morris, 1953-
Grope. VII. Jennings, Paul, 1943- Grope. VIII. Gleitzman,
Morris, 1953- Pluck. IX. Jennings, Paul, 1943- Pluck. X.
Gleitzman, Morris, 1953- Stiff. XI. Jennings, Paul, 1943-
Stiff. XII. Gleitzman, Morris, 1953- Nude. Jennings, Paul,
1943- Nude. Title.

A823.3

www.puffin.com.au

CONTENTS

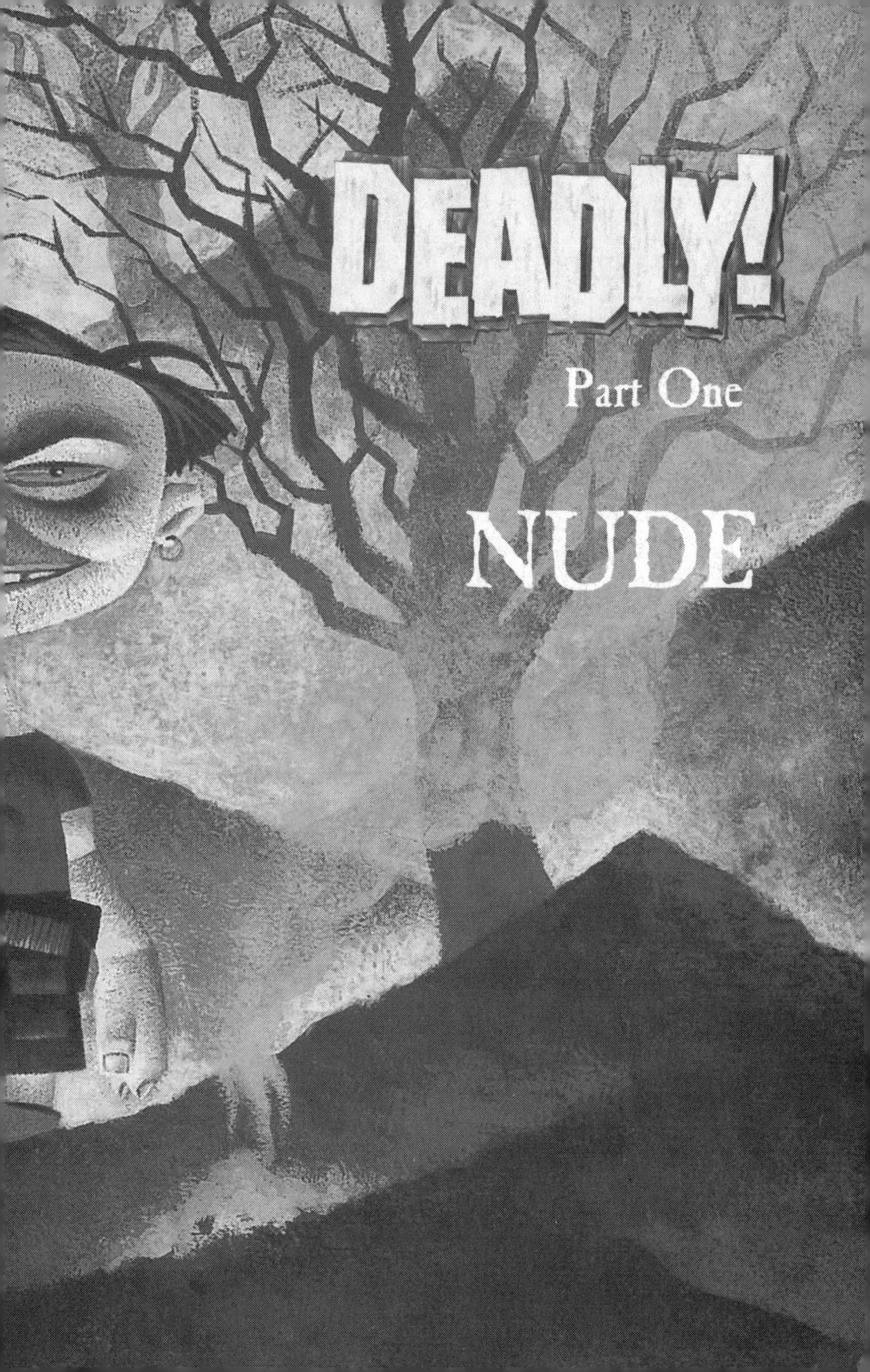
DEADLY!
Part One
NUDE

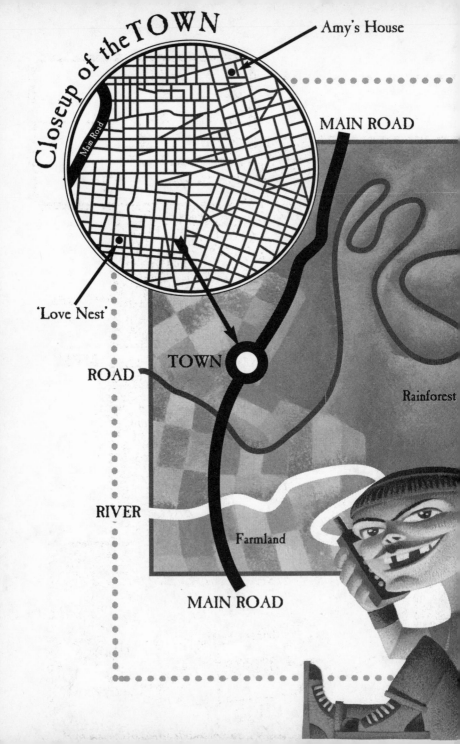

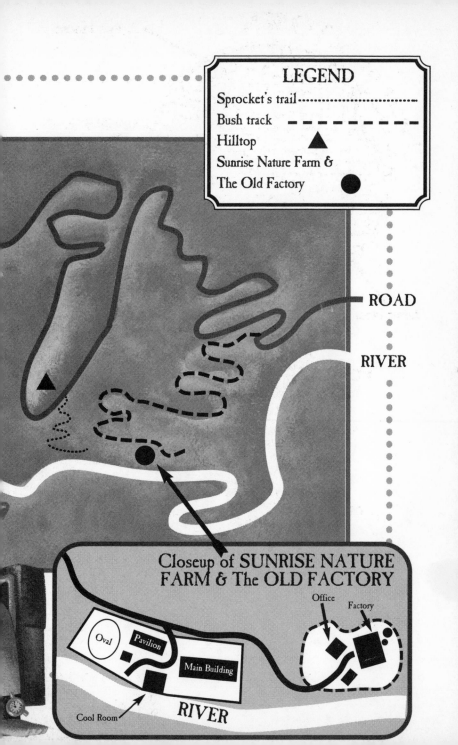

LEGEND

Sprocket's trail.............................

Bush track — — — — — —

Hilltop ▲

Sunrise Nature Farm &
The Old Factory ●

ROAD

RIVER

Closeup of SUNRISE NATURE
FARM & The OLD FACTORY

Oval   Pavilion

Main Building

Office   Factory

Cool Room

RIVER

SPROCKET

There were three things for sure.

I was naked.

I didn't know who I was.

And I needed to go to the loo.

Stones cut into my cold, bare feet as I hobbled across the narrow hillside track. I made my way to a rocky clearing and squatted down behind a tree. It would have to do. There was no toilet. And no paper. But when you have to go, you have to go.

'Ah,' I said. 'That's better.'

I cleaned myself up as best I could with some leaves from a shrub.

Then I picked up a handful of dirt to cover the large lump of poo I had deposited there.

'Drop that,' snapped a voice from behind me.

I turned around and saw a boy about six years old with a pretty face and curly blond hair. He wore an outfit like a jungle fighter. Not dress-ups – the real thing. Only pint-sized.

The dirt fell from my hand as I stared at him with astonishment. 'Hey,' I said. 'Where did you come from? Where's your mummy?'

Maybe I could help him and he could help me. I had woken with the dawn. Naked on the grass. That's all I knew about myself.

He didn't answer. He was an odd little kid. In one hand he held a small spoon. And in the other a mobile phone. He flicked the phone open, pressed a couple of buttons and spoke quickly into it.

'He's here,' he said into the phone. 'About half a kilometre along the track.' He glanced at my half-covered poop. 'And he's done a nice big one.'

A look of annoyance crossed his face and he began jabbing away at the buttons with his fingers. 'You're breaking up,' he yelled into the phone. He began pacing around trying to find a spot with better reception. Suddenly he threw the phone down on the ground and jumped on it. 'Pathetic,' he shouted. 'Cheap rubbish.'

'It's all right, Titch,' I told him. 'Your mummy can't be far away. Don't get upset. We'll find her.'

Maybe his mother could also help me. At least she might have some clothes I could borrow.

I tried to sound relaxed but I was worried. What was his mum going to say when she saw me in the nude?

The angelic little boy had a devilish smile. He didn't appear surprised that I was naked. And he seemed to know who I was. 'Just you stay there, son,' he said. 'You're not going to get away this time.'

Talk about weird. He should have been at kindergarten doing a finger painting or having milk and fruit. Not standing here in the rainforest ordering me around like a bossy bank manager. Maybe he was a relation. Maybe he was my little brother. He had hard eyes. But perhaps I had hard eyes too. I didn't even know what I looked like. It was a terrible feeling.

'Do you know me?' I asked.

'Just you take it easy,' he answered. 'There's no one around here to help you. Think about it. Consider your options. All alone in the bush, naked with no food. Better to give yourself up. This is rough country. You need clothes.'

He was right. The morning sun was just beginning to rise and I was shivering in the cool morning air.

And embarrassed.

He talked funny for a little kid. The words seemed too big for his mouth. I started to feel uneasy. But surely this little boy couldn't hurt me? He was only half my size.

The angel-faced brat reached into his pocket and took out a large white handkerchief. 'I think you have something that belongs to me,' he said.

He was crazy. I was stark naked. I had no pockets.

What could I possibly have that belonged to someone else?

Dimples appeared on his rosy cheeks. He grinned with delight, dropped to his knees and spread the handkerchief out on the ground. 'Good,' he said, motioning at my fresh piece of poop. He gently scooped it up with the spoon and placed it on the handkerchief. He looked at the big brown lump of poo with sparkling eyes. As if it was made of gold.

Oh yuck. He was pinching my poop. Shovelling up my . . . Disgusting. Gross. Surely this was a dream? It must be a nightmare.

The kid was too confident for his age. His eyes were old. They seemed to know things that they shouldn't. They weren't the eyes of a child. It just didn't make sense.

This couldn't be happening. At any moment I would wake up to find a smiling mother telling me that everything was all right.

I made one last effort to be friendly. 'What's your name?' I asked.

'Shut up,' he said. He was peering down the rough hilly track.

I put on a false grin. 'OK,' I said. 'If you won't tell me your name I'll call you Pooper Scooper.'

He didn't reply. He was listening to the sound of an engine. An engine with a loud, unfriendly growl.

Someone else was coming.

Pooper Scooper jumped to his feet as a truck

rumbled around the bend. It was a four-wheel drive, a khaki-coloured Hummer. A low, mean military vehicle with huge off-road tyres. It left the track and crawled right over a large rock in the clearing. I half expected to see soldiers staring through the narrow slit of its windscreen. But I couldn't see anyone. The glass was tinted black.

The driver jumped out onto the long grass. A girl. She was a little kid too. About the same age as Pooper Scooper – five or six at the most. What was she doing driving a truck? She must have been sitting on a pillow just to see over the steering wheel. She wore red and blue racing-car gloves, a baseball cap and a driving jacket fit for a Formula One champion. It was covered in advertisements and bright sewn-on patches. One of them read, REPTILE. The name suited her. She licked her lips with a flicking tongue. Just like a lizard about to catch a fly.

Someone inside lifted a canvas flap on the back of the Hummer. Two more infants jumped out. They were dressed in expensive walking gear. They had Nike boots and designer jeans. One wore a woollen beanie on his head. The other had spiky red hair and scowled a lot.

They carried backpacks with aluminium frames. Ropes, knives and whistles hung from their belts. The knives had big blades and burnt bone handles. Everything they owned was new and shiny – state of the art. Each of them had a mobile phone strapped on at the waist. They all sported military watches and compasses. The red-haired guerilla held a large net.

Each one had the same creepy, knowing eyes.

I just stood there gaping at the crazy sight. And as I did a feeling of coming danger crawled over my naked skin. An alarm bell rang inside my brain. I was naked but they didn't seem to care. I felt like . . . prey.

'Time to go,' I said to myself.

Too late. The little scowler's net fell over my head and wrapped itself around my naked body. I felt a rope being tied around my ankles.

The tiny hunters had me trapped.

The kid in the beanie shouted excitedly at Pooper Scooper. 'Where is it?'

Pooper Scooper pointed to his handkerchief on the ground near by. For a moment they lost interest in me. They all gathered excitedly around my piece of poop. Beanie was so worked up that he began jabbing at it with his bare fingers. Reptile pulled off bits of poo with her gloved hand. Scowler sliced it into sections with his Bowie knife. His wild cuts just missed Beanie's fingers. The whole four of them scuffled and pushed like a bunch of infants at a party trying to grab the biggest piece of cake.

'Get back,' snarled Pooper Scooper. 'I'm in charge here.' He shoved the others aside and recommenced investigating my poop with his spoon. He had a cute face but a nasty voice. Underneath those dimples Pooper Scooper was an ugly person.

'Sorry, Orson,' said Beanie.

'Careful,' said Scowler in a low voice. 'Don't damage it. This could be our last chance.'

I began to struggle inside the net. I had to get away from these insane children. But the more I struggled the more tangled I became.

'It's not there,' shrieked Pooper Scooper.

Now they were interested in *me*. Very interested. Scowler wiped his knife on the grass and joined the others as they formed a circle around me. Each one of them had a murderous expression. I looked for some sign of mercy. Only Beanie had a face with any suggestion of doubt. Behind his angry looks his eyes were not as hard as the others.

These little kids outnumbered me four to one. But I was twice as big as they were. If I could only get out of the net I might have a chance.

I was terrified but my brain was racing. I grunted and shrieked as if my senses had completely left me. I bucked up and down and squirmed and wriggled like a wild boar.

'He's panicking,' yelled Beanie. 'He might hurt himself.'

'We wouldn't want that,' said Scowler, sneering. He jumped up into the air and gave me a swift kick in the neck with the sole of his boot.

I gasped at the pain and held my hands to my throat. Then I collapsed with my eyes closed.

'He's choking,' said Reptile. 'We need him alive.'

'For now,' said Pooper Scooper.

'Don't damage him,' yelled Reptile. 'He's our last chance.'

'He's dead,' said Beanie in a worried voice.

Pooper Scooper picked up my wrist and felt for a pulse. 'No he's not,' he said. 'He's just fainted. What a weakling.'

I felt them undo the ropes, lift off the net and carry me to a patch of soft grass. Reptile forced a flask between my lips and poured in some cold water. I coughed and spluttered and sat up.

Scowler fixed me with an angry glare. His red spikes of hair whipped around like snakes as he angrily shook his head. 'Where is it?' he said. 'Hand it over and nothing more will happen to you.'

'Where's what?'

'Don't try that,' said Scowler. 'You know exactly what we want.' He looked ready to spring into the air.

'I don't,' I yelled. 'I don't even know who I am.'

'Very good. Very good indeed,' said Pooper Scooper sarcastically. I could see that he was their leader. 'We'll take him back with us,' he told the others. 'Where we can make him talk.'

I went cold all over. They were going to torture me.

'Aaargh,' I shrieked.

The child commandos fell back. Just for a second. Enough time for me to jump to my feet and dash between Scowler and Pooper Scooper. They both leapt at me but I was too fast. I bolted down the track like a rat out of a trap. The pain of the gravel under my bare feet was terrible but I couldn't stop. There was no way I was going to let these fiendish little terrorists take me prisoner. I jumped into the under-growth and pushed my way through the ferns and hanging vines.

And behind me, yelling and shrieking and crashing through the forest, came the Brats from Hell.

AMY

TWO

Mum tried really hard not to lose her temper on my birthday, but in the end she just couldn't help it.

'Where is your father?' she yelled, slamming the kettle down onto the kitchen table so hard all the cutlery jumped. 'What is he doing? He's been gone

an hour and thirteen minutes. It's only a ten-minute trip.'

It wasn't just the cutlery that jumped. The walkman Mum and Dad gave me for my birthday jumped too. Right off the end of the table onto the floor.

A couple of bits of plastic snapped off.

'Oh, Amy. I'm sorry,' wailed Mum, picking up the pieces. 'I'm sorry. I really am.'

I was pretty upset, but it wasn't Mum's fault. She'd had a really unhappy childhood. That can make you a pretty angry person. And a bit jealous when someone else is having a happy birthday. I'd seen it happen when kids at school had birthdays.

Plus I knew Mum was really stressed about Dad.

'An hour and fifteen minutes,' she yelled furiously. 'An hour and fifteen minutes to buy a birthday breakfast from a deli that's five minutes drive away and he's still not back.'

I looked at her angry, unhappy face and that's when I decided to do it.

What I should have done years before.

Make Dad confess.

Get it out in the open. The reason he was always disappearing on us.

Before I could even rehearse how I was going to do it, the back door flew open and Dad hurried in. 'Sorry,' he said, dumping a bag of take-away food containers on the table.

'An hour and sixteen minutes,' said Mum icily.

Dad looked at her sheepishly. 'I know what you're thinking,' he said. 'You're thinking I could have walked there on my hands in that time and hopped back carrying these pancakes on my head.' Dad put his hand on his bald patch. 'Which I could have done,' he said to me with a rueful grin, 'when I still had hair.' He gave Mum a nervous glance. 'I had to drop into work. Sorry.'

That's when I should have done it.

I should have looked him in the eye, or rather his steamed-up glasses, and said, 'Dad, I know you're having an affair with another woman.'

I took a deep breath and opened my mouth to say it. But before I could, Dad completely took the wind out of my sails.

He reached into his jacket pocket and handed me a birthday present. Another one.

'Happy birthday, Princess,' he said, and kissed me on the cheek.

'Thanks, Dad,' I stammered. I gave him a peck back. He was grinning at me expectantly. I tore off the paper.

It was a Swiss Army knife.

I needed a moment to pull myself together, partly because it was the biggest Swiss Army knife I'd ever seen, and partly because if I'd known I was getting a separate present from Dad, I'd have asked for a book token. So I could get Mum and Dad a book. *How to Repair Your Marriage After an Affair.*

'It's got twenty-seven implements,' said Dad enthusiastically. 'You'll be able to help all sorts of people with that.'

That's my dad. He loves helping people. Twenty-seven times if they let him.

Except for quite a while now he's been helping himself. To another woman.

'Thanks, Dad,' I said again, quietly.

Now, I said to myself, say it now.

But before I could, Mum cut in. 'Work,' she said bitterly. And she gave Dad one of her looks.

I'll say this for Dad, he didn't flinch. When Mum gives me one of her looks, my guts turn to soggy cauliflower.

'If work's more important than your own daughter's birthday,' Mum's look to Dad said, 'why don't you move in there?'

When three people have been together as long as me and Mum and Dad, you don't always need words. Sometimes looks are enough.

Mum glanced disdainfully at the Swiss Army knife. 'Don't you think Amelia's a bit old for a penknife?' she said to Dad.

I started to explain that it was more of a tool set than a penknife, but I didn't finish. Mum was looking even angrier than usual.

'Life's an adventure,' protested Dad, picking up the Swiss Army knife and pulling out an implement that looked like it was for removing kidney stones from small mammals. 'Amy can't get out there and explore life without the right tools.'

Mum didn't even answer him. She turned to me. 'Start on your cheese and asparagus pancakes, Princess,' she said. 'I'll go and mend your walkman.'

'Please, Mum,' I said. 'Leave it till later. Let's just all have our pancakes together.'

Suddenly Mum put her arms round me. I was startled because she hadn't done that for a while. It felt good.

'I just need a moment to calm down,' she said quietly. 'So I don't forget myself and kill your father on your birthday. I'll be fine when I've had a cup of tea.'

She grabbed the bits of walkman and went upstairs.

My insides sagged.

It was one of the signs, I knew. When parents start giving you separate presents, it was one of the signs their marriage was almost over. The kids at school had told me.

I had to get the repair work started.

Now was my chance.

I took another deep breath.

It was only ten twenty-five. I was born at ten thirty-two, so my birthday didn't really start for another seven minutes.

I could still keep the vow I'd made to myself. To confront Dad before another year of my life started. Another year of worry and sleepless nights and feeling sick half the time.

All I had to do was look at him across the kitchen table and say it.

'I know there's another woman,' I'd say. 'All those nights you come in late and think I'm asleep and creep into my room to give me a kiss, you pong of her perfume. You're just lucky Mum eats so much garlic or she'd smell it too.'

By now he'd probably be pale with shock, but I wouldn't stop.

'I know why you're doing it,' I'd continue. 'You think Mum doesn't love you any more. Well, she does. We both do. Mum can't help being a grouch. You know she had an unhappy childhood. Stop it, Dad. Give this other woman the flick. Come back to us.'

I knew every word of it off by heart. I'd rehearsed it under the bedcovers a million times. And now the moment had come to say it.

I took several deep breaths, gulped down some orange juice and cleared my throat.

'Dad . . .' I said.

He looked up from the deli box, a cheese and asparagus pancake wobbling on the fish slice in his hand. I cleared my throat again.

'Dad . . .'

I couldn't do it. The words wouldn't come.

I don't know why. Maybe it was because he looked so anxious and stressed and tired. Maybe I was worried that when Mum found out she'd kill him with the fish slice. Maybe I was a born coward.

If I'd been braver, maybe I could have stopped that day turning into a nightmare.

Maybe I wouldn't have ended up staggering down the street with my life in tatters.

Maybe, maybe, maybe.

The fact was, I couldn't say ninety simple little words.

Instead, Dad put the cheese and asparagus pancake on my plate and sighed. 'Listen, Princess,' he said. 'I know it's your birthday and I wish I didn't have to, but I've got to pop back into work and do a few chores and improve the state of civilisation as we know it. Sorry.'

'That's OK,' I said.

But it wasn't OK. It was Saturday. The vegie factory was closed for the weekend, and that included Dad's plant genetics laboratory.

He'd lied to me again.

We ate our pancakes in silence.

'When I get back this afternoon,' said Dad suddenly, 'we'll have a birthday tea. With a surprise.'

'OK,' I said quietly.

How, I thought miserably, can a highly educated scientist who's responsible for the health of most of the tomatoes, peas and carrots in this part of the state be so bad at observing stuff?

Like how sad my voice was sounding.

Mum was just as bad. She was studying ancient

history. It was a really hard course, specially doing it off the Internet. How could a person as intelligent as her not have noticed what was going on with Dad? She might have been good at ancient history, but she was really dumb at recent history.

'What have you got planned this morning?' asked Dad.

'I'm meeting some friends in town,' I mumbled.

I didn't like lying on my birthday, but Dad had lied to me enough, so I didn't feel too bad.

'That's nice,' said Dad.

I tried to smile but I couldn't.

'Dad,' I wanted to say, 'for the last five years I've been at a boarding school three hundred kilometres away. I'm only in town for a few weeks each year. How could I have any friends here?'

I kept quiet.

Upstairs I could hear Mum running a bath, so I didn't wait around for my walkman. Mum's baths could go on for hours.

Dad was in his bedroom when I yelled goodbye. Even from the bottom of the stairs I could see he was changing into one of his best jackets. The one with leather patches on the elbows that Mum reckoned made him look like a nerd.

'See you at your birthday tea,' he yelled.

I didn't answer. I was going to be seeing him before that.

After I slammed the front door, I crept over to the

carport, opened Dad's car, released the boot catch, climbed into the boot and closed the lid.

I lay in the darkness, smelling the rubber of the spare tyre and listening to my heart thump and having an awful feeling that this birthday wasn't going to be a happy one.

Then I heard Dad get into the car and start the engine and I felt us reversing out of the driveway.

I'd never been so scared and miserable.

There's a thing kids at boarding school do when they feel scared and miserable, which is quite often. They close their eyes and pretend they're someone who's even worse off than them.

I did that in the boot as I bumped along the road.

I pretended I was a kid who didn't have enough to eat. When that didn't work, I imagined I was a kid in a war. When that didn't work, I pretended I was alone and cold and naked on a hillside.

Even that didn't work.

It was strange.

The one thought that made me feel better was also the thought that terrified me the most.

That very soon I'd finally know the truth.

SPROCKET

THREE

Branches tore at my skin. Leaves and twigs whipped my face as I plunged through the bushes like a wild beast. Behind me came the wicked cries of the little soldiers.

The rainforest was cool and damp. The calls of kookaburras and bellbirds rang out as I forced my way over creeks and through strands of thick tree ferns.

I sucked in the cold morning air with great gasps. On and on, crushing and thumping, never stopping to look behind. But instinctively moving downhill. Heading towards the low land where I might just possibly get help. The shrill voices of the enemy grew fainter and fainter.

But I knew they were following my trail.

Finally I could go no further. I fell to the ground and tried to silence my roaring breath. The sound was like a terrible gusting wind. Surely anyone within a couple of kilometres could have heard it. I had to hide.

With my last remaining strength I pushed myself into a hollow log.

It was dark inside and there was only just enough

room for me to squeeze in. My arms were pinned to my sides. The log was only open at one end and my feet stuck out behind me. I was wedged in like a cork in a bottle. I just hoped and hoped that the bleeding soles of my feet could not be seen by any evil little child who might be out there.

As my eyes became adjusted to the dark, the rough shape of the rotting log became a little clearer. It was damp and smelt of musty fungi. I lay there shivering. Time passed. All was still. And silent. I used the time to think. I was alone in the world. There was not one face that I could remember.

'Mum?' I said. The word sounded strange to me. As if I had never used it. Who was my mother? Did I have one?

Suddenly two points of light glowed a few centimetres from my face. They blinked.

There was only one image inside my head. It froze my brain. It took over the log. It filled the universe. The vision of a slithering scaled horror.

Every nerve in my body called out. Get away, run, wriggle out. Better to be taken prisoner than to die and rot in a coffin-log in the depths of the forest.

'Hssss.'

The snake struck just below my right eye. Its fangs pierced my cheek like two super-heated needles. I shook my head wildly from side to side but it clung on, writhing in the darkness.

Somehow I managed to stifle my screams. I pushed

backwards, scraping elbows and knees in a wild reverse crawl. I sprang to my feet and grabbed the snake. I ripped it away from my stinging cheek and threw it into the ferns. Blood dribbled down my face.

The snake slithered out of sight but not before I had seen one thing. It was green. A grass snake. Not poisonous. Not dangerous.

Not deadly like the Brats who were even now searching the forest somewhere behind me.

I stood still, listening and rubbing my cheek where it hurt. The sun had grown warm where it filtered through the trees and the hum of insects filled the air. A million thoughts buzzed inside my head. But I gathered them in, carefully sorting out each new idea. Concentrating on what was important.

I was in a desperate situation. Naked and alone in the forest. There *would* be poisonous snakes around for sure. And the kid commandos were searching for me with ropes and knives.

And to make matters worse my stomach-ache was coming back. I felt as if something was jumping around inside my belly. It was swollen and gurgling as if I had drunk too much Coke.

Suddenly my heart stopped. *Snap*. The sharp sound of a twig breaking cracked through the trees. Someone was walking around. And not far off.

I stood still, moving only my eyeballs. I tried to be a tree standing still and silent. Out of the corner of my eye I could see someone moving.

A big person. That's all I could tell. Big and heavy. Moving slowly. I was saved. Help was at hand.

I opened my mouth to call out but something stopped me. Just in time. The person was searching. Pushing aside leaves and branches. Pausing to peer into logs and burrows.

Slowly, slowly, slowly I turned my head towards the intruder.

Amazing. Incredible. Impossible.

A naked man. A huge fellow with a great big belly. He had long greasy hair and a matted black beard. His chest was covered in tight curls. But apart from his own hair he wore nothing. Not a stitch. He was as naked as . . .

Me.

He continued to walk slowly in my direction, looking under each bush. It was only a matter of time before he saw me. At any second he was going to look up and see a tree that looked like a naked boy. Even though the day was cool my skin was clammy. Did I belong to this man? Was he searching for me – his long-lost son? Or was he with the child terrorists under orders from that bossy little Pooper Scooper?

Whatever it was, he was big enough to rip my head off with his huge hands. There was no way I could escape him if he saw me.

'Aha,' he suddenly bellowed. 'Gotcha.'

I gasped in terror. I was dead. I was gone. I was history. I was . . .

Saved.

He bent down, reached under some vines and grabbed something. He hadn't seen me at all. He had found what he was looking for. And it wasn't me.

A ball. A volleyball. He tucked it under his arm and went crashing through the trees at a great rate. Now I saw that he wasn't totally naked. He was wearing a pair of boots. How I wished they were mine.

I waited until he was almost out of sight and began to hobble after him. I couldn't show myself. He still might be with the enemy. Little kids liked balls, even kids with mobile phones and knives. He could be leading me right to them. I had to keep my distance. I couldn't trust anyone. But I had to stay with him. He knew the way out of the forest.

Suddenly I caught sight of something that made me feel better. Through a break in the trees I saw a dusty track curling its way up a distant ridge. A tiny speck was speeding up it in a cloud of dust. It was a long way off but I was certain that it was the Hummer.

Going the other way.

At least Hairy Chest wasn't leading me into a trap. I followed him carefully, trying as hard as I could not to make a sound.

I just hoped our journey was not going to be a long one.

It wasn't.

After only a few minutes the hairy searcher plunged out into a clearing. And not just any clearing. I saw an enormous compound surrounded by a high wire fence topped with razor wire. A small watchman's hut stood next to a gate. The guard was not there.

On the other side of the fence was a playing field with carefully mown grass and a high net stretched between two poles. A small pavilion overlooked the oval and in the distance, scattered between the towering mountain ash trees, were a number of other buildings.

Hairy Chest passed through the gate and jogged onto the oval. I watched in amazement as he placed the ball down on the grass. He put two fingers in his mouth and gave a loud whistle. A fantastic whistle. In response, a bunch of naked people ran out of the pavilion. They were all middle-aged.

There was a bald bloke who was sun-burnt. He was as red as a lobster – especially on his bottom. After him came a short, plump matronly woman. There was also a woman with long grey hair and a miserable-looking bloke about the same size as me.

The weirdest one was tall and thin and had a frizzy Afro hairdo. Without any clothes on he reminded me of a standard rose that had gone wild on the top.

The whole group lined up in front of the plump woman for an exercise session.

'We have to keep fit,' she said. 'By natural means if necessary. Stretch to stop the wrinkles. Jog to kill the fat. Run to beat Old Man Time. We have to hold our ground until help comes and the secret is known.'

'Whenever that is,' moaned the miserable guy.

'Don't be so gloomy, Silas,' said the bossy woman. She glared at the whole group. 'Twenty push-ups,' she shouted.

They all dropped to the ground and began to do frenzied push-ups. When they had finished she gave more orders. The whole group bopped and flopped. They sagged and dragged. They jumped and lumped. They puffed and panted and moaned and groaned. Hairy Chest's big belly drooped beneath him. He didn't seem used to such hard exercise.

An awesome sight. I didn't want to look but I couldn't help myself. I stared with wide-open eyes at this mass of naked jiggling flesh. There was no doubt about it at all.

I had stumbled upon a nudist colony.

FOUR

When the car stopped I lay in the darkness of the boot with my head on something soft and crinkly, listening.

I heard Dad get out and slam the door.

I heard him walk away.

Then nothing.

I gave myself three wishes.

One, that when I got out of the car I'd find we were at a vegie farm where Dad was checking the genetic health and emotional well-being of a crop of tomatoes.

Two, that we weren't outside a secret love nest because Dad didn't need one because he wasn't having an affair with another woman.

Three, that I could open the car boot from the inside.

The third wish didn't come true, and as I lay in the dark, my fingers sore from struggling with the lock, I knew the other two probably wouldn't either.

Then I remembered that the back seats of Dad's car folded down. I groped for the release catch and pushed one of the seats forward.

Sunlight jabbed into the boot.

I closed my eyes.

When I opened them again I saw something that made me wish I'd kept them shut. I saw what I'd been resting my head on. The soft crinkly thing that had stopped my head banging on the fuel pipe.

A big pack of disposable nappies.

I stared at them, feeling sick.

Then I crawled frantically through to the back seat, desperate to get away from them.

Nappies could only mean one thing.

A baby.

I prayed I was wrong.

Please, I begged silently, please let me be at a vegie farm. Because then there'll be a chance that the nappies were a mistake. That Dad was in a hurry at the supermarket and picked them up thinking they were microwave waffles.

I peered out the window.

It wasn't a farm. The car was parked outside a small weatherboard house in a street full of family homes.

I was at the love nest.

I stared at the house until my tears made it go all blurry.

I thought about bursting in and yelling at Dad and the Other Woman and throwing things at them. But I couldn't. It'd be too risky, chucking cutlery and knick-knacks and furniture around now I knew what else Dad had in there.

A baby.

A secret baby he'd had with another woman because he didn't love me and Mum any more.

Anyway, you can't throw things straight while your shoulders are shaking with sobs. I slumped back into the car seat and let them shake.

When they'd finished, I got out of the car.

A strange vehicle was parked a little way down the street. A big mean-looking military ute with dark tinted windows. For a second I had a wild thought. Maybe the Other Woman was a member of the armed forces. Maybe I could get her court-martialled for stealing a dad in peacetime.

I told myself to stop being silly.

A boy of about six wearing toy army pants was sitting on a nearby fence, watching me. The ute probably belonged to his dad. I wiped my eyes so the kid wouldn't see I'd been crying. He had blond curly hair and an angelic expression. He grinned at me.

I forced myself to smile back because I didn't want to hurt his feelings.

All right for you, I thought bitterly. Your dad's probably not a sex maniac. Your dad's probably content with just the one house and the one family. You've probably got a proper brother or sister to have fun with. You're probably not alone and abandoned.

I stopped torturing myself, turned away and started walking.

I didn't know which way I was going and I didn't care. Part of me wanted to walk straight out of town and up into the hills. Part of me wanted to stay up there for ever, living on curried insects. Because then I wouldn't have to break the news to Mum that Dad had replaced us.

I knew what it would do to her. Break her poor heart. Except Mum wasn't the sort of person who got sad, just angry. She'd probably never smile at me again, just scowl and bang take-away food onto tables and snap at me for the rest of her life.

As I trudged along street after street, I couldn't stop the flood of miserable thoughts. How my childhood was turning out to be as unhappy as Mum's. How fate was turning Mum into as big a meanie as her parents.

I gave a shudder.

I'd only met the Meanies once, when I was six and Mum and Dad and I went to stay with them on their property. They were the meanest grandparents I'd ever met. Just because I had a few mishaps, like accidentally letting twenty thousand head of sheep out onto the road, they reckoned I was uncontrollable and had to go to boarding school. And Mum had given in because she was scared of them. Which I couldn't blame her for. Not really. They used to hit her when she was little. It must have been awful, growing up with such mean parents. In the middle of thirty thousand hectares, nobody can hear you crying for help.

I'd just turned a corner into a street I recognised, when a horrible thought hit me. If the Meanies found out what a mess Mum's marriage was in, they'd probably make her go and live in a convent or somewhere. Which would leave me alone with a father who didn't really want me.

I started to sob again.

Then something happened that snapped me out of it.

As I stepped off the kerb to cross the street, out of the corner of my eye I saw a vehicle approaching in the distance.

Dad's car.

Without thinking, I ducked behind a hedge in someone's front yard. If Dad saw me in this part of town and realised I knew about the love nest, he'd probably offer me lollies and cash and a lifetime supply of cheese and asparagus pancakes not to tell Mum.

And suddenly I knew I was going to tell her. As soon as possible. So she and I could get out of town and start a new life.

I crouched behind the hedge, shaking with anger and determination, hoping Dad hadn't seen me.

His car sped past. Probably zooming off guiltily to get the surprise for my birthday tea, I thought bitterly. I hoped it was a big squishy cream cake.

I hurried home as fast as I could, thinking about the different things I could do with a big squishy cream cake. They all involved Dad and the Other Woman and a lot of dry-cleaning.

When I arrived at our street, I tried to prepare myself for what was going to happen next. Me breaking the news to Mum. Her either going into a cold fury or having a breakdown.

Or both.

I needn't have bothered.

Nothing could have prepared me for what was waiting in the house.

The first weird thing I noticed, as I opened the front door, was a strange sound. Then, as I stepped inside, I recognised it.

A baby crying.

My guts froze.

Dad had brought the baby here.

My brain spun. I realised what must have happened. Dad had decided to confess to Mum. To tell her he was moving in with the Other Woman. He'd brought the baby over to show her. And, I realised with a sickening jolt in the guts, to meet me. My new baby half-brother or sister.

This was my birthday tea surprise.

I almost turned and ran back down the driveway.

One thought made me carry on into the house. The awful thought of Mum, her face white with fury, trying to kill Dad with the fish slice.

'Mum,' I yelled, running into the house. 'Don't do it.'

Nobody answered.

I couldn't hear any sounds of a violent struggle, just the baby crying upstairs.

I went up. The baby was lying on the carpet in Mum and Dad's room, bare skin pink with rage as it howled and kicked. From its size, it looked to be about four months old. Or three, if it had been overfed.

Probably has been, I thought sourly. Other Women usually have big bosoms.

Mum wasn't in the room, or Dad.

Just their clothes. Strewn all over the floor. Which was usual for Mum, but not for Dad.

I stared down at Mum's robe and the clothes she'd been wearing before her bath. Plus the clothes she'd been wearing the day before. And about three days' worth of empty teacups. Next to them was one of Dad's business shirts and a pair of his work trousers. He always wore work clothes when he went to see the Other Woman so we'd think he was working.

The shirt and trousers had vomit all over them.

Serves you right, I thought bitterly. That's what you get with babies.

But where were Mum and Dad?

'Mum?' I yelled, running to different parts of the house with a growing sense of dread. 'Dad?'

They weren't there. The house was empty.

It was just me and the baby.

SPROCKET

FIVE

I couldn't stop myself staring at the exercising nudists. I peered through the wire fence at the disgusting sight. Everything was drooping and wobbling. Their naked bodies didn't look anything like the ones

35

on magazine covers. They had freckles and warts and hairs in all sorts of places. Some were skinny and bony. Some were short and fat. All sizes and shapes. The short, middle-aged lady was exhausted but she forced herself and the others to keep going.

I crouched behind a bush watching and thinking. I tried to put two and two together. And I always came up with an answer I didn't want – four.

These people were naked. And I was naked. I must belong here. Surely not. I had nothing in common with these fresh-air freaks. I didn't feel right walking around in the nude. And I was pale and they were brown. I couldn't be one of them. I was . . . I was . . . Who? I didn't have the faintest idea.

There was only one way to find out. I had to go into the nudist camp and check it out. There was nothing to be ashamed of. They didn't have anything different to me. Well, half of them didn't anyway. I walked past the empty guard post with a swagger.

At first no one took any notice. I suppose they thought I was just a naked spectator. But then Hairy Chest saw me. His eyes narrowed and his hands bunched up into fists. The others turned to see what he was staring at.

'So you've come back?' growled the plump bossy woman.

'The intruder,' gasped the guy with the sunburnt bottom.

'The thief,' muttered the thin man with the Afro.

They started to walk towards me with mean looks in their eyes. The nudists gathered around me, staring as if they had just caught a burglar. They knew who I was. And I was not someone they liked.

I decided to play the wimp. 'I need help,' I blurted out. 'I've lost my memory. I don't know who I am.'

Hairy Chest grabbed me roughly by the arm. 'You've come to the right place,' he growled. 'We're going to give you all the help you need. You're going to remember plenty.'

The other nudists began to mumble and grumble. Their mood was turning ugly. They began to close in on me. They looked as if they were about to tear me to pieces.

'Let's make him talk, Agnes,' said Hairy Chest.

'No,' said the bossy woman. 'Take him to Reception. I'll be with you in a moment.'

Hairy Chest started to drag me across the oval towards a large concrete building.

My guts were aching worse than ever. Something seemed to be fizzing inside my swollen stomach. I was starting to look like one of those men who drink too much beer.

Hairy Chest pushed me through a side door and called out in a loud voice, 'I've got him. I've got the . . .'

His voice trailed off. Standing inside the main doors were two more naked people. They didn't look like the other nudists – they had kind, innocent faces. One was a large, sad woman. She had purple hair with little silver moons and stars sprinkled through it. Next to her was a skinny guy with a shaved head. He wore four earrings in one ear and two in an eyebrow.

Hairy Chest didn't seem to know them. He let go of my arm. He didn't want them to see that I was a prisoner. I edged my way back towards the door. 'What do you want?' he asked them roughly.

The bald man with the earrings held out his hand to Hairy Chest. 'Me name's Con Rod,' he said. 'We're members of The Last Leaf. We were thinkin' we might stay a few nights. Reciprocal rights and all that.'

The large lady nodded her head and smiled. Her teeth were big and odd shaped. One was missing.

Hairy Chest glared and ignored Con Rod's outstretched hand. 'We're full up,' he snarled. 'No spare beds.'

Con Rod was disappointed. He nodded at his woman. 'Purple Cloud's getting over losing her boy,' he said. 'I thought a night here would do her good.'

Hairy Chest noticed me creeping towards the side door. He leaned towards the reception desk and spoke into a microphone. 'Agnes,' he said. 'Get here quick.' He switched off the mike and mumbled, 'She's probably running around after those little terrors again.'

Little terrors? Were they the Brats? My mind switched into top gear. I had to escape. I stared at the naked couple. They weren't part of this set-up. They were being turned away. Hairy Chest was trying to get rid of them.

The woman had lost her boy. That was enough for me.

'Mum,' I spluttered.

Her mouth fell open for just a second. Then her sad face lit up with a huge smile. 'Sprocket,' she said. 'Oh, Sprocket. It's you. It's really you.'

I was shocked. I was only pretending. Trying to get away from Hairy Chest. The name Sprocket didn't ring a bell. My mother wouldn't look like her. Would she? But she seemed to recognise me. And she had lost a boy. Maybe she *was* my mother.

She rushed over with wide-open arms. She was smiling and laughing. She grabbed my head and hugged it into her large wobbling breasts. It was terrible. Horrible. I couldn't breathe. It was like being drowned in jelly. My ears were blocked by her quivering flesh. The sounds of the outside world grew muffled, then disappeared. But I could hear a booming voice echoing through her bones.

'You've come back, darling,' she said. 'I knew you would. Where have you been? You've broken your mother's heart.'

I fought for air. She was smothering me. Suddenly all the pain, all the grief, all the terror seemed to grow into one big black cloud inside my head. I felt my eyes roll back as I slipped into unconsciousness.

The next thing I knew I was on the torture

rack. That's what it felt like anyway. Purple Cloud and Hairy Chest had an arm each. Con Rod held onto both legs. They were pulling in opposite directions.

'Agnes, Agnes,' shouted Hairy Chest. 'Where is the woman?'

'My boy, my boy,' screamed Purple Cloud.

'He's not your boy,' yelled Con Rod. 'Sprocket is dead. This is another kid. Sprocket had blue eyes. This kid's got brown.'

I felt as if I was going to break into three pieces. I bucked and kicked for all I was worth but they hung on like glue. The pain was terrible.

Without warning Con Rod let go of both my legs. Purple Cloud and Hairy Chest fell over backwards. I crashed painfully to the floor between them all. Quick as a flash I scrambled to my feet.

'Get out of here,' yelled Con Rod. 'Go, go, go.'

I didn't need a second invitation. I shot out of the front door like a nail out of an air gun.

I passed under a sign which read:

| SUNRISE NATURE FARM |
| STAY COOL |

Some memory, some fragment from my past, stirred inside my head. I knew without a doubt that I had seen that sign before. I felt like a convict escaping from jail.

On a small parking area was an amazing motor-home. I had never seen anything like it before. It was a truck with a double-storey van on the back. The whole thing was made of thick, rusty, plate steel. It had three sets of wheels on the back to take the enormous weight. Huge exhaust pipes snaked along the side. On the front was a rusty mermaid sticking out like a figurine on a sailing ship. Instead of windows the van section had portholes. There were rusty stars and moons and cupids all over the roof.

I tugged at the door trying to get inside. But it was locked. I looked around desperately for somewhere to hide.

There was nowhere.

A booming voice sounded over a loudspeaker.

'The intruder has escaped. Emergency. Emergency. The intruder has escaped.'

I held onto my naked, swollen stomach and headed for the gate.

And the world outside.

SIX

'Shhhh,' I said to the baby. 'I'm trying to think.'

The baby mustn't have liked girls of my age because it screwed its red face up and bawled even louder.

I made myself ignore it.

Don't let it panic you, I told myself. Babies like crying. It helps their voices develop. And their face muscles. Think, I told myself.

I stared at Dad's vomit-splattered clothes on the bedroom floor and tried to imagine what had happened.

Perhaps, while Dad was showing his love child to Mum and telling her that he'd be moving in with the Other Woman and taking half the kitchen utensils, the baby had thrown up over him.

I would have, I thought bitterly, if I'd been there.

But why weren't they here now?

A horrible thought hit me. Perhaps Mum had got so furious she'd whacked Dad with a utensil.

I gave the baby a quick once-over to make sure it wasn't having a coronary, then dashed all over the house, checking the floors for Dad's unconscious body.

Nothing.

I checked the kitchen for missing utensils. All the pots and pans were hanging in their normal places. The only things not put away were the kettle, the teapot and a half-empty take-away container of prawn and asparagus salad on the kitchen table.

Mum's lunch. I remembered she'd been getting herself treats from the deli quite often recently. Maybe she'd had suspicions about Dad after all. Maybe she'd been trying to blot out her fears with bought salads.

Suddenly I realised the house was silent.

The baby had stopped crying.

I dashed back up to the bedroom, desperately hoping it hadn't choked on one of Dad's socks.

It was OK. I sat down on the bed, weak with relief, until I saw what it was doing.

It was splashing its hands in a puddle of vomit and wiping its fingers on the carpet, frowning with cute concentration. I couldn't help smiling. It looked like it was trying to draw. Or write, even.

Then I pictured Mum's face when she saw the vomit smeared all over her white carpet. Hurriedly I picked the baby up and wiped its hands on one of Dad's business shirts.

The baby started bawling again.

I looked helplessly down into its angry, glaring eyes.

Perhaps it had wind. I tried to remember if you

were meant to pat babies on the front or the back.

'Sorry,' I said gruffly to the baby. 'I haven't had any experience at this. I'm an only child.'

Correction, I thought sadly. *Was* an only child.

'It can't be indigestion,' I said. 'Not now your lunch is all over the floor.'

What I actually said was 'Bub, bub, bub, goo, goo, goo, choo, choo, choo, bub, bub, bub,' but I think it got the message.

It stopped crying and started trying to grab my T-shirt.

I hardly noticed. I was staring down at the puddle of vomit. There were things in it I recognised.

Prawns.

Asparagus.

No wonder the baby had chucked up if Dad and the Other Woman had been feeding it solids dripping with garlic mayonnaise.

Then I realised what a dope I was.

It wasn't the baby's vomit, it was Mum's. She must have been having a rest after lunch when Dad arrived with the baby, and then when he told her the awful news, she threw up over him.

Shock could do that. I'd read about it. And anxiety.

Now that everything was starting to sink in, I was feeling pretty sick with worry myself.

Where had Mum and Dad gone?

Why had they left the baby behind?

I grabbed the bedside phone and rang Dad's mobile. A recorded voice said it was switched off or out of range. I dialled Mum's and heard it ringing down in the kitchen.

I picked up the baby and went downstairs. Suddenly I felt as though I had the weight of the world on my shoulders. And in my arms. The baby was getting heavier by the minute. Plus it was trying to pull my ear off.

I had one more desperate search. I looked in the back yard, right up the end past the compost bin. Mum and Dad weren't there. I went round to the front yard. They weren't there either.

Mum's car was in the carport, though, which was weird. She must have gone off on foot. Or in Dad's car.

Of course. That was it. She'd gone with Dad back to his love nest to meet the Other Woman.

And strangle her.

But why had they left the baby?

I felt something warm running along my arm. I looked down. The baby was peeing on me.

'You little rat,' I yelled, holding the dripping little tyke at arm's length. Then I realised it wasn't her fault she was naked. I couldn't believe it. Dad with a boot full of nappies and he hadn't even put one on the baby.

I didn't get it. Something wasn't right. I had to find out what was going on. And I could only think of one place to do that. The love nest. Even if Mum and Dad weren't there, the Other Woman would be and at least I could ditch the baby.

I carried the baby into the laundry, washed us both,

grabbed the laundry trolley, filled it with towels and pillow cases, put the baby in it, wheeled it into the kitchen, wrapped kitchen paper round the baby's middle, covered that with plastic wrap and set off.

On my way out I grabbed Mum's mobile and the Swiss Army knife. With so much weird stuff going on, I never knew when I might need an implement or twenty-seven.

I closed the front door behind me and that's when I saw the birthday card. It was tucked under the corner of the door mat. I must have missed it earlier when I got back.

My hands were shaking as I fumbled it out of the envelope.

'Dear Amy,' said the scribbled message inside. 'Sorry I can't be at your birthday tea. I have to go away for a while. I hope one day you'll understand. Love, Dad.'

I stared at the card for a long time, blinking back tears.

Then I set off for the love nest. If Dad and the Other Woman were leaving town, the least they could do was take their pesky baby with them.

I wheeled the laundry trolley down the driveway and was just starting to head along our street when I heard the growl of a vehicle coming up behind me.

I spun round, praying it was Dad's car, but I knew it wasn't. The engine was too loud and threatening.

It was the military truck.

It slowed down as it went past and I tried to catch a glimpse of the person behind the wheel. I couldn't, the tinted windows were too dark. That didn't stop me feeling a stab of jealousy.

Why couldn't I have a normal, dependable soldier dad? One who wouldn't be tempted by Other Women in case he got lipstick on his uniform?

I pushed the trolley to the end of the street and went into the corner shop to buy some nappies.

'Aren't you a bit young to be a babysitter?' asked the woman behind the counter suspiciously as she watched the baby grope wildly at the pay phone.

'I'm not a babysitter,' I replied. 'We're doing biology at school and for our end-of-term project we all had to have babies.'

After I'd left the shop and worked out how to get a nappy onto a baby who was yelling and kicking and trying to slap my face, I set off for the love nest.

We got lost a few times, but I remembered certain playgrounds and buildings, and finally I found the street.

The kid with blond curls was still playing on the footpath, talking urgently into a toy mobile phone. He was so caught up in his game he barely glanced at me.

My heart was thumping as I wheeled the trolley up to the front door of the small weatherboard house.

What would I find inside?

A love nest full of broken furniture and smashed crockery and rips in the wallpaper where Mum had tried to tear it off the walls with her bare finger-nails?

The Other Woman so grateful to have her baby back that she'd be shedding tears of joy even though her living room was wrecked?

I wondered if I'd be able to give her the lecture I'd prepared on not getting interested in married men even when they did know heaps about tomatoes.

I was pretty sure I would.

And, I thought hopefully, afterwards when she pulls herself together, perhaps she'll ditch Dad for being so forgetful and leaving the baby behind.

I rang the bell. Nobody came.

After ringing lots more times, I wheeled the trolley round the side of the house. The side gate was unlocked. The back door wasn't. I banged on it and shook the handle.

Still nobody came.

I remembered that at home Dad kept a spare back-door key in a small cavity he'd made by scraping out some mortar between two bricks in the wall near the door.

The walls of this house were wood, but I found a cavity all the same, between two planks. Tucked into it was a key.

I made a promise to myself that whatever happened I would not remove any of the Other Woman's major organs with my Swiss Army knife.

Then I opened the door and went inside.

SPROCKET

SEVEN

The voice from the loudspeaker bounced across the grounds of the nudist colony. At any moment the whole bunch of naked sun-freaks would be after me. I had to get away.

My aching belly was terribly bloated. I must have eaten something that had gone bad. I tried to push away the pain and raced towards the exit gate with a pounding heart. Hairy Chest, the man called Con Rod and the weird woman who thought I was her child dashed out of the reception area. There was a lot of banging and crashing. I dared not take the time to look back but it sounded like a fight was going on.

Loud yells followed me down the driveway.

'Let him go,' said Con Rod's voice.

'He's my boy,' shouted Purple Cloud.

'He's not, sweetheart,' shouted Con Rod.

'He's an intruder,' said Hairy Chest's voice. 'When I get my hands on him . . .'

I turned on the speed. There was no way he was going to get his hands on me without a chase. I must

49

have passed the oval. My surroundings were just a blur and it was hard to tell. I didn't see anything. Except . . .

Clothes. Hanging on pegs. In a sort of bus-shelter thing right next to the gate. A notice said:

> UNDRESS HERE
> NO ENTRY UNLESS NAKED

I knew that I wouldn't last long in the outside world. A naked boy would attract attention. And anyway, at night I might freeze to death. I threw a quick look over my shoulder.

The motorhome blocked the door to the reception building. No one seemed to be following.

Yet.

I whipped over to the shelter and stretched out a hand.

'There he is,' came Hairy Chest's booming voice from behind me. It was followed by the sound of a loud whistle.

I grabbed the nearest garment and a pair of slippers and fled out of the gate and down the bush track.

After about ten minutes I stopped and listened. Nothing. No one. All was silent. Except for the bell-birds.

I examined my piece of stolen clothing. Oh no. A dress. An old-fashioned, long, flowery dress decorated with a rainbow-coloured fringe around the hem. Not really me. Not really any boy for that matter. But it would have to do.

I stepped into the slippers and then pulled on the dress. I began to run in panic down the road with it hitched up to my knees. It was much too long for me but it was better than nothing. At least my private parts were covered.

I ran and ran and ran. My lungs were hurting and my breath came in great gasps but I managed to keep going for about five more minutes. Then I suddenly collapsed in the middle of the track. I couldn't go on.

It wasn't only my lungs that hurt. My stomach cramps were getting worse. Terrible stabs of pain shot through my swollen guts. It felt like red-hot nails were jumping around inside me.

I needed to go to the loo. Again. But this was not normal. Something was awfully wrong. The need to do a poop didn't arrive like this. Agony, agony, agony.

The road was still deserted but at any moment the nudists or the Brats might appear. Both groups seemed to hate me. What had I done? Why was I so alone? Where were my parents? I felt like a bird that had fallen from a deserted nest.

I pushed these thoughts out of my mind. There was no way I was going to be taken prisoner. I tried to run on. But I could hardly move. I was paralysed by spasms of pain. I staggered to the side of the road. My dress was soaked in sweat. Perspiration dripped from my forehead.

There was only one way to stop the pain. I had to have that bog. This was the worst constipation in the world. I pulled my dress up to my waist and squatted down, praying that this time no one would come while I was in the middle of it.

'Ouch, ow, ow. Aaargh.' It wouldn't come. It was like trying to force a pineapple out of my bottom. The pain was excruciating. 'Aaargh . . .' I fell onto my back, clutching my belly with both hands. My screams echoed down the hillside through the forest. I just couldn't help crying out.

I closed my eyes and forced my stomach muscles to push. I ignored the searing pain and ordered my bursting bowels to give up their treasure.

And they did.

There on the side of the road I passed a huge piece of poop. The pain immediately grew less but my stomach remained bloated.

I staggered to my feet. I had to get out of there. Fast.

Before I went though, there was one thing I had to find out.

What was it that the Brats were searching for in my poop? I grabbed a twig from the side of the road.

And began picking through the enormous pile of poo.

EIGHT

I went from room to room in the small weather-board house, looking for Mum and Dad. And the Other Woman.

They weren't there, but I could tell the Other Woman had been. I could smell her perfume. The house reeked of exactly the same whiff I'd noticed on Dad loads of times. An exotic pong like an expensive bathroom air-freshener, but with extra smells of vanilla and licorice and rubber. It made me feel a bit sick, but I could imagine people liking it, specially if it had a posh name like 'Happiness' or 'Other Woman'.

The house smelled like a love nest all right. The only thing was, it didn't look like one.

There was no visible sign that an Other Woman had ever been there. No furniture, no clothes, no makeup, not even a bra hanging from a light fitting.

Plus the place was full of fridges.

There were four in the kitchen. You could barely squeeze past them to get to the living room, where there were another six. And two in the hallway. Both the bedrooms had three each.

Eighteen fridges in one house.

I stood in the living room, staring at them. Some were old, some were almost new, some were big and some were medium-sized. From the humming and whirring and gurgling all around me, they were obviously all plugged in and switched on.

What was this place?

Had I stumbled on the headquarters of a fridge-stealing gang? Of which my father and his Other Woman were members? Possibly even the leaders?

It didn't seem very likely.

Get real, Amy, I told myself.

Trouble was, when you started suspecting a parent, anything seemed possible.

I opened one of the fridges. Inside was a baby's nappy. A wet baby's nappy. But it didn't look like it had ever been on a baby. It was lying on a shelf with a very bright lamp shining onto it. In the middle of the nappy, glistening in the light, was a small brown ball about the size of a pea.

I touched it with my finger. It was warm and rotten and mushy. It smelled like the Other Woman's perfume, only sour.

I opened another fridge. It had a nappy and a lamp in it too. The nappy was stuffed in a glass jar, half-submerged in dirty green liquid. Tucked into one of the folds of the nappy was another brown pea. This one was mouldy and rotten as well.

The other fridges all had nappies and lamps and rotting peas in them.

My mind was racing. I was confused. Dad was a top plant geneticist. One of the country's biggest frozen food companies paid him to help grow strong, healthy vegies, the sort you could leave boiling between commercial breaks without them going soggy. Dad had about three university degrees in vegies. And a big modern lab at the factory.

There must be some mistake, I decided. Dad would never do experiments in a dump like this.

Then I looked in the bathroom and saw just how wrong I was.

The bathroom was fitted out like a mini-laboratory, with test tubes and microscopes and other bits of scientific equipment cluttered around the sink. Almost hidden under some microscope slides was half a packet of butter menthols.

Dad's favourite lolly.

That wasn't all. On a shelf was our electric toaster-oven, the one Dad reckoned he'd chucked out three Christmas holidays ago after I'd tried to toast my old Lego blocks in it.

I didn't understand.

Dad had millions of dollars worth of equipment in his lab at the factory. Why would he set up another lab in a cramped bathroom with a dripping toilet cistern?

Then it hit me. The Other Woman. Maybe she was

a scientist too, trying to break into the highly paid world of nappy science. And Dad was trying to help her.

Typical, I thought bitterly. Dad just couldn't say no to a request for help. I'd seen it a million times. Stray dogs, charity collectors, broken-down motorists, and now a struggling industrial chemist.

I wondered if Dad had had affairs with any of the others.

I turned to leave the little bathroom in disgust and saw something hanging behind the door. Dad's jacket, the one with the leather patches on the elbows.

Suddenly sadness nearly choked me. I gave the jacket a hug and decided that if Dad did move away with the Other Woman, I'd ask him if I could have the jacket to remember him by.

As I hugged the jacket, I realised something was making a crinkling sound next to my ear. Something in the jacket pocket.

I put my hand in and pulled out another half-packet of butter menthols. And a letter.

It was just the last page, about four lines of elegant, old-fashioned handwriting.

'. . . this madness must stop, Drew,' it said. 'You are the only one who can bring it to an end. Please, I beg you, for all our sakes, no more.'

The letter was signed Charlotte Sampson.

My mouth was so dry I could hardly swallow. Drew was Dad's name. Charlotte Sampson must be the

Other Woman. And she wanted the affair to stop. Even though they had a baby.

I struggled to take it all in.

Then I heard a cry from the back yard.

Oh no.

The baby.

I'd forgotten about the baby. It was out the back in the laundry trolley.

I stuffed the letter into my pocket and hurried past the fridges towards the back door, straining anxiously to hear that the baby was OK.

Another shriek.

I flung myself out into the yard.

The laundry trolley was empty, towels and pillow-slips scattered on the ground.

I looked around wildly.

A little kid, a boy of about six with sticking-up red hair, was running off with the baby clutched to his chest.

He disappeared along the side of the house.

'Hey,' I screamed, sprinting after him. 'Come back. That's my baby.'

He ran down the driveway. My legs were longer than his, and I wasn't carrying anything, and I was desperate, so I caught up to him soon after he reached the street.

I was about to grab his collar when I realised the military ute was parked at the kerb in front of us.

'Help,' I screamed, hoping the soldier dad was still inside. 'This kid's got my sister.'

The boy pulled open the back door of the ute's big double cab and jumped inside with the baby.

I followed him in.

I expected him to be cowering on the back seat, making up excuses to a stern soldier dad, but he wasn't. He was just sitting there, looking grumpily at the other occupants of the ute.

In the front passenger seat was the kid with curly blond hair who'd been playing in the street earlier. Next to him, in the driver's seat, was a taller skinny girl, also about six, wearing some sort of racing driver's jacket.

The blond kid looked at me coldly, then turned to the red-haired kid.

'Why did you bring her?' he hissed.

'Couldn't help it,' growled the red-haired kid.

I grabbed the baby from him and held her to my chest.

'That was a very, very silly thing to do,' I yelled at the red-haired kid. 'You are a very, very naughty boy.'

'Actually,' replied the blond boy, turning back to me, 'you're the one who's in trouble.'

I realised another kid had climbed into the cab behind me. Another little boy, this one wearing a knitted beanie. He looked nervously at the blond kid and when the blond kid nodded he pulled the door shut. The engine roared into life and we sped off down the street.

'Stop,' I screamed, struggling to get a seat-belt

round me and the baby. I gave up and lunged forward and tried to grab the steering wheel.

'Sit down, lovey,' muttered the girl.

She spun the wheel and expertly changed gear. We screeched round a corner. I was flung back against the seat. Desperately I hung on to the howling baby.

'When your father finds out what you've done,' I yelled at the blond boy, 'you're for it.'

'My father's dead,' said the blond boy. 'What I suggest is that you concentrate on keeping the baby quiet. A much better idea, I would venture, than getting us all killed.'

I stared at them, trying to take it in.

I was being kidnapped at high speed in a military vehicle by a bunch of infants.

The baby couldn't believe it either. She was sobbing desperately. I managed to get the seat-belt round us both, then stroked her head. Gradually she stopped crying and lay against me, exhausted.

I saw we were speeding out of town, heading down back roads I didn't even recognise. Soon we'd be in the rainforest.

'You're all going to jail for a very long time,' I said to the four little kids. 'With no pocket money.'

The blond boy swapped smiles with the other three. His face was angelic and innocent, but his eyes were hard and angry.

I looked down at the baby and had a brilliant idea.

'She's hungry,' I said. 'She hasn't eaten or had a

drink for hours. If we don't stop and get her something she could die.'

The blond kid gave a weary sigh. Then he opened the glove compartment and handed me a baby bottle full of milk.

I gaped.

They'd planned this whole thing.

'Go on,' said the kid. 'Feed her.'

At first the baby wouldn't drink the milk. Then, after a lot of whingeing, she did.

I tried to stay calm so I wouldn't upset her and give her indigestion, but it wasn't easy.

Panicked thoughts flashed through my mind.

Who were these kids with their scary grown-up talk?

What did they want with the baby?

Where were Mum and Dad?

We sped further and further into the rainforest, bumping along endless dirt roads. I started to get really thirsty too. I was tempted to drink the rest of the milk myself, but I didn't.

The baby fell asleep and as I stuck the bottle in my pocket I remembered Mum's mobile. If I could dial without the kids seeing, and whisper without them hearing, and the phone worked out here in the rainforest, a police helicopter would be tracking us in minutes.

Except I didn't know where we were.

And the blond kid was watching me closely.

Then I remembered the Swiss Army knife.

Out of twenty-seven implements, there must be one for escaping from a speeding military ute.

Probably not, I decided.

So I tried something I'd seen in a movie.

Even though I was parched, I tried to look as though I had a full bladder.

'I need to pee,' I said. 'It's urgent.'

The blond kid gave me a long look. For a moment I thought he was going to tell me to put the baby's nappy on. Then he nodded to the girl and the ute skidded to a stop.

'Get the rope,' he said to the red-haired boy. 'From the back.'

The red-haired boy opened his door. Hoping the Bullying Counsellor at school didn't get to hear what I'd been doing in the holidays, I pushed him out of the cab as hard as I could so he went sprawling in the dirt.

Then I grabbed the baby and leapt out myself.

If only I'd thought.

If only I'd remembered how sitting in a vehicle for ages makes your feet go to sleep.

As soon as they hit the ground my legs crumpled and I collapsed into the mud. I tried to hang on to the baby, I really did, but as I fell she rolled out of my hands. I managed to break her fall, but I couldn't get a grip on her again.

The red-haired kid grabbed her and got into the ute with her and the ute sped away.

'No,' I screamed.

I struggled to my feet and sprinted after the ute, but it was already out of sight. I kept running anyway, the cool rainforest air ripping at my lungs, until I came to a fork in the road.

Now I couldn't even hear the ute's engine. There were other tyre-tracks in the mud, so I couldn't even see which way they'd gone.

It was hopeless. I stood there for I don't know how long, swearing at them and crying tears of anxiety about the baby.

Then I started walking.

I didn't know where I was or where I was going, so I chose the right-hand fork and just walked.

Trees and tangled creepers towered over me on both sides. There was hardly any sunlight in the thick rainforest, just lots of strange noises and shadows.

I tried not to think about Mum and Dad.

I thought about the girls at school, but they were hundreds of kilometres away. No, millions.

There was nobody else to think about. Not near by. Not a friend.

I walked on.

Then I stopped.

Up ahead I could hear a noise that was different from all the other noises in the rainforest. A sort of low muttering.

I was tempted to run, but where would I have run to?

So I crept forward, peering into the shadows.

I prayed it would be a responsible member of the community, a mature and dependable adult who could help me find Mum and Dad and the baby.

It wasn't.

I came slowly round a bend in the road and there, in a shaft of sunlight, was the weirdest thing I'd seen in a morning that had been the weirdest of my life so far.

A rough-looking pregnant girl in a dress, crouched under a tree, picking through her poo with a twig.

DEADLY!

Part Two

BRATS

The SKIN CREAM FACTORY

FOREST

FACTORY

OFFICE

ROAD

FOREST

SPROCKET

ONE

I squatted by the rainforest road in my stolen dress, feeling alone and terrified. I also felt ridiculous. What if some innocent traveller saw me picking through a pile of my own poo? They would run a mile. They would be scared out of their wits.

Even your *own* poo is foul. I tried not to breathe as I scratched through it. The child soldiers didn't want it for the perfume, that was for sure. So there must have been something in it. Something I had swallowed.

I tried to make sense of it all. Kid commandos. Old nudists. Poop pinchers. Mad hippies with a weird mobile home. Lost memory. No friends. Danger. Cold. And pains in my bloated belly. It was too much. I was trembling from head to foot.

Surely someone could help me? Surely someone could say, 'Hey, Robert or Mario or Doug,' or whoever I was, 'would you like a lift back home? Your mother is looking for you.'

But no one came. I was on my own. I had to think. I had to figure out who I was. What I was doing here. The word *mother* echoed in my head. Did I have one? Where was she? *Was* she here at the nudist colony? That woman with the purple hair *couldn't* have been her. But why were people chasing me?

I continued digging in my droppings with the stick. My fingers were shaking. I had to finish the search quickly. The crazy nudists or the little commandos might appear at any second.

Nothing. Not a thing out of place. Just an ordinary, everyday piece of poop. Oh no. My big belly began to throb again. Whatever was inside my stomach was still there. Surely there was no more poo? Maybe it was just wind. My guts felt as if they were full of swirling gas.

I remembered something about cows with swollen stomachs like this. Farmers stick hollow tubes into their guts to release the pressure. No one is allowed to smoke near by in case the escaping fumes ignite and blow up the cow.

Maybe I had the same disease. What if I exploded? I had to release the pressure that was building up inside me. I had to break wind before I burst open. But I couldn't. Something was blocking it off. Like a cork in a bottle.

More cramping pains ran up and down inside my bowels. I fell to the ground and clutched my belly.

'Aaargh,' I groaned. 'Ooh.' I let out a terrible scream.

'Push,' said a voice from nowhere. 'Take a deep breath and push.'

I looked up and saw a girl about my age staring at me. She was fumbling with a Swiss Army knife.

'Don't stick me,' I screamed. 'Please. No, no, no.'

The girl looked down at me with a worried face. She suddenly bent over and put the blade under the belt on my dress. She cut it with one quick movement, then folded up the knife and put it in her pocket.

'Don't be scared,' she said. 'You can't have a baby with that around your waist.'

'What baby?' I moaned.

She patted my stomach. 'This one,' she said.

'No,' I yelled. 'It's not that.'

The girl suddenly started wiping my forehead. 'Don't worry,' she said. 'I had a book about giving birth until Julie Spiros stole it. I know what to do. Push.'

This was crazy. She thought I was having a baby. The silly girl thought I was pregnant. Just because I was lying in the middle of the road in a dress clutching my swollen stomach and groaning.

'Get off me, you idiot,' I said.

Suddenly her expression changed. She peered at my face more closely. 'You're not a girl,' she shrieked. 'You're one of them.' She jumped to her feet and began to back away. She looked terrified.

The spasm of pain passed and with a sigh of relief I climbed to my feet. I took a few steps towards her.

'Don't be scared,' I said.

'Stay away,' she screamed. 'Don't make a move. My father has a black belt in karate. And he's just back there. He weighs ninety kilos and can lift a horse with one hand. And my mother's there too. She has a red belt in karate. And I'm a feng shui expert.' She pushed me away roughly.

'It's all right,' I said. 'I'm friendly. I'm harmless. I wouldn't hurt a fly.'

Quick as a flash she leapt forward and grabbed me around the neck. She started to wrestle me to the ground. She wasn't really a strong girl but I got tangled in the dress and my stomach got in the way. We fell to the ground with a crash.

This girl was beating me in a fight. Normally I could win against a girl. I knew that much even though I couldn't remember much else about myself.

'Where's my baby half-sister?' she yelled at me. 'Tell me or you're dead meat.'

'I don't know what you're talking about,' I squealed.

'You're with them,' she said. 'Those little kids with the mobiles. This is a trap.'

'No,' I yelled. I wriggled out of her grasp and

got to my feet. 'You're wrong. It's not what you think.'

The girl reached into the pocket of her jeans and took out her Swiss Army knife again. She began fumbling with it, trying to open out a blade.

She was dangerous. Everyone in this forest was dangerous. I didn't know what to think. She could be innocent. Or she could be a nudist in sheep's clothing. But if she was she wouldn't have tried to help me. Unless *she* was setting a trap. Everyone in this weird place seemed to hate me. It was like Malice in Wonderland.

Finally she managed to open the knife. She waved it in front of my face.

'Speak or die,' she said.

'You've pulled out the magnifying glass,' I said.

She snapped it shut and tried again with a shaking hand.

'A corkscrew,' I told her.

She had another go.

'Can-opener,' I said.

I started to laugh. I just couldn't help it. It was ridiculous.

'Kidnapping is not funny,' she said. 'Nor is under-age driving, false imprisonment or breaking into a love nest.'

'Kidnapping?' I yelped. 'Under-age driving?' Suddenly I knew who she was talking about. She had seen the little terrorists and was scared of them too.

She was an innocent bystander like me. Maybe we could help each other.

'You've got my half-sister,' she shouted. 'And she's just a baby.'

'I'm not with those little gangsters,' I said. 'They are trying to kidnap *me*.'

'Why?' she asked. 'What do they want?'

'They're after my poo.'

'Of course,' she said. 'Why didn't I guess? I'll bet your poo is worth bottling.'

I tried to think of a sensible explanation. Nothing came to mind. The silence was broken by the sound of an engine coming from the direction of the nudist colony.

'The Hummer,' I yelled. 'It's them. The under-age drivers. The Brats.'

'Right,' said the girl with a determined look on her face. She went to the middle of the track and stood facing the approaching noise. She selected the largest blade in her Swiss Army knife and held it ready.

'I'm going to get my half-sister back,' she said. 'And you and your friends better not try to stop me.'

'They're *not* my friends,' I shouted. 'And if the nudists are with them there will be too many for you. Hide.'

The growl of the Hummer was getting louder. I ran off the track and crouched down behind some thick ferns. The girl just stood there without moving.

'What nudists?' she said.

I whispered loudly through the leaves. 'They have a hide-out just down the road. Where I got the dress. They want to torture me. They are kidnappers too.'

The word *kidnappers* seemed to help her decide. At the last minute, just before the Hummer came into view, she dived in next to me.

The Hummer rumbled slowly by. The windows were wound down and I could see four titchy commandos jammed in the front cab.

I recognised the little girl who was driving. Her tongue was flicking in and out like a snake on the prowl. 'Reptile,' I whispered. 'And Pooper Scooper, Scowler and Beanie. They're dangerous.'

Reptile could only just see over the top of the steering wheel. The sight of a small girl driving a huge truck should have been funny. But the way she changed gears with so much confidence made a lump come into my throat. I held my breath as the Hummer growled by.

Once they were out of sight I was going to head cross-country and get as far away from the hills as possible. I had to find help and come back with normal people who could help me look for my mother. That woman I'd met in the nudist camp wasn't my mother – she was mixing me up with her dead child. I had a strong feeling my real mum had something to do with the nudists.

'They're the ones who kidnapped my baby

half-sister,' said the girl. 'And I'm going to get her back. See you.'

She suddenly bolted out from our hiding place and ran along behind the Hummer in a crouched position.

In a second she had lifted the canvas flap on the back and climbed in.

Who was this girl? There was something about her I liked. She spoke her mind and she had guts. Maybe she was one of them. Or maybe not. Perhaps she could be trusted. The Brats seemed to be her enemies too. I needed a friend. And by the sound of it, so did she. Perhaps I could help her find the baby. I had to make up my mind. And quick.

Without another thought I ran out onto the road, hoping that Reptile wasn't looking in the rear-vision mirror. It was hard to run with such a big belly but I managed to catch up with the slowly moving truck. I grabbed onto the tail-gate and hung on for grim death. Normally I would have had no trouble dragging myself up. But my swollen stomach kept getting in the way and my slippers fell off.

In the end I pulled myself over the tail-gate and fell into the truck. As I did, my guts were seized by another painful spasm. It hurt so much that I didn't even have time to wonder where in the heck I was going. Or what terrors might be waiting at our journey's end.

TWO

I crawled across the shuddering metal floor of
the Hummer and pressed my ear to the back wall of
the passenger cab, desperate to hear my sister make a
sound.

Preferably a happy gurgle.

Nothing.

Just the growl of the engine and the thump of the
wheels.

'If you've hurt her . . .' I hissed in the direction of
the mini-psychopaths in the cab.

Suddenly I felt very alone. I wished some of the
other girls from school were there. The cricket team,
with their bats.

I didn't want to be there. I wanted
to get as far away from those
evil kids as I could. But
they'd taken an innocent baby
and I wanted her back. OK,
she was only my half-
sister, but that didn't
mean my rescue attempt

was going to be half-hearted.

I dropped back onto my stomach and lay in the dark under the tarpaulin and tried to think.

When we got to wherever we were going, I had to be ready. Ready to act fast. Ready to grab the baby and get away.

I needed a plan.

I gritted my teeth and tried to have practical thoughts. It wasn't easy. In my life up till then I'd always needed a clear head to be practical, and preferably a diary with a planner.

Now my head felt like it was full of soggy pasta. In the last three hours I'd discovered my dad was having an affair with another woman, found their love nest, had both my parents disappear, been kidnapped by a bunch of infants, lost my baby half-sister, wrestled a boy in a dress, and stowed away on a giant military ute. My brain felt like it had been boiled, peeled, chopped and bottled.

Some birthday.

I felt for my Swiss Army knife in the gloom and double-checked with my fingertips that I had a blade this time and not a kitchen utensil. I had to smile. The boy in the dress had looked pretty surprised when I'd threatened him with a can-opener.

The Hummer gave a sudden lurch and I felt something that wiped the smile off my face.

A hand on my shoulder.

I rolled over, gripping the knife, ready to defend myself. How exactly I didn't know. The most violent thing I'd ever done was chuck an alarm clock at Julie Spiros when she put yogurt in my bed. Stabbing a six-year-old criminal psychopath was completely outside my experience.

'Back off and go to your room,' I hissed.

'Take it easy,' said a strained voice.

It was the boy in the dress. He must have followed me into the rear of the Hummer. A shaft of light from the open flap shone on his anxious face. He was eyeing the blade in my hand.

'Be careful with that,' he said. 'People can hurt themselves with sharp knives in moving vehicles.'

'Who are you?' I demanded.

I was trying to sound tough and confident instead of like a dazed kid whose parents had both gone missing. It wasn't easy. At school in drama they'd always reckoned I was a hopeless actor. The year I tried to get the part of Princess Leia in the *Star Wars* musical I ended up as the back half of a space camel.

'Who are you?' I repeated.

He hadn't taken his eyes off the knife, but suddenly he was looking confused and sad.

'Dunno,' he said. 'I can't remember.' He nodded towards the front of the truck. 'I'm hoping these little weirdos can give me a clue.'

I looked at him closely, trying to decide if he was telling the truth.

'You can't remember your own name?' I said.

He frowned unhappily. 'There's a theory I'm called Sprocket,' he said. 'Doesn't feel exactly right, but I s'pose it's better than nothing.'

He winced and held his stomach, which was still looking pretty swollen. More swollen than before, in fact.

I decided to ignore it. There was something more important I needed to know.

'The little weirdos,' I said. 'Who are they?'

'Wish I knew,' said Sprocket. 'They've been after me for as long as I can remember.'

I stared at him. 'What,' I said, 'years?'

'No,' he said. 'About three hours.'

The truck swung round a corner and we were both sent sliding. As I grabbed onto a spare tyre, the knife slipped out of my hand.

Sprocket leaned forward and picked it up.

And handed it back to me.

I stared at him in the gloom, surprised and confused. I didn't know much about violent criminals, but I was pretty sure they didn't do things like that.

'Thanks,' I said.

Before I could think of anything else to say, Sprocket got in first.

'Are you a nudist?' he asked.

I crouched there stunned while he straightened his dress. A nudist? That was the weirdest thing anyone had ever asked me.

'Why?' I said. 'Are you?'

He didn't say anything. The muscles in his face were straining. I could see it wasn't just the pain from his tummy. He was struggling to remember. He closed his eyes and shook his head in frustration and disappointment.

There was something about his haunted, pained expression. Maybe he was telling the truth. Maybe he was just a kid in as much trouble as I was.

I decided to take a risk. I put the knife away. 'I'm Amy Tunks-Livingstone,' I said, sounding tougher and more confident than I felt.

If Ms Rogers the drama teacher had seen my performance she'd have given me a standing ovation. Or at least the *front* end of the camel suit.

'G'day,' said Sprocket painfully through gritted teeth.

Before I could ask about his tummy, I realised the Hummer was slowing down.

Sprocket signalled me to follow him. He stuck his head warily out through the back flap. I peered over his shoulder. We were passing some long, low white-painted buildings behind a high wire fence. In among the buildings I caught glimpses of pink and brown things moving. For a crazy moment I thought they were naked people.

I looked again.

They were.

'The nudist camp,' said Sprocket grimly as we drove past. 'That's where the nudists tried to kidnap me.'

'I wonder if those nude kidnappers,' I said, 'are connected to our mini-kidnappers.'

Sprocket didn't say anything for a couple of minutes as we bumped along the dirt track. Then he tensed. The Hummer was slowing down even more. We felt the little driver changing down through the gears.

'I reckon we're about to find out,' said Sprocket. 'Follow me, and when you hit the dirt, try and roll into the bushes.'

He jumped out.

I gripped the back of the Hummer and felt sick. I was even worse at sports than I was at drama. Plus our school preferred cricket and netball to diving out of moving trucks.

I peered down. The dirt road was still speeding past, but getting slower.

I thought of my baby half-sister, and how I couldn't help her if I was caught in the back of the Hummer.

I jumped.

The dirt smacked me in the head and as I rolled I felt like several arms and legs were being ripped off. Then I found I was lying on cool under-growth with quite a lot of moist rotting leaves up my nose.

I sneezed a few times and rolled over.

Next to my face was the hem of a dress. Sticking out of it were two hairy ankles and two big feet. One of Sprocket's feet was scratched and bleeding.

Sprocket was crouched down low, peering at some-thing through the greenery.

I sat up.

'Are you OK?' I asked

'Keep down,' he grunted. 'They'll see you.'

I turned and saw we were at the edge of a clearing in the rainforest. The Hummer was parked in front of a group of low concrete buildings that looked at first like they were painted in green and grey camouflage. Then I realised they were covered in patches of moss and lichen.

I held my breath as the little kids jumped down from the Hummer cab.

They weren't carrying the baby.

That's good, I thought desperately. They must have already dropped her off. Maybe she's inside one of those buildings, warm and safe.

I prayed she was.

A big hairy man in a black apron was standing, arms folded, glaring at the little kids.

'Hairy Chest,' muttered Sprocket. 'I've met him before.'

'You're late for work,' the man shouted at the kids.

'Don't get your knickers in a knot,' growled the kid with spiky red hair. 'You know there hasn't been any work for weeks.'

The kids went into one of the buildings. Hairy Chest turned and followed them. I stared in disbelief at his retreating behind. His knickers weren't in a knot. He wasn't even wearing any. Under his apron he wasn't wearing anything at all.

I heard Sprocket give a pained gasp. I knew how he felt. I felt pretty nauseated myself.

'Come on,' I whispered to him. 'Let's check this place out.'

I didn't want to go. I didn't want to get any closer to those evil kids or to the bloke with the hairy buttocks. But I had to find out if my half-sister was there. And Dad. And maybe even Mum.

I followed Sprocket across the clearing to the nearest building. We pressed ourselves against the damp lichen-covered wall and listened.

Nothing.

Except, suddenly, a low angry growling.

'What's that?' I whispered, alarmed, peering into the tangled undergrowth near by. If it was a bush pig we were in trouble. When they were hungry they got really vicious. I'd seen it on TV.

'It's my stomach,' groaned Sprocket. 'I ate something that disagreed with me.'

I looked at him and it was my turn to gasp. His stomach was huge. It was so swollen it was stretching the fabric of his dress. The thin cloth didn't look like it was going to stand the strain much longer.

Sprocket didn't look like he was going to stand the strain much longer either. The poor kid's face was twisted with agony.

I had to get him some help. I looked around and saw a door in the side of the building. I couldn't hear any sounds coming from inside. I threw myself at the door, ready to kick it in if necessary, but it swung open when I turned the handle.

'Come on,' I said to Sprocket. 'Come and lie down while I think what to do.'

I could see he didn't want to, but the pain was so bad he didn't stop me. I led him into the small building and shut the door.

We found ourselves in an office with bare floorboards and a ramshackle paper-strewn desk. Paint was flaking off the walls.

I wasn't worried about the decor, though. I was worried about what was happening to Sprocket.

He was crouched down, panting with pain.

His stomach was getting bigger and bigger.

SPROCKET

THREE

We had a temporary hiding place in the draughty room. But for how long? At any moment we might be discovered.

Not that I was spending much time thinking about that. My main concern was my gigantic stomach.

'You look even more pregnant than before,' said Amy. 'As if you're having twins. I thought you were a girl when I first saw you. Are you sure you're a boy?'

I couldn't be certain but I thought she was trying to smother a smile.

'I'm a boy,' I said. 'I'll prove it if you like.' I flapped the hem of my dress as if I was going to lift it.

'Don't worry,' she answered hastily.

Before I could say another word I was gripped by another spasm of pain. The pressure was building up. At any moment I was going to have to release it. But I couldn't fart in front of this girl. She would think I was gross.

I clenched the cheeks of my backside together but it was no use.

'It's gas,' I screamed. 'I can't hold it in any longer. I'm going to let off. I just can't help it.'

'Don't worry about me,' said Amy. 'I once sat next to Stinky Harrison for a whole term. After that I could put up with anything.'

The pressure was increasing. And with it the pain. My belly was enormous. Far bigger than any beer gut. Far bigger than any pregnant woman's stomach. My dress stretched out like the covering of a hot-air balloon. I couldn't take it any more. It didn't matter what Amy thought. It didn't matter if I stank out the whole room. Or the whole country. I had to let go.

I was in agony. I fell onto my back and unclenched my buttocks.

Blrrp, blart, splat.

A small hard object shot out of my bottom and zipped across the room like a bullet. It hit the wall and bounced onto the floor. It was about the size of a large marble but shiny and blue.

'Ahhhh,' I cried.

The blue thing had been holding everything back. A disgusting, wet explosion followed it out between my legs. My dress billowed and shook like an exploding tent. Amy clapped her hands over her ears and closed her eyes. Thunder releasing from the backside of an elephant would have been a mere breeze in comparison to that terrible release of gas.

And not just any gas. It was bright blue.

The foul gust seemed to go on and on and on. Papers were whipped from the desk. Curtains flapped and shook. The lampshade fell like a power pole in a hurricane. The room was totally wrecked.

When it finally stopped, Amy opened her eyes. They grew wider and wider. The gas from my belly hovered like a boiling raincloud over the blue object. Amy pushed it with her toe and it rolled a couple of centimetres.

'Don't touch it,' I said. 'You never know where it's been.'

'I know where it's been,' said Amy. 'And I have no intention of touching it.'

'It looks a bit like a ball-bearing,' I said slowly. 'Or maybe a hazelnut.'

'It could be a marble,' said Amy. 'Felicity Moggs's little sister got one stuck up her nose once. Can you remember shoving it into any bodily recesses?'

'No.' I shook my head, trying to remember. Then I grabbed Amy and pulled her back. 'The cloud is moving,' I yelled.

The cloud settled down on the floor and completely covered the little blue object.

I suddenly felt embarrassed. This blue cloud had come out of my backside. 'Sorry about letting off,' I mumbled.

'At least it doesn't smell,' said Amy. 'It could have been an SBD. Stinky Harrison does them all the time.'

I looked at her, puzzled.

'Silent But Deadly,' she said with a grin.

I didn't smile back. 'I'm ill,' I groaned. 'I've got some terrible disease from that blue marble thing.'

Amy tried to make me feel better. 'Look,' she said, pointing at my dress.

My stomach was flat. It was back to normal.

'I think you're cured,' she told me. 'I think it's over.'

I couldn't take in what she said. I was staring at a huge huntsman spider that had crawled through one of the cracks in the wall. It was a whopper. Almost as big as a saucer.

So was the next one. And the one after that. And the one after that.

Five grasshoppers followed. After them came moths and butterflies. And caterpillars. And bull ants. And centipedes. And brown ants. And redback spiders and daddy longlegs. Tens, hundreds and then thousands of insects and creepy crawlies began to squeeze into the room.

They dropped down from holes in the ceiling. They came through the window. They pushed under the door. They scurried through cracks and holes and gaps.

In no time at all we were covered with scampering, crawling, hopping insects and spiders. We screamed and yelled and frantically tried to swipe them away. Amy jumped up and down, shrieking as a crawling black tide swept over her. She was completely covered. And so was I.

They were in my hair and eyes and earholes. I gasped and sucked in air. And with the air I drew in a huge spider. It squirmed and wriggled inside my mouth like a live, damp feather. I spat it out with a scream.

The crawling carpet moved over us.

And on.

The insects had no interest in me and Amy. We were merely in their way. They didn't even stop to bite us. They were being drawn to the blue cloud. They swarmed towards it as if pulled by a living magnet. In a flash they had gone. Disappeared into the blue, misty vapour. Every insect within a hundred metres must have been attracted to it.

There was a long silence. The last centipede wriggled into the cloud.

Amy was shaking all over. So was I. We held on to each other in our fear. Two terrified teenagers clinging together, totally defenceless. We couldn't take our eyes off the hungry cloud.

Suddenly the mist began to evaporate.

'Now what?' said Amy, her eyes wide.

As the cloud thinned we could see that the insects were still there. But every one was now blue. As if they'd been spray-painted.

Like a million bright-blue brooches they wriggled and squirmed in a huge pile which stretched halfway to the ceiling. The last of the mist vanished.

All that was left was a living blue pile. An enormous huntsman spider toppled down, rolled across the room and stopped right in front of us. It reared up, waved its front legs and then . . . and then . . . I couldn't believe it. The spider began to expand as if it was being pumped full of air. It grew bigger and bigger until it was the size of a mouse.

Pop. The spider exploded. Bits of blue leg and body splattered around the room.

Ping. A blue grasshopper shattered.

The whole pile began to expand and explode. A hail of bursting insect parts filled the air. Blue legs and shells and feelers hit us like sand whipped up on the beach in a storm. The blast stung and pitted our skin. The air was unbreathable. We huddled down and closed our eyes and mouths as the gale raged around us.

Then at last the sound of explosions grew less. The machine-gun spatter petered out and ended with an occasional lonely *pop*. I opened my eyes and saw that the softer parts of the insects were all that was left in the air. Feelers and spider fur and soft legs fluttered down like falling snow. Amy began to cough. She held her hands over her mouth. Her breathing stopped. Was she choking? Her face was purple beneath the blue fluff.

The only thought I had was that Amy might die if her lungs filled up with fuzz. I hesitated for a second. Then I jumped up and pulled off my dress. I spread it over her to keep the choking drifts away from her mouth and nose. She looked like a statue covered with a sheet in an empty house.

We stood there in silence until every last bit of fluff had settled. Everything including my naked body was covered in a warm blue snowdrift of insect parts. When it was over Amy pulled the dress off her head. She was gasping and looking at me with a strange expression on her face.

'Are you OK?' she asked.

I nodded, feeling my face blush.

She looked at me as I stood there naked trying to cover up my private parts.

'Shut your eyes,' she said.

'Why?' I said alarmed.

'Just do it.'

I did as she asked.

'OK,' she said a few moments later.

I opened my eyes and saw her standing with her back to me, facing the blue-spattered wall. She was wearing a dress. My dress. And on the floor, neatly folded in front of me, were her jeans and jumper.

'Hurry up,' she said. 'We have to get out of here.'

I put on her jeans and jumper, accepting the gift without a word. When I had finished I told her she could turn around. It felt so good to be wearing pants again.

We grinned at each other, both embarrassed.

I bent down and felt around among the blue insect parts. I touched something hard with the tip of my fingers. I grabbed it and held it out on my palm. It was the blue marble thing. Amy stared at me in disgust as I shoved it into the pocket of my jeans.

'I'll wash my hands later,' I said.

'You can keep the jeans,' Amy said icily.

I tried to change the subject. 'I wonder what that blue gas was all about?'

'Insect killer,' said Amy.

'I can see that,' I said.

'Maybe it's some sort of new ecological weapon,' said Amy. 'Maybe gene modification can make humans produce a natural insect repellent. You could put Aeroguard out of business with one flatulent release. Your bottom could become world famous. You . . .'

'Hang on a bit,' I said grumpily. 'How do you know all this?'

'Just guessing,' she grinned back at me. 'I know something else, too.'

'What?'

'You are definitely a boy.'

FOUR

We stepped shakily out of the office into the fresh air and crouched against the wall of the building. I tried to make sense of what I'd just seen. I couldn't. Dad was always going on about how amazing nature was, but even after three beers he'd never described anything half as amazing as that killer blue cloud.

Nervously I scanned the forest clearing for Brats.

I couldn't see any.

Something brushed against my arm.

'Giant spider!' I almost screamed. Then I realised it was just Sprocket, handing me the things from my jeans pockets. The Swiss Army knife. Mum's mobile. The ripped piece of letter from the Other Woman to Dad that I'd found in the love-nest bathroom.

'Thanks,' I said, stuffing them into the pockets of the ugliest dress in the world. If Julie Spiros ever saw me in it, I was dead meat.

Seeing the letter made me want to talk about Dad, but I didn't because there were too many other things to worry about.

Like finding him. And Mum. And the baby.

I peered around at the other buildings, looking for a clue. But it wasn't my eyes that found one, it was my nose.

'Hey,' I said to Sprocket. 'Can you smell that?'

Sprocket was busy stretching the arms of my jumper and the legs of my jeans to try and cover more of his bare wrists and ankles. He looked up indignantly.

'That wasn't me,' he said. 'I haven't done one for at least ten minutes.' He touched his stomach cautiously. 'I think I'm OK now. As long as I stay away from blue stones and baked beans.'

'I'm not talking about the gas,' I said, sniffing the air. 'I'm talking about that perfume smell.'

It was a smell I recognised. My pulse beat faster.

'My dad's been having an affair with a failed

industrial chemist,' I explained to Sprocket. 'This is her perfume.'

For a moment I thought it was coming from the letter, but it was too strong for that. It was coming from somewhere near by.

'I'd know it anywhere,' I said, looking around at the other buildings. 'It's like an expensive bathroom air-freshener, but with extra smells of . . .'

'Licorice,' said Sprocket suddenly. Now he was sniffing the air. 'And rubber.' He had the strained expression he got when he was trying to drag something out of his memory. 'And vanilla.'

'Exactly,' I said, my mind racing. A sudden thought made my insides ache. Why was the Other Woman's perfume here? Was she mixed up with the Brats? Was Dad? Was Mum?

'We've got to find out what's going on,' I said to Sprocket.

I realised he wasn't even listening. He was still sniffing the air, his face rigid with concentration.

'This smell,' he said. 'There's something that feels sort of . . . I dunno . . . familiar about it.'

I watched him struggling to remember, a poor kid who didn't even know who he was. Even though I was sick with worry about Mum and Dad and the baby, I forced myself to calm down. Sprocket had saved my life in the blue gas. The least I could do was spare a few brain cells to try to help him find out the truth about his life.

'Perhaps your mum used to wear a similar perfume,' I said.

'Perhaps she still does,' he said miserably. 'She could own a chain of perfume shops for all I know.'

I peered around again to try and see where the smell was coming from. It was too strong to have travelled far on the breeze. Near by was another building, a larger version of the one we'd just been in. One of its windows was open.

'There,' I whispered, pointing. 'Let's see what's in there.'

Or who.

As we crept over to the larger building, I tried to think of what I'd do if I came face to face with the woman who'd stolen Dad from us.

I decided I'd introduce myself politely, then whack her round the head with a used nappy.

We crouched by the window and peered in.

It looked like some sort of old-fashioned factory. There were big metal tubs with metal pipes connecting them. Some of the pipes had grubby cloth wound round them, like bandages. The tubs were scorched black, as if they'd once been heated by flames underneath.

The whole place was silent and empty.

No factory workers.

No Other Women.

Just the perfume smell, stronger than ever.

Sprocket and I looked at each other.

'Wonder what goes on here?' I said.

Sprocket swung a leg up onto the window sill. 'Only one way to find out,' he muttered.

I hitched up the dress and climbed in through the window after him.

It was cool inside, and there weren't many windows, so the whole place was in a sort of half-light.

I tapped one of the tubs with my knuckle. The faint echo told me it was empty.

Then Sprocket grabbed my shoulder so hard I thought for a second he'd remembered who he was. But instead of whispering excitedly in my ear, he roughly pushed me down behind a tangle of pipes.

'Hey,' I protested.

He was lying next to me. On the dirty floor. In my jeans and jumper.

'Shhhh,' he said.

I was about to make a brief point about the cost of washing powder when I suddenly heard it. The slap, slap of wet feet on the concrete floor.

Coming closer.

We held our breaths.

The smell was getting stronger.

Then a figure stepped into view.

It was human-shape and human-size, but despite having all the male human body parts, it wasn't human-looking. In the half-light its whole body seemed to be melting into a white pulp. The legs, the arms, the torso, all dissolving into a glistening slime. The featureless blob on top of the shoulders was only recognisable as a head because of the white-caked eyelids and the dull black eye-sockets.

I stared in terror.

The figure raised one terrible dripping hand and wiped it over its mushy face. Part of the hand wiped off on the face. Part of the face slimed onto the hand.

I desperately tried not to throw up.

Then, as the figure turned slightly, I saw what it was holding in its other hand. A small jar. It stuck its fingers, still with gobs of face on them, into the jar.

I couldn't believe what I was seeing.

This creature was collecting its own dissolving body and storing it in a jar.

I turned my head away, weak with nausea.

An angry roar rang out across the factory.

'Silas, how dare you?'

I looked up fearfully.

The big hairy man in the apron had appeared next to the melting figure and was glaring at it furiously.

'This is forbidden,' he roared.

The melting figure dropped its jar. Its shoulders sagged. And dripped onto the floor.

'I didn't mean any harm, Hubert,' it whined in the pleading voice of a middle-aged man. 'I just want to be young again. What's the harm in that?'

'The harm,' thundered Hairy Chest, 'is that I'm the foreman here and this produce is my responsibility.

And you are wasting it. Get a bucket and scrape it off.'

Hairy Chest led the sobbing Melting Man away.

Sprocket and I waited for several minutes to make sure Hairy Chest wasn't coming back, then dragged ourselves out of our hiding place and hurried over to where the jar lay on the floor.

Except there wasn't just one jar, there were lots, mostly empty.

Sprocket picked one up and we both studied it.

There was a label on the jar with the words Sunrise Skin Cream on it, and a photo of a woman rubbing skin cream on her face with great enjoyment.

'Skin cream,' I said, weak with relief. 'He wasn't taking it off, he was putting it on.'

The jar was still half full of cream. I stuck my fingers in and lifted them to my nose.

The perfume smell all around us was suddenly concentrated under my nostrils. Expensive bathroom air-freshener, licorice, rubber, vanilla, the whole Other Woman pong.

This must be the skin cream she used.

But where was the Other Woman?

With a sickening jolt I realised I was no closer to finding Dad or Mum or the baby. They could be anywhere.

'Sprocket,' I said, starting to tell him the awful news.

I didn't get any further. At that moment I heard the

sound of voices. Hairy Chest. And the Brats. Heading towards us.

Sprocket was staring at the label on the jar so intently he hadn't even heard. Then he ripped the label off the jar, stared at it one more time, and stuffed it into his pocket. I looked around wildly, saw an open doorway near by, grabbed him and dragged him into a storeroom.

Piled high all around us were hundreds of cardboard cartons, all with the skin cream label on them. Several cartons had been ripped open, and unopened jars were spilling out.

Sprocket stared at them in a daze. I could see he was trying to remember again.

I pushed the door almost closed and peeped through the crack just as Hairy Chest ushered the Brats into the factory.

'I want this place clean and tidy,' said Hairy Chest. 'Jump to it.'

'This is a complete waste of time,' grumbled Scowler, shaking his little head of spiky red hair.

'Monumentally stupid,' mumbled Beanie, not looking up at Hairy Chest.

'I fail to see the point,' muttered Reptile. She stuffed her little hands into the pockets of her racing driver's jacket and flicked her tongue disapprovingly over her lips.

'The point,' thundered Hairy Chest, 'is that Agnes is on her way.'

The Brats suddenly looked scared and started picking up the empty jars as fast as they could. Well, three of them did. Pooper Scooper gave a faint sneer and watched the others.

There was the sound of a vehicle drawing up outside.

'She's here, she's here,' squeaked Hairy Chest, his big muscular body jiggling nervously.

I felt Sprocket beside me, peering out through the crack. He was trembling, like I was.

Who was this woman who struck such fear into Hairy Chest and the Brats? A chillingly beautiful Other Woman with exquisite clothes and a ruthlessly vicious temper? A cruel and powerful gang leader with tattoos and fearsome weapons dragging Mum and Dad and the baby behind her in chains?

The outside door swung open.

A short, plump middle-aged woman wearing a light brown cardigan and a dark brown skirt waddled in.

She smiled sweetly at the trembling Hairy Chest and the nervous-looking Brats.

She was wheeling a tea trolley.

SPROCKET

FIVE

We stared out from our hiding spot at the scene before us. The woman in brown pushed her trolley briskly across the factory floor to where the Brats were standing in line.

'It's the bossy woman from the nudist camp,' I gasped.

I recognised her straight away – even though she was wearing clothes now. They made her look like an old-fashioned tea lady.

'She reminds me of the canteen lady at school,' whispered Amy.

'Shhh,' I said. 'This could be dangerous.'

On the front of her trolley hung a sign. It read:

> **TEA**
> Just four drops
> upon your tongue
> Is enough
> to keep you young.
> If you're bad
> I keep you small.
> Take your dose
> or – none at all!

The Brats stood facing her with their hands behind their backs. Hairy Chest looked on with his arms folded on his chest like a teacher waiting for the principal to inspect his class.

'Think yourselves lucky,' the Tea Lady snapped at the Brats in a brittle voice. 'This is the last dose. There is no more.'

Hairy Chest nodded. 'If you lot don't want it,' he said, 'you can give it to me.'

Pooper Scooper, Scowler and Reptile's eyes smouldered with hate and resentment.

Beanie smiled nervously. 'No more tea,' he said. 'Oh well, at least I'll be a teenager again. If only briefly.'

'You fool,' said Pooper Scooper in a scornful voice.

'I can get my driving licence again anyway,' said Reptile. 'I'll have a bit of fun before I go.'

'Idiot,' spat out Pooper Scooper.

'I can make up for lost time with the girls,' said Scowler in a slimy voice.

'What's wrong with you all? You're old enough to know what's going to happen,' said Pooper Scooper. 'Face up to it. The end is nigh. We'll all be dead before we can enjoy anything.' He gave the Tea Lady a savage glare. 'It's all your doing, Agnes,' he said. 'Just because we wouldn't do what you wanted you made us take too much. We've been stuck as children ever since and we've missed out on all the fun.'

'You should have thought of that when you were behaving like hooligans all those years ago,' said Hairy Chest.

'Let's get on with it,' said the Tea Lady. 'It's time for tea. Without your dose you'll all be dead. You know that as well as I do. Open up,' she commanded.

The four Brats opened their mouths reluctantly and stuck out their tongues.

The Tea Lady took the lid off a china teapot. She inserted a glass dropper that she filled with the tea. Then she squeezed out four drops onto each small tongue. The Brats swallowed carefully, not wanting to waste a drop, but hating what they were doing at the same time.

'What's going on?' whispered Amy.

'I dunno,' I replied. 'The tea must be some sort of medicine.'

The Tea Lady spoke to Hairy Chest. 'What sort of week has it been, Hubert?' she said.

'Terrible,' said Hairy Chest. 'They've been worse than usual.' He handed over an exercise book. On the front I could just make out the words.

> Punishment
> Register

The Tea Lady stood in front of Reptile who stared up at her with murder in her eyes.

Amy whispered to me. 'There's something about that girl that isn't right . . .'

I held my hand up over Amy's mouth to keep her quiet.

The Tea Lady looked around the room as if she had heard something. Her eyes narrowed as she listened. She stared straight at the storeroom door where we were hiding. She seemed to be gazing into my eyes. My heart was beating so loudly that it sounded like thunder in my ears. I held my breath.

The Tea Lady listened some more. Then, satisfied for the time being, she turned back to Reptile and read from the book.

'Hilda,' she said in a cruel voice. 'Using factory funds to buy a Hummer. Very clever of you to buy it over the internet.'

Reptile was angry. 'We had to go into town. We had to get the last tea plant before . . .'

The Tea Lady cut her off. 'And what if some nosey cop had seen what looked like a six-year-old driving an army truck?'

'I had the tinted windows up,' shouted Reptile.

The Tea Lady moved on to Scowler and turned to the next page in the book.

'Now to you, Stanley,' she said. 'Entering the main compound while still dressed. You know the rules. Everyone crossing the compound must be naked. You could have blown our cover.'

'It doesn't matter any more, Agnes,' Scowler said bitterly. 'What's the point? We're all doomed. Even you, little sister.'

'I'm still in charge here,' said the Tea Lady. 'And you'll do what I say.'

Scowler placed his hand on his Bowie knife. 'Soon, sister dear,' he said, 'very soon, you're going to have to deal with someone your own size.'

'But not right now,' said the Tea Lady.

I couldn't believe what I was hearing. The Tea Lady looked more like Scowler's grandmother than his sister.

The Tea Lady jabbed Scowler in the chest with an outstretched finger. She was just like a huge bully in the little kids' playground.

Amy was watching with big round eyes.

The Tea Lady moved on to Beanie.

'Disobeying the Foreman,' she said. 'Your trouble, Barnabus, is that you are easily led. You are weak. If you would just think for yourself you wouldn't be in this mess.'

Beanie stared at his shoes and shuffled his feet.

Amy and I watched the incredible scene, hardly daring to breathe. This woman had enormous power. I started to tremble. What would she do to us if we were discovered? The Tea Lady moved on to Pooper Scooper. He glared back up at her. He met her eyes fearlessly. I could see that his teeth were clenched. So were his fists. He looked ready to pounce.

'Orson,' she said in a biting voice. 'You're responsible for the whole mess. Letting the intruder escape. Again.'

'That's me,' I mouthed at Amy. 'I'm the intruder.'

Amy looked at me, trying to take it all in.

The Tea Lady continued reading. 'Losing the last seed. Again. Refusing to take off your clothes. Again. Leaving the compound without permission. Again.' She waved a fat finger under his nose. 'You're the ringleader, Orson. I hold you responsible for all this mischief.'

She handed a large jar to Hairy Chest. 'For punishment you get four spoonfuls of my special brussels sprouts each,' she said. The Brats all gasped.

'We're adults,' yelled Scowler.

'Then stop acting like children,' she said.

'Get lost,' snapped Reptile.

'Open,' commanded the Tea Lady. 'Or we'll make you.'

The Brats reluctantly opened their mouths. All except Pooper Scooper. He kept his firmly shut. Hairy Chest started to give the Brats four spoonfuls of soggy brussels sprouts. They pulled terrible faces and moaned and groaned.

'Urgh,' said Reptile as she wiped her tongue on her racing glove.

'Foul,' said Scowler.

'Disgusting,' said Beanie.

Finally Hairy Chest reached Pooper Scooper. The

tough little Brat shook his head decisively.

'I'm through obeying you, Agnes,' he spat out. 'You don't have any power over us any more. It's all over. We're all finished.'

The Tea Lady pointed her finger at the poem on her trolley. 'Take your brussels sprouts,' she said, 'or it's no more tea for you.'

'That won't work any more. There's none left,' yelled Pooper Scooper. 'I'm not swallowing one more brussels sprout.'

'Aren't you just,' said the Tea Lady in a menacing voice. She nodded at Hairy Chest. He jumped on Pooper Scooper and placed him in a headlock. Then he pinched Pooper Scooper's nostrils so that he couldn't breathe.

Amy and I watched the horrifying scene, amazed. She pulled my sleeve. 'My mother did that to me once when I wouldn't eat *my* brussels sprouts. I know how he feels.'

Pooper Scooper kept his jaws clenched and drew in a breath through the gaps in his teeth.

'Playing hard to get, are we?' said Hairy Chest. He used his free hand to prise open Pooper Scooper's mouth. Then the Tea Lady forced in a soggy green spoonful. Pooper Scooper squirmed and wormed but it was no good. Hairy Chest tightened his grip around poor Pooper Scooper's neck and held the little bandit's jaws closed. Now he couldn't breathe at all. He began to turn purple.

'Swallow,' ordered the Tea Lady.

Pooper Scooper seemed to swallow and Hairy Chest let him go. Straight away Pooper Scooper jumped up and spat onto the floor. Everyone stared at the mushy green gunk.

'Anyone who messes with me will get the same treatment,' he said. 'Chewed up and spat out.'

Hairy Chest shook his head in disbelief. 'You can lead a Brat to water,' he said. 'But you can't make him think.'

'I've outsmarted both of *you*,' yelled Pooper Scooper.

'We'll see about that,' said the Tea Lady. She grabbed him by his collar and threw him onto a bench. Then she grabbed his jeans and ripped them down, exposing his tiny bare bottom. *Whack, whack, whack*. She began spanking him with the flat of her hand. Pooper Scooper squirmed but he didn't make a sound. Not a yell. Not a scream. Not a word. He was tough.

'I wouldn't like to be her when he grows up,' I whispered.

Hairy Chest carried Pooper Scooper across the room by the scruff of his neck. Then he flung him into a smaller room and closed the door. On the door was a sign which read:

TIME OUT ROOM

'You wait,' shouted Pooper Scooper from inside. 'Without any tea I'll soon grow. I'll be ready to take you on any day now.'

'If you don't do what you're told,' said the Tea Lady, 'you're the one who will be dead. At least the rest of us will have a chance.'

'Don't be pathetic. You're history,' Pooper Scooper yelled. 'You're dead. We all are.'

The Tea Lady looked at the three Brats left in the room. 'No we're not,' she said. 'Not yet. If we catch the intruder there's hope.'

'Just let me get my hands on him,' growled Scowler. His face was twisted by an expression of terrible hatred. 'I'll make him talk.'

SIX

We crouched in the storeroom and watched the Tea Lady give a final stern glare at the sullen Brats. Then she did up her cardigan and wheeled her trolley out of the factory.

My brain was going like a turbine-driven vegie-processing machine. But instead of producing mashed turnips, it was producing indignation.

This was incredible. This was horrifying. This was an outrage.

Grown adults using kids as slave labour in their skin-cream empire. Beating them. Locking them up. Force-feeding them brussels sprouts. Giving them some sort of weird tea that made them think they were adults.

I could hardly believe it was happening in modern Australia.

How had my dad and my mum and my poor innocent little love-child half-sister got involved with such monsters? And more importantly, how could I find them and get them back to safety?

I looked desperately at Sprocket. I didn't dare speak because the burly Hairy Chest had moved right next to our hiding place. He'd have heard even a whisper.

I could see Sprocket was thinking the same as me.

We had to do something.

I pulled Mum's mobile phone from my pocket and mimed us getting out of there and me ringing the police.

Sprocket nodded and we both started looking round for a way out.

That's when I saw it. On the floor near our feet.

A nappy.

A used nappy.

The same brand I'd bought for my sister at the shop near our place. I smothered a gasp. She couldn't be far away. She might even be in this very storeroom. Asleep or drugged or . . .

Before my thoughts could run wild, there was a roar from the factory floor.

'Don't even think of it.'

I peered out. Hairy Chest was advancing towards Scowler, who had his hand on the bolt of the Time Out room.

Beanie, watching with wide anxious eyes, took a nervous step back.

Reptile didn't move. Her little eyes narrowed and the tip of her tongue darted in and out between her lips like a knife-blade aimed at Hairy Chest's throat.

Scowler didn't move either. 'Mind your own business, you little squirt,' he yelled, his face almost as red as his spiky hair. He glared up at the towering Hairy Chest. 'We're sick of you pushing us around,' he continued. 'Little brothers should be seen and not heard.'

Reptile hissed her agreement and Beanie stammered his.

I looked at Sprocket. Little brother? Hairy Chest was three times the size of Scowler.

Hairy Chest hesitated and looked uncertain. Just for a moment. Then he grabbed Scowler and pulled him away from the cell door.

'You lot need pushing around,' snarled Hairy Chest. 'All the while you do stupid things like kidnapping that baby.'

Scowler rolled his eyes. 'We did that for all of us, pea-brain,' he snapped at Hairy Chest. 'To get you-know-who to work harder. To make him a simple business offer. Solve our little problem, Mr Tunks-Livingstone, and you get your baby back.'

I stifled another gasp.

Dad was involved with all this. Working for them. Being blackmailed by them. My father was a skin-cream criminal.

I bet it's the Other Woman's fault, I thought, dazed and bitter. I bet she lured him into it with revealing dresses and Bunsen burners turned down romantically low.

While I was still struggling to digest all this, Scowler kicked Hairy Chest hard in the shin. Hairy Chest gave a yelp, let go of Scowler, staggered, slipped in a puddle of skin cream and crashed to the floor, banging his head on a metal pipe as he went down.

He lay groaning.

Scowler flung back the bolt and swung open the cell door.

Pooper Scooper walked slowly out, glowering under his angelic curls. But it wasn't his face that sent a jolt of anxiety through me, it was the pram he was pushing.

A big old-fashioned pram with a tasselled hood.

I struggled to see if my baby sister was inside and if she was OK. I couldn't. The sides were too high.

I strained to hear a cry or a gurgle. Nothing. I hoped she was asleep, blissfully unaware of who was pushing her.

Hairy Chest was staggering to his feet, holding his head. 'I'm telling on you lot,' he groaned, limping towards the door. 'When Agnes hears what you've done, you'll really suffer.'

Pooper Scooper yelled angrily after him. 'Count the days, Hubert. Count the days till we're fully grown again. Then we'll see who'll suffer.'

Fully grown again? I didn't get it. I looked at Sprocket. I could see he didn't either.

Scowler, Reptile and Beanie were glowering at the departing Hairy Chest.

'We'll send you to bed early,' Beanie yelled at him. 'And make you eat mud.'

Pooper Scooper gave Beanie a withering look. Beanie withered.

'We'll do considerably worse than that,' said Pooper Scooper quietly. And without any warning he gave the pram a violent push so it bumped and jolted across the factory floor and fell into the metal jaws of a large hydraulic machine.

'This is what we'll do,' said Pooper Scooper quietly, and went over to the machine and punched a control button.

With a terrible rusty squeal, the jaws of the machine closed, crushing the pram.

I stared from my hiding place, frozen with shock, a scream trapped in my throat. For the time it took Pooper Scooper to lead his psycho infants out of the factory, my body wouldn't work.

Then hysterical panic stabbed through me and I flung open the storeroom door and hurled myself over to the machine and dragged out the twisted, flattened pram.

I didn't want to look, but I had to.

I tried to.

I couldn't.

As I turned away, sick with fear, I felt Sprocket step past me and heard him gently pull back the torn fabric.

A long silence.

Then he spoke.

'It's empty,' he said. I turned slowly and looked. He was telling the truth. There was just twisted metal and ripped cloth and an unused nappy.

No baby.

I sat on the floor, weak and dizzy with relief.

Then I heard voices approaching. Hairy Chest and the Brats were coming back.

'Sprocket,' I hissed. 'Quick.'

He wasn't listening. He hadn't even heard the voices. He was staring at the pram, frowning. His eyes had the distant puzzled look they'd had when he'd first seen the skin-cream label.

Memories. Memories stuck somewhere he couldn't get at them.

I grabbed him and shoved him across the factory and back into the storeroom. I was about to follow him in when a thought hit me.

The pram. They'd see the pram had been moved.

I leaped back over to the machine, stuffed the wrecked pram back between the metal jaws and ducked down behind a vat just as Hairy Chest and the Brats came back in.

I was trapped. There was no way I could get over to the storeroom without them seeing me, and when they'd taken a few more steps they'd see me anyway.

Hairy Chest was holding what looked like a large electric cattle-prod. The Brats, eyeing him sulkily, were being herded back to work.

'Just remember next time you get too big for your boots,' barked Hairy Chest, 'Agnes has not only got the authority, she's also got the equipment.'

He prodded Scowler on the backside. Scowler yelped and leapt forward, sloshing soapy water out of the bucket he was carrying.

'Think yourselves lucky,' continued Hairy Chest. 'If she didn't have her hands full with that baby over in the main building, you'd probably be getting worse treatment.'

My heart experienced a two thousand megawatt power surge. The main building. So that's where my sister was.

And I was trapped here.

The Brats started half-heartedly scrubbing the factory floor and polishing the pipes and vats. Hairy Chest stood over them, watching them work. As each minute passed, they got closer and closer to the vat I was crouching behind.

I gripped my Swiss Army knife and wondered if it had an implement for overpowering groups.

Probably not.

Then suddenly a bizarre figure appeared behind Hairy Chest. The figure was covered from head to ankle in skin cream. It waved its arms and the cream flew off in gobs.

I stared in disbelief.

The Melting Man was back.

The Brats shouted in alarm and pointed and Hairy Chest spun round and roared.

'Silas, you mongrel,' he bellowed. 'I warned you.'

The Melting Man danced around the enraged Hairy Chest, flicking skin cream at him. As he darted away, I saw he had a bundle of clothes stuffed under one arm. It wasn't just any bundle of clothes.

It was my jeans and jumper.

Oh no.

Had something terrible happened to Sprocket?

'After him,' yelled Hairy Chest, giving chase, prodding the Brats to give chase too.

The Melting Man squished his way towards me, then veered away and led the others out of the factory.

For a few seconds he'd been close enough that drips of skin cream had spattered on the vat near my head. And close enough for me to notice with a jolt that he wasn't quite as tall as the first Melting Man.

And that he had a big scratch on his bare foot.

It was Sprocket in disguise.

Once I'd got over my stunned amazement, I glowed with gratitude for this strange boy who was risking himself for me. But I didn't glow for too long. There was too much to do.

As the cries of the chase faded into the distance, I crept quickly out of the factory and over to the edge of the rainforest. The setting winter sun was slanting through the thick foliage and I shivered in the cool air and prayed that some phone signals were slanting through too so that Mum's mobile would work.

It did, just.

I dialled the police station in town, thankful that Mum had made me learn the number years ago before I was allowed to go to the library by myself.

Sergeant Taylor answered.

'It's Amy Tunks-Livingstone,' I said breathlessly. 'From Wattle Street. My half-sister's been kidnapped by a ring of nude skin-cream criminals who have got little kids working for them as slaves. The crims have got my dad working for them too but I think his head was probably just turned by sexual infatuation. You have to send cars and helicopters urgently. And a social worker for my dad.'

Instead of asking for directions, Sergeant Taylor gave a cross-sounding sigh. 'OK, young lady,' he said. 'I'm going to let you off with a warning this time. Making prank phone calls is a serious offence, as is impersonating another person. If you do it again, you'll be in serious trouble.'

He hung up.

'I'm in serious trouble *now*,' I wanted to scream into the phone. 'Sprocket's in serious trouble too.' But I didn't in case the Brats were in earshot.

Desperately I thought about who else I could ring. I didn't know where Mum was and school was hundreds of kilometres away. There was only a caretaker there in the holidays. He probably wouldn't take kindly to me asking him to drive for seven hours to rescue me, not after I'd accidentally mixed All-Bran into his squash court paint.

Suddenly I felt very alone. Sadness gripped my throat and my eyes were suddenly hot and blurry. As I put the phone back into my pocket, I felt the scrap of letter from the Other Woman to Dad.

I pulled it out, wiped my eyes and stared at it.

'. . . this madness must stop, Drew,' it said. 'You are the only one who can bring it to an end. Please, I beg you, for all our sakes, no more.'

Signed Charlotte Sampson.

Was this the madness she'd meant? This evil skin-cream business Dad was a part of? With little kids so mentally abused they thought grown men were their little brothers. No wonder she'd had second thoughts about it all.

Anguish burned through me. Oh, Dad, I thought. Why didn't you take her advice? Why didn't you get out while you had the chance? Before your wife and both your daughters got dragged into this mess?

I took a deep breath. This wasn't going to help anyone. There was a baby over in the main building who urgently needed me. And possibly a mum and a dad too.

I looked down at my legs, which wouldn't stop trembling. It wasn't just the stress of everything that had happened, it was also because of what I had to do next.

Break into a camp full of hostile nudists.

I decided the main building must be part of the nudist camp Sprocket and I had passed on our way in. I started walking through the dusk, back along the entrance road towards the main building, peering anxiously into the darkening rainforest and listening frantically through the bird and insect noise for sounds of hostile Brats.

I sent a silent message to Sprocket's legs. Run fast. Climb high. Keep safe.

After a few minutes I came round a bend and saw in front of me in the gloom the long, low white building I'd seen on the way in. This time I noticed that at one end, overlooking a river, was an old tower.

I crouched near the fence, looking for naked bodies moving around inside the compound. I didn't see any, which was a relief in more ways than one. But there were lights twinkling in some of the windows.

I thought hard about the best way to get in. While I was thinkling I forgot to listen to the rainforest. When I realised the undergrowth was rustling it was too late.

There was somebody behind me.

I spun round, fumbling for my Swiss Army knife, trying to get an implement open that wasn't for catering.

I didn't need to. It was Sprocket, wearing my jeans, rubbing skin cream off his chest and face with my jumper.

'Gave them the slip,' he panted, grinning.

I was so pleased to see him I almost hugged him.

Instead I looked at his tummy. I was relieved to see it still looked pretty normal.

A thought struck me. The blue stone and the blue gas. How did they fit in to this whole mystery? How were they connected to the tea and the skin cream and the Brats and my missing family?

I made myself stop thinking about it. First we had to rescue my baby sister and any other family members who were in the nudist camp.

Sprocket was squinting through the fence at the white buildings.

'Getting in there won't be easy,' he said. 'The

nudists have seen me before. We'll have to try and blend in.'

'How?' I said.

Sprocket turned to me.

That day had been the scariest of my life, but nothing I'd seen or heard had scared me as much as the words he spoke now.

'Take all your clothes off.'

DEADLY!

Part Three

STIFF

The SUNRISE NATURE FARM

VILION

MAIN BUILDING
(including AMPS Room)

OL STORE

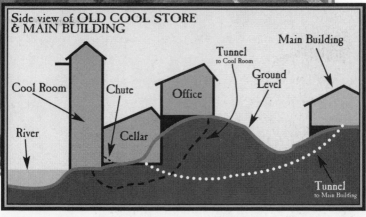

Side view of OLD COOL STORE & MAIN BUILDING

Cool Room

Chute

Office

Tunnel
to Cool Room

Ground
Level

Main Building

River

Cellar

Tunnel
to Main Building

SPROCKET

ONE

The shadows were growing long as Amy and I stood outside the nudist colony. There was no sign of life from the reception area and the weird mobile home had gone from the car park. The oval was empty.

I shivered at the thought of entering the place again. The people in there were dangerous. They weren't just fun-loving sun-seekers like other nudists. They were some kind of weirdos who drank a lot of tea that mucked up all their ages. The old ones were fanatics who trained their horrible brat children in guerilla warfare.

My instincts told me to run away. I didn't know who I was. Child soldiers were looking for a blue marble thing that had come out in my poop. I had been chased naked and alone through the forest by angry infants. They had kidnapped Amy's little half-sister.

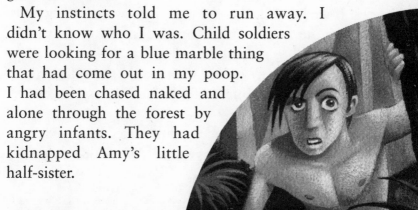

That really got to me. The thought of a baby separated from its family made me go cold all over. Anyone who would snatch a baby was a ratbag. A baby belonged with its mother. I had to help Amy rescue it. And to do that I had to go into the nudist camp with her and face whatever nightmare lay ahead.

Amy didn't like it when I told her to undress, though.

'You must be joking,' she said indignantly.

'We can't go in there with our clothes on,' I told her. 'You heard what the Tea Lady said. Naked bodies are their cover. No one is allowed to walk around the grounds wearing clothes. We will stand out like sore toes. Our only chance is to merge into the background. We might just get away with it in the dark. Come on, strip off.'

'You wish,' said Amy. 'I'm not joining a nudist colony. Not for anyone.'

'We're not signing up,' I said. 'We are spies. Intruders. If we have clothes on we might as well hang bells around our necks. This is a matter of life or death. It's no good being prudish.'

'I'm not letting you see me naked,' she said hotly.

'I'm not the slightest bit interested in your body,' I lied.

There was a long silence. She looked annoyed.

'You're no oil painting yourself,' she said. 'Anyway, look at that.'

We stared through the fence at a post littered with signs pointing in various directions. In the shadows I could just make them out.

I started to read aloud. 'Reception. I've already been there. Laundry, Gym, Oval, Workshop and . . . Cool Room.'

The last two words seemed to catch in my throat. I was already scared but now great shudders of fear ran up and down my body. The words bounced around inside my brain growing louder and then softer.

COOL ROOM COOL ROOM **COOL ROOM** COOL ROOM COOL ROOM.

I fell to a crouching position and put my head between my knees. An icy hand seemed to be squeezing my skull. 'Urggh . . .' I gurgled. I fell to the ground wheezing and fighting for breath. The very thought of a Cool Room had struck terror into me.

For a second I saw a huge steel door. Like a dream or a vision. Then it vanished.

'What?' whispered Amy. 'What?'

'Death,' I said hoarsely. 'Inside the Cool Room. I've been there.'

'Death. Whose death?' said Amy.

'I don't know,' I croaked. 'I've just got an image of a big steel door. And something terrible behind it. We can't go to the Cool Room.'

'Your memory is coming back,' said Amy urgently. 'Think, think. What else?'

'I'm trying to remember where I came from and how I got there,' I groaned.

'No, no,' she yelped. 'Tell me about death.'

'I can't remember,' I said. 'It's just a feeling. There's death behind the door. I know it.'

My brain was racing. Images of a dark tunnel and a steel door flashed through my head like reflections in a shattered mirror.

'Were there any prisoners down there?' squeaked Amy. 'Any babies?'

'I don't know,' I said.

'Maybe it's not a Cool Room,' said Amy. 'Maybe it's a cooler.'

'A cooler?'

'Yes. You know. A prison cell. My illegitimate half-sister might be locked up there. And death isn't getting its hands on *her*.'

'I can't remember what's in there,' I said. 'It's like trying to remember a dream after it's gone.' My body was still shaking.

'We have to go in,' said Amy. 'With our clothes *on*.'

I knew that it was crazy to enter the nudist colony. And dangerous. I wanted to leave there. To get help. To come back later and look for my mother. If I had one. I still felt in my bones that she was here.

But there was no way now that I was going to run off into the safety of the night. The idea of saving a lost and lonely baby took total possession of me. It was almost like I was trying to save myself. I had to go. Even if our search led us to the terrible Cool Room.

'You're right,' I said. 'We have to risk it. Follow me.'

We squeezed under the fence and started to creep towards the buildings, trying to stay out of sight of any watching eyes. We crouched low and scurried through the deepening darkness like a couple of rats. At any moment I expected a cry of 'Intruders'.

After about ten minutes we reached an ancient concrete building with a strong wooden door and no windows. It looked like an old warehouse of some sort.

'We'll never get in there,' whispered Amy desperately. She tugged at the handle and then shook her fists at the moon which was just starting to peep out. 'Someone help,' she groaned. 'My baby sister is in there.'

She didn't seem to think that I was going to be of much use. But I was. 'You stay there,' I said. I looked around to make sure the coast was clear and started to scale up a steel drain-pipe. I did it easily. As if I'd been getting in and out of buildings all my life. In no time I was on the roof.

'Tiles,' I whispered to myself. 'I can lift them off.'

I could see Amy looking up at me with a puzzled expression. Was she wondering if I was a burglar?

Maybe I was. *I* didn't know the answer – that was for sure.

I pulled off four or five tiles and clambered inside. I was in the space between the roof and the ceiling. The moon streamed down through the hole where I had removed the tiles. It filled the attic with a pale glow. The place was littered with dusty boxes, old toys, broken furniture and piles of newspapers.

I crawled around on my hands and knees looking for a trapdoor into the room below. I bumped into an old lamp and it fell to the floor with a crash. The noise seemed like the sound of a truck crashing into a glass factory. I froze and gritted my teeth, expecting a cry, a yell or a burglar alarm to break the silence.

But there was nothing. If anyone had heard me they were keeping quiet about it.

There, by a large box, I saw what I was looking for. The trapdoor. I was just about to lift it when I noticed something scribbled on the side of the box. I could just make it out in the pale moonglow. One word. ORSON.

That was Pooper Scooper's name, the worst of the Brats. I peered into the box. It was full of old-fashioned toys and other junk. A wind-up train. A sort of radio thing with an ancient set of earphones. A packet of used birthday candles and a box of matches. There was also a bundle of photos wrapped in a rubber band. I shoved the matches and candles in my pocket and crawled back under a moonbeam to examine the photographs.

Most of them were of people who lived long ago. Black-and-white prints and faded brown portraits. I found a face that seemed familiar. A young man with a hard face. He reminded me of someone I had seen recently. It hit me like a falling toilet seat. The person in the photo looked just like Pooper Scooper. It must have been his father or grandfather. He was sitting behind the wheel of an old English car. A Morris Major, I think. I shuddered. It was a cruel face. Just like Pooper Scooper's – only older.

I began to think about the tea. And the Brats who thought they were older than grown men and women. What if . . .?

The sound of a stone on the roof awoke me from my thoughts. Shoot. I had almost forgotten where I was. Amy must be worried. I moved around the cramped space trying not to make a noise. I crawled across to the trapdoor, pulled it open and peered through. It was dark below and I couldn't see what was there. I had to get down and let Amy into the building before she tried to kick the door in. She wanted that baby so badly that she was just as likely to kick up a fuss and get us caught.

I reached down and felt something. A coat-hanger.

Yes. It was a small cupboard with clothes hanging on a rack. Winter clothes, by the feel of them. Coats and jackets with thick woollen linings. I dropped down with a thump. If there was anyone around they must have heard me.

I stood still, trying to hold my breath. Nothing. Not a sound.

Gently I opened the door.

And froze in the bright light of the room beyond.

'Good boy,' I said in a trembling voice.

The dog jumped straight onto me. His lips were pulled back over his teeth. I felt his hot breath on my face. I fell backwards into the cupboard. There was nothing I could do to protect myself. All I had was my bare hands against his jaws. Hot canine breath filled my nostrils. Saliva dripped across my chin. I tried to hold his head away from the soft flesh of my lips.

For a few seconds I held him there. But my arms began to weaken. His bared teeth were almost upon me. Suddenly a thought flashed into my mind. I stared at him. I fixed him with a deadly glare. I tried to copy the look on Amy's face when I told her to strip off. I just peered into those doggy eyes with the fiercest look I could manage.

The dog started to gasp and wheeze. He fell to the floor and began clawing at his own throat. He made terrible gurgling noises. He seemed unable to breathe.

Could I make a dog choke to death just by looking at him? Was my glare so powerful? Surely I wasn't responsible for his agony. My fear turned to pity. The poor creature was dying in front of my eyes.

'It's OK, boy,' I said. I gave him my kindest look.

But it didn't do any good at all. If anything he was worse. His breathing stopped altogether. His eyes rolled back. I felt terrible. Even though it was a savage dog I didn't want to be responsible for its death.

I felt his neck for a pulse. 'Oh no,' I said.

That's when I saw it. His dog collar. It was too tight. It wasn't my glare that was troubling him at all. The collar was choking him. It was so tight that I couldn't even get my fingers under it. I quickly undid the wretched bit of leather and threw it onto the floor.

'Whoever did that to you is a monster,' I said. The dog just lay there for a bit with its eyes closed. Maybe it was dead.

Mouth to mouth resuscitation. Could you do that on a dog? I took a deep breath.

And so did the dog. It was alive. I jumped back. Would he attack again? I couldn't be sure.

The dog opened his eyes and then staggered to his feet. He rushed at me. And started licking my hand. He was grateful. I had saved his life.

'Good boy, good boy,' I said. What a relief.

I looked around, half expecting Hairy Chest or the Tea Lady to appear. But there was no one. The room was filled with filing cabinets. It was an office of some kind. I tiptoed over to the outside door and opened it.

'About time,' said Amy.

'Sorry,' I whispered. 'But I found this photograph.

I think that these people might grow backwards and . . .'

Amy wasn't in the mood for listening.

'My sister probably hasn't had her nappy changed for hours,' she snapped. 'Maybe she is hungry. Maybe at this very moment they are trying to feed her on solids instead of formula. And all you can think about are family snaps.'

She crept inside, shut the door quietly behind her and stared at the dog.

'It's OK,' I said. 'He's a friend.'

The dog wagged his tail. He was big and gangly and clumsy, not really vicious at all. He was a strange dog. He looked like a big, lolloping pup. A labrador. But his eyes seemed full of wisdom. Knowing.

I wondered what his name was.

The dog suddenly ran over to the door and began to growl.

'Someone's coming,' I whispered. I looked around for a hiding place. There was nowhere. We couldn't both fit in the cupboard and there wasn't time to get back into the roof. I ran to a closed door. A big wooden one with iron hinges. I pulled it open. A flight of stone steps led down inside a long low tunnel.

'Quick,' said Amy. 'Down there.'

I shook my head and pointed to an arrow painted on the wall. Underneath were the words: COOL ROOM.

'No, no,' I said. 'Don't go down there.' My breathing was shallow and fast. My skin was damp.

Amy stepped through the door and began to descend. I couldn't go after her. But I couldn't stay either. Footsteps were getting closer. I hurried through the door and the dog followed. I shut the door after him. We were in total darkness.

'You should have left him behind,' said Amy's voice. 'Now they'll know someone's here.'

'I'm not leaving him,' I said. 'Not after what they did to the poor thing. No way.'

I felt around and touched a wall. It was damp and cold. Water dripped from the roof. Every now and then a cold drop would land on my head. I grabbed the back of Amy's dress. The dress that had been mine.

'We have to stay together,' I told her.

The steps were slippery as we cautiously picked our way down. The soft sound of the dog's padding feet disappeared in front of us.

What was down there? My mind started to invent possibilities. Bodies? Foul bits from the grave? Nameless horrors? What if there was someone – something that could see in the dark? What if a hand or a bone or a feeler reached out and gently grabbed my throat? I felt sick with fear but pushed the thoughts away as best I could.

'I've got matches and candles,' I whispered.

'Don't, someone might see us,' Amy said under her breath.

The steps turned a corner and led into a cavern. A soft glow from a naked light bulb took the edge off the darkness. On the other side of the cavern the tunnel continued on.

But set in the side of the wall . . .

. . . was a huge steel door.

I began to shake all over. 'Don't open it,' I ordered. 'Death is in there.'

Amy didn't even hear me. 'I'm coming, baby,' she said.

She pulled the heavy door open.

TWO

Sprocket screamed.

I screamed.

The dog howled.

Inside the Cool Room, half-hidden in a swirling white mist, was a huge frost-streaked glass cabinet.

Inside the cabinet was a single solid block of ice taller than us.

Inside the ice, half-obscured by the frost but sickeningly unmistakeable in the ghostly light from the dim bulb, was the naked body of a man.

His arms and legs were splayed in all directions. He looked like he'd been snap-frozen in the middle of a fall or a fit or a disco. His skin was pale pink with a blue tinge that made my flesh crawl. His veins were sort of green.

Despite the freezing air stinging my face and the numb terror gripping my brain, feverish thoughts burned inside me.

What sort of people kept a frozen body in their cellar?

I thought *my* family were weird, but this lot left them for dead. Kids driving military trucks. Grown men wearing enough skin cream to moisturise an elephant. Compulsory afternoon tea. Little brothers who were forty years older than their big brothers.

What did it all mean?

Suddenly I noticed something about the frozen figure in front of me that drove all questions out of my head.

All except one.

The lower part of the man's face was obscured by the frost on the glass. But his red-rimmed eyes, staring as wide as mine and Sprocket's and the dog's, were clearly visible.

One anguished question seared into my brain.

Dad?

Dad's eyes had been red-rimmed for years. All those late nights with his Other Woman.

I'd seen it in movies heaps of times. A mild-mannered family man has a secret life of passion and romance and crime. Then the criminals he's working for get sick of him always ducking off home to fix the kitchen cupboards or attend his daughter's birthday tea and they do him in.

Now it was my turn to yell.

I threw myself at the glass cabinet and scrubbed frantically at the frost on the surface, trying to get a better look, trying to spot another feature I recognised.

Hoping desperately I wouldn't.

I wasn't that familiar with Dad's naked body. I'd always avoided looking if I could. But I did know he had a scar on his ribs where Mum accidentally swiped him with the cheese grater. The corpse in the ice didn't seem to. And the corpse had hairier legs than Dad's. Though I'd read, I remembered suddenly, sick panic rising up my throat, that hair kept on growing after death and perhaps that was also true of leg hair.

I fumbled frantically in the pocket of the dress for my Swiss Army knife, praying it had an implement for getting bodies out of blocks of ice.

Before I could find one, Sprocket, still pale and trembling, dragged me away.

'No,' I screamed, struggling. 'I've got to see if it's Dad.'

'Someone's coming,' whispered Sprocket shakily.

The door at the top of the stairs was creaking open. I could hear urgent voices and the scuffle of feet on stone steps.

Brats? Nudists? I couldn't tell and I didn't really care.

I tried to get back to the block of ice for one last look. You don't care about danger when it could be the last time you'll ever see your dad.

'If we stay here,' said Sprocket, 'we'll end up like him.'

I struggled in Sprocket's grip and glared at him, furious.

For a brief moment he looked at me with the sad eyes of a kid who couldn't even remember seeing his dad once, let alone for the last time. Then I realised the voices were getting closer and I stopped struggling.

Sprocket let go of me and bent down and grabbed a handle near the floor. He strained till his neck muscles bulged and started to lift up a sliding metal hatch in the wall. The grease on the runners was thick and sticky in the cold air. I stepped forward to help him.

'Get the dog,' said Sprocket. 'We can't leave him here to freeze.'

The dog was standing close to the ice block, whimpering and nuzzling the glass. Even when I picked him up he didn't want to take his eyes off the frozen man.

I knew how he felt.

Sprocket had the hatch high enough to scramble under. He grabbed me and pulled me through and forced it back down.

We stood in the darkness, listening to the footsteps and voices getting closer on the other side. The dog struggled in my arms. I held his jaws closed to stop him barking.

Chest heaving and eyes burning with grief, I said a silent prayer for Dad. Even though he'd strayed, I still loved him.

But now, wrenching my mind away from him, I had to think of the others who needed me. My baby sister, out there somewhere at the mercy of the Brats. And Mum, wherever she was.

Sprocket struck one of the matches he'd found. In front of us was a dusty old wooden chute, disappearing down into blackness. It must have been built for shifting meat and vegies and bodies out of the Cool Room.

'Come on,' said Sprocket. 'Don't think about it.'

The match went out. He pushed me to the top of the chute, positioned himself behind me and launched us into the darkness.

As we slid down I clung onto the dog and thought of the baby. Wondered what her name was. Anything rather than think about what new horror we were heading for.

Actually, it wasn't that horrible. Painful, but not that horrible.

It was a hard dirt floor and we hit it at speed.

We lay there for a while, winded. I felt the dog licking my face. Then Sprocket struck another match and helped me up and we looked around.

I could just make out a couple of vintage cars and some ancient farm machinery. Sprocket lit the stub of a birthday cake candle and I saw we were in a big old cellar full of stuff. Antique furniture, horse buggies, wooden butter churns, black-and-white TVs, gas lamps, old-fashioned fridges and several orange shag-pile rugs. And the sort of mouldy cardboard boxes families keep all the stuff in they can't bear to throw away.

I didn't get it. I always thought nudists were people who were more comfortable without worldly possessions. Who preferred to go through life uncluttered by uplift bras and jockettes. Why would they lumber themselves with enough junk to fill a museum?

Then I saw the prams. Two of them hanging on the wall, big and black and dusty.

And a clean patch on the wall where another one had hung. It must have been the one they'd put my sister in. Before Pooper Scooper had crushed it in the factory.

I was still shuddering at the memory when Sprocket grabbed my arm.

'Come on,' he said urgently. 'Keep moving. They'll still be after us.'

In the cellar wall near the bottom of the chute were a pair of big wooden doors. We headed for them. From the other side of the hatch came angry shouts. The dog suddenly struggled out of my arms and jumped down and ran over to the far side of the cellar. He looked back at us, wagging his tail.

'He wants us to follow him,' said Sprocket.

'Sprocket,' I said doubtfully, 'it's a dog.'

Sprocket was looking at the dog with a frown. He had the expression he got when he was struggling to remember. 'I trust him,' said Sprocket. 'Come on.'

We followed the dog behind an old-fashioned clothes wringer. He disappeared into a hole in the stone wall. We squeezed through after him and found ourselves crawling along a narrow tunnel that sloped upwards steeply.

'This is ridiculous,' I muttered.

'Keep going,' whispered Sprocket.

As the tunnel levelled out, I stiffened. Above our heads I could hear muffled voices and footsteps. We were under a floor. With nude kidnappers above us.

Sprocket blew the candle out.

We kept going. I made a mental note that next time I crawled over a dirt floor with sharp rocks in it, I'd make the boy I was with put his dress back on and give me back my jeans.

Finally the tunnel ended. The dog squeezed

between a couple of loose planks. We did too and emerged into a small room. Light spilled in under a closed door. The dog stopped and put his head down. Sprocket and I bent forward to see what crucial thing the dog had brought us to see.

It was a dog bowl with meat in it.

The dog was eating.

I turned to Sprocket.

'At the risk of being a bit obvious,' I said, 'can I point out that this is what happens when you let a dog take charge.'

Sprocket gave me a hurt look. 'I'm doing my best,' he said quietly.

I remembered how Sprocket had risked his neck for me. How he'd nearly been smothered by blue insect parts. And then been a human decoy covered in skin cream. Suddenly I felt ashamed.

'Sorry,' I said gruffly.

I slumped back wearily against the wall. Something hard dug me in the bottom. It was Mum's mobile in the pocket of the baggy old dress. Irritably I snatched it out. And saw something that made me gasp.

In the window of the phone was a message symbol. It hadn't been there when I'd rung the police station earlier.

Hands shaking, I punched in Mum's voice-mail number.

'You have one voice message,' said the pre-recorded operator. 'Message received at six-forty pm today.'

Then, miraculously, wonderfully, Dad's voice.

'Lesley, it's Drew. I'm sorry I left like that while you were in the bath. It's too complicated to go into now, but I'm OK and I'll explain when everything's . . .'

There was a crackle and Dad's message to Mum cut out. Frantically I dialled his number. A recorded voice said that his mobile was out of range or switched off.

I didn't care. I looked at my watch. Six-forty was about the time we were in the Cool Room. Dad must have phoned while we were out of range inside the concrete walls.

I wanted to scream with joy.

Men frozen in blocks of ice didn't make phone calls.

The corpse wasn't Dad.

I turned to Sprocket, trembling with delight and relief. But before I could tell him the good news and apologise again for being so grumpy, we heard a sound that made us both stiffen.

Somebody was outside the door, fumbling with the door handle.

There was no time to get back into the tunnel.

The door swung open. Silhouetted against the fluorescent light from outside was a small figure. It was obviously someone the dog knew well, judging from the loud and happy panting.

'Good boy, Matchbox,' said a boyish Brat voice. 'Wait till you see what I've got for you.'

I pressed myself against the wall, desperately hoping the Brat didn't turn on a light.

He did.

It was Beanie.

He blinked up at us, startled, looking like a kid who'd been caught doing something he shouldn't have been doing. For a second I had the wild thought that we could do a deal with him. Promise not to dob him in if he didn't dob us in.

But his eyes narrowed and he gave the scowl of someone who didn't do deals with kids. He stepped backwards out of the room and his shrill and urgent cry echoed around the nudist camp.

'Intruders.'

SPROCKET

THREE

Caught. Trapped. Discovered.
Beanie opened his mouth to shout out again and let the whole colony know where we were.

It was all over. We would never find the baby. We would probably end up frozen inside a block of ice. Like that poor corpse back there.

I had seen him before. I had been in this nudist camp before. But I had forgotten it.

The shock of seeing him on my first visit had jolted every memory out of my brain. And just as well too. I don't think I could have found the courage to return if I had known what lay ahead.

When Amy threw open that steel door and I got my second look it was like being brained with a sock full of ice cubes. A jangle of memories began to rattle around inside my head.

I recalled my first visit. Now I knew what I was doing in this crazy place. Now I knew where I had come from. Now I had a history. Now I was a somebody instead of a nobody. I wanted to tell Amy that she wasn't the only one who had lost a mother.

But there hadn't been time for talk. Not even any time for thought. My whole body was shaking. These . . . these . . . monsters had frozen someone. They had actually put a man inside an ice block. We had to escape.

Beanie had discovered us. He was about to call out for a second time.

But he didn't. He stopped. He was hiding something behind his back with both hands and he didn't want to let go of it.

He backed away from us with wide open eyes. A corridor stretched out behind him. 'You two stay there,' he snapped. 'Or you're dead meat.' He kept backing away. Matchbox followed him, wagging his tail as if he was about to get a biscuit.

What was Beanie hiding? And why did he care if we saw it?

Suddenly he disappeared around a corner. We heard a rattling noise and loud, running footsteps. They faded off into the night. The dog had disappeared with him.

Stay where we were?

'Not likely,' I said to Amy. We couldn't go back – there were voices behind us and they were growing louder with every second that passed. And we couldn't follow Beanie, that was for sure.

Another corridor led off to the left. It was dark. What was the matter with this place? Why didn't they have lights?

'This way,' I yelled.

The blood was pounding inside my skull. We had been seen. Capture was unthinkable. Amy was panting. Neither of us had enough breath to speak. We stumbled and bumped into each other as we ran down the long passage.

Crash, thump. 'Ow, shoot.' I thumped straight into a wall. Amy banged into me from behind.

'We're trapped,' I gasped.

'The candles,' said Amy's voice out of the darkness.

I fumbled around and pulled out the box. I struck a match against the side. It broke. With shaking fingers I tried again. The match flared briefly.

It wasn't a wall we had run into. It was a door. And something was written on it.

'What does it say?' whispered Amy.

'I'm not sure,' I said. 'I think it says AMPS.'

'I'm not going in there,' said Amy. 'Not after the Cool Room.'

'What could it mean?' I said warily.

'Something to do with electricity,' she said hoarsely. 'Maybe the Brats make people grow backwards by running electricity through them.'

A vision of a Frankenstein monster with wires running everywhere filled my mind. My whole body started to shake.

Suddenly a loud bell began to ring. The alarm had gone up. They were after us. There was nowhere else to go. Amy pushed into the room and I followed. I pulled the door shut behind us and felt around for a light switch. There wasn't one. We were in total darkness.

I was about to try the matches again when a terrible moan suddenly filled the air. Instinctively I dropped to the floor and crawled into a corner. It was pitch black. I could see nothing. Nothing at all. I reached out for Amy but she wasn't there.

I couldn't hear her because of the breathing. Not normal breathing. Loud, horrible, death-rattle breathing. Every gasp was like the last of a milkshake sucked up by a greedy child.

What type of creature could be making such

sounds? Half alive, half dead? Sucking the life from the room. What swivelling eyeballs were seeking me out? What sinewy fingers were clawing my way? What wired-up monstrosity wanted to shock me? Revolt me? Probe my brain?

I pushed myself further into the corner and tried to soften my own rasping breath. Could the creature see in the dark? Was it toying with us? I imagined long tentacles even now snaking their way across the floor.

I was only a boy. OK, I could put on a brave front. Especially in front of Amy. But I'd had as much as I could take.

Amy was somewhere in the room trying to breathe quietly. She was smart. She wasn't going to draw attention to herself. I thought about crawling across the floor to see if I could find her. But what if my hand fell on the unspeakable? What if my skin touched the horrible flesh of the unknown breather?

I could call out. I could whisper, 'Amy'.

But then IT would know where I was.

The stench in the room was terrible. Like some ancient grandfather's slippers wrung out and bottled. Like a perfume distilled from the sewers. A stinking smell of unwashed skin. The foul scent of rotting flesh from the grave.

What sort of creature were the infant warriors and their weird relations keeping in here? And why? Were they going to unleash it onto the world? Was it about to pop off a cloud of blue gas? Were we about to swell and burst like the insects in the skin-cream factory?

'Rasp, gasp, cough.' It was trying to clear its throat. I had to do something. I took a deep breath and closed my eyes. Slowly, slowly I began to crawl across the room. I had no idea where the door was. And outside it the enemy was waiting.

My fingers touched some sort of iron frame. I let them walk up it. Quietly, quietly. The stench seemed to grow worse with every breath from IT. I touched on something. Little ridges. Slimy. Curved in a horse-shoe shape. Set into a blob of sagging goo.

Oh, foul, foul, foul. What was I touching?

Teeth. I was touching ITS teeth. As I pulled away my hand they came with me. I was pulling ITS teeth out of ITS mouth.

'Aaagh.' I couldn't hold in the scream as I jammed them back into its horrible cake hole.

'Aaagh.' Another scream filled the air.

And another. But the last was the worst. An ancient cry. A gurgled groan from the grave.

I jumped to my feet and holding my hands out in front of me ran blindly across the room. *Crash*. My fingers were in another mouth. Oh, yuck. I thrust my fingernails back towards its tonsils. I could feel my invisible foe gagging. And biting me. A spray of vomit hit me in the face.

'Get your stinking fingers out of my mouth,' came an angry, choking voice.

It was Amy. I was attacking the wrong creature. I gasped as she punched me in the stomach. 'It's me,' I managed to say. 'Stop.'

'Sprocket?'

'Yes.' I started to feel her face in the darkness. It was her all right.

'Your fingers *stink*,' she spluttered.

'I know. I stuck them in something's mouth. It's in here with us.'

'What?'

'I don't know. Quick, find the door.'

We were hugging each other in the dark. Like a couple of little kids. Or a couple of big kids.

I took Amy's hand and started to pull her behind me. I stumbled forward. I couldn't tell which way I was going. My hand fell on something spongy. Like a living football bladder. Rising and falling.

A spidery object brushed across my face. A piece of rope maybe. Or a tube. Yes. A plastic tube. With my other hand I touched something soft. Material. It felt like a bed.

A bed. A plastic tube. Removable teeth. False teeth? Gargling and gurgling. Finally it hit me.

This was a sick room.

And whatever was in that bed was really sick. Such a stink of rotting flesh could only come from a near corpse.

Suddenly IT spoke. If you could call it speaking. The terrible growl was more like the noise of a plughole when the bath water is let out. Shivers ran right across my body.

I reached into my pocket with trembling fingers and struck another precious match.

In the flickering light I saw him. And he saw me.

His face reminded me of a flattened pat of wet cow manure. Shrunken, shrivelled and too collapsed to really be alive. Tubes ran into his nostrils and arms. Bottles of fluids dripped from above.

It was the most decrepit piece of flesh in the history of the world. This man should have been in his grave sixty years ago. He wasn't old – he was far beyond that – some sort of unnatural spectre that had lifted the lid of his own coffin, refusing to allow his bones to rest in peace.

His eyes lit up for a second when he saw me. He seemed to know who I was.

With a groaning voice a few words slipped from his wizened lips. 'Give the seed back,' he croaked in a terrible voice. 'Give the seed back. Or my grand-children die.'

The match suddenly burnt my fingers. I dropped it to the floor where it flickered and then sputtered out.

'Let's get out of here,' shouted Amy.

She burst through the door.

And I followed.

AMY

FOUR

We stumbled out of that awful room in shock.

Sprocket was ashen-faced. My whole body was trembling and clammy, so I must have been pretty pale too.

My brain tried to make sense of what we'd just seen.

Or rather glimpsed.

And heard.

And smelt.

I struggled to keep my stomach under control.

Who were these people who could allow that to happen to a human being? Who were these monsters Dad had got involved with?

The thought of my own dad being a part of that horror made my guts clench. Suddenly him having an affair with another woman seemed like peanuts. Even him replacing me with a love child seemed suddenly not so bad.

Not compared to *that*.

I realised I was running. Sprinting down the corridor away from the AMPS room. Sprocket was too. I could tell from his face he felt like I did. Nothing could have stopped me getting out of there.

Except one thing.

The distant frantic cry of a baby.

I grabbed Sprocket and dragged him to a stop.

'Did you hear that?' I hissed.

Sprocket frowned and we both strained our ears. There it was again. My baby sister. Somewhere in this scary nudist homestead. Wailing wordlessly for me to rescue her.

There were other distant sounds too. Adult voices calling to each other. And the shrill curses of angry Brats. They were still hunting for us.

'I've got to try and rescue my sister,' I said to Sprocket. 'If you want to get away from here I'll understand. You've done enough for me already.'

The colour had returned to Sprocket's face. And a hard gleam to his eyes.

'Little kids shouldn't be abandoned,' was all he said, and I knew he was with me.

Then we heard another sound. A Brat's voice, coming towards us along the corridor that cut across the one we were in.

'Here, mate,' the Brat was calling softly. 'Where are you, mate?'

I looked around desperately. There were only two doors in our section of the corridor. The AMPS door back down the other end, and what looked like a cupboard door about two metres away from us.

I pulled it open. Sprocket and I piled in. As I dragged the door almost shut, I prayed there were no more horrors behind this one.

There weren't. Just sheets, pillowslips, towels and pyjamas. All neatly folded on shelves. Barely visible in the gloom.

The door was open a crack and I peered out.

The Brat was in sight.

It was Beanie, creeping along furtively, clutching a china teapot. The same teapot the Tea Lady had forced the Brats to have afternoon tea from in the skin-cream factory.

'Where are you, mate?' Beanie was calling softly. His eyes were darting about nervously. He looked like a naughty little boy who didn't want anyone to see him. I recognised that look. The look of a person with a guilty secret.

One of the things I'd learned at boarding school was that people with guilty secrets can be forced to do things they don't want to do. I learned that the day I told Julie Spiros my guilty secret (that Dad was having an affair) and she threatened to tell the whole school unless I did something I didn't want to do (put curry paste in the principal's shoes).

Now, peering out of the nudists' linen cupboard, I knew from personal experience Beanie could be forced to do something he didn't want to do.

But first we had to capture him.

I whispered my plan to Sprocket. It was a good

plan, but a bit light on details about the actual capture.

That didn't worry Sprocket. He reached up and grabbed a pair of pyjama trousers off a shelf. With a flick of his wrist he whipped out the pyjama cord and expertly knotted it into a lasso. 'OK,' he whispered. 'Let's get him.'

Sprocket pushed the door open. Beanie was part of the way down one of the side corridors. We almost reached him before he heard us. He started to turn, but it was too late. Sprocket dropped the lasso over Beanie's head, flicked it down over the little bloke's shoulders and pulled it tight, pinning his arms to his sides just above his elbows.

Beanie yelped with fear, eyes wide, body trembling. Then, when he saw it was us, he seemed almost relieved for a second.

Until he remembered the teapot he was clutching in one of his trapped hands.

'Don't make me drop it,' he pleaded. 'Please, don't make me drop it.'

A familiar smell hit my nostrils. I took the teapot from Beanie and lifted the china lid. Inside was a small amount of tea. I sniffed it. And nearly fainted. It was the Other Woman skin-cream smell, but a hundred times stronger than I'd ever smelled it before.

While I waited for my eyes to stop watering, I realised Beanie was mouthing something at me.

'Don't drink it,' he was squeaking frantically. 'Don't drink it. Please don't drink it.'

Sprocket took the teapot from me and put the lid back on. 'He doesn't want you to drink it,' he said.

I crouched down so my eyes were level with Beanie's wide and terrified ones.

'A baby's being held here against her will,' I said to him. 'Take us to her.'

Beanie's eyes narrowed and suddenly he looked as outraged and angry as the principal at school had when she'd caught me putting curry paste in her tennis shoes.

'Who do you kids think you are?' spat Beanie. 'Coming in here and giving orders to someone like me?'

Something about the way he spoke made me shiver. I wondered if he'd been a school principal in a previous life. I tried not to let the thought stop me sounding tough and determined.

'The baby's my sister,' I said to Beanie, 'and I'll risk anything to rescue her. Including yelling so loud that the others come and find you with that teapot.'

Beanie turned even paler than Sprocket had been.

Just like I'd thought, a guilty secret. For some reason he didn't want to be caught with the teapot.

Beanie considered my proposal.

For about two seconds.

'All right,' he said. 'But only if you let me give this tea to my best friend first. If he doesn't get it he'll die.'

I looked at Sprocket. I could see he wasn't keen on the idea. But my mind was racing ahead to after we'd rescued the baby. To when we were trying to find our parents. So many of the mysteries in this place seemed to be connected to the tea. If we knew what was going on, it might help us find them.

Plus I saw Beanie's eyes had softened with concern. More than concern. There was obviously someone he cared about as much as I cared about my family.

'OK,' I said to Beanie. 'You've got two minutes.'

Even as I said that Beanie turned his head sharply at a nearby sound. A low whining gurgling moan that could only be coming from an ancient throat.

'He's in there,' said Beanie, straining at the pyjama cord to get to a half-open door a little further along the passage.

I signalled to Sprocket to stop holding him back. Sprocket hesitated and gave me the sort of look people give not very bright woodlice. I took his point. In this place, when you heard low whining gurgling moans from behind strange doors, you didn't go in.

'It's all right,' said Beanie. 'It's my room.'

On the door was a wooden plaque painted with the name Barnabus.

Sprocket and I followed him in, Sprocket still holding tight to the pyjama cord.

It was a typical kid's bedroom. Unmade single bed. Posters on the walls. Pile of empty soft-drink cans on the dresser.

Except, when I looked closer, I saw there was something wrong.

The posters were all of naked women, which I thought was pretty weird (a) for a kid and (b) for a nudist.

And the cans weren't soft drink, they were beer.

Then I saw something that was even more wrong. Beanie was on his knees in the corner of the room, crooning softly to an ancient figure lying sprawled on the carpet.

Not a person, a dog.

'It's OK, mate,' Beanie was saying. 'I've got your tea. The rest of the family don't care about you but I'm not going to let you die, Matchbox old mate.'

What was wrong wasn't just that it was a dog. What was wrong was that this was the same dog we'd first seen in the file room. And in roughly an hour he'd aged about six years.

The dog looked up at us with ancient rheumy eyes. His whole body seemed to have shrunk. His bones were visible under his skin like wire hangers inside moth-eaten old fur coats. His breathing was slow and painful. His nose was dry and wrinkled.

He was the oldest dog I'd ever seen.

Sprocket was as stunned as I was.

'The tea,' said Beanie urgently. He tugged on the pyjama cord to get Sprocket's attention. 'Pour the tea into his bowl.'

I couldn't watch.

This poor demented kid thought a bowl of tea was going to save his poor old dog that obviously had some rapid ageing disease.

I turned away and faced the dresser. And found myself staring at a faded, hand-drawn birthday card.

'To Barnabus,' it said in old-fashioned handwriting. 'Happy 70th Birthday.'

I didn't get the joke.

Suddenly I was having a strange feeling. It had been a long and very weird day, and a lot of things had happened that I couldn't explain, and suddenly I wanted to get them cleared up once and for all.

'Bean . . . um, Barnabus,' I said, 'how old are you?'

Beanie was anxiously watching the dog lap up the tea. He answered without looking up. Or thinking.

'Seventy-two,' he said.

I could tell he'd answered without thinking by the scared look he gave me directly afterwards. I stared at him, amazed. He glared back angrily.

'This wasn't my idea, you know,' he tried to snap, but it came out wonky, as if a deep weariness had suddenly welled up from inside him. 'It was our father who discovered the tea,' he went on, suddenly almost tearful. 'It was Father who made us kids take it. It was him who wanted us to be young for ever. Not this young though.'

I had to stop myself laughing. This was crazy. This was ga-ga. Tea that could stop people and pets getting old? Impossible. Totally nuts. This was a family in the grip of mass hypnosis. Mass hysteria. Mass lunacy.

I opened my mouth to say a few gentle words to Beanie, reminding him that this was planet Earth and that here we do our dreaming lying down with sheets over us. Before I could Sprocket grabbed my arm.

Hard.

'Look,' he gasped, pointing at the dog.

I blinked.

Slowly, amazingly, Matchbox was starting to change. As he stood there drinking, his body started to fill out. His coat became glossy. His eyes were suddenly bright. His whiskers weren't grey any more.

As Sprocket and I stood gaping in the brightly lit bedroom with not a single Hollywood special-effects person there, Matchbox became a young dog again.

'Urghhh,' I wanted to say, but I was too stunned to speak, or move.

Matchbox was still drinking greedily. Beanie must have been pretty mesmerised too, because he didn't move until it was almost too late. When he finally did lift Matchbox away from the bowl, what he was holding was a tiny yapping puppy.

I stared at them, mind whirling.

It was true.

What Beanie had said about the tea was true.

If I could believe my eyes.

Thoughts rushed at me, making me believe my eyes. Pieces of the mystery were suddenly explained. Kids who spoke like adults and drove cars. Younger brothers who were bigger than older brothers. Nudists who hoarded cellars full of ancient belongings because they weren't real nudists, they were . . .

My mouth was dry and my head was spinning.

It was incredible.

It was unbelievable.

It was happening.

. . . a family . . .

. . . a family with the biggest secret of all . . .

. . . a family that had discovered how to live for ever . . .

I reached out to shake Sprocket and stop him gaping at the dog and tell him what I'd realised, but before I could, another thought hit me.

Something must have gone terribly wrong for the family.

Because if everything was OK, why the kidnapping? Why the Melting Man frantically covering himself with skin cream? Why the corpse frozen in the ice? Why the awful dying thing in the AMPS room?

Before I could get these thoughts into any sensible order, the door of Beanie's room burst open and an angry crowd of adults and kids stormed in.

The Tea Lady and Hairy Chest were in front. Followed by Reptile and Scowler trying to push past their legs. Then the tall bloke with frizzy hair in a Jimi Hendrix T-shirt. And a bald bloke in shorts with lobster-red sunburned skin that was starting to peel. Plus a woman with long grey hair and a chin that stuck out like the figurehead on a ship. And a skinny bloke in a tracksuit with miserable eyes and sad drooping shoulders and gobs of skin cream in his ears who could only be the Melting Man.

All furious.

Beanie spun round to face them, half terrified, half defiant.

Sprocket dropped his end of the pyjama cord and stepped back, unsure.

'OK, I did it,' shouted Beanie. 'I took the last of the tea for Matchbox. But it's not my fault it was the last. It's not my fault Father drowned without telling anyone how to germinate the tea plant. It's not my fault we can't grow new ones.'

I glanced at Sprocket. Of course. The tea. That's what must have gone wrong. That's why the family were in a panic. It was the tea that stopped them ageing. And the tea had run out.

Beanie was still yelling, tearful now.

'It's not my fault you lot decided to let the pets die. Including Matchbox, who's been kinder to me than all of you put together. Even though you are my own brothers and sisters.'

Beanie stood glaring at them, panting and trembling.

Matchbox licked his hand.

'No, Barnabus,' said the Tea Lady with icy calm. 'None of it's your fault, and it's not you we blame.'

I realised with a jolt of fear that the members of this

weird and scary family had moved to all the corners of the small room, and it wasn't Beanie they were glowering at with open rage and hatred.

It was me and Sprocket.

SPROCKET

FIVE

We were trapped in the middle of a circle. A circle of hatred and fear. The Tea Lady, Hairy Chest and four other nudist family members closed in on us. The three Brats put their hands on the handles of their knives. The whole lot of them seemed ready to tear us to pieces. Lobster Bottom's face was redder than ever.

These people were incredibly cruel. They were probably experts in pulling out toenails. Or sewing up eyelids. They might even make us prisoners in a dungeon without a television set. There was no knowing to what depths their depraved minds could descend. After all, they had already frozen a man in ice.

Escape was impossible. There were too many of them. Nine family members crammed into one tiny bedroom and blocking off the door. I wondered where Pooper Scooper was.

Amy took out her Swiss Army knife and opened the largest blade. It looked small and weak in comparison to the Brats' Bowie knives. More like something you would use to clean your nails with than a weapon.

'Back,' said Amy. 'Retreat or die.'

Her voice shook and so did her outstretched hand. She was trying to sound tough. But she didn't. She sounded like a boarding-school girl who had been caught with her hand in the biscuit jar. No one was fooled. The mob were about to rush us.

But before they could, a figure stumbled through the door. A boy of about nine or ten years old with blond curly hair. He lurched across the room and threw himself at the Tea Lady.

'Give me tea,' he screamed. 'Give me tea.'

He was bursting out of his clothes. His army shirt was ripped across the back and his belt hung loose because the ends wouldn't meet. A compass and knife dangled dangerously from it. His runners had ripped open at the ends and his toes had burst out. The zip on his pants had split to reveal tattered boxer under-daks.

Everything he wore was tight. Was this another torture? Did these fiendish people dress children in clothes several sizes too small in order to punish them? I threw a glance at Amy. She was shocked. I could see she'd never seen anything like it before, not even at boarding school.

Was this an older Brat?

The answer was yes.

It was the same person in the photo I'd seen in the attic. Only younger.

'Orson,' yelled Beanie.

'Pooper Scooper,' I gasped. It was him. It really was. He had aged three years in just a few hours. Incredible. This was even worse than what had happened to Matchbox. Was this why he wanted the tea now?

The Tea Lady shook him off like a waitress removing a fly from her arm. Hairy Chest looked down at him scornfully. 'What's the matter?' he said. 'You knew the last plant was dead. We'll soon be ageing too. And anyway, I thought you wanted to be older. Now you're getting your wish. Why are you making such a fuss?'

Pooper Scooper pointed a finger at the Tea Lady. 'Ask her,' he yelled. 'Ask her.'

A silence fell over the group. They all stared at Agnes, the Tea Lady. She picked up the teapot. The lid rattled as she took it off. She tipped the teapot upside down and shook it.

'There's none left,' she said glaring at Beanie. 'Not one drop. Clearly Matchbox has had the last of it and now there's no tea left for anyone. And . . . and . . .' She lowered her voice a tone. 'I've just come from Gramps's room. He died of old age a few minutes ago.'

There was a disbelieving silence. Then a huge collective wail of grief filled the room. They all began to sob and scream. Every one of them except Pooper Scooper. He just looked on scornfully.

The woman with the long grey hair gave Jimi Hendrix a tearful embrace. Beanie threw himself onto his bed and pulled the pillow over his head. Hairy Chest tried to wipe the tears out of his beard. The Melting Man's face collapsed like a small child's after a fall. Lobster Bottom opened and shut his fingers as if they were snapping claws.

Reptile seemed to shrink. She looked like a kinder-garten kid whose mother has left her at the gate on the first day of school. 'Gramps was good to me,' she sobbed. 'When I was seventeen he used to let me clean his false teeth.'

'He gave up his life for us,' sobbed Beanie. 'He stopped taking tea so we could have more.'

'After the last plant died,' said the Tea Lady softly.

'He was the best man ever,' said Reptile as she wiped a tear from her eye.

'We're all going to die,' yelled Pooper Scooper. 'And it's *his* fault.'

He was pointing with an outstretched arm. Straight at me.

171

The room fell silent again. The family forgot their sorrow in an instant. They felt only rage. They wanted only revenge.

'Why did you come here?' spat the Tea Lady.

'He doesn't know,' shouted Amy. 'He's lost his memory.'

Amy didn't realise that I had the answers now. I hadn't had time to tell her that my memory had returned when I saw the frozen corpse.

'My mother,' I said. 'I came here to try and find my mother.'

'Your mother?' said the grey-haired lady. 'Why would she be here? We're all one family. We don't allow outsiders.'

'I was abandoned as a baby,' I started to blurt out. 'I don't know who my mother is. I was left in a cardboard box. A skin-cream box. It came from here.'

'A box,' shrieked Pooper Scooper. 'A box. That's ridiculous. Impossible.' His face had grown bright red. And he was trembling. He seemed to be fighting for breath. His head wobbled as if it was going to explode. Veins stood out on his forehead. The word *box* seemed to have sent him into an uncontrollable frenzy.

The others looked puzzled. No one knew why he was so angry.

Amy waved her knife. 'Calm down,' she said.

But Pooper Scooper didn't calm down. He grew worse. 'The only mother that's been here in sixty years is *our* mother,' he shouted. 'She went to the High Valley. Agnes is the oldest so she took charge. And there's no other mothers. We don't have children. Because we don't want to bring in outsiders . . .' He suddenly stopped. As if he'd said enough.

Agnes, the Tea Lady, took a step towards me. 'You stole the last precious seed,' she said in a dangerous voice. 'The seed from our one remaining tea plant. Why?'

'I didn't know it was a seed,' I yelled desperately. 'I took off my clothes because it was the only way to get in here.' Amy's eyes were popping out in amazement.

'You caught me,' I continued. 'You had me trapped. Like now. I was scared. I saw the seed inside some sort of open safe and I . . .'

'Stole it,' yelled Scowler.

'The blue thing looked valuable,' I said desperately. 'So I took it to bargain with.'

Jimi Hendrix shook his frizzy hair angrily. 'Why did you have to go and swallow it?'

'Well, I couldn't put it in my pocket,' I said. 'Not when I was in the nude. You would have just grabbed me and taken it back.'

They all started to grumble and mumble. 'Well, it worked,' I said. 'You were all so shocked that it gave me time to run away.'

'Down to the Cool Room,' gasped Amy.

'Where I lost my memory.' I added. 'Anyone would. After seeing that . . .'

Scowler took a step towards me. 'When you give us the seed,' he said, 'then we'll let you go.'

'No we won't,' shouted Pooper Scooper. 'He'll tell. Then our cover will be blown. We can still get the seed. Next time he poops.'

The whole lot of them began to advance, yelling and screaming in fury.

'Open him up.'

'Squeeze it out of him.'

'Give him an enema.'

They thought the seed was still inside me and they wanted it back. I had to do something. And quick.

I reached into my pocket and pulled out the bright blue seed. They all gasped and stopped in their tracks. They stared at the seed as if it was one of the Crown Jewels.

Suddenly my hand seemed to have a life of its own. Just like I had done once before I opened my mouth and popped the seed inside. The nudists and the Brats fell back with a terrible scream.

'No, don't do it,' yelled Beanie. 'Please don't. Not again.'

Even Amy was shocked. 'Think where it's been,' she said in a disgusted voice.

I looked at Pooper Scooper and the others. Then I pushed the seed against one side of my mouth and edged towards the door. 'We're leaving,' I said. 'If anyone follows – I swallow. Down the hatch for a second time. And that's it for your precious seed.'

'That's what you think,' said Pooper Scooper. He turned to the others. 'Let's get him. Like I said, even if he swallows it we can still get it back.' He waved his knife around in the air.

The family gathered around Pooper Scooper. They reminded me of a lynch mob in a Western movie. They didn't have a rope with a noose on the end. They didn't need one.

Bare hands and a knife would do the job nicely.

SIX

Pooper Scooper and the rest of the family started moving towards us, ancient eyes burning with fury.

I looked desperately around Beanie's bedroom. There wasn't much space to move with twelve of us in there. No windows to dive for. And several furious family members between us and the door.

Sprocket and I wouldn't be able to fight our way out. I'd have to use words.

I'd never tried to calm down a crowd of people who were going to eventually die if they didn't get a cup of tea. I wasn't really sure how to go about it. It's hard to be sympathetic with people who want to kill you.

'OK, everyone,' I said in the loudest voice I could manage. 'If we all stay calm and reasonable I'm sure we can think of something.'

That had worked at school camp when Angela Bishop had got her head stuck in a cow-milking machine. Though my voice hadn't been wobbling as much then as it was now.

Holding the point of his knife to Sprocket's chest, Pooper Scooper turned his hate-filled face to me.

'Give up, girlie,' he snarled.

I'd been spoken to unpleasantly by some pretty mean kids in my time, but it made it somehow scarier when you knew the nine-year-old threatening you was probably in his eighties.

'Don't ask me to be reasonable,' spat Pooper Scooper. 'I'm *un*reasonable. That's why sister bossy boots Agnes and my cretin big brothers forced extra doses of tea into me. To keep me little and easy to control. I'm the black sheep of the family.'

'We're black sheep too,' said Beanie indignantly.

'Yeah,' said Reptile and Scowler.

It wasn't working. Nobody was staying calm. Pooper Scooper looked like he could reach puberty and explode at any minute.

I looked at Sprocket for help.

I could see he was thinking desperately, shifting the seed from side to side in his mouth. I hoped he wasn't thinking of where the seed had been.

Then a thought hit me harder than a runaway Hummer.

Of course. That was it. The seed. That was the connection with Dad.

Suddenly I remembered all the dead and rotting seeds in the fridges at the love nest. Dad must have been trying to germinate them for this family.

But why? Love? Money? The desire to cross-breed cucumbers that would live for ever?

It didn't matter now. All that mattered was me stopping my voice wobbling too much.

'My father,' I said as loudly as I could, and I saw that instantly I had the attention of the whole family. 'My father has knowledge you desperately need.'

'He failed us,' said the Tea Lady flatly.

'But did he?' I said. My mind was racing, frantically trying to think of something to say next that would get us out of this hate-filled room.

Anything.

It didn't have to be true.

'What if somebody just wants you to believe that my father failed you?' I said to the Tea Lady. 'Somebody who wants a new crop of tea plants all for himself. Somebody who's been dropping round to my place for secret meetings with my dad for months.'

I looked hard at Pooper Scooper.

His eyes widened in fury.

'It's a lie,' he screamed.

It was a lie, and I felt guilty telling it, but I was desperate.

And it worked.

The other members of the family glared at Pooper Scooper. Hairy Chest grabbed him by the front of his split army shirt. Bald Lobster took his ear between a pink thumb and forefinger.

I grabbed Sprocket's hand and dragged him away from the point of Pooper Scooper's knife. Then I grabbed one of Beanie's empty beer cans.

Sprocket and I leapt for the door and flung ourselves through it. I slammed it shut and stamped on the can and wedged it under the door.

'That won't hold them for long,' I said. 'We've got to find the baby fast.'

Sprocket took the seed out of his mouth and put it in his pocket. 'I can hear her again,' said Sprocket. 'Listen.'

He was right. In the distance, above the clamour of voices in Beanie's bedroom, was the high thin wail of a baby in distress.

We ran along the main corridor and turned towards the sound. I was relieved to see we were going in the opposite direction to the AMPS room.

We sprinted down the corridor, my baby sister's howls getting louder and louder. Just before we reached the entrance foyer, Sprocket stopped.

He put his ear to a door.

'In here,' he said, flinging it open.

We found ourselves in a small library. It smelt of musty old books. On a reading table was a half-finished meal on a plate. And in the corner, red-faced and bawling in an old-fashioned wooden cot, was my baby sister.

I recognised her instantly, and not just because she was wearing one of the nappies I'd bought her. I recognised her voice. You do, when it's your sister.

Even when she's twice as big as when you last saw her.

I gasped. When the Brats had kidnapped her, she'd been about four months old. Now, less than a day later, she looked about eight months.

I didn't want to think about it. There wasn't time. I could hear that the Brats and the rest of the family had got out of Beanie's room. Their shouts were getting closer.

I grabbed my sister and the blanket she was sitting on and headed for the door with Sprocket close behind.

In the entrance foyer I stopped.

'Come on,' said Sprocket. 'Let's get out of here.'

'No,' I replied. 'They'll expect us to go tearing off into the forest. They'll be criss-crossing it all night with vehicles and spotlights. What they won't expect is for us to stay around here till they get tired and give up.'

Sprocket looked uncertain. There was no time for a debate. I saw a row of keys hanging behind the reception desk and grabbed one marked Cool Room.

'Come on,' I said.

Clutching the bawling baby to my chest I sprinted across the dark clearing and up the slope to the Cool Room building. One thought burned in my brain. How could Sprocket and I keep a scared and hungry baby quiet without a decent-sized breast between us?

It wasn't till we were inside the filing-cabinet room and I'd locked the door behind us that I saw that Sprocket had already thought of the answer.

He struck a match and lit another of his old candles.

'Keep it away from the windows,' I said. 'Or they'll see it.'

Then I saw he was holding the half-full dinner plate from the library. Cauliflower cheese. Peas. Carrots. Mashed potato.

I would have hugged him if he hadn't been a boy and if the baby hadn't been bawling in my ear and trying to get her fingers behind one of my eyeballs.

I prayed the baby was big enough for solids.

I needn't have worried. She ate half the mashed potato, two lumps of cauliflower and several peas. I watched her wolf it down. If she always eats like this, I thought to myself, no wonder she's growing so fast.

Sprocket and I finished the rest. Before that night I'd never liked carrots, let alone gulped them down.

Then, while Sprocket played on the floor in the moonlight with the baby and kept his ears open for approaching Brats, I took the candle and explored the filing cabinets.

Between us, Sprocket and I still had three parents to find, and I hoped there might be some clues in the cabinets.

There were, sort of.

I ploughed through loads of drawers, all full of old papers and files. I saw stuff that showed that the family had been taking the tea for over seventy years. I saw stuff about the huge amount of money they'd earned from selling the skin cream and how its 0.001% tea content made wrinkles disappear over-night. But nothing about Dad or Mum.

Then, just as I was about to give up, I found a bundle of letters at the back of one of the drawers. I glanced at the writing on the envelopes. My heart had a spasm. I fumbled in my pocket for the bit of letter I'd found in Dad's jacket at the love nest.

My chest had another spasm.

The handwriting was the same. These letters were from the Other Woman too.

With trembling hands I opened one and started reading.

'*My darling children,*' it said. '*I pray that in the months since I last wrote, you have come to your senses. That you have finally freed yourselves from the tea. That you have finally laid your father to rest. Because only then will you have the knowledge you need to join me here in the High Valley.'*

What I was reading took a while to sink in. Then the realisation hit me so hard I gasped.

The letter was from the mother of the family.

She was Dad's Other Woman.

Before I could read on, Sprocket gave a yell.

'Amy, look.'

I stuffed the letters into my pocket and hurried over to him.

Sprocket was crouching next to the baby, who was sitting on her blanket. 'Look,' he whispered, voice breathless with amazement. 'Look what she's done.'

Suddenly I saw what he was pointing at. It was something that drove all questions about the Other Woman out of my mind.

Smeared on the floor in wobbly cheese sauce were three letters.

'She did it herself,' said Sprocket. 'I watched her.'

I stared at the word. I stared at Sprocket. I stared at the baby. She was staring back at me.

That's when we heard the angry voices coming

towards us across the clearing.

'Oh no,' I said. 'I forgot about keeping the candle away from the windows.' Quickly I blew it out.

'Only one thing for it,' said Sprocket. 'We'll have to barricade ourselves in.'

At first I thought he meant barricade ourselves in the file room. Then I saw him moving through the moonlight towards the doorway that led down to the Cool Room.

A dread gripped my insides as I grabbed the baby and followed Sprocket down the dark stone steps.

'Careful,' said Sprocket. 'They're slippery.'

I didn't want to go back into that Cool Room. I didn't want to see the dead man in the ice again. But I couldn't let the Brats get their hands on my sister again.

Sprocket's voice was tight with fear. He didn't want to go in either.

But we did.

Sprocket pulled the big metal door shut behind us and the clang echoed in the darkness.

I forced myself not to think about the darkness. I forced myself to think about what I'd just seen on the file-room floor.

Those three wobbly cheese-sauce letters.

My tummy gave a lurch as I realised what had happened.

My half-sister was a child genius and she thought I was her mum.

SPROCKET

SEVEN

Once again we were in the dark. In more ways than one. We couldn't see anything at all. But we did know what was in the Cool Room with us. A corpse frozen inside a huge block of ice.

Outside were bloodthirsty Brats and the rest of their weird family. Pooper Scooper seemed to have a special hatred of me. Why did the word *box* send him into such a frenzy?

There was no time to concentrate on this question. My mind was obsessed with the frozen corpse lying somewhere in the dark inside its glass case.

What if the frosty body suddenly came to life? What if it possessed some terrible powers? What if we were turned to ice by the touch of a deadly frozen finger? I felt weak in the stomach. The first time I had been in the Cool Room it was so terrifying that I had lost my memory.

I just hoped that my churning stomach would settle down. I couldn't bear the thought of throwing up in front of Amy.

'It's all right,' said Amy. 'I'll look after you, darling.'

'Thanks,' I said. 'I'll look after you too.' I was a bit surprised that she liked me so much. We hardly knew each other.

'I was talking to the baby,' said Amy frostily. 'She's cold and wriggling around.'

I felt stupid. Really stupid.

The baby began to cry.

'Do something,' said Amy's voice in the darkness.

'There's only one match and no candles left,' I said, trying to sound confident.

I took out the match and tried to stop my fingers trembling. I couldn't. I struck the match against the box and it flared briefly. I just managed to catch sight of the corpse's terrible face before the flame expired.

'Did you see that?' I cried with a shaking voice.

'Yes,' said Amy.

There was a *click* and then a pale glow from high above filled the room. She had seen something different – a light switch. I felt stupid. I had let my imagination run wild but Amy had taken practical action. I had to get my act together.

The baby started throwing its arms around and screaming.

'Sh . . .' said Amy. She rocked the baby and smiled at it. The baby began gooing. It seemed to like her.

The Cool Room was less scary now that we had some light. I looked around. It was cold but only the corpse inside its glass case was frozen. We were not going to freeze to death. But how could we get out? I looked around for a weapon.

There was nothing there really. Only a large fire hydrant tap and a hose curled up below it inside a plastic box. I grasped the edge of the box. I was just strong enough to tip it up and empty out the hosepipe. I grabbed the large brass nozzle. It was really heavy. I put it on the floor and held onto the flat canvas hose. Then I swung the nozzle around and around like a parent giving their child a whizzy ride.

'Careful,' said Amy. 'You could hurt someone.'

'That's what I want them to think,' I said.

At that moment we heard a scratching noise coming from outside. Low down.

'The chute,' yelled Amy. 'They are coming up the chute.'

The chute door slid up and Pooper Scooper, Reptile and Scowler appeared in the hatch. Their faces were filled with desperation and hate. Their eyes were slits of anger. Their mouths were snarling caves out of which rumbled terrible rasping war cries.

'Charge,' shouted Reptile.

'Get them,' screamed Scowler.

'Kill,' yelled Pooper Scooper.

They tried to charge but they couldn't get a proper grip on the chute. They looked like crazy cyclists riding invisible bikes as their feet slipped on the shiny wooden surface. Reptile began to slide backwards.

She crashed into the other two with a loud yell. They all tumbled noisily back down the chute.

'Idiot,' raged Pooper Scooper.

'Quick,' I yelled at Amy. 'Turn on the hose.'

Amy began tugging at the large tap wheel with one hand while holding firmly onto the baby with the other arm.

'Put the baby down,' I yelled.

'No way,' she grunted. 'No one is going to separate me and my sister.' She kept tugging but just couldn't budge the tap. The Brats were scrambling back up. Scowler had already reached the top.

I began to swing the heavy brass hose nozzle to try and keep them at bay. But it wasn't going to be enough. I might get one of them. But then the others would be on top of me. They wouldn't be frightened of the water hose. They were filled with rage.

Suddenly Scowler stopped his charge. He started to shake. Reptile and Pooper Scooper froze where they were on the chute.

'No,' said Reptile in a worried voice. 'Don't. We'll give you anything you want.'

I couldn't work out what was going on. I was getting giddy from swirling around. Maybe it was affecting my judgement.

'OK, OK,' said Reptile. 'You win.'

Then I realised what they were looking at. Each time I swung the fire hose the huge brass nozzle just missed the corpse's glass case. I stopped swinging and grasped the nozzle with both hands. I held it high above the glass.

'Get back,' I said. 'Or I'll smash the case and take a chip off the old block.'

I didn't really know if I could do it. Attacking a dead man was not something I felt good about.

'I already told you,' said Reptile. 'Keep your hair on. We're going.'

'Who is he?' asked Amy. 'Someone you killed?'

'Don't be stupid. He's our father,' said Reptile.

'You froze your own father?' I yelled.

'You monsters,' screeched Amy.

'It wasn't like that,' said Reptile. 'He drowned in an accident. We preserved his body in ice. He was the only one who knew how to germinate the seeds.'

'Shut up, Hilda,' spat Pooper Scooper.

'Well, he's not going to tell you much now,' I said. 'He's a frozen stiff.'

'We're going to bring him back to life,' said Beanie. 'When science finds out a way to do it.'

'Get real,' I said. 'That will be never.'

'No,' yelped Beanie. 'It will happen. Randall was going to be . . .'

Pooper Scooper suddenly grabbed Beanie's leg and pulled him back down the chute. He was much bigger than Beanie and managed it easily. 'I told you to shut up,' he yelled.

Beanie fell into the chute and disappeared with a yell. Pooper Scooper scrambled towards me.

I started to shake the nozzle as if I was about to strike the glass case.

'OK, OK,' said Pooper Scooper. 'We'll leave you for now. But we'll be back. I know just how to handle *you.*'

He and Reptile slid back feet first down the chute on their stomachs. They reminded me of little kids who were too scared to go down a slide the right way. Only they weren't really little kids. And they were deadly.

Amy rushed over, still holding the baby, and closed the chute door behind them. She swung the heavy steel locking handle down into place with her free hand.

'We're safe,' I said. 'As long as we stay here.'

I looked around. The Cool Room was made of concrete. I walked over and checked the main door. It was firmly locked from the inside. Both exits had rubber seals to keep out warm air.

'They can't get in,' I said.

'And we can't get out,' said Amy. 'And it's cold.' She hugged the baby close to her chest.

The walls towered above us. The ceiling was impossibly high. It looked as if the Cool Room once had two storeys. But there was no top floor now. All that was left of the upper level was a door high in the wall above. I pointed up to it.

'We might get onto the roof through there,' I said hopefully.

'How could we get up there?' said Amy. 'It's way too high.'

Just then a muffled voice came through the main door. It was Pooper Scooper.

'Like Stanley said,' he called out. 'Give us the seed and we'll let you go.'

'I don't trust them,' said Amy. 'Once they get us away from him we will be in their power.' She nodded at the Brats' frozen father. 'He knows how to germinate the seed and make it grow.'

I nodded. The corpse was our passport to safety. But we couldn't get out of the lower door or the chute because the enemy was on the other side.

'We have to stay with him,' I said.

We stared at the dead man in silence. Suddenly I had an idea.

I walked over to the plastic hose-box and dumped it on the floor in front of Amy.

'A crib,' I said.

'That's very thoughtful, Sprocket,' she said. She placed the baby gently inside. The baby gooed and gurgled. Now it had its own little cot.

I grabbed the huge fire-hose tap in both hands and began to turn it. Water gushed out of the end. The nozzle began to writhe like a snake.

'No way,' screamed Amy. She knew what I was planning and didn't like it.

'It's better than falling into the hands of the kidnappers,' I shouted back.

She shook her head and pulled my hands from the tap. She started to turn it off. I recovered my grip and fought against her. It was a stalemate. Neither of us could move it one way or the other. The water continued to pour out of the nozzle. It was already up around our ankles and lapping at the baby's box. We struggled with the tap, our faces just a few centimetres apart.

'We'll drown,' she said. 'Then what will happen to my sister?'

'No,' I told her. 'Remember the Titanic.'

'The Titanic?' she yelled. 'That sank.'

'Yes, but the iceberg didn't.'

A couple of seconds passed. She stared at the frozen corpse. Then she understood.

'You're a genius, Sprocket,' she said.

I turned off the tap. 'Mind your face, Amy,' I said. 'Protect the baby.'

I took the heavy nozzle and smashed it against the glass of the corpse's case. It broke easily. Large shards fell inwards. In a few seconds I had broken every panel. A small cloud of cold air swirled out of the case and around our feet.

Amy splashed over to the tap and turned it on full bore. A huge jet of water immediately began to flood out.

In no time at all the water was around our knees. Then it was up to our waists. It was cold and dim. And dangerous. We began to shiver. Amy held on tightly to the floating crib. We were taking an enormous gamble. Three lives were at stake. But if we did nothing we would be captured. And some things are worse than death.

There was no sound from outside. The enemy didn't know what we were up to. The seals on the doors were keeping the water safely inside the Cool Room.

Soon the water had risen above the slab of ice.

'The ice block is frozen to the pipes,' said Amy.

The water continued to rise. Up, up, up. We began to swim, unable to touch the floor with our feet. Amy kept one hand on the plastic hose-box. The baby floated safely inside, lulled to sleep by the movement of the water.

I floundered around, keeping myself up by lying on my back and kicking with my feet. It was hard work.

After about an hour the water was halfway up to the door above. By now we were terribly cold. And tired. I was shivering so much that I sent tiny vibrations through the water around me. I felt myself growing weaker by the second.

Amy dog-paddled and kept her nose right up against the baby's little boat.

'Don't give up,' I said. 'Keep moving.'

'Nothing separates me and this baby,' said Amy. 'Not even death.'

I sank under the surface and then managed to come up for a breath of air. I spat out air and water. I coughed. My strength was disappearing. I couldn't last much longer.

Neither could Amy. She sank under the water and then bobbed up again. A look of terrible fear filled her face.

'It's OK,' I said. 'The box will float even if you let go.'

Amy nodded but her face was a picture of terror. The fear was not for herself. I knew that she would give up her own life for the baby if she had to.

The water continued to rise. Slowly. The walls of the Cool Room were smooth and there was nothing to grab on to. We were both cold and weak. My legs had gone numb.

Amy's head vanished from sight again. Then it bobbed up as before. Now she was really in trouble. She spat out water and spluttered. I looked up at the door. It was going to take at least another hour for the water to reach that level. I knew we could never last that long.

Suddenly Amy disappeared under the surface. She had gone under for the third time. It was no use. We were finished.

'So much for the iceberg,' I mumbled as I slid down into darkness.

DEADLY!

Part Four

HUNT

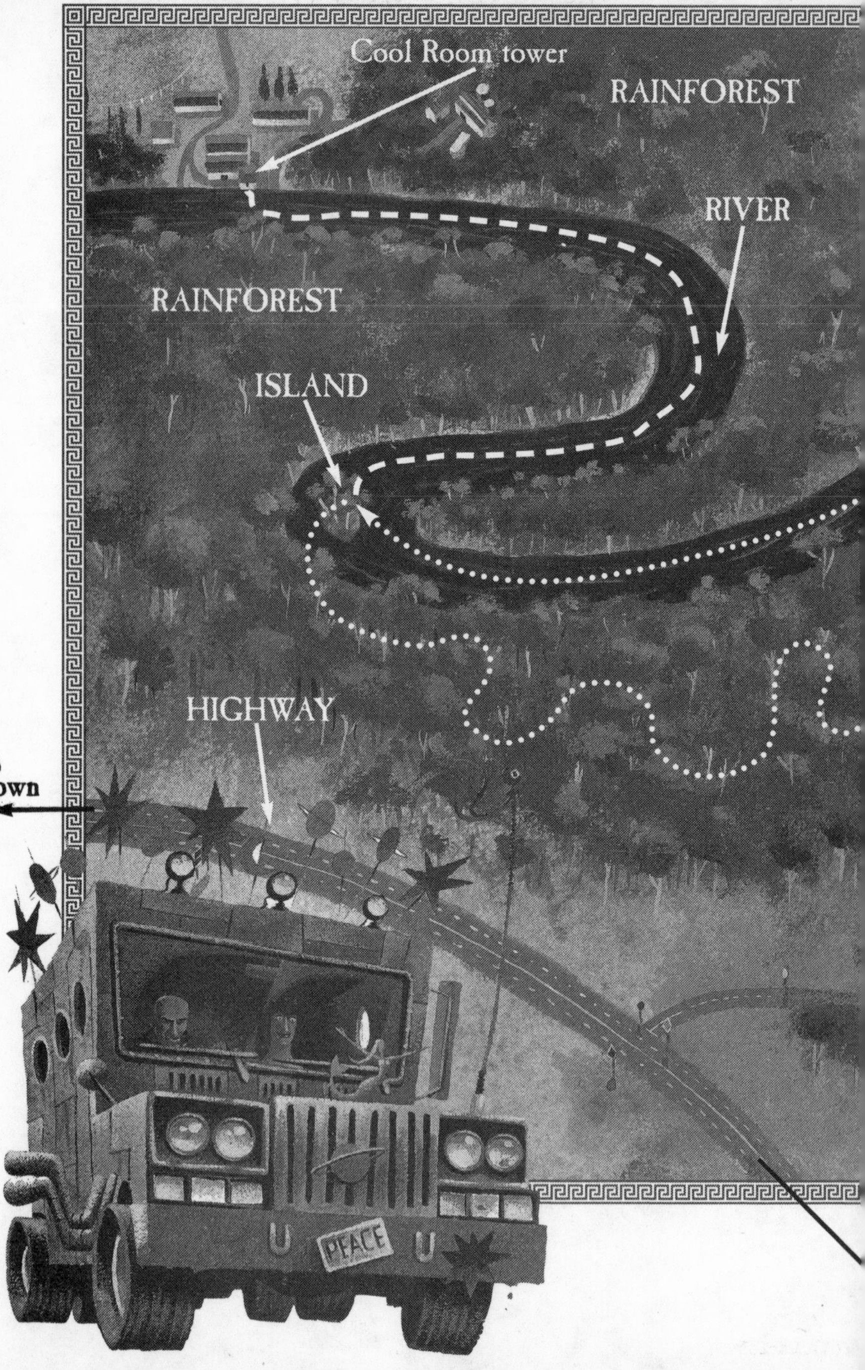

Cool Room tower
RAINFOREST
RIVER
RAINFOREST
ISLAND
HIGHWAY
to
the town
PEACE

LEGEND
Route of Amy, Sprocket and the baby
on the floating iceblock — — — —
Route of mobile home • • • • • • • • •

RAINFOREST

forest road

overnight stop

RAINFOREST

accident

The ESCAPE

to the
mountains

SPROCKET

ONE

I sank below the surface of the icy water that was rising to the top of the flooded Cool Room. My arms were like frozen lead. My feet and legs had lost all feeling. And my brain was barely working.

Drowning was weird. Not at all what I expected. I didn't see visions. I didn't dream dreams. I heard people speaking. Snatches of conversations from the recent past echoed inside my numb skull . . .

'*He's just fainted. What a weakling.*' The words of that little Brat Pooper Scooper when he and his brothers trapped me naked on the hillside.

'*Sprocket. Oh, Sprocket. It's really you.*' A voice from the nudist camp. That weird lady, Purple Cloud, who believed I was her dead child.

'*Push. Take a deep breath and push.*' Amy's instructions when she thought I was pregnant.

'*Give the seed back. Or my children die.*' The last few words from the rotting mouth of Gramps as I fled from his death bed.

'*We're leaving. If anyone follows – I* swallow. *Down the hatch for the second time.*' My own voice as I held up the bright blue seed and confronted Hairy Chest and the rest of the ancient but youthful family.

And then, finally, another voice. One I had never heard before. '*Swim, son. Swim. Don't give up.*' A golden voice. A glorious voice. The mellow tones of my unknown mother? Was she waiting for me? Did she know I was alive? Did she exist? Was she calling to me from far away? Or was I listening to the muddled ramblings of my own mind?

What was her connection to this strange place? Surely I wasn't going to die before I found out.

Feebly, and using the last tiny reserves of strength that remained in my cramped muscles, I flapped my arms. Slowly, slowly, slowly I began to rise through the water. The water that was calling me down to sleep and die in its chilly depths.

My head broke the surface and I managed to snatch a breath of air. Amy was doing the same. I knew that the thought of her baby sister floating alone in the plastic hose-box had called her back from the watery grave too. We had both been down three times and would have been dead but for those silent saving calls.

Still and all. There was really no hope. No boat. No raft. Only the baby's box and we couldn't cling to that. When we reached the roof we would die. And the Brats would get their precious life-giving seed back.

There was a gurgle. And an enormous roar. Like a sunken ship coming up from the depths, the ice block and its frozen corpse burst through the surface of the water. It splashed down with a *thwack*, rolled over a couple of times and then settled.

The frozen pipes below had released their grip on the ice coffin. The Germinator had risen from the deep.

Amy floundered towards the floating ice.

'Don't die. Live, live, live,' she gasped.

For a second I thought that Amy was talking to me. But she wasn't.

She managed to push the baby's box onto the frozen block of ice. Then she struggled up beside it. I dragged my shivering body after her. We lay there on our backs panting. The ice immediately began sucking the last few grains of warmth from our bones. But we were alive. The plan had worked.

Like I'd said to Amy – sure, the Titanic went down. But the iceberg didn't.

Water swirled and gurgled around us as we floated on the corpse. Neither of us spoke for a good five minutes. We were totally exhausted, needing every last drop of energy to draw in air. We lay there wheezing as the ice raft moved closer and closer to the upper door.

The water was freezing. The ice was freezing. And

we were freezing. I pretended to be hopeful. 'I think we're going to make it,' I said at last.

'All four of us?' said Amy.

Four? It took me a second to realise who she was talking about. Crazy, crazy, crazy. Inside the block of ice the frozen face of the dead man stared out at us. The father of everyone in the weird nudist family. And the son of Gramps who had died a grisly death back in his sick room.

'The Germinator,' I said, 'is the only one who knows how to make a nudist tea-seed grow.' I felt inside my soaked pocket. The seed was still there. And so was the skin-cream label I'd grabbed in the factory.

We were perched on top of the ice like a couple of ancient warriors on a funeral canoe. Amy fell silent – exploring some inner world of her own as she gazed at the baby. I shivered and took the chance to do some thinking myself.

I remembered.

I had been abandoned at birth. Passed from hand to hand. Foster home to foster home. Many of the people who had looked after me had been fine people. But they had their own children. They never gave me that special look of love. They spoke to me just that little bit more severely. They answered my cries just a little more slowly. And I had never uttered those magic words – not once in my life. I had never said, 'Mum' or 'Dad'. I took out the skin-cream label and stared at the woman's face drawn on it. Was my mother somewhere here? Who was my father?

Amy suddenly broke the gloomy silence. 'When this ice melts,' she said through chattering teeth, 'the old boy in there will start to go off. He'll begin to smell. Once he thaws no one will be able to bring him back from the dead no matter how much science advances.'

'I want to preserve him,' I said. 'I don't want him to rot away.' I was starting to become attached to this dead companion. He had been alive once. He had smiled and joked and loved. OK, he knew the secret of eternal youth and had started this weird clan. But still, he had belonged to someone.

In some ways he was like me. A dead man in an ice block is alone. But a boy without parents is lonely.

Amy interrupted my thoughts. 'Hey,' she said. 'We've almost got up to the ceiling.'

The water level had finally reached the door at the top of the Cool Room tower.

'Let the water rise above the door,' I said. 'We're taking the Germinator with us. The Brats need him. He's the only thing stopping them from attacking.'

We let the water lift our ice raft high up to the level of the door handle. Then I reached over and tried to open it. My fingers trembled from the cold. The handle had not been turned for years. It was as stiff as the poor Germinator. I groaned and used both hands to try and turn it.

Suddenly it moved. There was a *click* and the door flew open. Water began to pour out of the opening like liquid from a giant teapot. The sound of it splashing into the river far below drifted up through the night air. We began to float out with the flow.

Could we survive the fall? Was the water in the river deep enough?

'The baby,' screamed Amy. She grabbed her sister from the plastic box and held her tightly. The baby woke up and began to bawl like crazy.

Our frozen raft and its passengers swirled out of the door.

And stopped.

The ice raft had wedged on the edge of the door frame. It was halfway out. And halfway in. Far, far, below was the river. Above us the cold stars twinkled in the dark sky. Amy was outside and I was in.

The ice block started to rock like a see-saw as the water swirled out past it.

'Oh, shoot,' yelled Amy as her end of the see-saw dipped down. She clutched the baby under an arm and wriggled towards the centre of the ice block to stop herself from falling.

'Aaagh,' I screamed as I soared up towards the ceiling of the Cool Room.

Then the situation reversed. Amy's end rocked up towards the stars. And my end smacked down onto the water in the Cool Room.

Then I saw something weird. Unbelievable. Pooper

Scooper falling like an abseiling spider from a trapdoor in the roof. He dropped swiftly on a thin line which ran through a clip on his belt. A look of wicked glee was plastered across his twelve-year-old face. He'd aged another two years in the last two hours.

Another figure plunged down. It was Scowler. He seemed to be an expert abseiler. He gave a loud war cry as he fell. Reptile came hurtling after. They were followed by Beanie who seemed much more hesitant. He came down slowly with his eyes shut tight. Now they were aged around ten or eleven. They were growing quickly. Too big for their boots in more ways than one.

A face appeared through a trapdoor above. It was Hairy Chest. He was joined by Lobster Bottom. They both looked different. Like people who had been away for a year or two. Grey hairs and more wrinkles. They began pushing a large package through the trapdoor. It tumbled down and hit the water with a bang. There was a furious hissing sound as a small rubber dinghy began to inflate.

In no time at all Pooper Scooper and Scowler scrambled into the boat. They heaved Reptile in after them.

Beanie dangled halfway down on his rope.

'Hurry up,' screamed Pooper Scooper. He glanced over to us, stuck on our see-saw in the doorway. 'They're getting away.'

'I'm not coming. Pull me back,' came Beanie's trembling voice. 'You know I hate heights.'

High above, Hairy Chest stared at Beanie with a look of scorn on his face. He reached down and cut the rope with an ugly-looking knife.

Twang.

Beanie tumbled screaming into the water. The other three rowed furiously over to where he splashed and spluttered helplessly. They quickly pulled him aboard and started paddling towards us.

Amy stared at the river way below. 'We have to surrender,' she shouted. 'The baby will never survive the fall into the river.'

She was right. We could risk our own lives. But not Amy's baby sister.

'Crawl up to this end,' I said reluctantly. 'The weight will tip us back inside.' I began to move up and down, trying to refloat the ice. But Amy seemed paralysed. The Brats were almost upon us with their ropes and nets. Only a metre or so away. What the hell were they up to?

Suddenly there was a roar. The sound of an enormous gurgle filled the air. It was like the squealing of a giant bath after the plug had been pulled, a million times worse than the gurgle from the dying Gramps. A whirlpool had formed. It swirled around at an incredible speed.

Beanie began to howl with fear. Pooper Scooper gave a scream of fury.

'Aaagh,' shrieked Reptile.

Scowler said nothing. He was hanging on for his life as the rubber dinghy whizzed around the edge of the Cool Room. Faster and faster they spun, like flies clinging to a crazy merry-go-round.

The centre of the water turned into a huge, swirling funnel. The rubber boat entered the whirlpool and sped around so quickly that it was no more than a blur. The sound of the Brats' terror was lost in the roar of the water. Soon the surface had dropped to halfway down the Cool Room tower.

'The door has burst,' I screamed to Amy.

The top of the whirlpool continued to fall. The Cool Room was emptying. No bath ever emptied this quickly. But then no plug was ever the size of that steel door down below. The water rushed downwards and collapsed into a sucking, gurgling sea, flooding into the tunnels beyond the Cool Room.

The Brats' dinghy had lodged on a broken pipe on the wall about fifteen metres from the bottom. It suddenly deflated with a loud popping sound. The struggling figures dangled from it, desperately clinging on. They looked like terrified school kids.

They were terrified all right. But they weren't really kids.

And they were out but not down.

I had no time to wonder any more about them.

Our ice see-saw rocked wildly as we tried to cling to its cold, slippery surface. Up went Amy towards

the sky. Down I went towards the Brats and the
concrete floor far below. We were between the devils
and the deep blue sea. We could fall inwards towards
the Brats. Or we could fall outside towards the river.
Either way it was a long way down.

There was really only one choice.

I edged my way along the ice towards Amy and the
baby. The ice began to tip towards the river. In a
second we were airborne.

AMY

TWO

The four of us fell through the night air
towards the dark river.
Me.
My baby sister.
Sprocket.
The frozen Germinator in
the block of ice.
I had one arm wrapped
desperately around the

baby in her blanket and the other wrapped just as tightly around Sprocket's waist. Sprocket was hugging the ice block like it was his long-lost mother.

Three of us were screaming.

They say that just before you die your life flashes before your eyes. Not the whole thing, just edited highlights like the footy on TV.

That's what happened to me. I saw a quick flash of Mum yelling at Dad. And a quick flash of Dad sneaking off to see his Other Woman. But I didn't get the flash I desperately wanted – the one showing where Mum and Dad had disappeared to.

Instead all I could see, right in front of my face, was the wide-open mouth of the yelling baby. Pink gums glistening in the moonlight.

And something else. Something white emerging from one of the gums.

A tooth.

I stopped screaming for a moment and stared.

A tooth, appearing from nowhere, fully grown in about two seconds.

Impossible.

Get real, Amy, I said. Snap out of it.

I didn't say it out loud, just to myself.

Out loud I said, 'Aaarghhhhhh.'

We hit the water.

The force of the impact should have been enough to jolt me out of any hallucinations I was having. So should the time I spent thrashing around underwater.

The daze of stars and bubbles. The weed dragging at my legs. Sprocket dragging at my arms.

I kicked as hard as I could and my head burst through the surface of the water. I realised with relief that I was still clinging to the baby. Sprocket hauled us back onto the block of ice. Air rushed into my aching lungs.

Then I saw the baby wasn't breathing.

'Breathe,' I screamed at her, pleading, desperate.

She didn't breathe. Instead she projectile-vomited a jet of warm river water into my face. After that she started wailing, taking deep shuddering breaths between each wail.

I held her tight against me and stroked her wet head in the moonlight. Gradually she started breathing in time with me. And shivering just like me.

I looked around us. Our ice raft was floating in a patch of calm water next to a large overhanging rock. Sprocket was sitting astride the ice block, hands above his head, gripping onto a bush growing out of a crack in the rock, stopping us from drifting into the roaring current of the river.

The warmth of the water from inside my sister made me realise how cold I was, how cold we all were, sodden and shivering on that lump of ice. We were in a desperate situation. The Brats would be after us. To get their frozen father back. And to get the precious tea-plant seed Sprocket had stolen from them. And to make sure we would never tell the world about their sinister secret of eternal youth.

It was a desperate situation but it wasn't desperate enough to make me forget what I'd seen.

I looked into my baby sister's mouth again.

And gasped.

There were four teeth now. And while I stared, my own shivering mouth open wide with astonishment, a fifth tooth appeared out of one of her gums like a tiny target popping up in a fairground shooting gallery.

'Sprocket,' I yelled over the rushing water. 'Look. In her mouth.'

Sprocket glanced into the baby's mouth and gave me an exasperated glare. 'Very nice,' he shouted. 'I'm sure you're a very proud big sister. But right now we've got slightly more important things to worry about than baby teeth.'

'They're growing too fast,' I shouted at him. 'Look.'

I slid myself closer to him and held the baby up in front of his face. The poor little thing was bawling. I hoped the cold was numbing some of her teething pain.

Sprocket glanced into the baby's mouth again. Just as two more teeth appeared.

'Shoot,' he exclaimed, squinting in disbelief at the two white newcomers. 'What's going on?'

Thoughts were rushing through my head faster than the water swirling around us. 'Look at her,' I said. 'It's not just her teeth that are growing too fast.

All of her is. She's about five kilos heavier than when we rescued her a couple of hours ago.'

Sprocket stared at the baby. I could see his mind was racing as fast as mine. 'You don't mean . . .?' he said.

I nodded, my guts churning harder than a beetroot-canning machine.

'The tea,' he said. 'She must have drunk some of the tea. Now it's wearing off she's ageing really fast, just like Pooper Scooper and the others.'

I nodded again and pressed her sobbing head to my chest. I knew what Sprocket was going to say next. I'd already thought it and the thought was making me feel ill.

'Which means,' continued Sprocket, looking a bit ill himself, 'that if the tea's made her younger than she really is, your baby sister's not really a baby.'

We both looked at her, shivering and sniffing in my arms.

'How old do you think she is?' asked Sprocket.

I did some quick maths. How long had Dad been seeing the Other Woman? Five years? Ten? More? Their love child could be a love teenager.

'I dunno,' I said miserably. 'She could be older than me.'

If Dad had appeared on the ice block with us at that moment, I'd have hugged him with relief. Then I'd have pushed him in the river.

How could he do it? How could he deceive me and

lie to me and let me think I was his only daughter for all that time?

Suddenly angry shouts rang out from the distant riverbank. Torch beams sliced across the dark water.

'The Brats,' I gasped.

'Oh no,' said Sprocket. 'I was hoping the whirlpool in the tower would have slowed them down a bit longer. We've got to get moving.'

'Get moving?' I squeaked. 'How?'

Sprocket didn't answer. We both knew we only had one option.

'Hang on tight,' he said.

'Wait,' I said, and ripped the edge of the sodden baby blanket with my chattering teeth and tore it into three strips and used them to tie the baby to my chest. 'OK,' I said.

Sprocket pushed hard against the rock and we spun out into the roaring torrent.

'Are you all right?' yelled Sprocket as we clung to each other and the ice.

'I'm fine,' I shouted. 'Thanks.'

But I wasn't, and neither was Sprocket. Cold was searing our bodies. We were hurtling down a roaring, rushing, rock-studded river in the dark. Our craft was a block of ice. You can't steer a block of ice, not even when it's got an ancient and probably very wise bloke frozen in it.

I clung on and tried to think of things that would give me strength. Reasons for hanging on. Saving my baby sister. Finding Mum and Dad. But how? Where?

We hit a rock.

Sprocket and the baby and I slid off the ice into the water.

I grabbed at the rock, frantically trying to haul myself far enough up to keep the baby's head out of the water. It was too dark. The rock was too slippery. I couldn't see a hand-hold. I needed light.

I got it. Suddenly we were lit up by a dazzling searchlight beam. Just as the baby's head was slipping back under the water I saw a crevice in the rock. I squeezed my numb fingers into it and hauled with all my strength, dragging my torso and the baby's head out of the water.

In the distance, behind the dazzle, I heard the growl of outboard motors. I realised I didn't care that the Brats were coming. I'd have welcomed the bogey man and Darth Vader if they could have rescued us from that freezing rock.

Sprocket didn't see it that way.

'This isn't good,' he yelled, clinging onto the rock next to me.

The block of ice had skidded off the rock and was bobbing away from us down the river, glittering in the searchlight beam.

Sprocket stared after it, distraught. 'Once the Brats see we haven't got the Germinator,' he said, 'we're goners.'

He was right. The only reason Pooper Scooper and

the others hadn't jumped us the first time in the Cool Room was that Sprocket had threatened to smash the ice and cause their father to go off.

And now the river was trying to do the job for us.

I could still see the block of ice bobbing downstream. It seemed to be in one piece. I couldn't see any big cracks or blue limbs sticking out.

Then it stopped bobbing.

I hauled myself further out of the water and peered downriver.

The block of ice had run aground on a small island. It wasn't really an island, just a group of rocks and gravel, but it was enough to stop the ice.

'I'm going down there,' said Sprocket. 'Before the Brats get to it. You stay here. They won't harm you if I've got their father.'

Before I could say anything, he let go of his rock. The foaming current swept him away. I clung onto the rock and watched him go, a sodden helpless kid carried along by forces stronger than both of us.

The baby, still strapped to my chest, was sobbing pitifully.

'It's OK,' I panted to her, trying to breathe warm air onto her poor frozen face. 'He knows what he's doing.'

But it wasn't OK. The Brats were getting closer. Their yells were getting louder and their outboard motor sounded like a chainsaw coming to slice off my frozen fingers.

HUNT

I heard Sprocket give a yell.

With a surge of relief I saw he was on the island next to the ice. Then I saw he was sprawled on the gravel. Not moving. With his head in the water.

My insides went as cold as the rest of me.

Sprocket must have been knocked unconscious.

I had about two minutes to get his face out of the water.

I let go of the rock.

The water sucked me forward. Desperate to protect the baby's head, I managed to fend off the rocks that loomed at me, but unfortunately I only had my hands and arms to do it with.

Soon they hurt a lot.

The current was swinging me too far to the left. It was going to sweep me past the island. For a second I was tempted to give up, to let the river carry me where it wanted to. To somewhere I could sleep for ever and not feel the cold.

Then I got angry. I was too young to drown. So was my sister, whatever age she was. I wanted to get to know her better.

I sucked air into my mouth till my cheeks bulged. I clamped the baby's mouth to mine, holding her head there with one hand. Then I swung my head round to face the island, and with my other arm and both frantic legs, started to swim.

I felt my churning feet catch in my dress and rip it, but I didn't stop.

Slowly, slowly I beat the current. By the time I dragged us onto the gravel next to Sprocket, the baby and I were both gasping air and whimpering with fear and exhaustion.

I snatched Sprocket's head out of the water. His eyes were closed and his face had a blue tinge, even in the golden glare of the searchlight.

I would have given him the kiss of life, but I didn't have the breath, plus I was sobbing, so I just gave him a good shake. His head flopped around like a netball in a string bag. Then his eyes opened and he grimaced.

I turned away in case he projectile-vomited river water.

And saw something even worse.

About fifty metres away, powering towards us in a big old barge with two huge outboard motors screaming angrily behind them, were the Brats. They were close enough that I could see the fury on their faces. And it wasn't just because of their ripped and sodden clothing. Pooper Scooper looked about thirteen now, but with decades of rage and hatred burning in his eyes. Scowler, Reptile and Beanie had aged to about eleven, but they were more furious than any eleven-year-olds I'd ever seen, even ones that had been sent to bed early.

Hairy Chest was there as well, wrapped in a long fur coat, towering over the Brats, dark eyes flashing as he waved his fist at us. And Lobster Bottom, struggling into waterproof sailing gear, mouthing things at us I was glad I couldn't hear, his angry pink skin pinker than ever. And the Tea Lady, brown cardigan billowing out behind her, mousy hair flecked with grey now and plastered by the wind across her wrathful face.

The only one in the barge not gripped by fury was Matchbox. He had his paws up on the front and was peering at us, tongue out, panting excitedly.

Pooper Scooper was gripping a machete with a big gleaming blade. Several of the others were holding a large net. Must be to haul in the Germinator, I thought. Then, as I looked again at the hatred on their faces, I realised with a stab of panic that it was probably to haul in me and Sprocket and the baby as well.

I looked wildly around the little island. Over to one side, wedged between two rocks, was a hefty gnarled driftwood log.

I turned to Sprocket to ask him to grab it with me. My plan was to show the Brats how easily we could bring it smashing down onto the ice coffin. How if they didn't back off they could forget reviving their dead father and learning the secret of germinating the tea seed.

It had worked in the Cool Room.

But before I could get the words out, Sprocket did something completely crazy.

He flung himself at the block of ice and pushed

and heaved it back into the water so it bobbed and banged and scraped its way downriver.

I screamed at him.

'Why? Why did you do that when threatening to defrost Old Father Bird's Eye was our only hope? Our only way of stopping the Brats turning us into old-fashioned hamburger mince?'

Sprocket didn't say anything.

He just stood there as the ice coffin floated away.

Leaving us, two kids and a sodden shivering whimpering baby, alone and defenceless as the big black Brat-filled barge roared closer and closer.

SPROCKET

THREE

In no time at all the human ice block was in the grasp of the current and racing downstream. Pooper Scooper gave a howl of fury. Scowler shouted so loudly that a piece of bubblegum he was chewing fell into the river. Lobster Bottom ran back and forth in helpless rage. Hatred and disbelief filled the voices of the whole mob. They ran about like ants in a dug-up nest.

'Suffer,' I said under my breath.

Hairy Chest was yanking at his grey beard as if this would somehow give him strength. Reptile's knuckles were white with fury on the rudder as she kept the barge powering in our direction. The Brats and the rest of the murderous crew were coming to get us. We had sent their father, the Germinator, and his secret towards oblivion and they would never forgive us.

Suddenly Beanie pushed Reptile away and grabbed the rudder. He pointed the barge downstream. White water sprayed up behind it, thrown up by the enormous outboard motors.

My plan had worked. The family had decided to leave us and follow the ice man. It must have been a difficult decision. They wanted me so that they could get the tea-plant seed. But they didn't know how to make it grow. The Germinator knew the secret but he was going to keep it until they figured out a way to bring him back to life.

I watched with relief as the distant barge began to enter a bend in the river. It was bobbing furiously in the strong current. I could just make out the heads of the Melting Man, Lobster Bottom, Scowler, Reptile and a couple of others. I couldn't see Pooper Scooper. Maybe he had gone below deck. Then the moon went behind a cloud. I couldn't see anything.

Amy collapsed onto the ground with the baby still

tied to her chest. I dropped down next to her.

It's only after the immediate danger is gone that your body starts to punish you. We were both shaking all over. Aching and shivering. It was partly from the cold. And partly from fear. My stomach was churning. I felt really sick.

I bent over and threw up on the muddy bank. Carrots and mashed potato mainly. Possibly a bit of cauliflower. Those left-overs from the library where we found the baby were the only food I'd had for two days. Well, except for a seed. And that didn't count.

I took the small blue sphere out of my pocket and stared at it. A seed that could give eternal youth. I realised that it must be worth a fortune. If it fell into the wrong hands wars would be fought over it. Brother would turn against brother. Country against country. There were plenty of people in the world who would kill to have eternal youth.

The seed was a seed of death and destruction. Maybe I should throw it in the river. Whoever found out how to germinate it would have enormous power. They could have whatever they wanted.

I wanted something.

My mother and father. If they were alive.

Thirteen years ago my mother had placed me in a skin-cream carton. And left me on the doorstep of a police station. And now I wanted to find her – my real mum. The Brats might know something about her. After all, there were skin-cream boxes in the factory. And the mention of the box had sent Pooper Scooper into a terrible temper tantrum. So he at least must know something. But he would never tell. Unless I used the seed to bargain with him.

I put the seed back in my pocket and tried to work out what to do. Amy and I were stranded on the small island. But we couldn't stay there. If they got their ice block back the Brats would return. For us. And the seed.

I stared gloomily at the quickly running river. Neither of us had the strength to get to the other side. We would drown for sure. And the baby with us.

Amy was kneeling over the little tyke. Like us, the baby was shivering. Her blanket was soaking wet and her face was turning purple.

Amy unstrapped the baby and began rubbing her briskly. I looked around for something dry. Something warm. But there was nothing. The island was cold, bleak and bare.

'Please don't die, baby,' said Amy.

The infant was too weak to cry. Too weak to even struggle. A tear ran down Amy's cheek.

'Give her to me,' I said. Amy gently handed her over. I took the baby and placed her inside the wet jumper I was wearing. The baby's skin was freezing cold against mine.

'What are you doing?' yelled Amy.

'Body heat,' I said. 'It's her only chance.'

Amy nodded and wriggled towards my side. She

tenderly embraced me. What was she doing? This was no time for romance. This was no time for love. Well, not that sort of love.

'Two lots of body heat is better than one,' said Amy.

She had a point. We lay there with our arms wrapped around each other. The baby was between us like the meat in a hamburger.

After a bit the baby started to wheeze and gasp. The three of us were shivering. I knew beyond question that this infant could not last much longer. None of us could.

Amy and I were shaking worse than ever. Our bodies heaved and trembled and our teeth chattered noisily. I didn't like to say anything but I knew that shivers of that sort meant only one thing. Our bodies were making one last desperate effort to produce heat.

Suddenly I heard a voice inside my head. *'Don't give up, son. Don't give up.'* An image came into my mind. A young woman. Pretty and kind. She hugged me tight and smiled at me with the sort of smile that only a mother can give.

I didn't want to die. I wanted to find her. She was out there somewhere. I was sure of it.

At that moment I hoped that the Brats *would* come back. It would be better to fall into their hands than to perish on this little island in the middle of nowhere. Especially for the baby. She hadn't had any life at all yet.

My thoughts were suddenly chased off by a noise. The sound of an engine. I broke away from Amy and stared down the river. At first I couldn't make out who it was. Then as it came closer I could see. A strange vessel was making its way around the bend. It was heading against the current right in the middle of the river.

'Look,' gasped Amy.

'What on earth is that?' I said.

I couldn't make sense of it. What I was looking at was like some crazy image out of a dream. No, not a dream. A memory. I had seen this boat before.

Only it wasn't a boat then. It was a mobile home. The whole thing was made of thick, rusty, plate steel. Huge exhaust pipes snaked along the side. On the front was a rusty mermaid sticking out like a figurine on a sailing ship. Instead of windows the van section had portholes. All over the roof there were rusty stars and cupids sparkling in the moonlight.

I started to jump up and down and wave my arms.

'Help, help, help,' I screamed.

'Over here,' yelled Amy.

A door opened in the side of the mobile home and a figure appeared. It was the weird woman who had hugged me to her breasts in the nudist colony. I could see the little stars and moons twinkling in her thick dark hair.

She started to wave back. She had seen us.

Her voice floated across the water as the strange vessel turned and headed our way.

'Sprocket. My boy, my boy . . . I'm coming. I'm coming.'

Man, was I glad to see her. We were saved. I knew she wasn't my mother but right now that didn't matter. In a few seconds we would be aboard the floating mobile home on our way to safety. Amy was grinning like mad.

The weird craft powered towards the muddy shore. And powered and powered and powered. Faster and faster. What were they doing? Why didn't they cut the engine? Instead of easing up they were speeding up. Purple Cloud hung out of the door waving furiously. Wasn't there anyone at the wheel? They were going to strand themselves on a mud bank.

I hung my head and groaned as they ploughed into the mud. And ploughed and ploughed and ploughed. The mud covered the bumper bar and the radiator and the headlights. But still it came. Filthy water churned up under the mudguards, thrown up by the wheels.

Wheels. Of course. The mobile home had wheels. Like a drunken seal it lumbered up onto the bank and stopped with a watery squeal.

'Anyone for Surfers Paradise?' yelled a cheery voice. It was Con Rod, the bloke with the shaved hair and earrings. He jumped down from the cabin and didn't seem to mind getting mud over his flared jeans. He walked jauntily across to where we stood shivering on the bank. 'I reckon you . . .'

His voice faded away as he stared at the baby.

Purple Cloud, who had been looking at me with wide eyes, followed his gaze.

She gasped and jumped down and grabbed the baby from inside my wet jumper. 'Start the heater up, love,' she said. 'This baby is blue.'

'The heater's busted,' said Con Rod. 'Flamin' Weasel Dixon sold me a crook one.'

'Come on,' yelled Purple Cloud. 'Climb aboard. Hurry.'

We quickly followed Purple Cloud into the mobile home. It was like the inside of a gypsy's caravan. Rose-scented candles burned and spluttered from bottles that had been glued to the bench tops. The whole thing was lined with red velvet curtains covered in pictures of princesses, queens and mermaids. Huge trails of flowers and creepers grew from jars and pots. Sticks of incense sent out lazy curls of sweet smoke which drifted up towards a sleeping platform.

Purple Cloud began rubbing the baby with a soft towel.

'We have to get out of here,' I said to Con Rod. 'Those Brats are vicious. When they were little they tied me up in the forest. And kidnapped Amy's baby sister. They're as mad as hell. Who knows what they can do now they're bigger.'

Con Rod stared at me without answering. For a moment he looked puzzled, but then he jumped into the driver's seat and put the mobile home into gear. In a second we were lumbering back into the water.

Amy stared down at the baby with worried eyes. 'She's still blue,' she said.

'Losing the last of her body heat,' said Purple Cloud. 'This calls for emergency measures.'

She reached into a cupboard and pulled out a jar filled with some light brown goo. She massaged the baby all over with it and then wrapped her in a blanket. She handed the baby to Amy who took her with a smile.

'Don't worry, love,' said Purple Cloud. 'She'll be OK now.'

Amy began tickling the baby, trying to get her to smile. She started sniffing at the brown goo. 'Hey,' she said. 'What is this stuff?'

'Peanut butter,' said Purple Cloud. 'I'm out of massage oil.'

'You can't do that,' gasped Amy.

'Why not?' shouted Con Rod. 'It's not the crunchy sort.'

There was dead silence. Then Amy and I started to laugh.

Purple Cloud turned her attention to me. She started pulling off my wet clothes. I grabbed onto my jeans to stop her tugging them down. I had been naked in a nudist camp and it hadn't worried me too much. But this was different. This was close range. And Amy was looking.

'It's all right,' said Purple Cloud with a loving smile. 'You don't have anything to hide from your mother, Sprocket dear. I've wiped your little bottom many a time.' She tossed over Con Rod's leather jacket for me to put on.

'You're not his mother,' said Con Rod from the front. 'You have to face it, love. Sprocket's dead. I already told ya. This is another kid.'

The smile fell from Purple Cloud's face. 'I know,' she said sadly. 'But he looks like he needs a mother. And he answers to Sprocket.'

I was just about to tell her that was because I didn't know who I was when we last met. For all I knew then I *could* have been Sprocket.

But right at that moment we began to bounce around. The front of the mobile home jolted upwards. It was almost vertical. Like a space shuttle about to take off. Amy and I and the baby slid towards the back. My heart missed a beat. What was happening?

'Just going ashore,' yelled Con Rod.

He was trying to get the van up a steep bank. The wheels spun at an incredible speed. We were losing grip. It was too steep.

Suddenly the van slipped backwards. Down, down, down.

Underwater.

We were totally submerged. I couldn't believe it. I thought I saw a fish dart past a porthole.

Amy clutched the baby to her chest in terror.

But it only lasted a second. Then, like a cork, we bobbed up to the surface.

'Whoops,' said Con Rod. 'I forgot to engage four-wheel-drive.'

There was a bit of clunking and grinding of gears. Then we mounted the bank again. And were on dry land.

Con Rod pointed to a burning stick of incense. 'You were right, love,' he said. 'Lavender stops the van sinking.'

Purple Cloud shook her head.

'Lavender stops the van *stinking*,' she said.

We all started to laugh again. For just a second we felt safe. And forgot that somewhere out there in the cold night, killer children and their hundred-year-old brothers and sisters were searching.

And lusting for our blood.

FOUR

It felt good to laugh. But only for a moment. Then I remembered the danger we were in. I remembered what I'd seen in the eyes of that desperate, tragic family. How they'd go to any lengths to keep their secret safe. Including making sure that an innocent love child who'd drunk some of their anti-ageing tea would never get to blab their secret to the outside world.

If they could get their hands on her.

I hugged my baby sister to me and peered anxiously out of a porthole into the darkness as Con Rod drove the mobile home deep into the rainforest. Finally he stopped and pulled on the handbrake.

'I reckon we're safe from them hoons here,' he said. 'But just in case they do get close, time for a bit of camouflage.'

'I'll give you a hand,' said Sprocket.

While they worked in the moonlight, covering the mobile home with branches and fronds, I wondered what we'd do if the evil Brats and their frenzied brothers and sisters did find us.

The baby started shivering again.

So did I.

What was that?

I strained my ears, desperately hoping I hadn't just heard distant angry shouts and the revving of a Hummer engine.

Nothing.

Just insects and frogs and Con Rod swearing at a splinter in his thumb.

A hand touched my shoulder.

I jumped.

It was Purple Cloud.

'Your name's Amelia, right?' she said with a kind smile.

I nodded, wondering how she knew that. Perhaps she was psychic. She looked as though she might be, with her sparkly hair and her soft eyes and her pink and purple satin and velvet dress-kaftan-robey thing.

'Sprocket told me,' she said. 'Why don't you get out of that wet dress, Amelia, and into something warm and dry.'

'I want to make sure the baby's OK first,' I said.

Purple Cloud gently prised her out of my arms. 'I'll look after her,' she said, pulling dry clothes out of an overhead locker and steering me behind a plastic shower curtain with an Indian temple on it. 'You get yourself fixed up. How old is she, about twelve months?'

I hesitated wearily. Suddenly I didn't have the

strength. There was too much to tell. I'd only just met this person. I couldn't just blurt out that for all I knew my baby sister could be older than me. 'I'm not sure exactly,' I said.

I didn't like letting the baby out of my sight, so I stripped off the wet dress and pulled on some old pants and a big windcheater as fast as I could.

When I emerged, the baby was lying on a towel on the dining table and Purple Cloud was gently massaging her again with the peanut butter.

'Anything oily's good for a massage,' said Purple Cloud. 'Except the stuff Con Rod uses in the motor.'

Two minutes later the baby had stopped shivering and was gurgling happily.

'You have a go,' said Purple Cloud, 'while I warm her up some milk.'

This is crazy, I thought as I gently massaged the baby's back. But it was working, so I kept on doing it.

Until I saw something in the flickering candlelight that left me suddenly unable to move. Something that shocked and stunned me so completely, I couldn't even lift my hands.

It was on the baby's back, down low where I'd just rubbed away a smear of peanut butter.

A birthmark.

A birthmark in the shape of Tasmania.

I'd seen that birthmark before, the time I'd burst into the bathroom one holidays and Mum had been naked with her back to me.

Same birthmark.

Same position.

I forced my hand to move. I tried to wipe the birthmark off the baby's back, hoping it was just a big piece of peanut skin.

It wasn't.

My head spun.

Why did this baby, who was the love child of Dad and his Other Woman, have the same birthmark as Mum?

Unless . . .

Could Mum be the mother of this baby?

I stood there in a daze, too stunned to speak, trying to work out if a birthmark could be passed on from a mother to one of her daughters.

I became dimly aware of Purple Cloud feeding the baby milk. Then Con Rod and Sprocket came back in and helped her make a cot out of a cardboard box and some towels.

'Scuse me asking,' said Purple Cloud, frowning with kind concern as she laid the now sleeping baby in the cot, 'but who exactly is this bub?'

'I'm not sure,' I said quietly.

Sprocket gave me a strange look.

'Poor love,' said Purple Cloud, stroking my hair. 'She's too tired to think.'

'No more questions,' said Con Rod as he and Sprocket dragged boxes and old tents off a couple of sleeping platforms at the back of the vehicle. 'All questions to be saved till the morning by order of the bloke with his name on the rego papers.'

But even though I was desperate for sleep, there was one question I couldn't leave till morning. I lay on Purple Cloud's old fur coat for ages, one hand on the edge of the cardboard cot, watching the moonlight twinkle on some crystals hanging in front of a porthole, thinking about whether the baby next to me could really be Mum's daughter.

It didn't make sense.

It took nine months to have a baby and I was home on school holidays every two and a half. I'd have noticed if Mum had been pregnant, even though angry people did often hold their tummies in.

How could she have had a baby without me knowing?

My exhausted brain couldn't come up with an answer.

I wished Dad was around. Perhaps he could tell me what was going on. But I didn't even know where he was. He could be anywhere. Iceland. Mars. Somewhere with his Other Woman. Who, I remembered with a sick jolt, was the Brats' mother. I shuddered at the thought of Dad pashing on with a twenty-three-year-old blonde bimbo tea-guzzler who was really a hundred and something.

Suddenly I just wanted to hand the whole thing over to someone big and official. Like the police. But I knew that wouldn't work. Sergeant Taylor hadn't even believed me when I'd rung him and told him about Dad and the skin-cream factory. He'd choke on his chewy when he heard me going on about an invisible pregnancy.

I heard Purple and Con stirring in their sleeping area up the front.

'I'm not doin' nuffin', Officer,' Con Rod mumbled dreamily. 'These hub caps are me Dad's, honest.'

Anyway, I was pretty sure Con Rod wouldn't want anything to do with the law. In town there were blokes with exhaust pipes about one tenth the size of Con Rod's and they were always getting pulled over by the police.

Perhaps Sprocket could think of an answer. I glanced over at him. He was awake too, lying on a blanket on the other rear sleeping platform, staring at something he was holding up in front of his face. I could tell from his expression he was churning stuff over as well. Probably thinking about his mum. I didn't want to burden him with any more of my problems, not tonight, not after he'd helped me so much.

'Thanks,' I whispered.

At first I didn't think he'd heard me.

Then he whispered back. 'Thank you.'

I saw what he was staring at.

The blue seed.

I'd never been interested much in seeds. Anything that sprouted gave me the yawns basically. It was probably all the happy moments Dad had spoiled by being more passionate about his flowerpots than his family.

This was different though.

I gazed across at the blue seed in Sprocket's hand and a shiver went through me.

This wasn't just some new strain of supermarket tomato that was resistant to fruit-flies and shelf-packers.

This was possibly the most amazing piece of nature in the world.

Sprocket turned the blue seed in the moonlight. Carefully. As if he was holding the lives of an ancient family in his fingertips. Even though some of them had done awful things to us, I felt myself trembling. They were people after all. And unless the seed could be germinated, they would die soon.

Which would stop them harming any of us, that was true. But I still didn't feel good about it.

I looked at Sprocket. I could tell from his face he was feeling the same as me.

Suddenly I was glad he was my friend.

Parents, even though I loved mine heaps and was desperately hoping they were OK, were always just parents. Friends were different. There was no limit to how far a friendship could go.

As my eyelids grew heavy and my brain started to shut down, I had another thought.

In a world where anti-ageing seeds were possible,

perhaps invisible pregnancies were possible too.

I must have slept after that because the next thing I knew sunlight was streaming in through the porthole next to my head.

I rolled over and rubbed my eyes and saw Mum's mobile lying next to me on the pillow. I'd left it in the pocket of the wet dress. Purple Cloud must have retrieved it.

Then I saw that the message symbol was showing again.

Frantically I dialled Mum's voicemail.

Dad's voice crackled in my ear with another message for Mum.

'Lesley,' he said. 'Something I forgot before. This is very important. Do not, repeat, do not use the little plastic bag of herbal tea on the kitchen table. I was in such a rush to get away I left it there by mistake. Just don't touch it, and tell Amelia not to touch it either. I'll explain when I see you. Have to go now, my battery's . . .'

The message ended. I stared at the phone. Dad had called me Amelia. He only called me that when he was really stressed.

Then, slowly, the significance of his message seeped into my sleep-fuddled brain.

The tea on the kitchen table. Dad had been doing research work for the ancient family. It could have been their anti-ageing tea.

Mum could have . . .

Suddenly I realised the cardboard cot wasn't next to me on the sleeping platform any more. I looked around wildly. There it was, down on the floor, torn into pieces.

I couldn't see the baby anywhere.

Then, from outside the mobile home, I heard squeaky laughter.

I leaped down and flung open the door.

Blinking in the morning sunlight, I peered around.

No baby.

Just a small figure, three or four years old, wearing a big T-shirt as a dress, sitting on the grass. Purple Cloud, Con Rod and Sprocket were standing open-mouthed, staring at her.

My stomach gave a lurch.

Could my sister have grown that much in eight hours?

The small figure saw me, stared a moment, then stood up and put her hands on her hips.

'Melia,' she yelled at me in a squeaky toddler's voice. 'Melia.'

My blood froze.

No.

It wasn't possible.

Con Rod bent down and tried to pick a twig out of the toddler's hair. She pulled her head back. 'Wong way, silly ididit.'

Con Rod's shoulders sagged.

So did my insides. The way the toddler was

snapping angrily at him sounded sort of familiar.

I shook my head. 'It's not possible,' I croaked.

Con Rod turned and saw me as I went over to them.

'You'll think I'm nuts,' he whispered, glancing nervously at the toddler. 'She's been growin' in front of our eyes. Purple Cloud reckons it's a group hallucination, but I know it's real. She kicked me.'

The toddler stared up at me and threw a tantrum.

'Melia,' she shouted. 'Bad girl. I very angry. Naughty Melia.'

She's playing, I thought desperately. Purple Cloud must have told her my name's Amelia and she's including me in her game.

'Melia in big tubble.'

Or, I thought with a wild stab of hope, perhaps her name's Amelia too. Except why would Dad give both his daughters the same name?

The toddler's face suddenly crumpled into tears and she rushed at me and threw her little arms around my leg.

'Lezzy scared,' she bawled. 'Lezzy scared.'

I was swamped by a rush of thoughts and feelings. I remembered the vomit with Mum's lunch in it next to the baby when I first found her. The way the baby had grabbed at the phone in the corner shop. The way she'd written the word MUM with cheese sauce.

And of course, the birthmark.

And that's when I knew, even before I saw the

shocked realisation dawn on the faces of Sprocket and Con Rod and Purple Cloud, that the little kid sobbing pitifully into the legs of my pants was Mum.

SPROCKET

FIVE

The steel mermaid on the mobile home was coloured gold and red by the morning sun. I wouldn't have been surprised if she had suddenly flapped her tail. Crazy, crazy, crazy things were happening.

But at that moment I was far away. Inside my head. Thinking.

If you had to pick the world's most loved word what would it be?

Dying soldiers call it out on the battlefields.

Old men and women whisper it as they say their last goodbyes.

It is the first word spoken.

And the last.

Mum.

And here was Amy calling the baby *Mum*. Because the baby was her mother.

Only she wasn't a baby any more. Amazing. Incredible. The little tyke has grown into a toddler right in front of our eyes. She could walk. And talk. 'Fanks,' she said to Amy. 'Fanks for saving Mum.'

Amy hugged the small child to her chest. Tears were running down her face. 'You're not a love child,' she sobbed. 'You're not my half-sister. You're, you're . . .' Her voice trailed off and then she added. 'You're a married woman . . .'

Purple Cloud and Con Rod looked on in amazement.

'Your mum?' said Con Rod. 'Pull the other one.'

'It's the nudists' tea,' I said. 'It can make you young.'

'Like lilac water?' said Purple Cloud doubtfully.

Mrs Tunks-Livingstone scrambled up onto a chair and pulled Amy's head onto her little chest. 'Mummy here now,' she said. 'Everyfing will be OK.'

'Yes,' said Amy, dazed. 'I'll look after you.'

'I don't fink so darlink,' said Mrs Tunks-Livingstone. 'I in charge now. I muvva.'

Tears still streamed down Amy's face. She was weak with relief. 'You haven't changed,' she said. 'You're still the same inside that little body.'

Amy picked her mother up like someone lifting a child to dance with them at a grown-up's party. 'Nothing will ever separate us,' she said quietly.

Mrs Tunks-Livingstone glared at Amy. 'No time for dat, young lady,' she said. 'It'th time to talk. But not in front of hippieth.'

Purple Cloud and Con Rod looked hurt at being called hippies but they didn't say anything. Mrs Tunks-Livingstone struggled out of Amy's arms and waddled into the sleeping area at the front.

'Come Melia,' she ordered.

Amy wiped away her tears. 'Don't mind her,' she said. 'She's always been grumpy. Her last childhood was a really unhappy one. But I'll bring her up with proper manners this time.'

She took a deep breath and followed her mother into the bedroom. As she closed the door I couldn't help noticing the smiles on both faces. Mother and child were together again.

A great wave of sadness came over me. Amy had found her Mum. But I didn't even have one. Well, I might have. That's about all I could say. And I was going to find her. If she was alive.

Purple Cloud ran her fingers through my hair. She really wanted me to be her son. She just couldn't get the idea out of her mind. It made me feel uncomfortable. As if I was a traitor.

I moved away and sat down on the lid of a long window seat near by. It was cold. Very cold. My backside started to ache from it.

Before I could shift, Purple Cloud reached over, grabbed my head and pulled it into her chest.

'Sprocket,' she said. 'My darling Sprocket. I know you're looking for your mother. But until you find her I thought *I* could be a mum to you. I know you're not my boy. He died. I was just . . . hoping. Me and Con Rod, well, we could look after you.'

Con Rod was examining a map. Purple Cloud couldn't see his face. But I could. He looked up and started nodding and winking at me. He wanted me to be nice to her. He wanted me to go along with it. I rubbed my cold bottom and tried to think.

A big tear ran down Purple Cloud's face. It smudged her eyeliner and made a long black track down her cheek. She rubbed it with her fingers and made it worse. She began to sniff, trying not to cry. One of the pieces of glitter in her hair shook loose and spiralled down onto a rose-scented candle. The candle began to splutter and then died.

I didn't know what to say. I wanted to be kind. I wanted to say, 'Yes, yes, yes. You can be my mother. We will all live together happily ever after.' But I couldn't. She wasn't my mother. I did like her even though she was a bit weird. She was kind and loving, but she didn't match up with the picture of my mum that I had in my mind.

And Con Rod. A great guy, but he was a bit weird too. I looked at his pointy shoes and flared jeans. He had a silver pendant hanging on his hairy chest. He was mad about all these old Elvis songs like 'Blue Suede Shoes'. He thought he was a rocker. It didn't matter. He had a heart of gold. But he wasn't my father.

I stared at these two lovely people and knew what I had to do. I had to be cruel to be kind. I had to set them straight so that they didn't get their hopes up. I had a terrible ache in my own heart.

'I'm sorry,' I said. 'But I can't think about anything except my real parents. Wherever they are.'

Purple Cloud and Con Rod fell silent. They suddenly seemed tired and old and beaten. I felt terrible. I had hurt their feelings. And they were such nice people. Purple Cloud wiped away her tears with a red and green silk handkerchief. Maybe she didn't believe in tissues because they were made out of trees. She smiled at me, trying to be cheerful.

'It's all right, Sprocket,' she said. 'We'll help you find your Mum. Won't we, Con?' He looked up from where he had been stowing things away in preparation for our journey.

'Course we will,' he said.

I gave her the kindest smile that I could manage. 'Thanks a mill . . .'

Suddenly the coldness became more than I could bear. I sprang to my feet. The cheeks of my backside were so cold that I had lost all feeling in them.

'Jeez, that's cold,' I said. 'What have you got in there?'

Con Rod went red. He was hiding something.

I lifted up the lid of the window seat and stared inside.

An old friend peered back.

SIX

I heard Sprocket give a cry of alarm and hurried out of the small bedroom.

At first I couldn't work out what the thing in the mobile home window seat was. Your brain doesn't work very fast when it's still trying to get used to the fact that the sleeping toddler in your arms is your mum.

Then I realised.

I stared at the large block of melting ice.

Or rather, at the wide-eyed Germinator frozen inside.

Or rather, at the fingertips of the Germinator's hand, which were poking out of the melting ice like bloated raw sausages.

Very old ones.

My insides went even more wobbly than they already were.

At boarding school you see plenty of grubby fingers, but I'd never seen any that exact shade of bluey-greeny-grey.

Then Sprocket and I stared at Con Rod.

We'd last seen the Germinator floating away down-river the previous night. How had he got here?

We didn't have to ask the question. Con Rod could see it in our faces. But before he could answer it, we heard something that made us stiffen with fear.

The sound of an angry throbbing military engine.

'The Hummer,' said Sprocket, squinting frantically out of the window. 'Can't see it, but it sounds like it's getting closer. The Brats must be heading this way.'

My insides churned. I hugged Mum to me. I didn't want to think what that awful desperate family would do if they got their hands on us.

Lock Mum away so the world couldn't discover the secret of their tea.

Lock us all away. Or worse . . .

I had a sudden urge to grab Con Rod and shake him hard and scream that we had to get Mum to a hospital.

I didn't.

Chances were, medical science couldn't do any more for Mum than it could for the Germinator. And if the TV news found out about her, she'd end up being gawked at by the whole world. Labelled for life as a freak.

No, she was better off with me. At least I could give her the loving childhood she'd never had.

As long as we could escape the Brats.

Con Rod must have seen the terror in my face because he leaped into the driver's seat.

'Moving out,' he yelled as he turned the ignition and gunned the motor. 'Batten down the hatches and the under-fives.'

Sprocket hurried to the back window and peered out, trying to see how close the Brats were. Purple Cloud dashed around clicking seat-belts over cupboards and shelves.

I dropped into a beanbag chair with Mum and held her tight. The mobile home jolted off through the forest. Branches scraped at the windows as we lurched over rocks and fallen timber.

Mum slept on. In her innocent childish sleep, she must have felt safe.

Con Rod swerved to avoid trees, and water from the Germinator's melting ice block sloshed across the floor.

'You'd be wondering,' said Con Rod, glancing at us in the rear-vision mirror, 'how it got here?'

'I'm wondering,' croaked Sprocket, still peering anxiously out the back window, 'whether we can go any faster.'

Con Rod either didn't hear him or pretended not to.

'I seen them hoons chasing that block of ice down-river last night,' said Con Rod. 'It hit a bit of a whirlpool and got snagged under some overhanging trees. Hoons was in such a hurry to catch it they whizzed straight past. I got a couple of cables round it and Con Rod's yer uncle. Lucky I've got the ninety horsepower winch on board. Weasel Dixon reckoned I'd only need a fifty-five, but I'm glad now I told him to nick me a decent one.'

Con Rod spun the steering wheel, did a couple of quick gear changes and glanced back at Sprocket.

'You're probably wondering,' said Con Rod, 'why I done it?'

Sprocket looked like he could hear the Brats getting closer and was wondering why Con Rod didn't just concentrate on driving.

'I ain't been to university,' said Con Rod, 'but I know this much. When a person's carked it they deserve to be laid to rest decent and not left at the mercy of young hoons. So I'm gunna drop this bloke off at the cop shop. Anonymous, naturally, and real late at night.'

I saw that Purple Cloud was looking at Con Rod and her face was glowing with love and pride. She blew him a kiss.

'He's been collecting junk for thirty years,' she said, 'and I've never been prouder of him.'

Con Rod shrugged modestly. 'World's a weird place these days, what with global warming and too many hormones in the chicken nuggets and parents who suck their thumbs,' he said, nodding back towards Mum who was still asleep in my arms. 'Helps a bloke stay sane, giving another bloke a bit of a hand.' He glanced back at the frozen Germinator. 'Pity, probably never even know who he is.'

Sprocket and I decided to tell him. Perhaps once his curiosity was satisfied, he'd pay all his attention to getting us away from the Brats.

We told Con Rod how as a young man the Germinator had discovered the tea plant in the mountains. How he'd put the tea on the family menu so he and his wife and kids could all live for ever. How he'd died unexpectedly without telling any of his family how to germinate the seeds of the tea plant.

'A hundred-and-ten years old?' croaked Con Rod, turning and staring at the frozen Germinator in amazement. 'He doesn't look a day over thirty. Except for the fingers.'

He turned back and accelerated through a tangle of vines.

'Poor things,' said Purple Cloud, struggling to take it all in. 'They must be desperate now their tea's run out. I've got some rosehip and lemon-flower tea they can have if it'd help. It's very high in vitamin C.'

Con Rod hit the brake and steered the mobile home across a creek bed. Then he turned round and stared at the Germinator again. He was struggling to take it in too. 'You're sure it's not chicken hormones?' he said.

'No,' said Sprocket. 'It's this.' He held up the blue seed. 'Problem is, nobody knows how to grow it.'

Con Rod squinted at the seed in his mirror. Purple Cloud gazed at it, fascinated. Then she took it gently from Sprocket. 'Looks healthy to me,' she said. 'Mind if I have a go at getting it to shoot?'

'How?' asked Sprocket, doubtfully. 'Organic fertilizer?'

'No,' said Purple Cloud. 'Positive visualisation and a grain-sprouting chant.'

'Any sign of them hoons?' said Con Rod as we crashed through a rotten tree trunk.

'Can't see them,' said Sprocket. 'But this forest's so thick they could be getting closer all the time.'

'We should reach the road soon,' said Con Rod. 'I reckon I can outrun that jumped-up jeep on the flat. That's if me overdrive's working.'

We jolted over a fallen tree. Saucepans clattered in cupboards and incense holders bounced off the shelves around us.

Hope we get to the road soon, I thought desperately. Much more of this and we'll wake Mum.

I didn't want her getting terrified too.

Mum woke.

'Firsty,' she said, rubbing her face with her fists.

'There's water,' said Purple Cloud, 'and milk and my homemade rose-petal cordial.'

'Water,' I said. This was no time for treats.

Purple Cloud undid her seat-belt and got up out of her beanbag chair and lunged over to the sink. She staggered back with half a glass of water.

'Not firsty of that,' lisped Mum, tossing her five-year-old curls. 'Only firsty of soda, lime and bitters.'

I sighed.

Then I stared.

Mum was about a year older than she had been an hour earlier. Was this how it worked? As the tea wore off, would she age faster and faster?

I felt sick with fear and dazed by the unreality of it all. I stroked Mum's hair and prayed that she would make it back to her right age. That she wouldn't age too fast and end up with mental trauma or extra wrinkles.

I tried not to think about the Germinator's fingers.

I turned away so I wouldn't see them and that's when I saw something else. Above my head. A row of damp crumpled envelopes pegged to an indoor clothes line.

The writing on the envelopes looked familiar.

I jumped to my feet and hung onto some shelving and took a closer look. And recognised the writing. They were the letters I'd found in the nudist camp filing cabinet.

'I rescued them from the pocket of your dress,' said Purple Cloud. 'River water's not the best for letters. Thought I'd better dry them out. I left them in the envelopes in case they're private.'

'Thanks,' I said and gave her a grateful smile.

I didn't tell Purple Cloud they were from the Brats' mother. I didn't want her knowing that the Brat's mother was also the Other Woman that Dad had been having an affair with. I was ashamed, I guess. Plus I didn't want Mum to hear.

I turned to Sprocket, silently begging him not to say anything. He was busy peering out of the back window.

I unpegged one of the envelopes and carefully jiggled out the letter. The ink had run, but I could just read it.

'*My darling children,*' it said. '*I pray that in the months since I last wrote, you have come to your senses. That you have finally freed yourselves from the tea. That you have finally laid your father to rest. Because only then will you have the knowledge you need to join me here in the High Valley.*'

My mind raced. She sounded like she knew a lot about how the tea worked. Maybe she knew enough to help Mum safely back to her right age.

Come to that, I thought with a jolt, maybe Dad does too. He's a top plant geneticist. He was doing research work for the Brats and their family. He must know about the tea or he wouldn't have sent that frantic message to Mum not to drink it.

I found myself praying that Dad was in the High

Valley with the Other Woman now, safe and healthy and achieving excellent research results on how to get tea-affected people back to their right ages without their heads exploding.

They were my only hope. I had to find them. Once we'd escaped from the Brats, I had to get Mum to the High Valley.

Wherever that was.

'Firsty,' yelled Mum.

'There's water, young lady,' I said to her. 'Take it or leave it.'

I didn't like being so strict, but we were fleeing for our lives. Plus I didn't want to spoil her.

'Diculous,' yelled Mum. 'Lezzy get my own drink.'

'Road coming up,' shouted Con Rod. 'Hang on.'

We bumped up onto the road with a violent lurch. The glass of water sloshed in my face. Mum wriggled out of my arms.

'Mum, come back,' I yelled, blinking and wiping my eyes.

She ignored me. I saw her blurred little figure waddle over to the fridge.

I leaped after her, but it was too late. She reached up and pulled the fridge door open just as Con Rod braked sharply on a corner. The contents of the fridge flew out and splattered all over Mum.

She clung to the door, yoghurt dip, lentil curry and spinach soup dripping off her.

'No fair,' she yelled tearfully and slammed the door

as hard as she could.

There was a blue flash from the fridge motor.

'Hey,' called Con Rod. 'Easy with that fridge. That cost me forty dollars.' He glanced back and saw smoke wafting up from the back of it. 'Aw, no,' he groaned. 'Weasel Dixon only gave me a month's warranty and it didn't extend to the motor.'

'Look out,' screamed Purple Cloud. 'You're going off the road.'

I felt the mobile home go into a skid.

'Aaaargh,' yelled Con Rod.

There was an eye-snapping thud, the cupboard doors flew open, and half the junk Con Rod had collected in thirty years was hurtling through the air. I threw myself over Mum as hub caps and plastic milk crates and bags of frozen peas and Elvis Presley CDs and an old dressmaker's dummy bounced and clattered around us.

Then there was silence, except for the dripping of yoghurt in the fridge.

'Everyone OK?' asked Con Rod shakily.

'I think so,' sighed Purple Cloud.

'We're in a ditch,' groaned Sprocket from the back window.

The floor was at a forty-five degree angle. Mum was still safely under my arms.

'Are you OK?' I whispered.

'That driver am an idiot,' said Mum.

I lost it.

'That,' I yelled at Mum, 'was a very, very naughty thing to do. You will never, never open a fridge again without asking me first, do you understand?'

I tried not to think about how I'd opened the door of the Cool Room in the nudist camp without asking anyone.

Mum's little face crumpled and the waterworks started.

I took a deep breath, determined to stay firm.

Then I noticed that Mum's eyes weren't squeezed shut like sobbing kids' eyes usually are when they've been yelled at. Hers were wide open and staring at something over my shoulder.

In terror.

I turned.

The bluey-greeny-grey face of the Germinator was centimetres from mine.

I screamed.

Then I saw he was still frozen in his block of ice. Except now not only his fingertips were thawed, the front of his face was too. He must have slid out of the window seat when the mobile home went into the ditch.

I turned away and cradled Mum's head against my beating chest. Her little shoulders were heaving with sobs and her whole body was trembling.

Suddenly my eyes were hot and wet too. Suddenly I was little again myself, lying in bed late at night sobbing with unhappiness as I listened to Dad creep out of the house. And suddenly I knew what it must have been like for Mum when she was little, crying in her lonely bed after her parents had yelled at her. Alone, with nobody to comfort her.

I hugged her to me and stroked her head.

'It's OK,' I whispered. 'I love you and you're safe.'

I tried not to think about the Brats roaring towards us.

There was movement behind me. I looked up to see Sprocket staring at the Germinator's face. Purple Cloud gently took Mum from me. 'Come on, love,' she said. 'I'll get you that drink and you can help me with my seed-sprouting chant.'

But then, from outside, came a sound.

We all looked up, startled.

There was something on the roof, whining.

An animal.

Sprocket hurried outside. I followed, jumping out the door which was at a crazy angle. The front wheels of the mobile home were deep in a ditch and the back wheels were spinning in the air.

Con Rod was already outside, dragging logs around.

The animal whined again.

I looked up. There were water tanks lashed to the roof, and huddled behind them, looking down at us reproachfully, was Matchbox.

'Good boy,' croaked Sprocket, amazed. 'You're still guarding your original master. Good boy.'

Matchbox jumped down, barking excitedly. He wasn't the puppy we'd last seen. He was fully grown again. It was incredible. He must have leaped out of the Brats' barge as they overshot the ice block, and then got on Con Rod's roof while he was winching the Germinator aboard.

My throat felt suddenly tight with emotion. If a dog could overcome all odds, I reckoned we could too.

I had a big grin on my face as I patted him. Then my grin faded. In the distance, getting louder, I could hear the angry growl of the Hummer.

I turned wildly to the others.

Before I could yell at them about running and hiding, Purple Cloud appeared in the doorway of the mobile home with Mum in her arms.

'Look everyone,' she said. 'Look what Les found.'

'Not Les,' said Mum crossly. 'Lezzy.'

I stared at the plastic bag of frozen peas Mum was holding.

On it lay the blue seed.

Which had sprouted.

SPROCKET

SEVEN

I stared in disbelief. Amy stared in disbelief. The Brats and the other nudists had been trying to find out how to germinate a seed. They had even kept the Germinator frozen in a block of ice hoping to bring him back to life and learn the secret.

And now Purple Cloud had made it sprout. By chanting.

'What did you sing?' I gasped.

Purple Cloud started to chant in a soft voice. '*Mighty moon with magic glow. Stroke this seed and make it grow.*'

'That's it?' I yelped.

Purple Cloud nodded with a happy smile. 'I made it up,' she said.

'It rhymes an' all,' said Con Rod proudly. 'It's good. Elvis would have bought it off ya. If he was still alive.'

'The Germinator didn't know your song,' I said. 'So that couldn't be the secret.'

Their faces fell. They knew what I said was true.

I picked up the seed and examined it. If we could

keep it alive there would be more seeds and more plants and tea for everyone. If only we could figure out what had made the plant start to shoot.

I had only just put the seed back on its frozen peas cushion when the Brats' Hummer screeched round the corner. We could have run off into the surrounding forest to escape them but Mrs Tunks-Livingstone would never have kept up with us. And Amy wouldn't abandon her, that was for sure.

'Quick, inside,' yelled Con Rod.

The mobile home was still on a crazy angle but we managed to scramble in and slam the door. Tins of food, plates, candles and anything that was loose had been thrown all over the place. We had to hang onto whatever we could to stay upright. Amy grabbed her little mother's hand to stop her slipping. Matchbox scrambled over to the Germinator's ice block and stood guarding his frozen master.

The whole scene was like a battlefield after a big fight. I put a towel over the seed to hide it.

'Give yourselves up,' boomed a loud voice. We all scrambled over to the window as best we could.

It was Beanie. At first I didn't recognise him. He was growing older. Fast. He was a young man now and wasn't a gawky teenager any more. Pooper Scooper was with him. He was even older than his brother – maybe twenty-three or twenty-four. He still had curly blond hair but his angel looks had gone. What was on the inside was starting to show on the outside. He was a real mean dude, that was for sure. His muscles were bulging like those on a weightlifter. I would be no match for him now. He was much too big.

Reptile and Scowler jumped down from the cabin. Reptile still wore racing gear but she had changed her other outfit for a larger size now. She probably had suits left over from earlier times. She gave a wicked grin. I noticed that one of her front teeth was missing. But there was no sign of the other nudists.

Scowler dragged out nets and ropes from the back of the Hummer. I felt sick in the stomach. I was reminded of my battle with them on the hillside. Only this time the Brats were not little kids.

And this time they weren't going to let me escape.

Mrs Tunks-Livingstone climbed up onto a bed. She peered out of the window. 'I go. She ate,' she said.

'Speak slowly, Mum,' said Amy.

Mrs Tunks-Livingstone snorted and jumped down off the bed.

Purple Cloud lit another aromatic candle. 'Peach blossom for peace,' she said.

I stared outside. Scowler had a small jar in one hand. Something was moving around inside it. It looked like a spider to me.

Con Rod slapped his knee. 'I know how to get rid of 'em,' he yelled.

He dragged his ghetto blaster over to the window and pointed it out through the fly screen. He pressed a button and turned up the volume. Elvis's mellow voice boomed out through the gum trees.

' "Wooden Heart",' said Con Rod appreciatively. 'Lovely tune.'

There was a bit of talking and grumbling between the Brats but the music didn't drive them off.

'That's funny,' said Con Rod. 'It got rid of a noisy mob of teenager campers in the Fitzroy Crossing caravan park. They hated it. No taste in music.'

'This lot are not what they seem to be, remember,' I told him. 'They could be as old as you. They could even be a hundred years old. They probably *like* Elvis.'

'They're not all bad then,' said Con Rod.

'Don't be too sure,' I said.

We continued to peer out of the window. The Brats were glaring at the van with cloudy grey eyes. It was the eyes that made them look so evil. They had youthful faces but old, old eyes. Eyes that had seen too much. Suffered too much. Done too much. Desperate, angry eyes. I shivered. The Brats would do anything to get the seed and the Germinator back. They were not going to grow old and die. Not for anyone.

Just then the van door slammed.

We all turned around in shock.

'Mum,' screamed Amy. She threw herself towards the door. Mrs Tunks-Livingstone was running across the clearing towards the Brats. 'I go. She ate,' she yelled back at us.

'Oh no,' cried Amy. 'She's going to negotiate.'

She tried to follow her miniature mother but Con Rod held her back.

'It's too late,' he said. 'They've already grabbed her. We'd better see what they have to say.'

Scowler quickly tucked Mrs Tunks-Livingstone under his arm. She began to kick and yell. Beanie shook his head, puzzled. Mrs Tunks-Livingstone was hard to understand. Her brain knew more than her mouth could get out. Pooper Scooper made a gesture to Scowler who reluctantly put Amy's tiny mother on the ground. Pooper Scooper squatted down and talked to her. She was about the same size now as the Brats had been when I first saw them stalking through the forest the day before.

Then Pooper Scooper came towards the van. 'We've made a deal,' he shouted. 'You give us back the seed *and* our father and we let the little brat go.'

'Say yes,' Amy whispered desperately.

'We accept,' I yelled through the window.

'First I inspect the goods,' said Pooper Scooper.

'Fair enough,' said Con Rod. He threw open the door and Pooper Scooper stepped in.

Matchbox gave a growl.

Pooper Scooper stared at the Germinator in horror. Melted water was running across the floor. The Germinator's head was sticking out of the ice. So were his fingers and the toes of both feet. His flesh was grey and flabby.

Once again the Germinator's face reminded me of someone but I couldn't think who. Pooper Scooper stared at the Germinator. Then he looked at me.

He suddenly seemed to make up his mind about something. 'Father has melted,' he said in a low voice. 'You've let him melt. Decay has set in. We'll never bring him back to life now.' He raced out of the van and across to the other Brats.

For some reason his voice sounded false. He seemed to be putting on an act. He didn't really look as if he cared about the Germinator at all. Something else had upset him when he looked at *me*.

The others did care about their father though. There was a lot of yelling and screaming. Beanie threw back his head and wailed at the sky in grief. The others were as angry as a nest of bees.

We were in big trouble. At any moment they might charge.

I turned back to the dead man whose face was now even further out of the melting ice.

That's when I noticed it. Weird. Really weird.

'What's that?' I said.

'A nostril,' said Con Rod.

'No, inside,' I yelled.

There was something up his nose.

It looked like a tightly rolled piece of paper wrapped in thin plastic. I quickly grabbed it and gave a tug. The small cylinder was frozen and wouldn't budge. I bent down and blew warm air into the stiff nose.

Slowly, slowly, like something I didn't want to think about, the long object slid out of his nostril.

At that very moment a terrible scream echoed around the clearing. It was Mrs Tunks-Livingstone. Without even looking at it, I shoved the object into my pocket.

'The monsters,' said Purple Cloud. 'What are they doing?'

I ran to the window. Scowler was holding the jar open in front of the infant Mrs Tunks-Livingstone. She was yelling and trying to get away but Pooper Scooper held her in his strong hands. The Brats were trying to lure us out by frightening the poor kid.

'What on earth's in there?' gasped Purple Cloud. 'The poor little thing. We have to help her.

'I'll go,' said Amy.

'No,' said Con Rod.

He picked up a large spanner and headed for the door. I shoved out a foot and tripped him. He skidded across the sloping floor and stopped at Purple Cloud's feet.

'It's me they want,' I said. 'This is my fight.'

The thought of falling into the hands of the Brats again terrified me. But after all we had been through I couldn't let the enemy frighten a child. Plus I was beginning to like Mrs Tunks-Livingstone. She had guts.

If I gave myself up they might let her go.

Might. That was the word.

They might be happy to take the seed and run. But

I didn't think so. They wouldn't know how to germinate any new seeds. They would want the secret. The one I didn't know. They would probably grab me and try to force it out of me.

I didn't want to be tortured. I didn't want to die. But I had to save Amy's mum. And find my own. I was sure Pooper Scooper could lead me to her.

Another loud wail floated across the clearing. It was now or never. I grabbed the seed from its frozen peas cushion and, holding it high above my head, stepped out of the door and ran towards the Brats.

'You can have it,' I yelled. 'Just let her go.'

The Brats stared at me, dumbfounded. They were mesmerised by the little green shoot that was sprouting from the seed.

'It's growing,' yelled Beanie.

'We're saved,' shrieked Reptile.

'It's yours,' I said. 'And I know how to germinate it. Take me and let the others go.'

Without warning the Brats began to howl and shriek like a mob of hungry dingoes. Scowler charged at me with outstretched hands. He and Reptile grabbed me and held me high in the air. Pooper Scooper snatched the seed from my clenched fingers. Then they bore me off towards the Hummer.

Con Rod and Amy stumbled out of the van. 'Drop him, you mongrels,' shouted Con Rod.

Pooper Scooper waved his knife. 'Stay back,' he yelled. 'Or the kid gets it.'

Mrs Tunks-Livingstone broke away and ran towards Amy. The Brats didn't care about her any more. They had what they wanted.

The excited terrorists quickly tied my hands and feet. Then they threw me into the back of the Hummer and strapped down the rear canvas flap. In an instant we were bouncing off down the road. I could just make out the shapes of the four Brats through the window of the driver's cabin.

The mobile home and Amy and Mrs Tunks-Livingstone and Con Rod and Purple Cloud and Matchbox were soon only a speck in the distance.

As we sped away a lonely thought came into my mind.

That group of weird people back there were the nearest thing to a family I had ever known. I really liked them. Every one. Even if they were a bit strange. And now I was losing them.

I thought of my mother and stifled a sob.

Maybe Pooper Scooper would take me to her. Maybe he would have mercy now that he had the seed. Suddenly his face appeared at the rear window of the cabin. He stared down at me with a cruel smile.

Then he held up his index finger.

And drew it across his throat.

DEADLY!

Part Five

GROPE

The Hidden Map

I am going to the High ...
tea plants. I may still be ...
... beg you to come to me. ...
I have failed ...

SUNRISE
FARM

TOWN

━━━ HIGHWAY
〜〜〜 MINOR ROAD
┼┼┼ RAILWAY
••• BY FOOT

...ley to destroy any remaining
...iue when you find this.
...finish the task if
Love,
    Mother

HIGH
VALLEY

AMY

ONE

Sprocket had sacrificed himself for Mum. He'd given himself to the Brats so she could go free. And now they were driving away with him as their prisoner.

'Stop,' I yelled. 'Bring him back, you vicious monsters.'

The Brats didn't stop. I squinted helplessly into the early morning sun as the Hummer roared away down the rainforest road. They were taking the boy who'd saved my life three times and saved my mother's life at least once and given me his only dress, and I couldn't do a thing.

Except yell.

'Come on,' I screamed at Con Rod and Purple Cloud. 'We've got to get after them. We've got to rescue Sprocket before they do horrible things to him.'

Normally if I'd seen my best friend being carried off in a military four-wheel-drive by a bunch of ninety-year-old thugs with the muscles of twenty-five-year-olds, I'd have sprinted after them.

But this wasn't normal.

I had Mum clinging onto me with her arms round my waist. You can't drag your mum on a chase after armed thugs when she's only six. Plus I was weak with relief that the Brats hadn't harmed her.

Con Rod wasn't chasing them either. He was staring mournfully at his mobile home, which was in a ditch at a forty-five degree angle with its back wheels spinning in the air.

Purple Cloud was leaning against a tree, her head in her hands. She looked sort of weak too, with sadness. I couldn't tell if it was because Sprocket had been kidnapped or because he didn't want her to be his replacement mother. Both probably.

It was Matchbox who got us moving. He forgot he wasn't as young as he had been half an hour earlier. As the Brats' Hummer roared away, he barked furiously and raced after it, only giving up his rescue attempt when he realised the Hummer was twice as fast as him and not scared of being bitten.

The rest of us sprang into action. Con Rod flung his winch cable over the branch of a tree and hooked it up to the rear axle of the mobile home. Purple Cloud packed dead ferns under the front wheels so they wouldn't spin in the mud.

I tried to prepare Mum for the chase ahead.

'Scary,' she sobbed into my pants, her whole body trembling. 'Those fishy monster people had a scary spider.'

I crouched down so our faces were level. 'That was a very brave thing you did,' I said, 'trying to negotiate with those vicious monster people. I'm very proud of you.'

Mum stared at me, startled and a bit pleased at the same time. She looked like a kid who'd never been told she'd made anyone proud before.

I gave her a hug. 'When we catch those vicious monster people, I won't let them hurt you,' I whispered.

I wasn't sure how exactly I was going to manage that, but I meant it.

The winch motor revved noisily and I turned to see the mobile home slowly dragging itself out of the ditch.

'Bewdy,' yelled Con Rod. 'C'mon, let's get after Sprocket before those mongrels get chopsticks under his fingernails.'

Purple Cloud looked stricken and we piled into the mobile home.

Mum screamed.

At first I thought that like me she was picturing the awful things the Brats could be doing to Sprocket. Then I realised she was staring at the large block of melting ice. The one with the bluey-greeny-grey corpse of the Germinator in it.

Fingers and toes were sticking out.

And something else.

'I can see his willy,' said Mum.

'Jeez,' said Con Rod. 'You'd think they'd have left his undies on when they froze him.'

Then something else occurred to me. Con Rod and I exchanged a look. I could see he'd had the same thought. The lighter our load, the faster we could go after Sprocket. Should we ditch the ice man?

Con Rod screwed up his face. 'Don't seem right,' he said. 'He's the Brats' dad. Perhaps we can swap him for Sprocket.'

'Less talk,' yelled Purple Cloud, face frantic with concern for Sprocket, 'and more fast driving.'

Con Rod revved the engine and accelerated us away down the rainforest road. Purple Cloud brushed cooking utensils and tinned food off the beanbags.

I clicked a seatbelt round Mum, then Purple Cloud and I slid a big tarpaulin over the ice block and lashed it to the legs of the dining table. Matchbox watched us warily. I hoped some insulation would slow down the melting. Even if it didn't, at least the private bits would stay private. The last thing I wanted to have to do in the middle of a dangerous high-speed chase was explain the facts of life to my own mum.

I sat down next to her in a beanbag and clicked my seat belt round me.

And nearly fainted.

Mum's head was almost level with my shoulder. She

was ten centimetres taller than when I'd last looked.
I'd heard parents complain about kids having growth
spurts whenever their backs were turned, but this was
mind-boggling.

'Amelia,' said Mum quietly, looking up at me with
big anxious eyes. 'Will I go like him?'

She pointed to the tarpaulin.

I took a deep breath. I wanted to say no. I wanted
to say that she'd quickly and painlessly grow back to
her proper age. But I'd never had a mother drink
nudist tea and turn into a baby before, so I didn't
honestly know.

'He died in an accident,' I said quietly. 'You're not
going to die in an accident because I won't let you.'

Mum looked relieved, but only a bit.

I tried to calm myself down. As the effect of the tea
wore off, I told myself, Mum would probably have
bigger and bigger growth spurts. Her T-shirt was
looking very tight already. Soon she'd be big enough
for Sprocket's dress.

But what if she got to her right age and didn't stop?

What if Mum just kept getting older and older,
faster and faster?

Until she died?

Con Rod slammed on the brakes which jolted me
back from the brink of panic. The road had ended
and we were at a T-junction with a highway.

'I reckon they've taken him back to the nudist
camp,' said Con Rod. 'Quickest way's through town.'

Purple Cloud and I nodded. Con Rod glanced at the compass on his dash and swung the mobile home round to the right.

Matchbox stood up on Mum's lap, barking and scrabbling at the window. 'Matchbox says Sprocket went this way,' said Mum, pointing in the opposite direction.

Con Rod hit the brakes and everyone in the mobile home over eight looked at each other. It was the urgent decision of three mature people against the opinion of a dog.

'Dogs know,' said Mum, stroking Matchbox's greying neck fur. 'Dogs know where their people friends are.'

A dog and a little kid.

I remembered how, the day before, Matchbox had led us to a bowl of dogfood. Now Matchbox gave a low, mournful whine. An old dog whine. So low and so mournful that suddenly I had tears in my eyes. Tears for Sprocket, who'd given himself to the Brats to save Mum. Tears for Dad, who'd disappeared trying to save the lives of eleven people. Tears for Mum, who just wanted to be a normal grouchy thirty-four-year-old mature-age student again. And I knew that like me Matchbox cared more about Sprocket than any amount of dogfood.

'You're right, Les,' said Purple Cloud to Mum. 'Dogs do know.'

'Lesley,' said Mum crossly.

'Righty-ho,' said Con Rod, swinging the mobile home round to the left. 'Towards the mountains it is.'

As Con Rod accelerated down the highway, Purple Cloud hung onto shelves and started tidying up the mobile home. 'I don't worry so much if I'm busy,' she said, struggling to strap her dressmaker's dummy into a beanbag.

I was busy too, thinking. I knew why the Brats were taking Sprocket towards the mountains.

'The High Valley,' I said.

'Sorry?' said Purple Cloud.

From my pants pocket I dragged the letter I'd found in the nudist camp filing cabinet.

'This is from the Brats' mother,' I said, and read aloud from the damp, crumpled page.

'*My darling children. I pray that in the months since I last wrote, you have come to your senses. That you have finally freed yourselves from the tea. That you have finally laid your father to rest. Because only then will you have the knowledge you need to join me here in the High Valley.*'

Purple Cloud took the letter from me and read it again to herself.

'I think my father's in the High Valley too,' I said.

Mum stared at me. 'How do you know?' she demanded.

I took a deep breath and pointed to the letter. 'That's the woman Dad was having an affair with,' I said quietly. Now Mum was eight it was time she knew.

Mum's little jaw tensed. Purple Cloud and Con Rod exchanged a look. Purple Cloud patted me sympathetically on the arm. Then she did the same to Mum.

'We have to get to the High Valley,' I said. 'It could be our only hope of finding Sprocket and my dad.' And, I thought desperately, the Brats' mother's tea knowledge could be my only hope of saving Mum if her ageing went out of control.

In the rear-vision mirror I saw that Con Rod was frowning.

'Never heard of any High Valley,' he said. 'Have you got a map?'

I jumped up and pulled the rest of the letters off the indoor clothesline Purple Cloud had pegged them on to dry.

They were all similar to the first one. None of them contained a map.

'We'll have to keep after them Brats,' said Con Rod. 'Mountains are about five hours away.' He glanced back at the water trickling from under the tarpaulin. 'Dunno if that bloke's gunna last that long.'

Same with Sprocket, I thought miserably. And Mum. And maybe even Dad.

As we sped on, water from the melting ice sloshed over our feet.

'We need more ice,' said Con Rod. 'Stop our passenger ponging. Keep your eyes peeled for a servo.'

We pulled into a service station about fifty minutes later.

'Fill 'er up?' asked the proprietor.

'We're in a bit of a hurry,' said Con Rod. 'Just make it two hundred litres and thirty bags of ice.'

The proprietor stared.

Quickly I made Mum take off the tight T-shirt and put on one of Purple Cloud's shortie tie-dyed kaftans. Then, while Con Rod handed bags of ice in through the window to Purple Cloud, I rushed Mum to the toilet.

Crossing the forecourt, we passed two boys of about ten in the back of a ute. They sneered at us. My heart jumped. But there was no sign of the Hummer parked near by. And I remembered the Brats were adults now.

'You're weird,' said one of the boys to Mum.

'You're an idiot,' replied Mum.

'Ignore him,' I hissed at Mum. 'We haven't got time.'

I hurried Mum into the Ladies. She insisted on going into the cubicle on her own.

'I'm hungry,' she said once she was inside. 'And thirsty.'

'Stay there,' I said. 'I'll be back in two minutes.'

When I got back with a cheese sandwich and an orange juice, Mum was gone.

The cubicle was empty.

I searched frantically. Both the other cubicles were empty too.

Then I heard a commotion coming from out by the pumps.

I hurried outside. Mum was standing with the two boys. I felt faint with relief. But only for a moment.

'They've got a dead body in there,' one of the boys was yelling, pointing to the mobile home. 'Call the cops.'

My guts went tight. If the police saw the frozen Germinator, we'd never catch up with Sprocket. By the time we got out of jail, the Brats would be in the High Valley and we'd never find them.

The two boys and the proprietor were trying to see inside the mobile home. Purple Cloud was pulling the curtains closed.

'That girl told us,' said one of the boys, pointing to Mum. 'A dead body.'

Mum glared at him.

The proprietor looked suspiciously at Con Rod. Over in the office, the proprietor's wife was watching us with the phone in her hand.

'Dead body?' said Con Rod, scratching his nose. 'Yeah, we got one of them.'

The proprietor's mouth fell open.

So did mine.

Con Rod glanced through the window at Purple Cloud, who nodded. He climbed into the mobile home. My brain was racing. If I ran for it now, perhaps I could get away before the police arrived. Except what about Mum? She couldn't run as fast as me, and I couldn't carry her like I had the night before when she was a baby.

Con Rod and Purple Cloud clambered back out of the mobile home, carrying a human-sized figure between them.

I stared.

It was green.

It had no head.

It wasn't the frozen Germinator. It was the dressmaker's dummy with pins sticking out of it.

'Purple Cloud uses it for making her kaftans,' said Con Rod. 'Don't ya, love?'

Purple Cloud nodded. 'I call her Kylie,' she said.

I leaned against a petrol pump until my heart calmed down.

The proprietor glared at the two boys. 'Reece, Waylon, get inside,' he snapped. 'You're grounded. No telly for a week.'

I grabbed Mum and we all piled into the mobile home.

'Go,' said Purple Cloud urgently, 'or we'll never catch the Brats.'

While Con Rod sped us away down the highway, I helped Purple Cloud pack ice bags around the Germinator.

Then I turned angrily to Mum.

She was huddled in a bean bag, eyes downcast, and even though she'd grown since I last looked, she seemed smaller.

'Those boys were laughing at me,' she mumbled. 'I just wanted to shut them up. I'm sorry.'

Without looking up, she held something out to me.

It was one of Con Rod's leather belts.

I stared.

Then I took the belt and put it down and gave her a hug.

Mum looked stunned.

I was stunned too. Was this what she'd got when she was naughty as a kid? A beating with a belt? I knew she'd had an unhappy childhood, but I hadn't realised it had been this bad.

I didn't want to think about it. I hugged her tight and forced my mind back to the present.

We were speeding along, the Hummer still out of sight. Matchbox, peering out the front window, was panting and wheezing eagerly and seemed happy at the idea of heading towards the High Valley.

But what would we find there? Ageing Brats bent on violent revenge? Dad in a love nest with a woman who was a hundred and two but had the body of a thirty-three year old? Sprocket in a torture chamber?

Purple Cloud must have been thinking the same thing. About Sprocket anyway.

'Oh, Sprocket,' she moaned quietly to herself. 'Don't do anything to upset them.'

That's when it hit me.

The terrible danger Sprocket was in.

The Brats and their brothers and sisters needed more tea plants to stay alive. The seed they'd grabbed with Sprocket was their only hope. But they needed more. They needed to know how to germinate future seeds. They'd do anything to Sprocket to make him tell them.

And Sprocket didn't know.

'Oh, Sprocket,' I moaned as we hurtled towards the mountains.

SPROCKET

TWO

The Hummer bounced along at a terrifying speed. Amy and Con Rod and Purple Cloud were somewhere far, far behind us. I was tied up in the back of the truck. In the front were my deadly enemies, Pooper Scooper, Beanie, Reptile and Scowler.

They were now well and truly middle-aged. Pooper Scooper's muscles had started to turn to fat. Reptile was missing two of her front teeth. Her tongue flicked nervously in and out of the gap. The pimples around Beanie's mouth had been replaced by dry flaking skin. Scowler's frown lines were deeper than ever. The three men all had short whiskery beards.

I had to get out. I had to go back and find my friends. They were the nearest thing I had to a family. And they would be worried about me.

I strained at the knots that held my hands firmly behind my back.

I twisted and twisted and twisted, trying desperately to get free. But it was hopeless. The ropes were well tied.

There was a window between the cabin and the rear of the truck. Through it I could see the back of the Brats' heads as they stared out at the deserted mountain road which rushed beneath the wheels. I guessed that it was nice and snug in the cabin. I could imagine the heater blasting out hot air onto warm toes.

The canvas cover of my mobile prison shook noisily around me. The back flap was held down with leather straps. It kept out the view of the surrounding country. But not the cold. I shivered constantly as the truck climbed higher and higher into the snow-covered mountains. We must have been travelling flat out for four or five hours.

'Hey,' I screamed desperately. 'Let me out. I have to have a pee.'

They ignored me completely. Maybe they didn't hear. More likely they didn't care. I grew colder and colder and my bladder began to scream for release.

Finally the truck slowed and stopped.

The cabin doors banged. I could hear voices through the canvas.

'Don't horse around,' said Pooper Scooper. 'We don't want to waste time.'

There was the sound of splashing.

'Ah, lovely,' said Scowler's voice.

'That's better,' said Beanie with a sigh. Then he added, 'Look at Hilda. Trying to hide behind a bush.'

Pooper Scooper gave a coarse laugh.

The splashing continued. It nearly drove me crazy. The Brats were taking a leak.

'What about me?' I screamed. 'I need to go, too.'

'Shut up,' came a savage hiss from Pooper Scooper.

'Better help him out,' said Beanie.

'Let him suffer,' I heard Scowler say. 'What do we care?'

I couldn't hold it in any longer. I had to let go. A huge torrent of pee shot down my legs and soaked into my jeans. Oh, relief. Oh, shame.

It was humiliating. But at least it was warm.

The Brats finished relieving themselves and climbed back into the Hummer. But before Reptile could even turn the key there was a loud shout. I struggled to my knees and peered through the window into the cabin. I could hear their voices clearly now that the engine wasn't running.

'It's still alive,' said Reptile.

'Careful, careful, you fools,' shouted Pooper Scooper. 'Don't kill it. It's our last chance.'

A terrible commotion was going on. Beanie was trying to force the left side door open but couldn't. Scowler leaned across him, pulling at the lock.

The seed was lying on a rag on the huge console that covered the gearbox.

And it was moving.

Tiny roots had appeared, and the shoot was quite long. It poked about five centimetres out of the blue seed. It was waving around like an arm. It suddenly gave a little push and rolled itself over a couple of times. I had never seen anything like this in my entire life. A seed that could travel.

My brain began to grow numb.

I couldn't take much more of this.

One weird, horrible thing after another kept wriggling into my life. All I wanted was to find my parents. I wanted to put the foster homes and lone-liness behind me. I wanted a mother's loving smile. I wanted ordinary everyday family where you watch TV and read books and go to the footy. But all I could find on this terrible journey was fear and hatred.

Except for Amy and Purple Cloud and Con Rod of course. I wondered if I would ever see them again.

Beanie finally managed to push the Hummer door open. He burst out and landed on the roadside. Scowler followed. Reptile had already jumped out of the driver's door. The seed gave another thrust and plopped onto Pooper Scooper's lap.

'Coward,' he yelled at Beanie. He quickly grabbed the seed as if was a hot coal and dropped it into an empty take-away chicken container. He folded down the lid and put his ear to the box. He smiled wickedly. I sensed that he could hear the trapped seed rolling around inside.

'The ruddy thing's moving,' said Scowler's voice.

'What the hell is going on?' yelped Reptile.

'Father knew this would happen,' said Beanie. 'Why didn't he tell us?'

'He wouldn't even let us near the plants,' said Reptile. 'He was germinating them somewhere. But how?'

'Get a shovel,' commanded Pooper Scooper.

The flap of the truck lifted and daylight poured in. Scowler glanced at me briefly. Then he climbed in and unclipped a folded spade from the wheel arch. He gave it to Pooper Scooper who opened it up and dug a shovel-full of cold earth from the side of the road.

He lifted the lid of the chicken carton and shook some soil on top of the wriggling seed.

Beanie stepped back.

'Pathetic,' Pooper Scooper said to him. He held the plant out for them to see. 'What are you scared of? This is what we want, you morons. The thing is growing. Fast.'

It was incredible. The plant was sprouting so quickly that you could see it move. It was like one of those nature movies where the film of a flower opening is speeded up. Only this was real.

'Brilliant,' said Reptile. 'It might grow a seed.'

'Which we won't know how to germinate,' said Beanie gloomily. 'And we can't use the leaves from this one until it's matured.'

'We'll get it out of the kid,' said Scowler nodding in my direction. 'He made the seed sprout. I'll make him talk.'

I was in desperate trouble. I didn't know what started the seeds growing. I looked past them along the road, wildly hoping to see someone who could save me, a friendly policeman, anyone.

Not very likely on a deserted country road. Clumps of frozen snow littered the edge of the forest like dirty cotton wool. Small puffs of fog hung in the air with every breath, and my wet pants were freezing cold.

Not far off was a clearing and a small log cabin with smoke curling out of the chimney. A Land Rover was parked outside. I closed my eyes and sent out a silent message to the owners. 'Please come and help me,' I said.

The door of the log cabin remained closed. No one was going to help. Not unless Con Rod, Purple Cloud and Amy managed to catch up with us. I had to stall the Brats. I had to keep the Hummer parked by the side of the road until they came.

Suddenly I had an idea. Anything to stop them hurting me.

'I've got something you might be interested to see,' I yelled.

'What?' spat Pooper Scooper.

'Untie my hands,' I said. 'And I'll show you.'

'Search him,' ordered Pooper Scooper.

Reptile and Scowler climbed into the Hummer and roughly rolled me over. For a moment I thought that they were going to untie my hands. But my hopes died as quickly as they were born. Reptile and Scowler rummaged through my pockets.

'Ha,' yelled Reptile. She pulled out the small paper cylinder I had found in her frozen father's nose.

I suddenly realised my mistake. If this piece of paper gave them what they wanted they wouldn't need me any more. They had kept their father frozen so that they could bring him back to life and learn his secret.

Pooper Scooper put the plant in the container down on the side of the road and snatched the paper from her hand. He unrolled it and began to read aloud.

My Dear Children,

If you find this note it means that you have thawed out the body of your father. It means that you think that science has reached the point where you can bring him back to life and find his secret.

I beg you not to. Let him rest in peace.

None of you were wise enough to hold the secret. I'd hoped that Randall – my innocent baby – would grow up to be that wise son. But he drowned in the river with his father.

When I lost my child I realised what a treasure a baby is. The tea brings eternal youth. But the price we have agreed to is to keep the secret from outsiders. This means you can have no children. That price is too high. It is not worth it. The tea brings a false promise of happiness. It is dangerous.

I am going to the High Valley to destroy any remaining tea plants. I may still be alive when you find this. I beg you to come to me. And finish the task if I have failed.

Love,
Mother

Reptile looked over Pooper Scooper's shoulder at the flattened piece of paper. 'There's a map,' she said. 'It shows the way to the High Valley.'

'But Mother's been gone for years,' said Scowler. 'She's probably grown old and died by now.'

'She had enough time to destroy all the plants first,'

said Reptile, licking her wrinkled lips with a flicking tongue.

'The cow,' spat Pooper Scooper.

'Don't call her that,' said Beanie. 'She's still our mother.'

'You dropkick. You fool. You nincompoop,' yelled Pooper Scooper. 'She can die if she wants to. She can get old and horrible. But what about us? The same thing is going to happen. Remember what happened to Gramps. All we have left is a few lousy days at the most. Think about it. Your bowels are going to fail. What's left of your hair will fall out. Your teeth will rot. Your bones will break. You will stink of your own pee.'

'Like he does,' said Scowler, nodding at me. 'It's all his fault. Let's get rid of him.'

The four Brats stared down at me angrily.

I shuddered. This was like an old gangster movie. I almost expected them to put me in concrete boots and throw me into a lake.

'If I die,' I said desperately, 'so does the secret. I know how to germinate nudist tea seeds and you don't.'

'And you *will* tell us,' said Pooper Scooper slowly. He pulled the fingers on his right hand one at a time making each knuckle crack in turn. Then he turned to the others. 'You three can go back and see if you can get something out of those other pests. They must have seen how the seed was germinated too.'

'Where will we meet up?' asked Scowler.

Pooper Scooper jabbed at a point on the map.

'Here,' he said. 'Then we'll go on to the High Valley. And see if there are any plants left growing in the wild.'

Reptile stared at the map. 'I'll phone Hubert on the mobile as soon as we get into range,' she said. 'So the others can come too.'

'No,' said Pooper Scooper. 'Leave them behind. There might not be enough tea. We can't save everyone.'

Reptile shook her head. 'I'm calling them,' she said. 'They're family.'

The others nodded their heads in support.

Pooper Scooper threw them all a filthy look but decided not to take them on.

'We haven't got any wheels,' said Reptile.

Pooper Scooper pointed to the Land Rover next to the nearby cabin. 'You know what to do,' he said.

'I sure do, Brother,' said Reptile. She pulled a pair of pliers out of the pocket of her driving outfit.

From the back of the Hummer I watched as the three middle-aged Brats headed across the road to steal the car. They walked cockily, like a mob of gangsters hoping to meet someone to beat up. They were tough but I didn't want them to go and leave me alone with Pooper Scooper. He was not only tough.

He was also evil.

With a shock I realised why Pooper Scooper didn't want the others around. He didn't want them to see what he was going to do to me.

I looked into his eyes. They were hard and cold and merciless. At that moment I knew without a doubt that he was a killer.

I strained against my ropes. The knots didn't budge.

Pooper Scooper disappeared from sight. He didn't even bother closing the flap on the back of the truck.

'Don't think you can just jump out,' I heard him say. 'Because I'll just back up and run over you.'

A moment later the Hummer began to move off.

He was a worse driver than Reptile. Much faster. We rocketed along the road at an enormous rate. Frozen ferns and snow-covered gum trees blurred by. After about another hour of this the truck did a quick U-turn and screeched to a stop.

Where were we? What now? Pooper Scooper appeared. He dropped the tail gate with a crash.

I stared out into the late afternoon shadows. We had arrived at a small railway station surrounded by bushland. It was totally deserted. The railway tracks were narrow and the station quaint and old-fashioned. An ageing locomotive and several carriages stood a little way off, covered in snow. A guard's van sat silently on a track not far from the platform.

A large sign read:

```
CHUFFING BESSIE
CLOSED FOR THE WINTER
```

'Damn,' said Pooper Scooper when he saw it.

He held the container with his precious plant in it in one hand. He carefully put it on the ground. Then he suddenly grabbed me by the feet and pulled me out of the Hummer with one cruel tug. I fell to the frozen surface heavily, striking my head on a lump of ice. My skull was a ball of red hot pain.

'Well, Little Brother,' he said. 'I let you live when you were a baby. That was a mistake I won't repeat again.' He cracked a knuckle on his left hand.

I looked around for help. But it was hopeless.

Pooper Scooper could do what he liked.

There was no one to stop him.

THREE

Sprocket was out there somewhere.

The four of us sat in the front of the mobile home, grim and anxious as we hurtled along the highway.

Me.

Purple Cloud.

Con Rod.

Matchbox.

We all peered desperately at the road ahead, hoping each time we swayed round a corner or lurched over a crest that we'd see the Hummer up ahead before they reached the mountains.

So far we hadn't.

Our big cluttered vehicle felt tiny under the vast white sky. An hour passed, then another. The mountains appeared as a smudge on the horizon, then as a cluster of distant snow-covered peaks, stunted but getting larger.

Still no sign of Sprocket.

'Flamin' mongrels,' muttered Con Rod. 'They must be using premium unleaded.'

Matchbox gave a worried whine. I knew how he felt. I'd only known Sprocket for one and a bit days, but the thought of anything bad happening to him churned my guts almost as much as the thought of anything bad happening to Dad or Mum.

I glanced back at Mum to check she was OK, and nearly fell off my seat.

She was where I'd left her, strapped tight to a beanbag chair with a seat-belt, but she'd taken off the sandals that Purple Cloud had lent her and was clipping her toenails.

With my Swiss Army knife.

'That's not a toy,' I said, hurrying back and taking it from her. In a rolling, bouncing mobile home she could have snipped a toe off before she knew it.

'Hey,' yelled Mum. 'Do you mind? I'm not a little kid.'

We glared at each other.

With a weird feeling in my guts I had to admit she was right. She was almost as big as me now. But I was still responsible for her.

'It's not safe,' I said. 'End of discussion.'

I closed the Swiss Army knife and put it in my pocket.

'I don't care,' muttered Mum sulkily. 'It's a dumb knife anyway. I've had better toenail trims from your dad's gardening clippers.'

'There they are,' yelled Con Rod.

I rushed back to the front, straining my eyes to see the Hummer.

'Sorry,' said Con Rod. 'My mistake.'

Purple Cloud and I gave strangled screams of frustration as we overtook a stock-feed truck.

'It's the same colour,' said Con Rod defensively.

'Sorry love,' muttered Purple Cloud. 'We're a bit stressed, that's all.'

She was speaking for me as well. I'd never felt so stressed. And not just about Mum and Sprocket. Dad was on my mind too. What if he was in the High Valley helping his Other Woman destroy the tea plants and the Brats caught him? What would they do to him?

I tried not to think about it. I tried to concentrate

on looking after Mum. But it's hard to be a good parent when you're that stressed.

I made Mum a cheese sandwich for lunch. As soon as my back was turned, Mum fed it to Matchbox.

'Why?' I said angrily. 'Why did you do that?'

'It had onion in it,' replied Mum sulkily.

Then I saw what Mum had done to the overalls Purple Cloud had lent her an hour earlier when she'd grown too big for the kaftan. She'd ripped the arms off at the shoulders and the legs off at the knees.

'It was daggy,' muttered Mum.

I started to explode.

Purple Cloud put her hand on my arm. 'It's just a difficult stage she's going through,' she said. 'I was like that when I was ten.'

I hoped Purple Cloud was right. At the rate Mum was growing, I hoped she'd only be difficult for another hour or so.

I was wrong.

An hour and a half later we still hadn't caught up with Sprocket and the Brats.

If it wasn't for Matchbox, standing with his front paws on the dashboard whimpering expectantly at the road ahead and the looming mountains, I'd have wondered if we were heading in the wrong direction.

I saw how grey the fur on his face was getting, and how droopy the skin under his eyes. He was an old dog again, and getting older. If he didn't have some tea soon . . .

GROPE

Coming up was another petrol station. Just a ramshackle general store with two pumps and some windswept flowerbeds.

'Con Rod,' I said. 'Do you think we should stop and ask someone if they've seen the Hummer come this way?'

'Good thinkin',' he replied.

He pulled up next to the pumps.

The outside of the place was deserted except for a Land Rover and three elderly tourists in plastic raincoats and floppy hats inspecting the flowers.

'They look a bit past it,' said Con Rod. 'Let's try inside.'

'Hummer?' said the woman behind the counter, folding her brawny arms. 'What, you mean like an entertainer? Haven't had any of those in today. And if we have he wasn't humming.'

Con Rod explained about the sort of Hummer we were looking for.

The woman's eyes lit up.

'Yeah,' she said. 'Sylvie up at the Esso, about thirty k's north, had one of them earlier. Rang me up just now to tell me about it. Bunch of blokes in a big army jeep thing. Rude blighters, some of them.'

'Thanks,' I said, grabbing Con Rod's arm and steering him towards the door.

We were just about to step out the door when the woman gave an angry shout. 'Stay right where you are,' she yelled.

300

We froze. I'd thanked her for the information, what else did she want? Then I saw it wasn't us she was yelling at.

It was Mum.

Mum was standing at the back of the shop, next to the shelf with sun lotion and baby nappies on it. She was staring in panic at the woman, who was striding towards her.

I stared at Mum in shock. She'd aged another two years. Not that I could tell for sure because she was dressed like a teenager off to the sort of party where there wouldn't be any parents around.

Green lipstick.

Buckets of mascara.

Tiny clinging skirt and top.

'Jeez,' said Con Rod. 'She's been at Purple Cloud's festival gear. With a pair of scissors by the look of it.'

Suddenly Mum bolted towards the door.

'Stop,' yelled the woman. 'I'm gunna do you.'

Con Rod grabbed Mum as she tried to run past and held her to him protectively. She struggled and a tub of hair gel fell from under her top and clattered to the floor. And a couple of lipsticks. And several pots of nail varnish.

'Right, you little thief,' hissed the woman when she saw them. 'It's the cops for you.'

'Lesley,' I said to Mum angrily, 'I told you to stay in the mobile home with Purple Cloud. Get back in there immediately and get those ridiculous clothes off. We'll talk about this later.'

I was doing my best to sound like a responsible parent. I saw the woman staring at me, and I remembered I didn't look like one.

Mum stood there for a moment, glaring at me, pale and trembling and furious. I remembered how I'd felt like that when Mrs Noakes the gym teacher had caught me in the sports storeroom drawing bottom cracks on the basketballs.

I held Mum's mobile phone out to her.

'If you want to do something useful,' I said, 'try ringing Dad's mobile. He might be in range now.'

Mum snatched the phone and stamped out of the shop.

For the next few minutes I worked hard with Con Rod to persuade the woman to drop the charges and let us pay for the things. She finally agreed, as long as Con Rod spent another fifty dollars on top of the total.

'Got any ice?' asked Con Rod.

I glanced out to the forecourt to make sure Mum was safely in the mobile home with Purple Cloud.

She wasn't.

Purple Cloud was hurrying out of the mobile home, peering around in alarm.

Mum was standing next to the Land Rover. She was talking to the elderly tourists. I couldn't see their faces, but I could see that Mum was pointing

indignantly back towards me and doing an exagger-
ated pantomime of somebody telling somebody else
off.

The elderly tourists were nodding sympathetically.

Mum was complaining to complete strangers about
me being too strict.

Right, you little madam, I thought furiously as I
strode towards her. You're grounded.

That's when Mum's feet left the ground.

The elderly tourists had grabbed her and were
throwing her into the back of the Land Rover.

I screamed and ran towards them.

So did Purple Cloud.

The elderly tourists scrambled into the Land Rover,
slammed the doors and the engine roared into life.

'Stop,' I yelled. 'Mum.'

The Land Rover hurtled forward, and for a
moment it headed straight for me. Then it swerved
with a squeal of tyres, and just before it flashed past
and roared away up the highway towards the mountains, I caught a glimpse of the old people's faces.

The ugly scowl on one of the men looked sort of
familiar.

So did the anxious look in the other man's eyes.

But it was the old woman driving, or rather her two
missing front teeth, that made me realise with a stab
of terror who they were.

SPROCKET

FOUR

Little Brother?

That's what Pooper Scooper had called me. Just before I realised that he was going to kill me.

I lay there in the darkening evening. Tied up helplessly on the ground next to the deserted railway station. My mind was spinning like the chamber of a revolver with two targets and only one bullet left. I wanted so badly to find out what Pooper Scooper knew about me. And I wanted to live. I didn't want to discover who I was and then die a couple of seconds later.

Suddenly it clicked. The imaginary bullet slid into the imaginary chamber. There was a way I could hit both targets at once. Keep him talking.

'You're full of bulldust,' I yelled. 'I'm not your brother.'

'Aren't you, Randall?' he said with a sneer.

'Randall?' I gasped. 'The little baby who drowned?'

'You didn't drown, Little Brother. Daddy Dear did.'

Pooper Scooper was mocking me. Putting on a baby voice.

'Little bubbums was ill. Daddy was taking his little sweetheart to hospital.'

His words flew to my ears like metal filings drawn to a magnet. He was answering all my questions. But for a second I was distracted.

An amazing sight met my eyes. The plant growing out of the blue seed had used its own tiny branches and roots like little arms and legs to pull itself out of its container. Some tiny leaves had appeared. The plant flopped onto the side of the road and began to roll slowly towards the forest. Pooper Scooper hadn't seen it. I threw him another question.

'How did . . .? How did . . .?' The next word was difficult to say. 'How did . . . I get to the police station?'

Pooper Scooper gave an evil smile.

'I know you're stalling, Randall. Trying to keep me talking. But no one is coming to help you. No one will find us up here. This train line is closed for the winter. But you might as well know. The three of us were crossing the river in a row-boat. You were a newborn baby. I was eighty-three.'

He felt no guilt. No sorrow. He cared only about himself. He gave a proud smirk.

'I looked twenty, of course,' he said. 'Anyway, the boat capsized. Father Dear managed to swim to shore with you. Then the idiot came back for me. I couldn't swim. He just managed to push me onto the bank before he sank under the water. The others came and put up a search. They finally found his body and took him back to base.'

My brain felt as if it was about to burst out of my skull. Pooper Scooper was my brother. So were Scowler and Beanie. And the other freaky nudists, Hairy Chest and Lobster Bottom. The Tea Lady, Reptile and the woman with the long grey hair were my sisters.

The frozen Germinator was my father. And, and . . . my mother was . . . their mother. Darkness began to fill my head. I was going to faint. But I couldn't. I struggled against the safety of oblivion.

Pooper Scooper's words came to me distantly. 'I dumped you off at a police station and told everyone that you had drowned. My big mistake was putting you in one of our skin-cream cartons. To the police it was just a box that some single mother had found in a bin. But it led *you* back to us.'

'But why?' I said. 'What did I ever do to you?'

Pooper Scooper seemed to struggle with some inner demon. Instead of an answer he gave me a look of hate. His wrinkles turned down, making his mouth seem like the arch of an ancient bridge.

By now the plant had managed to haul itself on top of a pile of frozen snow. More tiny white roots started to appear from the bottom of the seed. Seven or eight little branches immediately began to sprout.

The nudist tea bushes were definitely the fastest growing plants in the world. No wonder the Brats were ageing so quickly now that they had no tea.

All those years in the foster homes I had wanted to know who my mother was. I had thought that she might have been a single mother. Never in my wildest dreams would I have believed that I could have come from such a weird family. I couldn't take it in. It was mad. Crazy. Impossible.

I wanted to run screaming into the forest. But I was tied up on the ground next to a deserted railway station. And anyway, there was still one question that was going to shatter my skull if I didn't let it out.

'What about my mother?' I shouted. 'What about her?'

Pooper Scooper gave a loud laugh. 'Probably dead,' he chortled. 'If not she'd be . . . let me see . . .' He calculated on his fingers. 'One hundred and five years old. People go back to their real ages quickly when they stop taking the stuff.'

'Why did she stop?' I said. I knew some of the answer. And I had to keep him talking. Before he killed me. I glanced over his shoulder at the plant.

It had grown to a height of about half a metre. It was really thriving on the frozen ice. Two flowers had started to open. In the middle of each was a bud about the size of a marble. Between the folded leaves of each bud I could see flashes of blue.

Pooper Scooper still hadn't seen them. He snorted scornfully. 'After Mother heard you were dead she was never the same again. Went all funny. She stopped taking the tea years ago. Ran off up into the High Valley where the plants came from in the first place. Said she was going to destroy any that were left.'

A look of disgust came over his face. 'She was sentencing us to death. Her own children. We knew the High Valley was up in these mountains somewhere but we could never find it. Now we know exactly where it is. Thanks to you, Brother Dear.'

Pooper Scooper waved the note that I had taken from my father's nose when his body had started to thaw in Con Rod's van. Pooper Scooper shoved it into a pocket and pulled a large Bowie knife from its sheath.

'That's enough chit-chat,' he said. 'It's time for you and I to part.'

This was it. This was the end. I was going to die without seeing my mother. Or even knowing whether or not she was alive. I wriggled and squirmed but the knots were still as tight as ever. How much would a knife in the guts hurt? I knew that I had never known pain like it. I was seized by a wave of terror.

Suddenly Pooper Scooper's eyes grew round. He was transfixed. Bewildered. Like someone waking up in a smoke-filled house. He began to sniff.

I threw a quick look at the plant in its bed of frozen snow. The two flowers had fully opened and in the middle of each one was a bright blue seed. A sweet sickly perfume filled the air. Pooper Scooper turned from me at last and saw the plant.

'Yes,' he shrieked triumphantly. 'Yes.' He waved his fists over his head and gave a cry like the last warrior left alive on a battlefield. Then he staggered towards his prize.

As he did so my mind was seized by a terrible urge. The words, *Eat me, eat me*, pierced every brain cell. I thrashed about like a tied crocodile thrown alive onto a fire. Every part of my body, inside and out, burned with pain. I had to get to that plant. I was lost in a hurricane of agony. My whole body felt as if it would explode into shreds. I had to eat that seed. The sweet smell drove me crazy.

'Eat,' it demanded. 'Eat. Or die.'

Pooper Scooper was filled with the same fury. He grabbed a seed from the largest flower, shoved it in his whiskery mouth and swallowed.

'No,' I screamed. 'No. It's mine.'

Pooper Scooper gave a satisfied burp. Immediately the flower which had held the seed began to wilt. In a few seconds it was dead. The frenzied look disappeared from his eyes.

He calmly walked over to the plant and plucked the second seed. He held it up to his mouth.

I strained and stretched and bucked up and down.

'Mine,' I shrieked. 'Mine, mine, mine.'

Pooper Scooper seemed to be going through some incredible battle with himself. His right hand was trying to force the second seed into his mouth while his left hand was pulling it away. His knife had fallen to the ground. The plant was exerting its enormous power over him once again. But this time it was trying to stop him from swallowing the other seed.

Suddenly he began to lurch towards me like a sleep-walker. He couldn't help himself. His limbs obeyed another master. He was a zombie.

I lay on my back with my mouth wide open like a bird about to receive a worm from its mother. With a terrible groan Pooper Scooper dropped the seed into my mouth.

And I swallowed.

Immediately the scent disappeared. Pooper Scooper shook his head and looked around with a puzzled expression. Then, like light rushing into a room when the curtains are opened, the truth hit me.

The seeds were germinated inside the guts of people. One person – one seed. It made sense. The terrible perfume attracted any nearby humans. The strongest of them would swallow one seed and carry it away to grow in distant fields.

I looked at Pooper Scooper to see if the truth had hit him too, but it hadn't. He was crouching over the tea plant, tugging at it gently. He was trying to see how firmly it had taken root.

Snap.

'Damn it,' he shouted.

The tea plant had broken off at ground level. The whole thing immediately began to shrivel in Pooper Scooper's hands. He fell to his knees and tried to dig the roots out with his knife. But it was no use. They were shrivelled as well.

Suddenly I smelt the scent of rotting vegetation. Pooper Scooper gave an angry wail. No tea could be made from the remains of this dead plant.

My stomach had already begun to swell. And I knew why. This had happened to me before. My belt was too tight and I had no way of releasing it with my hands tied. The pressure from the gas in my stomach was terrible. Last time this had happened I had swollen like a pregnant cow.

'Help me,' I groaned.

Pooper Scooper had already loosened the front of his own trousers. His belly was beginning to bulge out like mine. He patted it like a greedy guzzler at a banquet. Then he reached down and cut my belt without a word.

Oh relief. Wonderful. My stomach plopped out like a bag full of jelly. The pain disappeared.

Only to be replaced by another.

Without giving it a thought, my evil brother grabbed my hair. He pulled my trussed body across the frozen ground as if I was no more than a sack of potatoes.

'Aagh,' I shrieked.

He ignored my screams and dragged me across the tracks towards the empty guard's van standing at the deserted station. He pushed me inside. I groaned in agony. My scalp was on fire with pain.

'Shut up,' he said. 'You're damned lucky the seed is inside you. Otherwise . . .'

Night had fallen but in the light of the moon I saw him, once again, draw a finger across his throat.

Before he could say any more there was a squeal of brakes. The stolen Land Rover bumped across the small car park and came to a halt. Pooper Scooper jumped out of the carriage and walked towards the strong headlights.

It was the rest of the Brats. Scowler stepped out into the moonlight. He had a tough, sexy-looking girl with him.

She looked about eighteen. She was dressed all in black. Her lips were covered in green lipstick. She wore chunky high shoes and a tiny mini-skirt. A little diamond twinkled in her navel. Her tight tank top didn't leave much to the imagination.

She pouted in a sulky fashion and clutched a ghetto blaster in one hand. I could just make out the strains of a tune about someone called Mrs Robinson.

Beanie and Reptile joined the others. There was a heated conversation between them all but I couldn't make out the words. They examined Pooper Scooper's bloated belly.

Without warning an argument broke out. They started shouting at each other. There was a lot of yelling and pointing towards my carriage. Someone used the word, 'Tigress'.

Suddenly the girl slapped Scowler right across the face.

Reptile and Beanie packed up laughing. They thought it was a great joke.

Scowler held a hand to his raw cheek. Pooper Scooper muttered at the girl under his breath. But neither of them hit her back. How could she get away with it? They all looked in my direction.

Suddenly I realised what they were arguing about. Me.

They were deciding who was going to torture me.

Which one was going to get out of me how to germinate the seed.

And the winner was . . .

The Tigress.

She strode cockily towards the train.

I had heard about things like this before. Women can be as cruel as men. Worse sometimes. She was like a female tiger. A man-eater.

'I'm glad I'm not him,' I heard Beanie say.

The Tigress stared down at me. She stepped into the carriage and slammed the door behind her. Then she gave a deadly smile and licked her lips.

'No,' I cried. 'No.'

I was tied up, helpless. The Tigress knelt down next to me and put her face so close that her plucked eyebrows went out of focus.

As quickly as a pouncing big-cat she made her move. She grabbed my head and pulled my ear up to her sharp teeth. She was going to bite my ear off.

I gasped and tried to pull away. Out of the corner of my eye I saw someone at the window. It was Scowler. He had come to gloat. To watch me being tortured.

I was tied up and helpless. I felt the warm breath of the Tigress in my ear.

'Kiss me,' she whispered. 'And make it look good.'

What, what, what?

She suddenly pulled back my head and kissed me.

Oh, yes. Oh, man. Those lips. Soft and supple. She was kissing me wildly.

I relaxed and let myself go. I had never felt anything like it before. She wasn't trying to torture me. She wasn't a tigress. She was an angel. What a kiss. My first ever. For a second or two I didn't respond. I was dumbstruck. A frozen dork. Then the wild passion of the moment overtook me and I started kissing back.

I wanted it to go on for ever.

But it didn't.

She pulled away. 'Is he still watching?' she whispered.

I shook my head.

She jumped up and peered out the window.

'They think I'm having my wicked way with you,' she said. 'But I've come to save you, Sprocket.' She was still staring out into the dark night. Her skimpy tank-top rode up revealing her bare waist. That's when I noticed the birthmark of Tasmania on her back.

Suddenly I realised who I had been kissing.

'Mrs Tunks-Livingstone,' I screamed.

There was a scuffling sound from outside.

'Quick,' said Amy's gorgeous young mother. 'Someone's coming.'

She threw herself onto me.

And once again locked her sweet lips . . .

Onto mine.

FIVE

'Stop,' I screamed.

The mobile home shuddered to a halt at the side of the dark highway.

Con Rod gave me a bewildered look. He obviously couldn't understand why anyone would want to stop in the middle of trying to rescue Mum and Sprocket from their evil abductors. Unless it was an emergency.

'Did something drop off our rear end?' asked Con Rod.

'Did we hit something?' asked Purple Cloud.

'We're going the wrong way,' I said. 'We should have turned left back there.'

'How do you know?' asked Con Rod, bewildered again.

'Look,' I said, pointing at Matchbox.

The ancient dog was straining in my arms, frail body rigid and trembling with urgency, droopy wet eyes staring into the darkness behind us. The sound bubbling in his throat was half growl and half whimper.

Half anger and half fear, which was exactly what I was feeling.

Con Rod reversed the mobile home back along the highway until, in the headlights, we saw a dirt road winding off to one side.

Matchbox's growls got louder and he tried to struggle free. He'd have jumped out and gone running up the side road if I'd let him. I held onto him and his growls turned to wheezes.

Con Rod and Purple Cloud looked at each other, perplexed.

'Come on,' I said frantically. 'We've trusted Matchbox's nose this far.'

'She's right,' said Purple Cloud.

Con Rod's eyes suddenly widened with excitement. 'Jeez,' he exclaimed, pointing at the dirt road through the windscreen. 'Look at the size of those tyre tracks. They're Hummer tracks or my name's not Constantine Rodwell. And there are smaller ones on top of them.'

AMY

'The Land Rover?' I said.

Con Rod nodded grimly.

As we sped up the bumpy road into the mountains, I dialled Mum's mobile phone for the millionth time since Scowler, Beanie and Reptile had driven off with her.

It was still switched off.

Worried sick, I dropped Con Rod's mobile back into its cradle.

I didn't even want to think about what horrible things could be happening to my poor, innocent teenage mum at the hands of those ancient brutes.

'Scowler,' muttered Con Rod. 'I wouldn't like any daughter of mine going round with a bloke with a name like that.'

Purple Cloud put a supportive hand on my shoulder.

'Con Rod,' she said. 'You're not helping.'

I stared through the windscreen at the road ahead. It was getting narrower, and steeper, and twistier. The trees looked white and ghostly in the high beam of the headlights. There was no sign of the Land Rover.

'Please,' I said desperately. 'Can't this thing go any faster?'

Con Rod leaned forward in the driver's seat and put all his weight on the accelerator pedal. The engine thundered even louder. I braced myself for a surge of extra power.

There wasn't one.

317

'Flamin' Weasel Dixon,' said Con Rod. 'That's the last time I let him sell me pre-loved piston rods.'

He changed down a gear and stamped on the accelerator again.

There was a loud hiss, the whole mobile home gave a neck-snapping jolt and the engine died.

'Or reconditioned gaskets,' said Con Rod as he pulled off the road and we bumped to a stop on a steep, scrubby hillside.

Con Rod jumped out and flung open the engine cover. I jumped out after him. My head was spinning with panic. Here we were, stranded at the side of a dark deserted mountain road while Mum was in the clutches of psychopathic hundred-year-old ex-dwarves with the muscles of crocodile-wrestlers.

'There's the problem,' mumbled Con Rod, lifting his head out of the engine and taking the torch out of his mouth. 'What I need is something to bung up that crack.'

'Glue?' I said frantically. 'Welding stuff?'

'Cumquat-and-peanut butter,' said Purple Cloud, handing Con Rod an earthenware bowl. She gave me a squeeze. 'It worked last time, and with some positive visualisation it just might work again.'

She stared up at the stars. I did too, trying to help. But all I could think of were three graves side by side. One was marked 'Mum', one was marked 'Dad', and one was marked 'Sprocket'.

Then I heard a faint chugging of an engine coming

out of the darkness. At first I thought it was the mobile home motor drowning in peanut butter, but the sound was coming from the wrong direction for that.

Suddenly I saw a pair of headlights, winding towards us up the road.

I was about to grab Con Rod's torch and wave it and yell frantically for help.

I didn't.

As the vehicle got closer I saw it was a vintage car. A Ford from the nineteen fifties or sixties. The only time I'd seen an old car like that was in the storage cellar next to the ancient family's Cool Room.

As the car rumbled past, I peered at the driver, ghostly in the headlights of the mobile home.

It was the Tea Lady. She looked about eighty, white-haired and frail as she clung onto the steering wheel, but she had exactly the same sad, determined expression on her face as she'd had when Pooper Scooper had refused to drink his tea.

I caught glimpses of the other people in the car, all wrapped in old-fashioned coats and scarves. Lobster Bottom. The Grey Hair Lady. Jimi Hendrix. The Melting Man, without his skin cream this time, but with so many wrinkles on his face he still looked like he was melting. A stooped and toothless Hairy Chest.

Not one of the elderly brothers and sisters so much as glanced at us as they passed. They were all staring in the direction they were going, as if somewhere ahead of them was the most important thing in the world.

'Jeez,' said Con Rod, 'not a very helpful bunch.'

'It's the rest of the family,' I said, my chest thumping with excitement. 'If we follow them, they'll probably lead us to the High Valley. To Mum and Sprocket. Maybe even to Dad.'

Con Rod stuck his head back into the engine, swearing and banging urgently at things. 'There's a bit of gasket stuck in a valve,' he said. 'I can't get at it with my tools. A corkscrew'd do it, but.'

'We left it at the campsite,' said Purple Cloud. She swore as well.

I handed Con Rod my Swiss Army knife.

After a bit, the engine coughed into life.

'Bewdy,' said Con Rod. 'God bless the Swiss Army and peanut butter.'

We followed the old car at a safe distance. Actually it wasn't that safe because we had to leave our head-lights switched off, but Con Rod managed to stay on the road most of the time and luckily there wasn't any oncoming traffic.

Suddenly, Con Rod's mobile phone rang.

'Can someone get that?' said Con Rod. 'I can't touch it while I'm driving cause I've only got one point left on me licence.'

I grabbed the phone out of its cradle, hit the button and put it to my ear.

And nearly fainted.

I could hear moans. And heavy breathing. And people trying to talk with what sounded like something against their mouths.

It was Mum.

And Sprocket.

They sounded as though they were wearing gags.

Whatever was happening to them, something must have pressed on Mum's mobile phone in her pocket and it was returning the last call.

'Mum,' I screamed into the phone so loudly Con Rod nearly drove off the road. 'Mum. Are you OK?'

There was no answer. They couldn't hear me.

'Mum,' I yelled. 'Hang on. We're coming.'

More groans and breathless muffled words. I couldn't bear to listen. I switched off the phone.

'It's Mum and Sprocket,' I sobbed to Con Rod and Purple Cloud. 'I think they're being tortured.'

At that moment, the old car turned off the road down a narrow rock-strewn track. Con Rod swung off after them, then stopped.

'Go,' I yelled. 'After them.'

I was pounding the dashboard with my fists. Con Rod grabbed my hands in his stringy tattooed ones and held them gently but firmly.

'Don't you blow a gasket,' he said. 'That old rust bucket'll be taking it real slow over them rocks. We don't want to come round a corner and give 'em one up the backside.'

He had a point. I took several deep breaths. Purple

Cloud smoothed my hair. I looked at their crumpled, concerned faces in the dark, and suddenly I felt jealous of their son, having two parents like them.

Except he was dead.

Con Rod slipped the mobile home into gear and we moved slowly along the bush track.

We didn't bump into a single old car.

After a few minutes, Con Rod suddenly pulled off into the trees.

Ahead of us was a large clearing. Against the moonlit sky I could see the dark shapes of three parked vehicles.

The old car.

The Hummer.

The Land Rover.

And another shape I didn't recognise at first, until a figure hurried past it with a torch and I caught a glimpse of rusty railway tracks.

Train carriages. Old wooden train carriages, flaky varnish shining dully in the moonlight.

Other dark figures with torches moved around the three parked vehicles. Stooped, ancient figures, groaning and wheezing as they dragged suitcases out of the boot of the car.

The whole scene had the atmosphere of imminent departure.

One thought stabbed through me.

Find Mum and Sprocket.

I moved so quickly Purple Cloud and Con Rod

didn't have a chance to stop me. Before they realised what was happening, I was out of the mobile home and running across the clearing at a crouch.

I kept close to the trees and headed for the parked vehicles. I needed to get a look inside the Hummer and the Land Rover without being seen. I was still working out how to do this when a torch snapped on near my shoulder and I froze.

It was the ageing Brats in a huddle near the Land Rover.

I couldn't see if Pooper Scooper was with them.

I pressed myself against a tree, sick with fear.

'Hey, Barnabus,' Scowler was saying to Beanie. 'What's happening in the carriage with the kid and the girl?'

Beanie shook his balding head and shuddered. 'I can't look,' he said.

Reptile glared into the darkness. 'I don't like it,' she said. 'I don't like the way Orson does things any more.'

Scowler just grunted.

I was dizzy with panic again. They must be talking about Mum and Sprocket. What couldn't Beanie look at? The horrible, battered condition of poor Mum and Sprocket's bodies?

I realised 'the carriage' must be one of the old train carriages. Once the three Brats had moved away, I crept over to the carriages. The compartments were dark and silent.

Except one. I saw the flicker of candlelight inside what looked like a guard's van standing separate from the other carriages. The window was half raised and I could hear the faint sound of music.

The vicious brute. Pooper Scooper had probably used music to cover Mum and Sprocket's cries as he'd tortured them.

I stood up and peered in through the window of the guard's van, bracing myself for what I was going to see.

I didn't brace myself hard enough.

My legs almost buckled.

Inside the guard's van, on a green leather seat, were sprawled Mum and Sprocket, eyes closed.

Kissing.

'Mum,' I yelled. It came out as a sort of squeak.

Mum opened her eyes, saw me, and kept on kissing.

Then Sprocket opened his eyes and saw me too. He tried to wriggle away from Mum, licking green lipstick off his mouth. 'Amy,' he said wildly. 'Keep calm. It's not what you think.'

I opened my mouth to let him have it, but my voice had disappeared. Then I saw to my amazement that he was tied up. This is crazy, I thought weakly. Why hasn't Mum untied him?

Suddenly my strength returned. 'How dare you, young lady,' I yelled at Mum. 'You're a married woman.'

Mum rolled her eyes at me through the window.

'I'm not doing anything your father hasn't been doing for years,' she said. Then she frowned. 'Anyway, you said you'd look after me. Not let horrible men drag me into their cars.'

Suddenly Mum looked close to tears. I didn't know what to say.

I tried to get a foothold to climb in through the carriage window. The train wheels were caked with old grease and my feet kept slipping off.

Sprocket managed to sit up. He slumped back wearily against the seat. He wasn't even struggling to untie himself.

Then I saw why. His stomach was bloated and swollen. He must have swallowed another seed. At least he didn't seem to be in pain this time.

'Sprocket,' I said. 'You've got to escape. Come on, both of you, move it. We've got to get away from this crazy evil family.'

Sprocket didn't move. He just looked sadly at me through the window.

'They're my family,' he said quietly.

I stared at him.

'The Germinator was my father,' he said.

My head spun. Then I remembered Pooper Scooper's reaction in the mobile home when he'd seen Sprocket and the Germinator together. He'd looked as stunned then as I felt now.

Sprocket was still looking at me, but not so sadly.

'I'm glad you're OK,' he said.

I was glad he was OK, apart from his poor stomach, but I was too dazed to show it.

All I could hear was a low murmuring sound.

At first I thought it was just my brain struggling to digest the amazing news. But after a few moments I realised it wasn't me.

The noise was coming from stooped figures advancing towards me out of the darkness.

Hairy Chest. Lobster Bottom. Jimi Hendrix. The Tea Lady. The Melting Man. The Grey Hair Lady.

They were glaring at me and their wrinkled mucus-strung mouths were moving with murmured threats as they came closer.

'She's the one,' muttered Hairy Chest. 'She's the one who stopped her father helping us.'

I stared at them, stunned. That was crazy. They'd got it totally wrong. But I could see they weren't in the mood for explanations.

Their bodies may have been bent and wizened, but the ancient anger burning in their eyes and the furious energy trembling in their scrawny limbs left me frozen with terror.

Sprocket's brothers and sisters were coming to get me.

SPROCKET

SIX

Amy looked at me with a stunned expression. 'What are you two *doing*?' she yelled.

She didn't like me kissing her mother – that was for sure. I opened my mouth to explain. But before I could speak, a muscled arm wrapped itself around Amy's neck.

It was Hairy Chest.

At that very second the air was filled with an unmistakable sound. The hiss of steam under pressure.

I struggled to my feet and hopped across to the window. Lobster Bottom and Hairy Chest were dragging Amy across the tracks towards the station platform.

Mrs Tunks-Livingstone ran to the front door of the guard's van. 'Leave her alone,' she shrieked. She began shaking at the handle. She couldn't get the door open.

The chuffing noises grew louder. And louder.

Amy bucked and kicked but the men were too strong for her. They pulled her up onto the platform. Just in time.

An ancient locomotive steamed right onto the spot where they had been standing on the tracks. I caught glimpses of Amy's struggle as the engine and a small red passenger carriage rumbled between us. Steam poured out between the wheels. I could make out Reptile's face in the glow of burning coal from the engine's furnace. She was pulling levers and turning wheels. Pooper Scooper was furiously shovelling coal into the boiler.

I wanted to yell out. I wanted to tell Reptile that she was my sister. So that she would unlock the door and let us out. But Pooper Scooper was keeping all three Brats well away from me.

The engine chugged on and disappeared from sight. Now I could see Amy clearly. She was still fighting with Hairy Chest and Lobster Bottom on the platform.

'Let her go,' said an angry voice. It was Con Rod. And with him was Purple Cloud. They were immediately surrounded by more members of the family. The Tea Lady threatened Con Rod with a broomstick. And the Melting Man held a large rock above his head. Jimi Hendrix and the woman with the long grey hair were trying to grab Purple Cloud.

Con Rod charged forward, waving a wheel wrench above his head. I just managed to hear snatches of what he was shouting at them.

'Flamin' mongrels . . .'

'Kidnappers . . .'

'Our boy Sprocket . . .'

'Weasel Dixon . . .'

I hopped around the carriage helplessly.

'Untie me,' I shrieked.

But Mrs Tunks-Livingstone had no time for me. She was kicking the door handle like a cop in a movie.

Through the window I saw Jimi Hendrix grab Con Rod from behind and put him into a headlock. Quick as a flash Hairy Chest joined in and they both wrestled him to the ground. The woman with the long grey hair pounced on Purple Cloud, helped by Lobster Bottom.

Purple Cloud struggled furiously. She began to spin around like a top. Lobster Bottom spun off and fell onto the train track.

This was terrible. Amy, Con Rod and Purple Cloud weren't a match for my frenzied brothers and sisters. They didn't have a chance. I had to do something. But I was tied up.

Mrs Tunks-Livingstone threw her whole body against the door. It burst open.

'Amy,' she yelled. 'I'm coming.'

In a flash she was gone. I struggled against the ropes but just couldn't free myself. I hopped with two feet towards the door. There was an enormous crash and I fell backwards. The locomotive had joined onto the guard's van. By the time I managed to get up again it was too late. The train was already moving. I would have fallen beneath the wheels if I had jumped. And the back door of the guard's van was closed. There was nothing I could do.

Rip. My pants suddenly split right down the seams. My stomach was now growing and swelling at an enormous rate. The seed and the gas were pumping me up like a balloon. I had to get the ropes off before they cut me in half.

I shouted through the window.

'Con Rod, Purple Cloud.'

They were too busy with their own problems to notice me.

Closer by I could see desperate figures running. It was Beanie and Scowler. They were shouting at each other and trying to jump on the rear platform of the guard's van.

They disappeared from view. The back door of the guard's van suddenly flew open and they tumbled inside.

Beanie looked out behind him into the dark night.

'Silas and Agnes and the others,' he yelled. 'They're getting left behind. Stop the train.'

'It's Pooper Scooper,' I yelled. 'He won't stop for anyone.'

They stared at me with puzzled eyes.

'Orson,' I shouted.

'The selfish ratbag,' screamed Beanie.

They knew what Pooper Scooper was doing. But not why.

There were only two seeds. And they might not

produce enough tea for everyone in time. If no new plants were found, these ancient people were going to die of old age. And Pooper Scooper was not going to be one of them. He was leaving his brothers and sisters behind on purpose.

Reptile started to move towards the front of the train.

'Take me with you,' I yelled.

Scowler threw a brief glance in my direction and snorted. They were going to leave me there. Why should they take me? After all, I was the intruder.

'I'm your brother Randall,' I yelled.

Scowler and Beanie looked at me in disbelief. Their mouths fell open. Their eyes grew round.

'Randall?' gasped Reptile.

I nodded. 'Orson dumped me at a police station in a skin-cream box when I was a baby.'

'Randall's dead,' said Scowler.

The train was gathering speed. My friends were somewhere behind in the middle of a terrible fight. The murderous Pooper Scooper was kidnapping me again. My other brothers and sisters were being left behind to die of old age.

'I've swallowed another seed,' I yelled. 'My guts are killing me. My pants are too tight. Don't leave me to die.'

Scowler threw a glance at my bloated body and grabbed my shoulders. Then he nodded at Beanie who took hold of my feet. They staggered through

331

the passenger carriage towards the locomotive with me dangling between them like a pregnant kangaroo on a hunter's pole.

We hurried through the next carriage and poured into the cabin of the locomotive.

Reptile was unconscious on the floor. She must have tried to stop the train. But Pooper Scooper had obviously stopped her. He was still furiously shovelling coal into the fire. He was laughing. His wrinkled, twisted face glowed red in the light of the flames. He was like a crazy devil laughing on a journey to hell.

When he saw us he lifted the shovel above his head. He was going to smash anyone who approached. There were more of us. But we were unarmed. And I was tied up.

The two Brats dropped me heavily on the hard metal floor.

'Stop the train, Orson,' yelled Beanie. 'You're not going to leave the others behind to die.'

Pooper Scooper stopped all right. He stopped laughing.

He suddenly doubled up with pain and grasped his swollen stomach with his hands. At that exact moment a pain shot through my own guts.

Our time had come. There on a steam train. In the snow-covered mountains. In the middle of the night. Two bloated bellies . . .

Were about to pop off.

Reptile suddenly groaned and opened her eyes. Just

in time to see Pooper Scooper doubled up in pain. He pulled the tattered remnants of his pants and under-wear down to his ankles and cried out in agony.

'Aagh, my guts,' he groaned. 'What's happening to me?'

I had no time to answer even if I'd wanted to. The pain in my own enormous belly was unbearable. We were both about to pass the seeds.

And I was glad.

I wanted them both. I wanted to plant the little blue pellets of eternal youth in ice. And cultivate them. And grow more nudist tea. Not for myself. For my unknown mother. If she was alive. At one hundred and three years of age she would not have long to live. I wanted the tea to make her young again and save her. So I could have a mother.

Pooper Scooper wanted the seeds too. For himself. So he would never die.

'What's wrong with him?' shouted Reptile.

None of the Brats seemed to know about the swallowed seeds.

Pooper Scooper was crouching down, almost touching his shoes with his fingers. His buttocks were warmed by the roaring flames of the boiler.

'Aagh,' screamed Pooper Scooper. 'Help. It's killing me.'

But there was nothing I could do. And anyway, fate lent a hand.

Pop.

Pooper Scooper's seed spat out of his backside.

Straight into the flames of the furnace. There was a brief flare like the last gasp of a distant star exploding. Then a tongue of flame licked out of the boiler door and swept across the instrument panel.

'No, no, no,' shrieked Pooper Scooper. He grabbed a long poker and jabbed feverishly into the furnace. But it was no good. The seed was burning with a strong flame. It was too late.

Pooper Scooper turned to me. His face was convulsed by a wave of sheer hatred. He raised the poker high above his head. Its end was glowing red.

'You interfering little mongrel,' he shouted. Spit dribbled down his chin. 'I'm going to finish you once and for all.' He waved the poker in front of my terrified face.

'Don't, Orson,' yelled Beanie. 'He says he's our brother.'

Pooper Scooper paused. But Beanie's words only enraged him more. 'Lies,' he screeched. 'All lies.'

He raised the poker to strike. When . . .

An enormous squirt of blue gas blasted out of his backside. Reptile and Scowler jumped back in terror. They had never seen anything like it. I had. But not what followed. The swirling vapour swept across the instrument panel where the burning seed's flame was giving its final lick. In an instant the vapour ignited. In front of our horrified eyes Pooper Scooper was transformed into a human flame-thrower.

He screamed and dropped the glowing poker.
He hopped around the cabin howling in agony as a
scorching blue flame whooshed out of his rear end.
Scowler and Reptile dived to the floor as the crazy
flame raked the locomotive cabin, charring everything it touched.

And then it was gone. As quickly as it had come.
The blue gas had burnt itself out. Pooper Scooper
stood trembling, gasping for breath and clutching his
burnt backside with blackened fingers.

He slowly picked up the glowing poker, pulled up
his trousers, and stepped towards me. Death was in
his eyes. My death. Pooper Scooper cared nothing for
seeds. Or brothers. Or eternal youth. He was totally
out of control.

I snatched a glance out of the train. The dark forest
rushed by crazily. The frozen ground blurred into a
dirty white sheet. The locomotive was gaining speed –
rushing down a steep slope, faster and faster.

There were two choices open to me.

Stay with Pooper Scooper and his red-hot poker.

Or jump.

I was in a desperate situation. History. Dead. Gone.

Pooper Scooper's face boiled with rage. His eyes
were puffed up. Frozen spit covered his chin. His
words tumbled over each other angrily like notes
ejecting from a crazed automatic teller machine.

'Jump, and do us all a favour, Intruder,' he shouted.

'Don't kill him, Orson,' said Hilda. She put one of

her driving gloves on his arm. Her tongue flicked in and out of her wrinkled mouth like a reptile watching an ants' nest.

'Shut up,' said Pooper Scooper. 'I'm going to finish him.'

I stared at the glowing red tip of the poker. The sight made me tremble. My legs felt as if they were going to collapse beneath me.

'You can't, Orson,' said Beanie. 'Not if he's our brother.'

Pooper Scooper waved the poker in his brother's face. 'You're an idiot, Barnabus,' he yelled. 'He's not our brother. It's just another lie to get himself off the hook.'

'You're the liar, Orson,' I yelled.

Scowler stepped between them. 'It doesn't matter who he is,' he shouted. 'Only one thing matters. That was a seed you shot into the boiler, wasn't it? This kid's all swollen up the same as you. He's swallowed one, too. If you push him off the train, Orson, our last hope goes with him. We're all going to die unless we get that seed.'

Pooper Scooper glared at his fellow Brats with eyes full of fury. First Stanley, then Barnabus, then Hilda. They all nodded their heads. I could see that Pooper Scooper was trying to control himself. In a fit of temper he threw the poker onto the floor.

Then under his breath he said, just to me, 'The time will come, Little Brother, the time will come. Just wait till we get to the end of the line. I'll have you then.'

SEVEN

It's not easy, fighting an enemy to the death when you're trying not to harm them.

The ancient family members were vicious, clawing and scratching and gouging. My face and arms were raw and bleeding. I decided to try and knock one of them out to calm things down.

Then suddenly they all stopped fighting.

The significance of the loud hissing and clanking that had been going on for several minutes finally got through to them.

And me.

And Con Rod and Purple Cloud and Mum.

We all stood staring as the train hissed and clanked away from us up the mountain track.

The old folk started wailing and stumbling after it.

I ran towards the mobile home dragging Mum behind me.

'Come on,' I yelled at Con Rod and Purple Cloud. 'We've got to go after the train.'

Yes, I was concerned about Sprocket. Deeply, gut-wrenchingly concerned. Despite what he'd just been doing with Mum.

But I was concerned about something else too. The Brats had the only map to the High Valley. If we lost them, we might never find our way there. We might never find Sprocket's mother. Or my dad. And if my mum's body couldn't take the physical stress of ageing at eight thousand times the normal rate, if her skin started shrivelling up and her bones started disintegrating, who else could I turn to for help?

'Jeez,' said Con Rod as he swung himself into the driver's seat of the mobile home. 'I've never done this before. Not driven along train tracks. Not for more than a couple of hundred metres anyway.'

'You can do it, love,' said Purple Cloud, tightening his seat-belt.

Con Rod gunned the motor and we shot across the clearing towards the tracks.

Then I saw the sad huddled group, doubled over, gasping for breath. Hairy Chest and the Tea Lady. Lobster Bottom and Jimi Hendrix. The Grey Hair Lady and the Melting Man. Their attempt to catch the train hadn't lasted long.

They stared up at us, shivering and aged and mournful.

Sprocket's family.

'Wait,' I yelled.

Con Rod hit the brakes and we skidded to a stop next to them.

'We can't leave them here,' I said to Con Rod. 'Who knows how long they'll survive without tea.'

'Poor things,' said Purple Cloud. 'Perhaps if we can help them get up to the High Valley, they might find some plants there.'

'They can come on one condition,' said Con Rod. 'No more kicking me in the groin.'

Purple Cloud slid open the door and we helped the elderly folk clamber in. There was a lot of groaning and moaning and wheezing, but finally they were all aboard. Matchbox, huddled on the floor next to the Germinator's tarpaulin, whined happily to see them.

The Tea Lady gripped my hands with her knotty wrinkled ones. 'Up till now,' she said in a thin wavering voice, 'I thought you were a nosy inter-fering pest, but I'm changing my mind about you.'

'Thanks,' I said.

With an apologetic smile, the Tea Lady touched the scratch on my temple where she'd tried to remove my left eyeball.

We set off again.

'Everyone grab a beanbag and a seat-belt,' called out Con Rod. 'If there aren't enough, wedge yourself in with cushions. OK, let's hope these tyres can grip snow.'

The mobile home gave a lurch as we mounted the tracks. Con Rod accelerated. We sped forward, wheels drumming over the frosty wooden sleepers.

The elderly folk gave a feeble but excited cheer.

I peered through the windscreen. Con Rod was driving with the headlights off. The tracks gleamed in front of us in the moonlight. I couldn't see the train, but I could hear it, chugging somewhere ahead in the darkness.

I went and sat next to Mum. She was stroking Matchbox and staring out the window at the dark snow-dusted trees flashing past.

She'd wiped her make-up off and was wearing a pair of Con Rod's overalls. Suddenly she didn't look a day over seventeen. I opened my mouth to give her a talking to about shoplifting and kissing unsuitable boys, but she was looking so sad and I was so sick with worry I couldn't bring myself do it.

'Do you think we'll ever see him again?' said Mum.

'Who do you mean?' I said. 'Sprocket?' I paused. 'Or Dad?'

We looked at each other for several moments. Then she looked away.

'Both,' she said quietly.

Con Rod gave a yell. 'There it is,' he shouted.

I hurried up to the front. The train was about twenty metres ahead of us chugging up the mountainside, wreathed in smoke and steam.

The elderly folk gave another cheer and Hairy Chest started singing, 'She'll Be Coming Round The Mountain When She Comes'. The others joined in, including Matchbox.

Then the mobile home jolted violently. And again. The whine of spinning rubber drowned out the community singing. The train started pulling away from us.

'Our wheels are slipping,' said Con Rod. 'Snow's getting too deep.'

I hung on to the back of Con Rod's seat, willing the tyres to grip.

For Mum's sake.

For Sprocket's sake.

For all our sakes.

Con Rod changed gear and the engine revved. We started to catch up with the train again. I wanted to scream with relief.

Then the jolting started again.

And the whining from the wheels.

My stomach tightened with despair.

Slowly, shudderingly, the gap between us and Sprocket, the space between us and the precious map, started to widen as we slipped back and the train pulled away from us into the night.

'I think I know how to fix it,' said Con Rod. 'But I'll need someone to take the wheel.'

Purple Cloud and I looked at each other helplessly. Neither of us could drive, and none of the old folk looked up to handling a four-wheel-drive gearbox with a truck clutch.

'I'll do it,' said Mum.

I stared at her.

'It's OK,' she said to Con Rod. 'I'm over eighteen and I've had a licence for sixteen years.'

Mum grabbed the wheel and slid into the driver's seat. While she did stuff with the clutch and gears that she used to do when we were running late for my train to school, Con Rod pulled on a large pair of scuffed leather gloves.

Then he wound down the front passenger window. Icy wind blasted into the mobile home. The elderly folk huddled deeper into their coats and scarves.

'Get as close to the train as you can,' Con Rod said to Mum. 'Purple Cloud, love, when I give you the signal, reverse the winch.'

Before we could stop him, he swung himself out of the window and onto the bonnet. Purple Cloud screamed. Con Rod dropped onto his stomach and wriggled his way to the front of the lurching windswept vehicle. He reached down behind the bullbar and grabbed the end of the winch cable and held it up triumphantly.

On the end of the cable was a big rusty metal hook.

Mum was changing gear and working the clutch even faster than the times she'd lost her temper in the supermarket carpark.

Gradually we caught up with the train again.

Con Rod was hanging off the bullbar now, reaching forward with the cable, straining to get the hook into the coupling loop at the back of the guard's van.

I couldn't look.

I couldn't not look.

Con Rod vanished.

Then he appeared again, waving frantically at Purple Cloud. The hook was in the coupling loop.

Purple Cloud threw a switch on the dash and the winch motor whined furiously as it paid out the cable. Mum took her foot off the accelerator and struggled to get the mobile home out of gear.

'Neutral,' she yelled. 'I can't find neutral.'

She found it. For a few seconds the train seemed to be hurtling away from us. Then the cable went tight and with a mighty jolt that rattled every pair of false teeth there, we were suddenly skimming over the snow, towed by the thundering train.

For a horrible moment I thought the jolt had flung Con Rod into the trees, but his wind-flushed face appeared at the open window and we dragged him inside.

Purple Cloud gave him a tearful hug, and all the old folk wanted to as well, but Con Rod hastily slid back into the driver's seat.

'There's no steering,' said Mum as she squeezed out and let him take over.

'Don't matter,' said Con Rod. 'The tracks are between our wheels. They'll keep us on the straight and narrow.'

'Won't the Brats see us?' asked Purple Cloud, peering anxiously at the train ahead.

'Too much smoke and steam,' said Con Rod. 'And

old chuffers like that don't have rear-vision mirrors.'

We swayed and skimmed over the snow into the night, the world's biggest toboggan with some of the world's oldest passengers.

I made sure all the old folk were securely strapped in, then took Mum aside. We both hung on to the sink. Mum was as tall as the fridge now. It didn't seem long since she'd barely been able to reach the handle.

'I'm very, very proud of you,' I said. 'Even prouder than I was this morning.'

Mum looked down at me, and gave me a happy bashful twenty-year-old grin. 'Thanks,' she said.

Then Con Rod gave a yell. 'Hang on, everybody,' he shouted. 'End of the line. The train's stopping.'

We stopped too. But only after we hit the back of the guard's van with a thump that threw everything and everybody in the mobile home into a tangle of arms, legs, beanbags, crockery and meditation equipment.

'Jeez,' said Con Rod. 'Just as well I fitted the economy-sized bullbar.'

It took us a while to calm the old folk down. While Mum and Purple Cloud and I checked them for injuries and brushed the brown rice out of their hair, Con Rod peered anxiously out the window.

'No sign of the Brats,' he said. 'Funny, but. They must have felt the thump. Hang about. There they go.'

I looked to where he was pointing. Five figures were struggling up the snowy slope of the mountain that towered over us. In the moonlight I could just make them out. It was Scowler, Reptile and Beanie.

They were slightly ahead of Pooper Scooper, who was dragging the fifth stumbling figure across the snow by a rope tied to his hands.

'Sprocket,' I screamed as I flung myself out of the mobile home. At least he was still alive. My anguished wail echoed through the dark mountains. So did Matchbox's anguished howl.

Pooper Scooper stopped and turned, peering down at us. Then he turned away and made urgent, angry gestures to the others. They hurried on up the slope.

'Come on,' I yelled at Con Rod. 'We've got to go after them.'

Con Rod grabbed my arm. 'I can't drive up there,' he said. 'I haven't got chains for the wheels. And we'll freeze if we go up there without rugging up.'

He was right. The mountain air was bitterly cold. I saw that Purple Cloud had dragged a big old army kitbag out of the mobile home. She unzipped it. Huge shapeless brightly coloured woollen jumpers and socks spilled out.

'I knew my knitting would come in handy,' she said as we pulled them on.

I was stuffing my socked feet into the rubber boots Con Rod gave me when a chorus of moans and wails rang out from the mobile home.

'Poor loves,' said Purple Cloud. 'They've just found their melting dad.'

'At least they'll be warmer inside,' I said, and we set off up the mountain.

Snow started falling again, thick and blinding, and we lost sight of Sprocket and the Brats.

'Just keep heading uphill,' panted Con Rod. 'It's all we can do.'

'It'll be dawn soon,' said Purple Cloud.

'Have we got any weapons?' asked Mum.

Nobody answered her.

We plodded upwards through the freezing darkness. Then Purple Cloud slipped and fell.

'Easy, girl,' said Con Rod as we helped her up.

'Why don't you go back down to the mobile home,' I suggested to her, concerned. 'You don't have to come with us.'

'No,' said Purple Cloud, glancing up towards where she'd last seen Sprocket, 'I want to come.'

I understood as I glanced over to check that Mum still had her jumper on. I was a stand-in parent myself.

We plodded on. Time got lost in the dark swirling snow.

To stop myself worrying about Sprocket, I thought about the High Valley we were heading towards.

And started worrying about Dad. Even a top scientist with a quilted anorak would have trouble surviving in this bleak wilderness.

I knew Dad. If he was up here looking for any remaining plants, he'd go to the highest, most dangerous peak to find them if he had to, and he'd keep on searching till he was in worse shape than the Germinator.

Do anything to help, that was my dad.

Fear and anxiety churned inside me like the snow squalls that were stinging my face.

'Jeez,' said Con Rod. 'I'd kill for a hot rum and coke.'

Then, slowly, the sky lightened. The snow stopped falling. Feeble sunlight crept over the peaks. A chill breeze sprang up and parted the mist.

To reveal an incredible sight.

Below us, plodding slowly up the mountain, were Hairy Chest and the Tea Lady and the others, six stoop-shouldered figures each wrapped in a brightly coloured jumper.

They were dragging something behind them up the snowy slope with ropes made from knotted curtains.

The Germinator in his ice block. With Matchbox sitting on top.

'They must be trying to get their father up higher to where it's colder,' said Purple Cloud. 'Stop him melting.'

'Or return him to his High Valley,' I said.

Con Rod didn't say anything.

He just gave an alarmed squeak.

347

I turned round to see what had alarmed him. And gave an anxious gasp myself.

Above us the mountain slope was topped by a row of rocky peaks. Between two of them was a deep narrow passage, the only way through.

About to enter the passage were Pooper Scooper, Scowler, Reptile and Beanie, still with Sprocket as their prisoner.

Once the Brats were in the passage, we wouldn't be able to see them. They could ambush us. Or we could lose them for ever.

And Sprocket.

And the map.

Desperate, frantic, I started to move towards them. I didn't know what I was going to do, but I had to do something.

Then I stopped.

A flash of movement caught my eye.

A figure had appeared from nowhere. A mysterious figure in a blue quilted parka with the hood up, hurtling along the ridge towards Sprocket and the Brats.

On a snowboard.

SPROCKET

EIGHT

Tramping up that mountainside, I'd lost all sense of time. Suddenly I realised Pooper Scooper and the other Brats were dragging me into a high mountain passage between two rocky peaks. I snatched a glance down below in one of the brief clear moments. The stars had faded and the rising sun was painting the snowy slopes with bright red rays. My heart leapt.

It was the mobile home. Down there behind the train. Amazing. Incredible. Somehow or other Con Rod had managed to hook it on to the back of the guard's van.

And there was Con Rod. Struggling up the hill behind us with Amy and Purple Cloud and another woman. Further back but following as fast as they could were Hairy Chest, the Tea Lady and the rest of my weird family. They were pulling some sort of box behind them. I held my breath. I didn't want Pooper Scooper to see them. I had to distract him. He might decide on an ambush.

I was too late.

'You two go ahead,' Pooper Scooper yelled. 'I'm going to send a little present down the hill.'

He began to make a round ball of snow. A very large one. My heart missed a beat. He had seen the others. He was going to roll a snowball down the hill. It would grow larger and larger as it plunged down the steep slope. It might even start a landslide. Anyone coming up from below would be wiped out. I had to stop him.

The misty clouds closed in and blotted out the valley below.

I yelled at Scowler, Beanie and Reptile. The three Brats were my only hope.

'Hairy Chest is down there,' I told them. 'And Lobster Bottom. And the Tea Lady.'

They stared at me, not understanding. I tried desperately to remember the real names of their brothers and sisters. *My* brothers and sisters. But I just couldn't think of them.

'He's lying again,' said Pooper Scooper. 'It's only that brat of a girl. And her mother. And the other two pests.'

'Someone's coming,' shouted Reptile. Her tongue flicked in and out nervously. She was pointing to the frozen slopes above us. A distant, solitary snowboard rider was heading our way.

As the figure descended I could see that it wore goggles and a parka. There was something strange about the way the figure was moving over the snow, confident, flying into the air and making risky jumps. But when it landed he or she was wobbly and nearly fell several times. Maybe the person was injured or weak from being lost in the snow. I hoped like hell that the snowboard rider might be able to help me.

'Untie him,' said Pooper Scooper. 'We don't want to attract attention.'

Scowler undid my ropes and whispered in my ear. 'Say nothing. Absolutely nothing. Understand?'

My stomach began to growl. I was gripped by a sudden pain. The seed was moving. At any moment I might have to crouch in the snow and let it burst out of my bowels.

The spasm passed and my attention went back to the figure on the snowboard.

Suddenly I was overtaken by an incredibly powerful image, a premonition . . .

I reached into my pocket and pulled out a wet, crumpled piece of paper that I had shoved into my pocket at the skin-cream factory. It was a label from one of the jars. On it was the photo of a young, beautiful woman. She was a picture of youth and beauty with clear, glowing skin.

At that moment I knew without a doubt that the snowboarder was the same person. Don't ask me how. It was just a feeling. But I knew I was right.

Pooper Scooper tried to snatch the label from my hand but I was too quick for him.

Beanie looked on, puzzled.

I held the picture up to his face. He stared at it with a frown.

'Mother?' he said.

My heart seemed to stop. The world seemed to stop.

The woman on the label was Beanie's mother. The woman on the label . . . was my mother.

Was this the end of my long journey? Was my feeling about the mysterious snowboard rider right? Was she the same person as the photo on the skin-cream label? Was I about to find happiness for the first time in my life?

Right at that moment, when all my dreams seemed as if they might come true, at the end of my long and dangerous journey . . .

A terrible thought hit me for the first time.

If this was my mother . . .

Would she like me?

The snowboard rider skidded to a stop.

And pulled off her goggles.

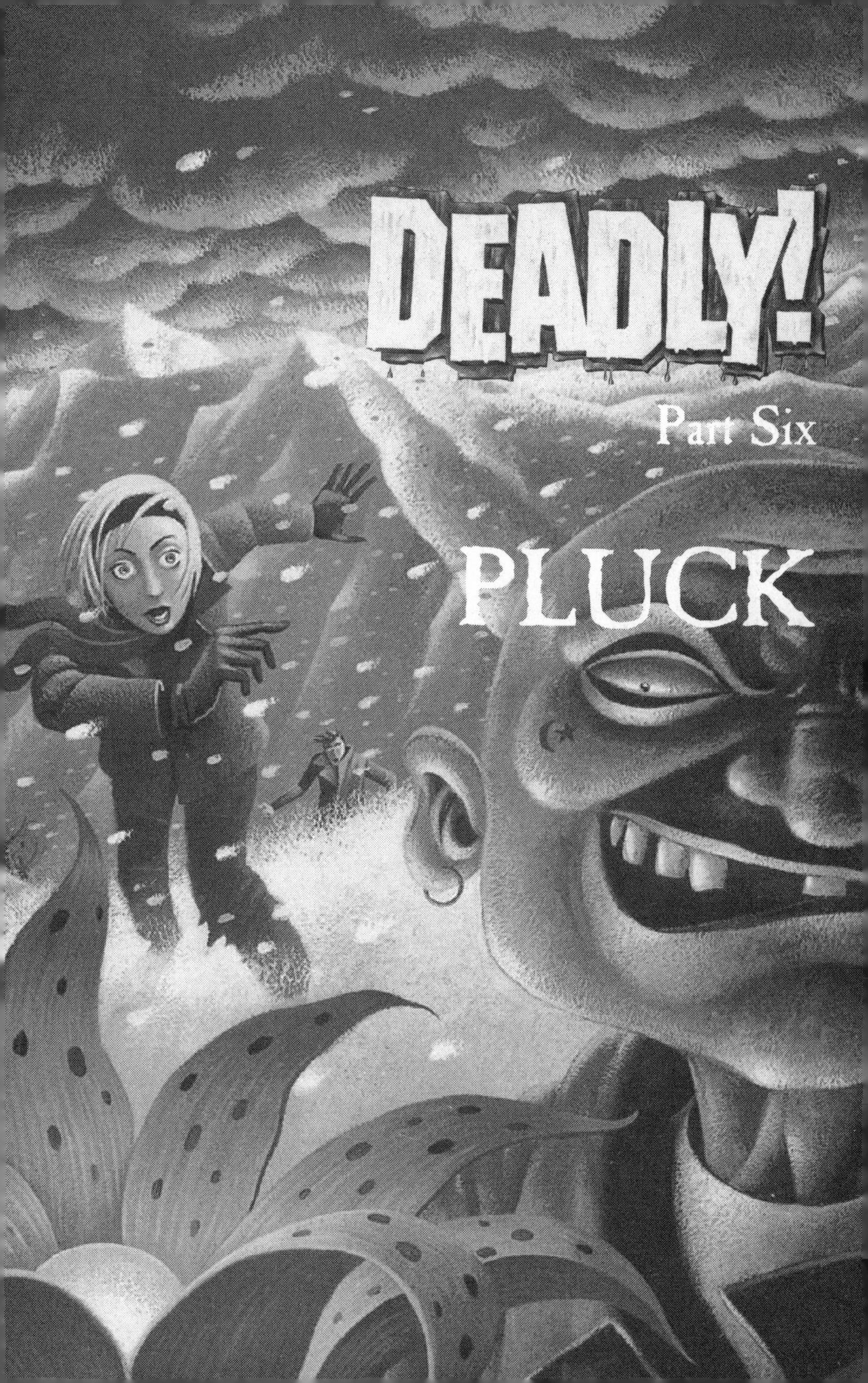
DEADLY!
Part Six
PLUCK

The HIGH VALLEY & the GREAT CHASM

CHASM

GOAT TRACK

FLOWERS

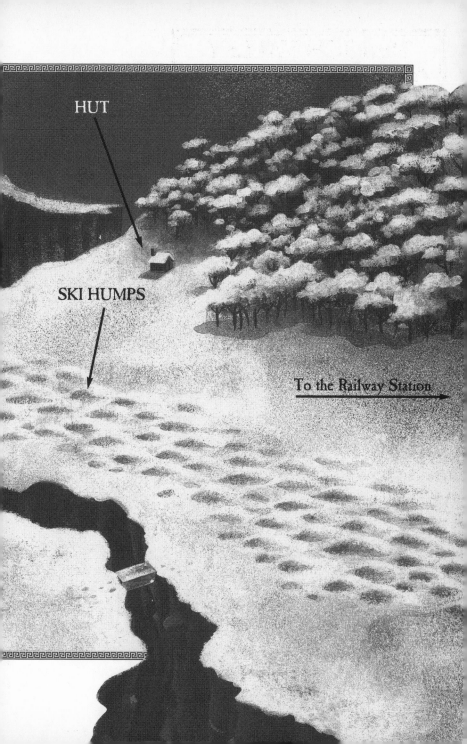

HUT

SKI HUMPS

To the Railway Station

SPROCKET

ONE

I stopped dead. Paralysed with shock.

So did the ageing Brats – Beanie, Scowler and Reptile. I was their prisoner, but for the moment they weren't interested in me. The sight of the snowboard rider standing there in the High Valley had frozen them in their tracks.

Their brother, the evil Pooper Scooper, let out a strangled cry. It echoed down the slope to where my friends Con Rod, Purple Cloud, Amy and Mrs Tunks-Livingstone were struggling towards us, coming to save me from certain death. Behind them came the rest of the crazed family, pulling some sort of snow-covered box behind them.

But now I stared in amazement at the snowboard rider as she took off her goggles. She was at least one hundred years old. Wrinkles ran like crazy rivers in every direction across her face. Her bright, white hair was cut very short in a trendy fashion. Her eyes sparkled as she gazed at us.

The four old Brats looked as if they had seen a ghost. They all yelled out the same word at the same time.

'Mother.'

At the sound of that word a feverish heat swept through my body. My legs began to tremble. I felt as if my burning feet would melt the snow and send me sinking from view. I tried to speak but no words would come.

Their mother was . . .

My mother.

My dream had come true.

Dream? Was the whole thing a dream?

Like a sleeper trying not to wake up, I tried to keep the vision of this woman alive. I clung to her image, not wanting it to vanish. But she began to shimmer and fade as a million questions swarmed around in my tortured brain. Had I really swallowed a seed that could give eternal youth? Was it even now germinating inside my swollen stomach? Were these ageing warriors really my brothers and sisters?

As if from a long distance I peered at Reptile's wrinkled mouth and thinning hair. And Beanie's grey beard. And Scowler's angry red-lined eyes. Had they really gone from six to sixty in three days?

Was there really a girl called Amy whose mother had turned into a baby? Was Purple Cloud a middle-aged dream-hippy or a real person?

A vision of Con Rod and his weird mobile home drifted into my mind. Only to be replaced by a picture of me and Amy fleeing from hostile nudists. Floating down the river on the frozen corpse of . . .

My father.

The Germinator had been this dream-woman's husband. The man in the ice block was my dad.

It *was* a dream. It couldn't be true.

Loud voices rang in my head but the words had no meaning. I was unable to speak or listen. The figures in the snow around me gestured and jumped like living shadows. Then they began to fade. I blinked my eyes and tried to call them back. I didn't want to wake and find myself in the bedroom of a lonely foster home.

I wanted my dream-mother.

A hand fell on my shoulder.

A real hand.

I struggled to bring its owner into focus. It was one of the Brats. His words bored into my brain.

'He claims he's Randall,' said Beanie.

The wonderful old lady was staring deep into my eyes. She was not a character in a dream.

She was a dream come true.

Her lips trembled. A tear ran down her cheek. She was unable to speak. Words were not sufficient. She held out her arms.

'Randall,' she choked. 'My son.'

Every nerve in my body seemed to fire at once.

A wave of joy and happiness like I had never known before lifted me up and carried me forward.

'Mum,' I cried. 'Oh, Mum.' I rushed into her embrace. My search was over. She pulled my wet cheek against hers and held me tight. We just stood there hugging in silence. The cold chill of loneliness that had made my bones ache since before I could remember, seeped away into the snow.

My mother's arms were . . . like the walls of a solid house, like the keel of an unsinkable boat, like the blankets on a soft bed. For the first time in my life I felt safe. And loved.

My mother's arms were . . . a mother's arms. There was no other place to be. We stood there hugging each other. For minutes. For an hour. I couldn't say. But it wasn't long enough.

Finally we pulled apart. My mother's happy smile suddenly faded. She stared at my swollen stomach.

'Oh no,' she said in a shocked voice. 'Randall, you haven't?'

'Yes, he has,' said Beanie. 'He's swallowed a seed.'

We were surrounded. Not just by the Brats but by my whole new family. The older ones had caught up with us. The Tea Lady and Hairy Chest. The two I called Lobster Bottom and Jimi Hendrix. And all the rest of my ageing brothers and sisters. They had made their way up to our mountain valley.

And my friends were there as well. Amy and her mum Mrs Tunks-Livingstone, Con Rod, Purple

Cloud and dear old Matchbox, too. Amy and her mum were smiling. 'You've found your mum at last,' said Amy. 'Your journey is over.'

I was too filled with joy to remember that Amy was on her own journey. To find her father if he was still alive. And to re-unite him with her mother.

Mrs Tunks-Livingstone was now at least twenty-five years old. And growing older by the minute. She winked at me and I fleetingly wondered if she was recalling our kisses in the dark guard's van last night when she'd been a teenager.

Purple Cloud had watery eyes. She gave a little sniff. I wanted to give her a hug too but this wasn't the time. I knew that she was happy for me. And sad for herself because I didn't need her for a mother. I had found my real mum.

My mum beamed around, staring in happy amazement at each of her children. She didn't seem to mind that they had all grown old. 'I hoped it was you, Children,' she said quietly. 'You've come to your senses at last. You've given up the tea and let yourselves grow old gracefully.'

She ran to Beanie and peered into his eyes. Then she hugged him. 'I'd know you anywhere, Barnabus.'

Beanie hugged her back with tears in his eyes. 'Mother,' he said. 'Look at you, you're, you're ...' He couldn't seem to bring himself to say the word.

'Old,' she said. 'Yes, I'm old. And what's wrong with that?'

'Everything,' said Beanie. He held up the label from the skin-cream jar. 'In only a few years you've gone from beautiful to . . .' He couldn't bring himself to finish the sentence.

Mother moved among her elderly children, dragging me with her. She didn't want to let go of my hand. She went to each one in turn, giving them a hug and a kindly comment.

'Stanley, you look good without hair.'

'Hilda, are you still driving fast cars?'

Then she turned to the Melting Man. 'Silas, you look miserable. Come on, cheer up.'

She even had a friendly word for the Tea Lady and Hairy Chest. 'You seem to have looked after the others well, Agnes and Hubert,' she said.

There was a lot of mumbling and grumbling when she made that comment. Especially from the Brats.

'They made us into six-year-olds. That's not looking after us,' yelled Scowler.

'You were always hard to control, Stanley,' said my mother. Finally she came to the last of her children. 'Orson,' she said slowly. 'You told us that my baby died in the river. You were the only other one there. You dumped your own brother.'

'So what?' hissed Pooper Scooper. 'You were going to pass the secret of the seed on to him. Instead of me.'

Reptile was angry with her brother. 'Orson. You told us he drowned in the river with Father,' she yelled. 'You lied.'

'You shouldn't have done it,' said Beanie.

'You can't abandon your own kin,' said Lobster Bottom. 'That was unforgivable.'

'So was nicking off with the train,' added Jimi Hendrix.

The others were all staring at me in a different way now. I wasn't the intruder any more. I was their brother. But they were shocked out of their brains.

'Orson,' my mother said. 'You have a lot to answer for.'

'Rubbish,' snorted Pooper Scooper. 'You're old and decrepit. You're going to die of old age. So are we if we don't get more tea. We haven't come here to grow old like you. We came to see if there were any more tea plants up here in the mountains. We want to be young again. We're not going to die. Not like Gramps. Not like you.'

My mother smiled at him sadly. 'Life is a circle,' she said. 'We must return from where we started. Everyone has to make the whole journey. No one can stay young for ever.'

Pooper Scooper grew redder and redder in the face. He spat viciously into the snow. 'Bulldust,' he shouted. 'Old is ugly. Old is painful. Old is senseless.'

I stared at them both. Pooper Scooper's description of my mother was right. My mother was old. But it was he who was ugly. He who was full of pain. And he who had lost his senses.

A wave of anger suddenly overtook me. This

wicked brother of mine, now an old man, had dumped me at a police station when I was a baby. And told my family that I was dead.

'You stole my life,' I yelled.

Pooper Scooper ignored me and shouted at the others. 'Idiots, idiots, idiots. Father was going to pass the secret of germination on to him.' He pointed at me with a gloved hand.

'Because none of us could agree who should be the new Germinator,' said Scowler. 'We all accepted that.'

'Not me,' said Pooper Scooper. 'I was the smartest. I was the natural heir.'

He looked from face to face but no one gave him any support. They were on my side. I was family. For the first time in my life.

'I'm going to find more plants,' he spat. 'Who's coming?'

There was a long silence. Scowler and Hairy Chest shuffled their feet. 'No one,' said my mother. 'It's all over.' I could see that they wanted to go but Mother's words held them back.

'Suit yourselves,' shouted Pooper Scooper. He turned and began running towards a forest of snow-covered gum trees. I wanted to go too – my mother needed those tea plants.

But there was another reason. My blood began to boil. He was getting away. He had robbed me of thirteen years with my mother. He had sentenced me to a childhood of loneliness. There was no way he was going to get off so easily. Red clouds of rage swirled behind my eyeballs. It was time for a reckoning.

I began to run through the snow after him. Con Rod and Amy and some of the others started to follow me.

'Don't, don't,' came my mother's voice. 'It's between Orson and Randall. Let him go. Let them sort it out.'

Had she known the dark depths of Orson's soul she would never have let me go after him alone. But she was his mother too.

And she didn't know.

That he would kill.

For the bright blue seed that was about to burst from my tortured bowels.

AMY

TWO

I **squinted** into the early morning sunlight, trying to catch a glimpse of Sprocket among the trees.

Nothing.

I wanted to go after him so badly. We'd come so far together and the thought of him alone in a freezing forest with the murderous Pooper Scooper was more than I could bear.

I could see Con Rod and Purple Cloud felt the same way. So did Mum.

I took a few determined steps towards the trees. Then I saw old Mrs Sampson looking at me.

She shook her head again.

There was great sadness on her face, but great wisdom too. For three days I'd been trying to imagine what Dad's Other Woman would be like. I hadn't even got close.

I stopped moving forward and Purple Cloud squeezed my arm.

'Mrs Sampson's right, love,' she said. 'This is between Sprocket and Pooper Scooper. It's something Sprocket's got to do on his own. What *we've* got to do is get these old folk somewhere warm before we cop another blizzard.'

She was right.

In the distance, a bit further along the valley, I could see Mrs Sampson's hut, smoke fluttering from its chimney.

We were a wheezing and exhausted group as we stumbled across the snow. Reptile and Beanie and Scowler dragging the Germinator. Matchbox sitting on the ice block, too ancient to move. Me supporting the frail and trembling Tea Lady. Purple Cloud with her arm round the waist of the woman with the long grey hair. Mrs Sampson lovingly steering the stooped Hairy Chest. Mum lagging behind with Jimi Hendrix leaning on one shoulder and Lobster Bottom on the other. Con Rod giving the Melting Man a piggy-back.

'Not much further,' I said to the Tea Lady.

'Thank you, my dear,' she croaked. 'You're very kind.'

I didn't feel very kind.

I felt scared.

Scared of what might be happening to Sprocket.

Scared of what terrible things Mrs Sampson might tell me if I asked her about Dad.

Suddenly I decided it was better to know than not to.

'Mrs Sampson,' I said, the words hurting my throat even more than the bitter cold. 'Is my father here?'

Mrs Sampson didn't answer for what seemed like an ice age.

'Perhaps she didn't hear you, love,' murmured Purple Cloud.

'I heard you, Amy,' said Mrs Sampson gently. 'I was just deciding how to break the news to you.'

My insides gave a painful spasm.

'Your father arrived two days ago,' Mrs Sampson continued. 'He had finally realised that the plants are a menace, and he responded to my plea. He came to help me destroy the last of them.'

She pointed up at the highest mountain towering over the valley. Sheer wind-blasted snow-cliffs and looming jagged faces of black icy rock.

'The last plants are up there,' she said. 'Too high for me to reach. Your father set out to find them yesterday morning.' She hesitated and her voice dropped. 'I haven't seen him since.'

I stared up at the freezing mountain, wondering how a person could survive up there overnight. My hot tears, blurring it from sight, told me a person couldn't. Then I felt Purple Cloud's spare arm squeeze my shoulder.

'Try not to fret, love,' she said. 'He could be OK.'

'Try and think positive,' said Con Rod gently. 'You can't be sure he's carked it.'

I took a deep breath. They were right. And I didn't want Mum to know. Not till she was older. Not till we were sure.

I was glad she'd fallen behind. She wouldn't have heard any of this.

I glanced back.

And saw Mum standing there, sobbing, with Jimi Hendrix and Lobster Bottom staring at her with bemused concern.

'You reassure her,' said Purple Cloud as we hurried back to her. 'The rest of us'll take a breather.' She steered Jimi and Lobster back to the main group.

Mum saw me approaching and wiped her swollen red eyes on the sleeve of her purple and green jumper.

With a jolt I realised the tea must be wearing off faster. She'd aged several years since we'd got to the valley, and we couldn't have been there more than an hour. She didn't look too many years away from her real age now, though that could have been partly because her cheeks were all blotchy from crying.

I wasn't sure what to do. Even though she wasn't back to her real age, she was twice as old as me. Suddenly I wanted her to be my mum again, to hold me so I could cry some more about Dad.

But I could see she wasn't ready for that yet, so I forced those feelings back down.

'Don't fret, Mum,' I said softly, putting my arms round her. 'Dad'll be OK.'

'I'm not crying about Dad,' sobbed Mum.

I was confused, but relieved.

'What is it, then?' I said gently, reaching up and stroking her hair. 'You can tell me.'

'You'll think it's stupid,' sniffled Mum.

'No, I won't,' I said, and gave her another hug.

Mum held out her hands. 'Look,' she said.

I looked. I couldn't see what the problem was. They were perfectly normal hands for a twenty-five-year-old, and as she was thirty-four I would have thought she'd have been pleased.

'I'm getting old,' she said.

I stared at her. Near by, Sprocket's ancient brothers and sisters, some of them over eighty years old, were stumbling around poking pathetically in the snow,

371

desperately searching for tea plants to keep them alive for a while longer.

Suddenly I realised what Mum was anguished about.

It was the thing I'd been trying not to think about for the past day.

What if, once Mum got back to being thirty-four, her ageing didn't slow down to the normal rate? What if the tea had stuffed up her ageing process so completely, she ended up dead at ninety-three in two weeks time?

Desperately I tried to reassure her. 'That won't happen,' I tried to say. But I was so swamped with dread I couldn't get the words out.

Luckily I didn't have to.

That wasn't what she was worried about.

'I'm getting too old for you to look after me,' she sobbed, 'and that makes me very sad. You're the best mum I've ever had.'

I needed a moment to digest this.

'Thanks,' I whispered, and stroked her hair some more. Then I forced myself to stop worrying. I forced myself to look on the bright side.

My mum was growing up. She was nearly ready to be a mum again.

But first there was one more job I had to do.

Tell her about what might have happened to Dad.

I took a deep, painful, icy breath and opened my mouth to break the awful news.

SPROCKET

THREE

My breath was visible in the cold morning air as I panted up the snowy slope. I ran after my brother with a heart full of hate. Pooper Scooper was slow but he had a long start. He easily vanished into the trees.

I entered the forest and followed his footsteps. Snow began falling and the swirling flurries were quickly covering his prints. If I didn't hurry I would lose track of him. But my swollen stomach was slowing me down. I was like a pregnant wombat ploughing through the drifts.

I staggered on between the thick trees for about ten minutes. Then I stopped. Pooper Scooper's footprints had vanished.

Right at that moment, that very moment, I needed to go. I had to relieve myself. The seed was coming. My bloated belly ached like crazy. I had been through this before when Amy and I had hidden in the skin-cream factory. I knew what to expect.

373

I lurched towards a small hollow under a tree. I needed to poop out the seed. If there were no more plants growing up here in the mountains I would be able to plant it. And get tea for my mother. She was not going to die of old age. Not while I was in possession of a plant which could restore her youth.

I pulled down my jeans and underpants and squatted in the freezing snow. Great spasms rippled across my belly. The pressure was building up inside me. A huge force of gas was waiting to be released. But something was stopping it. And I knew what it was.

I groaned and moaned and tried to force the seed out.

There was no one to help me.

And the enemy was near by.

Something flitted in the corner of my eye. Someone was hiding behind a tree.

I sensed that it was Pooper Scooper. He was not going to let me poo in peace. No way. He knew what was going on. Only last night he had burned his own bum after shooting a seed into the furnace. Now he wanted my seed for himself. He wanted to stay young for ever.

I half stood from my squatting position, my jeans still down around my ankles. I bent over and stared through my legs. Everything was upside down. Even Pooper Scooper who was running menacingly towards me through the snow.

I moved my cold bottom around and lined him up

like a soldier sighting a tank with a bazooka. I pointed my rear end straight towards him and squeezed my stomach muscles. The pain was terrible. The gas had reached maximum pressure.

My backside trembled. I held my breath and took careful aim.

Pyee-ow.

The blue seed shot out of my rear end with the speed of a bullet. *Thunk*. It hit Pooper Scooper fair in the forehead and knocked him off his feet. He lay without moving. I had done it. I had stopped him. A soft groan came from his lips. Oh no. I had to stir myself. He was still alive even if he wasn't kicking. The seed lay near by in the snow.

I hastily started to pull up my pants as Pooper Scooper sat up and stared around, dazed. He focussed on me, his eyes swimming with hate. He touched his bruised forehead and then searched around with his eyes.

'Aha,' he yelled. 'Got it.'

With one swoop he snatched up the seed in his gloved hand and held it high in his clenched fist.

I wanted to race over and grab the seed but the awful pains in my belly stopped me from moving.

My heart sank. He had beaten me. He had what he wanted. The seed was his. He would take it off and grow more and more new plants. He would keep himself young for ever. There would be no tea for my mother. Or anyone else.

PLUCK

Suddenly my bursting bowels let go.
Phwow, blurt, blarp.
Just as before, in the skin-cream factory, blue gas billowed out of my bottom like steam from a kettle. A huge cloud formed behind me and hovered over the brilliant white snow.

It was very close to Pooper Scooper. He ploughed through the snow, leaving deep footmarks sometimes down to the depth of his knees.

The blue cloud followed. Uncanny. Unstoppable.

In a flash Pooper Scooper was engulfed. Completely swallowed by the cloud. I could hear him gasping and coughing inside it.

A large scorpion dropped from a tree and disappeared into the mist. Then a spider. And a centipede. Huge blue ants emerged from their hiding places in the cold ground. Blind white termites erupted by the million from rotting logs and crawled towards the seed. They swarmed towards Pooper Scooper and then vanished into the blue gas.

A scream erupted from inside the cloud. I gave a shiver and tried not to think about what was happening to my wicked brother.

Pooper Scooper must have realised that the cloud protected the seed from insects. The seed suddenly shot out of the cloud and flew overhead in a low curve. It landed a few metres from where I lay.

But he was too late to draw off the blue cloud. The gas had done its work. It began to fade just like it did the first time. All that was left was a huge blue pile of dead insects.

I knew what was coming. I had to move away. And quickly. I dragged myself over the snow and crouched behind a tree.

Three beetles rolled down the pile and began to swell. *Pop, pop, pop.* They exploded like three crackers going off at once. Blue bits of beetle spattered through the air.

Then the whole pile began to go off. With Pooper Scooper still on the inside. Insect parts rained into the sky and fluttered down. The nearby trees were coated in blue snow.

Pooper Scooper lay moaning and groaning in the middle of the popping pile. He staggered to his feet and tried to sweep a coating of blue body parts from his skin. Then he lurched into the forest like a tortured soul that had crawled from a brightly coloured grave. My hatred evaporated. He had been punished enough. He was alone and defeated.

And I had my mother.

As my stomach pains subsided I pulled my pants over my freezing backside and walked back to the edge of the forest. Far below I could just see some tiny figures. They were making their way slowly towards a distant cabin. I knew that it must be Amy, Con Rod and the others.

I thought I could see one of them waving to me.

I bet it was Mum.

I waved back with my closed fist. In my hand I had a gift which I knew she would not want to accept.

Somehow I had to make her take it.

A seed that could cheat death.

For ever.

FOUR

Mum took it pretty well, the news that Dad could be frozen to death on the icy peak above us.

She didn't say anything at first.

Just stared up at the distant black rock walls for a long time as we trudged through the snow.

Then she sighed.

'I reckon we'll have earned some happiness,' she said. 'Me and your father. If we get through this.'

My eyes filled with tears. I blinked them away before they could freeze, and gave her a hug.

Now I'd finished telling Mum the awful news about Dad, I'd just realised there was some good news too.

Dad hadn't left us to have an affair, he'd left us to try and right a wrong. He'd realised the plants were evil and that his attempts to germinate them were misguided. Helping Mrs Sampson destroy the remaining plants in the High Valley was his way of making amends. He hadn't left us for a love nest, he'd left us for a noble mission.

Excitedly I turned to tell Mum this.

Before I could, Sprocket came running towards us across the snow, panting and wild-eyed.

'Sprocket,' I yelled with delight and relief.

'Where's my mum?' he said. 'I've got to find her.'

I squinted around at the others. I could see Scowler and Reptile and their ancient brothers and sisters poking in the snow with twigs, but I couldn't see Mrs Sampson.

'She's over here,' said a low, sneering voice behind us.

We spun round.

Pooper Scooper, still a scowling brute in his fifties, hate-lines etched into his face, muscles knotted like a hangman's rope, had one brawny arm round Mrs Sampson's throat and with the other hand was holding an ancient flare gun to her head.

He had blue insect parts all over him.

'The seed,' he rasped, glaring at Sprocket. 'Give it.'

Sprocket stood rigid with horror, his hand in his pocket.

'Don't give him anything,' said Mrs Sampson

softly, her face clouded with sadness. She sighed a
ragged, mournful sigh. 'Oh, Orson, son, what
happened to you? You were always an angry one, but
never like this.'

'The seed,' repeated Pooper Scooper, cocking the
hammer on the gun.

'You hurt her,' shouted Sprocket, 'and I'll do you.'

'So will I,' yelled Mum.

Con Rod and Purple Cloud hurried over. 'Flamin''
mongrel,' said Con Rod. 'Come over here and take
on someone your own age. Approximately.'

'Randall,' said Mrs Sampson, so calmly it was
almost as if she didn't have a psychopathic son
half-strangling her. 'Give me the seed.'

Sprocket stepped forward unwillingly.

'It's to keep you alive, Mum,' he said. 'So we can be
together.'

'Please,' said Mrs Sampson, holding out her hand.

Sprocket placed the round blue seed into her hand.

Pooper Scooper released his grip to grab the seed,
but before he could, Mrs Sampson placed her fingers
over the end of the gun barrel and pushed it away
from her head. She turned and looked Pooper
Scooper square in the face.

'We're old, son,' she said gently. 'We're old and it's
nearly our time to die. Accept it.'

'Gimme,' rasped Pooper Scooper, aiming the gun
between her eyes.

'I'm not scared of you, Orson,' she replied sadly.

'And that old mountain rescue gun has been getting damp in my hut for years. It probably doesn't even work.'

Pooper Scooper's finger tightened on the trigger. Sprocket tensed, about to leap. Suddenly Pooper Scooper pointed the gun up into the air and fired it.

A flame leaped out of the barrel and a loud explosion echoed through the mountains. A pink flare burst above our heads, brilliant for a moment, then quickly fading to nothing.

'Now,' hissed Pooper Scooper as he rammed another flare cartridge into the gun. 'The seed.'

'I haven't got it,' said his mother quietly. 'I put it in the gun barrel.'

Pooper Scooper stared at her and then at the barrel.

His furious, anguished roar was so loud it blotted out the gun noise that was still echoing through the peaks. I saw why the anguished yell was so loud. It was coming from Sprocket's mouth too, and the mouths of all his brothers and sisters.

Their last seed was destroyed.

Then another noise started. A deep rumbling noise a hundred times louder than the sounds we puny humans had been making. I looked up and what I saw stopped my heart.

The side of the mountain was falling towards us.

A great wall of white was sliding and buckling and tumbling, breaking into huge clumps, disappearing into a billowing white mist, but judging from the terrible sound that got louder and louder, still coming straight for us.

'Avalanche,' someone screamed.

We turned and ran.

The swirling snow-mist was on us already and as I grabbed Mum and dragged her away from the thundering white wall, I caught a glimpse of Sprocket and Con Rod and Purple Cloud doing the same with Mrs Sampson and the Tea Lady.

Mum and I ran till my lungs were cramped with fear and cold.

All the time the noise got louder.

Then Mum slipped and sprawled on the ground. I grabbed her and tried to drag her to her feet but she was too heavy and I went sprawling myself and suddenly snow was all over me and darkness was pressing in.

The last thought I had was, I'm too young for this.

Too young to die.

Too young to be a parent.

Too young to do this on my own.

That was the last thought I had before the noise stopped.

Suddenly there was complete silence. For a moment I thought it was because I was dead. Then I realised I wasn't and pushed frantically at the snow over my head and daylight appeared.

I stood up.

Next to me Mum was doing the same, brushing snow off her hair. And near by, Sprocket and Con Rod and Purple Cloud and Mrs Sampson were helping each other to their feet.

I could see other members of the ancient family struggling out of the snow, several of them complaining about how avalanches weren't good for their arthritis. But it wasn't them I found myself staring at. It was the figure limping slowly towards me through the last of the settling snow-mist.

A familiar figure in an anorak with leather patches on the elbows.

I stared, hope and disbelief starting their own avalanche inside me.

'Dad,' I screamed, and hurled myself towards him.

I knew there were probably such things as snow mirages, but I didn't care. And when I reached him and flung my arms round him and pressed my face into his chest, I knew he wasn't a mirage.

Mirages don't smell like dads. Not dads who haven't had a shower for three days.

'Princess,' he said, 'Thank God you're all right.'

I opened my mouth to tell him Mum was too, then closed it again. I needed him to myself, just for a minute.

'I thought it looked like you,' he was saying, 'but I couldn't believe it. What are you doing here, Princess?'

I didn't answer. I just hugged him, my body trembling with happiness.

Then I realised everyone was staring. Mum, Sprocket, Con Rod, Purple Cloud, the old folk, everyone.

'Drew,' gasped Mum. 'What are you doing here?'

I waited for him to reply, desperately hoping it would be a convincing answer that didn't include any references to mountain-hut love nests.

But before Dad could speak, a very strange thing started to happen.

I started to have a powerful feeling that I should go up the mountain. That I should walk away from the dad I'd only just discovered was alive and run up the mountain. My brain was hurting and the only way I could stop it was to fling myself up the mountain.

I struggled to shake off the awful feeling, to ignore the familiar perfume that was pricking at my nostrils. Everyone else could smell it too, I could tell. Rheumy eyes were starting to open wide and ancient feet were starting to shuffle.

Dad held me tight and I saw his eyes dart anxiously towards the peak.

'Oh no,' he said. 'It's starting.'

'What?' I said, struggling to get away from him.

'I found a crop of plants up near the peak,' he said, gripping me tighter. 'They've just started seeding. I couldn't get to them to destroy them. That's what I was coming down to warn you all about. Before the avalanche gave me a ride. Here, sniff this.'

From his pocket he took a lump of yellowy-brown fungus and crushed it under my nose. I sniffed. It smelt of new-mown grass.

Suddenly the craving stopped. I didn't want to go up the mountain any more. I sagged against Dad weakly.

'What is that?' I croaked.

'In nature,' said Dad, sniffing the fungus hard and pulling more lumps from his pocket, 'toxic plants often have something growing near them that acts as an antidote. Like stinging nettles and dock leaves. Mrs Sampson told me about this.'

I saw that Sprocket's mother was sniffing her own lump of fungus, and trying to give some to her elderly children. They were pushing it away, eyes on the mountain peak.

I grabbed the extra fungus from Dad and started passing it out to Con Rod and Purple Cloud and Mum. Except before I could get to Mum, Dad stepped over to her. I decided to let them have their reunion in private.

Sprocket had his back to me, staring at the huge crevasse that had been torn open by the avalanche along the base of the mountain.

'Here,' I said, holding some crushed fungus under his nose.

He pushed my hand away. He didn't even look at me. But I was looking at him. I could see the expression on his face.

It was the expression of a boy who knew there was still something that could keep his mother alive, and who was going to get to it, even if it killed him.

SPROCKET

FIVE

Amy gasped as I pushed the fungus from her hand. What was she thinking of, sticking bits of toadstool up my nostrils? Whatever it was I had enough thoughts of my own to cope with.

My mother was over one hundred years old. I had only just met her. I wanted more years than she had left in front of her. I had to find another seed and grow more tea.

She was determined to let nature take its course.

In more ways than one.

Nearby was a block of ice. And inside was the body of the dead Germinator. Mum wanted to put him to rest. After all, he was her husband.

And Pooper Scooper's father.

And Lobster Bottom's father.

And the Tea Lady's father and Hairy Chest's father . . .

And . . .

My father.

An incredible wave of sadness swept over me as I stared at his stiff, cold face. He had died saving me from the swollen river. I would never know him. And he would never know me.

We had been dragging him all over the place. We had floated up the flooded Cool Room on him. We had used him as a boat and paddled him down the river. We had pulled him way up here into the mountains. His own children had kept him frozen so that they could bring him back to life and find out how to germinate . . .

'Tea plants,' shrieked a desperate voice. It was Amy. 'Sprocket,' she yelled. 'Sniff this stuff. Quick.'

What was she going on about? Something was happening. I couldn't figure it out. A sudden calm had fallen over the whole mountain valley. The snow seemed whiter. The chasm at the bottom of the slope below appeared deeper. The cliff on the other side towered impossibly high. And the air was filled with . . .

The most beautiful scent in the world. I had smelled it before when the plant had flowered by the side of the road. And on the train on the way up to the Hidden Valley. But it hadn't been as strong then. This was fantastic. Wicked.

The others were enjoying it too. Lobster Bottom, Jimi Hendrix, Hairy Chest and the rest of the family including Scowler, Beanie and Reptile were looking at the mountain peak and sniffing. Their eyes were wide and staring. Like hypnotised chickens they took lurching steps down the slope towards the foot of the cliff face. And the chasm that lay before it.

But not Con Rod and Purple Cloud. They were holding the crushed fungus under their noses. So were my mother and Amy. They were alarmed. For us.

I heard my mother's voice. It seemed far, far away as if she was at the other end of a long tunnel. She was speaking to Amy's dad. 'The last plants,' she said. 'You couldn't get to them to destroy them.' Her voice began to fade inside my head. The last thing I remember her saying was, 'Save my boy. Save Randall.'

I took a deep breath, pulling the wondrous perfume deep into my lungs.

'Chocolate Magnum,' I said. It was my favourite food. But this was better. My lips began to drool. Somewhere up on the mountain was the mother of all Magnums. Sweeter, bigger, juicier. It made every nerve in my body tingle. I trembled with delight. My feet took me unknowingly towards the prize.

Scowler, Beanie and Reptile were lurching forward with me. So were the other ancients. They were all seeing wonderful visions.

'Hamburger,' said Beanie. He licked his lips hungrily.

'Apple pie,' shouted Reptile.

'Potato chips,' groaned Scowler.

'Earl Grey,' slurped the Tea Lady.

Every one of us was imagining our favourite food. We were being called to the mountain top by false hungers. Our own appetites were so strong that we could not resist. The ageing Jimi Hendrix was even mumbling for brussels sprouts.

Suddenly I fell forward on my face. Someone had tripped me. It was Purple Cloud. She held the life-saving fungus under her nose with one hand and had the other wrapped around my ankle.

'Sprocket, darling,' she yelled. 'That scent is bad for the soul. Fight it.' Her voice came to me from far off like the sound of a distant sailor calling through the fog.

The perfume seemed to give me the power of a hundred men. I sprang to my feet and shoved her aside as if she was no more than a feather. I turned towards the mountain and strode forward. I was out of my mind – not knowing what I was doing.

In no time I was about a hundred metres down the slope. Nothing could stop me now. Nothing except . . .

My mother . . .

Hurtling down the slope behind me. Riding like the expert snowboarder she had been in her recent youth.

Riding without a snowboard.

She was standing unsteadily on my father's icy coffin. With one hand she clung to a snow-covered rope. With the other she grasped the fungus. She was red in the face from holding her breath. She was bringing me the fungus that could stop the smell of the plants.

And she was hurtling down the slope on the top of her dead husband.

Amazing.

But, but. Why wasn't she stopping? She was about to crash into me. I was going to be mowed down like a sparrow on a train track.

At the last second Mum flew up the side of a mound of snow and became airborne. The ice block went one way and she went the other. The icy coffin dived down into the snow and stopped like a plane that had tipped up on landing.

My mother plunged down towards me. She crashed into my shoulders and sent me reeling backwards. Before I could move she crawled onto my chest with a pained expression on her face. The fall must have hurt her elderly body but she found enough strength to shove the fungus under my nose. I grabbed her wrist and held her gloved hand away. Nothing, not even my dear mother was going to keep me from the mountain.

Suddenly, far in the back of my mind, a small grain of sense called to me. A tiny voice from within spoke in only a whisper. 'Don't be stupid,' it said. 'Your mother and Purple Cloud care for you. Go back, go back, go back.'

But there was another voice. A more powerful voice. It was saying, 'Breathe deeply. Smell. Taste me. Take me. Eat me.'

I stood there on the cold mountainside like a pin between two magnets. First pulled one way. And then the other.

The plants were calling, calling, calling.

The chasm was about two metres across and hundreds deep. My elderly brothers and sisters were still stumbling towards the chasm mumbling about food as they went. They would never be able to jump that far. Especially in those old bodies. They lurched down the snow-covered hill towards the gorge. They were completely in the power of the plants' aroma.

I was being held back. Sense began to seep into my crazy brain. The image of Purple Cloud and my mother was faint and far off. But it was overcoming the power of the plants. I took the fungus from my mother's outstretched hand and held it under my nose.

Immediately the power of the scent was gone. The world became normal. I looked into my mother's eyes gratefully. She had saved me.

But who would save her?

She would soon die of old age. It wasn't fair. It wasn't right. We had only just found each other. We needed time together. Someone had to save her. And that someone was me. There was only one way. I had to get to the tea plants first. I pushed my mother aside and quickly threw the fungus to the ground. I breathed deeply once more. I drew the over-powering scent down deep into my lungs. It was beautiful beyond belief.

Perfume. I had smelled it before. Only yesterday. The sweet aroma of Mrs Tunks-Livingstone's hair when she was just sixteen. Her image filled my crazed mind. A vision of the most gorgeous girl in the world suddenly beckoned me. In my head I saw her dressed in the tank top, a diamond in her navel and green lipstick on her soft lips.

Suddenly my mother and Purple Cloud seemed ugly. The perfume distorted their images in my mind. Purple Cloud's face seemed to bloat and twist so that she resembled a witch. The wrinkles on my mum's face appeared to unite into a grotesque and monstrous snarl.

I jumped to my feet and crazily stumbled towards the ice coffin where it was angled into the snow.

'Mrs Tunks-Livingstone,' I whispered hoarsely. Here I come.'

Lobster Bottom and Jimi Hendrix were calling out names, too. So were all the others. Like lovesick dogs they followed the fatal scent.

'Kylie Minogue,' mumbled Beanie with vacant eyes.

'Ricky Martin,' gasped Reptile.

'Marilyn Monroe,' whispered Scowler.

'Ringo Starr,' crooned the Tea Lady.

The Melting Man was calling out for someone called Vera Lynn. Lobster Bottom was mumbling about Nicole Kidman.

Wonderful visions of the sixteen-year-old Mrs Tunks-Livingstone filled my head. Crazy fantasies took hold. I saw her standing on the mountain top with arms held out waiting for me. Her soft lips were . . .

Oh no. The others were far ahead. Scowler, Beanie and Reptile were approaching the chasm. And the rest of my ancient brothers and sisters were not far behind. They would get to Mrs Tunks-Livingstone before me. That's what my crazy mind thought, anyway.

I bent and grabbed the rope attached to the front of the ice coffin. It tore away in my hand. I tried to raise the ice but it was as heavy as a car. Normally I could never have budged it. But the scent gave me strength.

I bent down and lifted. I ignored the pains shooting up and down my spine and tried to block out the sight of my father's face. Gradually the front of the ice block began to move. I raised it about half a metre and pushed snow under it with my shoe. Slowly at first and then faster and faster it slid down the slope.

I just managed to scramble on top before the ice block sped down the hill out of control towards the chasm. Desperately I swept aside the soft snow coat looking for something to cling to. Yes. My father's frozen fingers were projecting out of the ice. I grabbed them and held on like crazy. Once before I'd used him as a boat on the river. Now he was my sled.

We flashed past the startled faces of my ancient brothers and sisters. They began to stagger even faster, desperately calling out the names of their fantasies.

Looking down towards the chasm I could see a patch of frozen snow humps. The ice block began to buck and jump wildly as it ploughed through them. Suddenly it became airborne. I was losing my grip. I was going to fall.

I clutched my father's fingers and stared at his face. Was he trying to tell me something? Could he save me? I wasn't interested. The power of the nudist tea flowers allowed no real emotion. I closed my eyes and held on for grim death.

Wham.

The ice block shot out over the chasm and hit the ledge on the other side. Then it slipped. About half a metre. The ice coffin had wedged itself across the yawning gap. The shock threw me to one side and I felt myself slipping down into the chasm. Something sharp caught my belt and saved me. I unhooked myself from Dad's bent frozen fingers and crawled to the other side.

I lay there winded while my ancient brothers and sisters swarmed towards the ice bridge. The Tea Lady and Hairy Chest were now in their eighties. They were getting left behind and didn't like it.

The scent of the plant had removed the last bit of common sense from our brains. We were not ourselves. We were desperate animals. The scent of the plant was calling for the strongest and fittest to eat the seeds. To carry them afar to new and fertile fields.

The mob tottered across the bridge, drawn to the mountain that called our befuddled brains.

I stared up the sheer cliff. It loomed over me, huge and impossible, covered in ice and snow. Was that a face far above? Was that a green smile? Her wonderful perfume called me forwards.

'Mrs Tunks-Livingstone,' I gasped. 'Wait for me.'

SIX

I stood rigid with horror as the frenzied old folk pushed and clawed their way up the steep mountain track, feeble arms flailing, haunted hollow eyes desperately searching for the distant plants high above them.

'Wait for us,' they yelled furiously at Sprocket and Scowler and Reptile and Beanie who were scrambling ahead of them up the mountain slope.

Their mother, fungus held under her nose, stood above the chasm on her husband's ice coffin, defeated, helpless, watching. The Germinator lay there, still and cold and sightless, while the sons and daughters he'd hoped would live for ever ignored him completely and moved closer and closer to plummeting to their deaths.

The morning sun must have thawed my brain, because suddenly I jerked into action. I set off as fast as I could down the slope towards the chasm. I had to get across and try and stop the frenzied old folk, or divert them somehow, or at least get them into an orderly queue.

'Stop,' I screamed across at them while I was still fifty metres away from the ice bridge. 'Stop pushing.' They ignored me, just like the Year Two kids had the time I'd been canteen monitor.

Purple Cloud and Con Rod and Matchbox must have had the same idea. They were panting down the slope next to me. None of us was moving very fast. Matchbox was too old and the snow was too deep and none of us humans could use both our arms for balance because we were all holding fungus to our noses.

Then suddenly a figure dashed past us, sprinting and leaping through the snow, both arms pumping.

It was Mum.

She wasn't holding fungus to her nose. As she ran past I saw why.

She was gone, ga-ga, perfumed-out. Her eyes were locked on the distant plants like gun-sights in a video game. And I glimpsed something else in her eyes. The determination of a kid in her late twenties who was having a happy childhood at last and would do anything not to grow up.

Even climb a mountain of black frozen rocks with her bare hands.

Even slip and fall and die.

'Mum,' I screamed. 'Stop. Don't do it.'

She didn't even slow down.

I looked around frantically for Dad. He was hobbling after her, hampered by his avalanche limp, moving way too slow to catch her. Mum must have got away from him before he could get any fungus under her nose.

I stopped, scooped up a handful of snow and rubbed it and the fungus into a yellow paste. Begging my nose not to start running, I smeared the paste under my nostrils and across my chin.

Con Rod and Purple Cloud stopped and stared at me. I realised I probably looked like an Australian fast bowler, but there was no time to explain.

'Try and stop those oldies falling and killing

themselves,' I begged them. 'Chuck ice at them if you have to.'

Then I breathed in big lungfuls of cut-grass fumes and set off after Mum.

Now I could run with both arms, I sped through the snow like a sprinter at the Winter Olympics who was late for breakfast.

But Mum wasn't just fast, she was cunning. She wasn't going to risk being grabbed by Mrs Sampson on the Germinator bridge. She veered away to one side and ran straight at the chasm.

And leaped over it.

For a moment, when she hit the other side, she started sliding back and I though she was a goner. I tried to scream but I didn't have the breath. Mum scrambled and grabbed at a bush and dragged herself forward and started clambering up the side of the mountain.

I had no choice.

To keep up with her, I had to jump too.

I did it with my eyes closed.

As I hit the other side and started heaving myself up the icy black rocks, I thought of Mrs Newsome, the sports teacher at school. Mrs Newsome reckoned once that what I needed to improve my athletics performance was more school spirit. She was wrong. What I needed was a mother risking death.

Mum was about twenty metres above me, hands and feet moving up the rock face in quick frenzied movements. Sometimes one of her feet slipped, and a shower of stones and bits of ice bounced off my shoulders and head.

'Mum,' I yelled. 'Stop. Climb down and we'll get Dad to grow some more plants at home and you can stay young and I'll be your mum and let you watch "The Simpsons" all day.'

I'd have promised anything at that point, even Pokémon.

Mum didn't even glance down.

The evil perfume might have been making her cunning, but it was also making her stupid. Instead of doing what the others were doing, picking the way up the mountainside that had the least death-spots, her plant frenzy was making her take the shortest route regardless of the risks.

Straight up.

Peering through the frozen grit peppering my face, I could see that the steep ridge Mum was on was leading her to a dead end. A sheer shiny cliff-face dropping away into frozen mist.

Then I saw something else, over to the right of us. The figure of a man. He wasn't climbing straight up in a plant frenzy. He was zig-zagging his way along what looked like an old goat-track, picking his way carefully on thick knotty legs that were only half-covered by the ragged strips of cloth that had once been greasy jeans.

Pooper Scooper.

My gasp must have carried through the thin mountain air because he stopped and looked down at me.

What I saw made me almost forget to cling on to the rock. His face had mutated into a bloated misshapen leathery horror with huge dark eyes and a cylindrical snout with about twenty nostrils.

That's what I thought, anyway.

It was only after I'd stared at him in revulsion for about half a minute that I realised he was actually wearing a gas mask. An old-fashioned World War One gas mask. I guessed it was so the plant perfume wouldn't affect him.

By then it was too late.

He'd already kicked a big rock down towards me. Not a round boulder, but a jagged blade of a rock that had been splintered off the face of the mountain by vicious frosts.

I pressed myself into the ice and the rock shattered near my head and I felt a hot stab of pain in my cheek as a knife-edge shard of rock slashed me on its way past.

I felt blood running down my face and I hoped it wouldn't wash the fungus paste off. I hugged the ice until I dared look up.

Pooper Scooper had gone.

OK Amy, I thought. A plan. You need a plan.

I made a plan.

Stage One. Hug rock till trembling stops.

Stage Two. Get after Mum.

I started Stage One, but I didn't get very far because after about five seconds, directly above me, Mum started screaming.

I looked up. She'd reached the dead end of the ridge. And gone past it. She was hanging off the end of the ridge, legs kicking desperately in the air, trying to get a grip on the sheer shiny cliff face that fell away into misty nothing.

'Mum,' I yelled. 'Hang on.'

My frantic breathing burned my chest as I climbed up towards her, praying that Pooper Scooper wasn't waiting at the end of the ridge to fling me and Mum off.

I dragged myself to the edge of the ridge and grabbed the back of Mum's jumper and tried to pull her up. I couldn't do it. She was nearly fully grown now and she was too heavy. Her weight was dragging me along the slippery rock towards the brink.

'Hang on, Mum,' I shouted, and let go of her.

I could see her hands slowly sliding on the ice. I fumbled in my pockets and pulled out my Swiss Army knife and prised open the implement for opening bottles of wine.

Praying the ice layer on the rock was thick enough, I screwed the corkscrew into it as far as it would go. Then, gripping the knife with one hand, I grabbed Mum's jumper again with the other and pulled.

I wondered which would snap first, Swiss Army metal or my shoulder muscle.

Neither did. Slowly, painfully, I pulled Mum back up onto the ridge.

We both collapsed back onto a flat ledge and lay there, gasping and groaning. Well, I was. Even though she was completely exhausted, Mum was still trying to drag herself up towards the plants.

'Wobbly Bottom,' she was whispering. 'Button Head. Wind Machine. Princess Possum.'

With a stab that went right through me, I realised she was saying the nicknames Dad used to call me when I was a baby. That was the desire the plants were evoking in her perfume-fuddled brain.

Not for food or romantic fantasy.

For me.

I put my arms round her and hugged her tight. She must have got a whiff of my fungus paste, because suddenly her eyes cleared and she gazed at me with a look of love and concern.

I hadn't seen that look for days.

I wasn't sure I'd ever really seen it.

'Amy,' she whispered. 'Your poor face. It's bleeding.'

Then our eyes clouded, mine with tears and hers with evil perfume.

I blinked my tears away and saw that Mum was staring over my shoulder, up the mountainside. Her exhausted face was shining with crazed desire.

I saw what she was looking at.

On another ledge about a hundred metres up were smudges of bright green. I wiped my eyes dry and squinted and saw what they were.

Plants.

Tea plants.

Suddenly I lost it.

How dare you, I screamed silently at the plants. How dare you seduce people with the promise of eternal life and turn them into kid-neglecting zombies just so you can get your seeds into their bellies and have eternal life yourself.

I scanned the mountainside above me. Way over to the right I saw the hunched form of Pooper Scooper scuttling along a narrow track, following its winding route towards the plants. Over to the left his ancient brothers and sisters were doing the same on theirs. So, I saw, ahead of them, was Sprocket.

They were all further up the mountain than me, but I suddenly realised that if I climbed in a straight line I could get to the plants before them. So could Mum, but she was lying on her back exhausted, groping a feeble hand towards the plants and croaking things like 'Droopy Drawers' and 'Farty Pants'.

I gazed up at the distant ledge.

A powerful desire surged through me. More powerful even than when I'd smelled the plant perfume, before Dad had given me the fungus.

But this wasn't perfume that was drawing me up

the rock face now, giving me the strength to claw my way up towards the plants.

It was anger.

I wasn't going to eat the plants, I was going to destroy them.

SPROCKET

SEVEN

As I clawed my way desperately up the sheer, frozen cliff-face my crazy desire grew stronger. All I could think of was reaching the gorgeous teenage Mrs Tunks-Livingstone. She wasn't really there, of course. And anyway, even if she had been she was over twenty years old.

The teenager with the green lipstick was only a picture created in my mind by the powerful scent from the tea plants. All thought of my mother had been swamped by the incredible odour. I was like a boy drowning in his own dream.

And I couldn't wake up and see the real world.

Far below the feeble Scowler, Beanie and Reptile,

now well into their sixties, were trying to follow. Further back their even older brothers and sisters were desperately climbing. Every now and then a loud yell would fill the air as one of them slipped or lost their footing. By some miracle none of them fell. The sweet perfume of the tea plants drew them on and up. It drove them crazy with the false promise of eternal youth and imagined lovers.

Finally I reached the top of the cliff and found myself on a flat plateau of jagged white rocks. The longing for Mrs Tunks-Livingstone was suddenly replaced by an even stronger desire. Now only one image possessed my mind. Seeds. Tea seeds. Calling me. Calling everyone. 'Eat me, eat me, eat me.'

The seeds needed us to help them survive. They could only germinate in the guts of a human being. The plants promised life but what they really gave was living death.

At that moment something happened that changed everything. The gently falling snow turned into a blizzard. It swirled around my face biting and nipping at my hands. Each snow-drop seemed armed with its own set of tiny teeth.

I couldn't see through the swirling eddies. The valley beneath disappeared. The scent grew fainter in the strong wind. Every now and then a flurry would be followed by a lull. Then the perfume would grow stronger and I would once again be desperately driven on.

I staggered forward. My feet sank deep into the soft snow. At times I plunged down to my knees and even my waist. All feeling disappeared from my toes and fingers. A snowy beard gathered around my lips and chin. Father Christmas eyebrows hooded my stinging eyes.

The cold air seared my lungs and filled my chest with pain. At times when the scent of the plants grew fainter a small voice tried to speak to me. 'Go back,' it said. 'You are dying. Go back to your mother.'

'Shut up,' I yelled at the voice of reason.

I struggled on through the blinding snowstorm, growing weaker and weaker but unable to resist the call of the plants. Just as my strength was about to fail, I found a track. Footprints in the snow. Two sets – one large and one small.

The sight of the footprints filled me with fury. Someone was ahead. Someone was going to reach the plants before me. This person would take all the seeds, leaving me with nothing. That's how it seemed to my crazed mind, anyhow. I tried to run but fell and stumbled.

The snowstorm stopped as suddenly as it came. The mountaintop was bathed in sunlight. A clear cold sky stretched blue over the valleys and peaks. A wonderland of cold beauty. But I saw none of that. I was not in heaven. I was in hell. My mind was not my own. And my body was cold and weak.

A terrible squealing, squeaking noise seemed to fill

the air. Somewhere ahead someone, something, was in terrible agony. It sounded like the cry of tortured pigs. A litter of tiny voices screamed in protest.

At what?

'Save us, save us,' said a voice in my head. A voice wafting on the scent which filled the mountain air.

'I'm coming, I'm coming,' I cried to the unseen callers.

Murder was happening. Just ahead. I climbed over a snowdrift and there in the sunlight was the killer.

Amy.

She had beaten me up the mountain and was killing the plants. She stood on the edge of the yawning cliff. It swept down not just to the valley but deeper into the chasm where my father's ice bridge breached the terrible depths. A jagged bottomless cavern with jaws of rock and a mouth with a ghastly appetite.

And into these jaws nudist tea plants tumbled and fell. One after another they dropped. Their blue seeds made a blurred trail like the tail of a jet stream.

Amy was throwing herself onto the plants and furiously trying to pull them up. She couldn't get the roots out of the frozen ground but the stems were breaking off at ground level. Like hunted animals the plants weaved and ducked trying to avoid her furious grasp.

'Leave my mother alone,' she screamed. 'Leave Sprocket alone.' Tears were streaming down her face as she grabbed the plants of death and flung them into the abyss.

Not far away a figure was creeping towards her. A man wearing a gas mask. He was going to get the plants before me. It could only be one person – Pooper Scooper.

The plants were calling both of us to fight a deadly duel. The fittest would win and swallow a seed. But first Amy would have to be stopped.

Inside my fevered brain I heard the call. 'Live for ever, Sprocket. Make your mother young again. Save her. Save us. Save yourself.'

I lurched forward. Red fury possessed me. I muttered to myself. 'Stop Amy. Save the seeds.'

By now there were only four plants left. Pooper Scooper was nearly upon her. With his help I could save the plants. 'Stop her,' I screeched, 'Stop her.'

Amy looked up briefly and then snapped off three of the remaining four plants. She pitched them over the edge but one fell only a metre or so and wedged itself on a rock. Amy dropped down onto her stomach and began swiping wildly, trying to dislodge it so it would fall into the chasm.

Pooper Scooper fell to the frozen ground and began chipping around the last plant with an ice pick. He was trying to save it. He wanted to get it out, roots at all.

Amy flayed her arms wildly.

Pooper Scooper dug furiously.

I ran crazily towards them. Stop Amy. Defeat Pooper Scooper, and then the plants would be mine.

'Aha,' yelled Pooper Scooper as he levered the nudist tea plant and its icy root ball out of the earth. The plant screeched and squealed inside my head. Then it closed its petals protectively around the blue seed which grew in the middle of its only flower.

At the same moment Amy managed to dislodge the stuck plant from the cliff face and send it tumbling after the others. I gave a scream of misery. Amy turned, saw the intact plant in the hands of Pooper Scooper and dived on him.

Together they rolled towards the edge of the ravine, struggling and grunting over the prize. I was seized with panic. They were going to fall. And take the last plant with them.

I stumbled forwards. Nothing entered my mind but the call of the plant. I reached out and – yes, yes, yes. I snatched it from Pooper Scooper's gloved hand. Then I turned away and raised a victory cry that echoed across the valley. The plant was mine. And so was eternal youth. My mother could be young again. The flower seemed to give a satisfied little murmur.

Pooper Scooper and Amy continued to struggle on the very edge of the precipice.

'Sprocket,' Amy screamed. 'Help. Please help.'

Her cry was but a tiny whisper in the back of my mind. The call of the plant was a roar in my ears.

Pooper Scooper's eyes glared out through his gas

mask. His face was a vision of hate. He had Amy against the edge of the cliff. She was helpless. His fingers grasped her throat. She was choking. He was going to throw her to her death. Somewhere, somehow, the tiny whisper inside my brain grew louder.

I could see Amy's lips moving. Silently forming words with the last of her strength. 'Help me, Sprocket.'

For just a second I remembered who she was and what she meant to me. A daggy girl who had been my friend through terrible times. A mate. A comrade. She had given me her jeans in exchange for my dress. She had listened to me whingeing about my mother with great kindness even though her own father was missing. In the darkness of the nudist colony she and her Swiss Army knife had always been there. Even now she was trying to save me from the plants. At the cost of her own life.

I suddenly realised something, there on the top of the mountain, in the middle of that terrible conflict. Right through the whole journey all I had thought about was me. While Amy had always worried about us. Me and my missing mother. Me and my sad life in the orphanage. It was all I ever thought about.

But Amy. She had saved the baby – who had turned out to be her own mother. And she had agreed to help me find my mother. But I had never said one single word about her missing father. Not one.

She sure was some girl.

And now this monster was trying to kill her. I was filled with shame and rage. I couldn't let her die. There was only one thing that would release Pooper Scooper's grip of steel. Only one thing that meant more to him than life itself. I held the disgusting plant high above my head. My fingers trembled around its frozen root ball.

I pitched it into the air over Pooper Scooper's head. Not too high. Not too low. Just enough to make him leap.

Pooper Scooper released his hold on Amy's throat. He jumped up and backwards like an ancient footballer taking a mark. He seemed frozen in mid-air as his hands safely took the plant. Then he fell to the ground with a yell of triumph. A yell that turned to a scream as he tottered backwards. His feet scrabbled to gain a grip on the icy surface. Like a demon dancing on hot coals he fought for a foothold. And failed. Down he went, tumbling and turning into the gaping jaws of the crevasse below.

'Suffer,' I screamed into the chasm.

Then, suddenly, the crazy madness that had possessed me left. The last plant had gone. The perfume of terror vanished. Only clean, clear mountain air filled my nostrils. I realised what I had done.

'I killed him,' I whispered hoarsely.

'No,' gasped Amy. 'You saved me.'

She got to her knees, exhausted. I dropped down in front of her and put my arms around her. The fog from our breath mingled in the cold air.

Holding Amy wasn't like being in Mrs Tunks-Livingstone's arms that time in the train. Or on the island when we tried to keep the baby warm. This was different.

'What are you doing?' said Amy in an embarrassed voice.

'Giving you a hug,' I said.

For once Amy couldn't think of anything to say.

So she just hugged me back.

EIGHT

I should have spotted the trouble brewing. I should have seen it on Scowler's face. The bitterness that twisted his wrinkled mouth as he stood at the bottom of the mountain waiting for the rest of us.

But I was thinking about other things. Worrying that Mum was OK. As she'd come down the mountainside and across the Germinator bridge she'd been silent and thoughtful. She'd looked sad, and I knew how she felt. It could take a bit of getting used to, accepting you were never going to be eleven again.

Then Scowler grabbed me and I saw the fury burning under his sagging eyelids.

'You've killed our brother and condemned us to death,' he shouted, gripping my arm with surprising strength for someone nearly seventy. 'You've destroyed our only chance of living. How does that make you feel?'

It made me feel terrible. I looked at his ancient face, his watery eyes bulging, his fury turning to panic, and I realised he was right. In my desperation to save Mum and Sprocket from the plants, I'd condemned ten other people to death.

'Does it make you feel good?' yelled Scowler, jabbing me hard in the chest with his bony fingers.

I didn't know what to say. It made me feel sick. I felt as though I'd be haunted by the guilt of it for the rest of my life.

'Are you satisfied?' shouted Scowler, jabbing me again.

I staggered backwards and my feet slipped from under me and I thumped down onto the hard-packed snow.

Before I could get to my feet, there was a blur at my shoulder and someone stepped forward and thrust their face close to Scowler's.

It was Mum.

'Listen, Buster,' she said. 'I sympathise with your predicament, but if you touch this young lady again, I'll forget you're a senior citizen and hang you from the top of that mountain by your short and curlies.'

'Yeah?' snarled Scowler. 'And who might you be?'

'Her mother,' said Mum, putting her arm round me.

Even though a freezing wind was blowing down the valley, I glowed. Mum was back. It was the happiest moment of my life.

I gazed up at her loving face and saw she'd finally returned to her right age. But something was different. As she winked at me with a familiar thirty-four-year-old eyelid, I noticed something was missing from her face. The anger and stress lines that had lived at the corners of her eyes and mouth for as long as I could remember.

Gone.

Vanished.

Gazing down at me was the relaxed face of a thirty-four-year-old who'd had a happy childhood.

Dad limped up to us and brushed the snow off my orange jumper and gave Scowler a stern look. 'Everything my wife has said goes for me too,' he announced.

Scowler wasn't cowed.

He started to go for me again. Out of the corner of my eye I saw Con Rod and Sprocket tensing themselves to leap forward, but before they could, Beanie and Reptile grabbed him.

'Leave it, Stanley,' said Beanie to Scowler. 'Hurting the youngster isn't going to help us.'

'It's over,' said Reptile quietly. 'We might as well accept it.'

'No,' yelled Scowler. 'I won't accept it. For Pete's sake, we're not talking about going to bed early, we're talking about dying. I'm not going to accept that, why should I?'

Beanie and Reptile didn't know what to say. They frowned, crinkling their bushy grey eyebrows. I could see they were thinking that Scowler had a point.

The other old folk thought so, too. The Tea Lady and Hairy Chest and the others started murmuring in low anguished voices.

I looked at their poor wrinkled faces, angry and scared and bewildered. The awful guilt swept through me again. Scowler was right, I'd condemned them all to death.

'Why?' Scowler yelled again, his voice cracking and his eyes filling with tears. 'Why should I accept my own death?'

Their mother stepped into the centre of the group. She took a deep breath, and it was almost as if she was drawing strength into her ancient body from the mighty mountains around us.

'Because you have to, son,' Mrs Sampson said quietly to Scowler. 'We all have to. Living things grow old and die. It's as simple as that.'

'No,' spat Scowler. 'It's not as simple as that. The plant gave us eternal life.'

Mrs Sampson shook her wizened head sadly. 'The plant didn't give you anything,' she said. 'The plant was only interested in itself. Your father and I were wrong to place you lovely children in its power. Yes, we all had some extra years, but they were scared, unhappy years. Scurrying around with no clothes on getting ulcers and sunburn. That isn't my idea of eternal life.'

While she was speaking, Scowler's eyes were slowly growing wider. I gripped Mum and Dad's hands tighter, fearing he was going to explode with violent anger.

'Show me one good thing the plant has given us,' said Mrs Sampson. She looked at Sprocket with loving eyes. 'Something even half as wonderful as what I've been given today.'

Scowler raised his arm and pointed beyond the circle of shadowy figures standing around us. His eyes were wide with amazement.

We turned and looked.

My eyes went wide with amazement too.

Amazement and terror.

'Holy underdaks,' croaked Con Rod.

Dragging itself up over the rim of the chasm was the most incredible thing I'd ever seen, even in the three days since I'd met Sprocket.

'What is it?' yelped Purple Cloud.

It was a snowman.

But not a snowman like I'd seen on Christmas cards. Not a smooth white snowman with a smiley face and a carrot nose.

The one hauling itself to its feet at the edge of the chasm and lumbering towards us was ragged with icicles and streaked with dirty ice. Its eyes were black holes and its mouth was a green smear of hatred.

As it thudded through the snow towards us, I started to shiver, and not because of the icy wind cutting through my jumper. I'd recognised the boots on the snowman's feet.

So had Sprocket.

'Pooper Scooper,' he gasped.

'Orson,' squeaked Beanie. The rest of the ancient family gasped and held on to each other.

The snowman suddenly stopped in mid-stride.

Its foul frozen body started to shudder, as if something violent was happening inside the frozen crust. I imagined rage building up, rage that would eventually want to find a target.

Then I noticed something about the green mouth. In one corner was a half-chewed leaf.

Pooper Scooper must have hung onto the last plant. He must have fallen into deep snow at the bottom of the chasm. He must have eaten the plant and made himself young enough to climb out.

How much had he eaten, I wondered. What age would he end up?

The shuddering stopped.

We all stood there for ages, still stunned by what we were seeing. We didn't run. Most of us couldn't, and anyway there was no point. Pooper Scooper had come back from the dead. We all knew we couldn't get away from someone who could do that.

After a long while, Pooper Scooper still hadn't moved. His black eye-holes hadn't shifted their malevolent frozen glare from us.

Finally Beanie spoke. 'Or-Orson,' he stammered. 'Is that you?'

Pooper Scooper didn't reply. Scowler gave Beanie a nudge, and Beanie crept fearfully across the snow to the icy hulk of his brother.

'Or-Orson,' he stammered again. 'Don't be angry. You can be the head of the family. You can take over from Father like you always wanted to.'

As Beanie spoke, he reached up with a trembling hand and tried to grab the half-chewed leaf from the corner of Pooper Scooper's mouth. He got a grip on it and pulled.

Pooper Scooper's head came off.

Beanie screamed and dropped the head. It shattered against his boot. I stared at the fragments of frozen crust on the snow, trying to make sense of what I was seeing.

The head was hollow.

Everyone gasped. Con Rod swore in amazement.

Nobody could make their mouths work to ask the burning question.

Where was Pooper Scooper?

We found out seconds later.

Mrs Sampson strode forward and swung her snowboard with all her might against the snowman's body. The filthy frozen torso and legs shattered into a thousand ice fragments and fell in a pile onto Pooper Scooper's boots.

She rummaged in the pile and pulled out various items of Pooper Scooper's clothing. Then she found what she was looking for. She straightened up and held it out to her ancient children.

'Is this the eternal life you want?' she demanded.

In her hand was a clear block of ice about the size of one of those plastic domes you shake if you want to see snow on Sydney Harbour Bridge.

Frozen in the ice was a tiny baby.

Nobody spoke.

Nobody made a sound.

'Is this the eternal life you want?' repeated their mother.

I could tell from the faces of her ancient children it wasn't.

SPROCKET

NINE

My mother led Beanie, Scowler, and Reptile down to the crevasse. Hairy Chest hobbled behind using a branch for a crutch. The Tea Lady, Jimi Hendrix and the rest of the family were now over eighty years old but still able to walk. Their faces were lined and the skin hung loosely from their necks.

Amy, her parents, Purple Cloud and Con Rod stayed behind in the cabin. They seemed to know that what had to be done was a very private affair.

My family stared thoughtfully at our frozen father who was still wedged across the chasm in his ice coffin.

Mother spoke quietly. 'Your father has earned his rest,' she said. 'You hoped to bring him back from the dead. So that you could find the secret of eternal youth.'

'He would have given it to us too,' said Scowler.

'There's another secret,' said my mother. 'And it's this. The universe gives what it will. We should take what life offers and live it to the full. Without worrying about when it will end.'

I nodded but I didn't altogether agree. I didn't want her life to end for a long, long time.

'I don't want to be old,' said Scowler bitterly.

'You look fine,' said Mum. 'When you appeared young you were imposters. Now you have dignity. Now you are yourselves.'

The rest of them stayed silent. This wasn't the time for them to speak their minds. This was our father's moment and there was no place for quarrelling.

My mother held up a long steel bar that she had brought from the cabin. 'My dear husband, your father, deserves his rest,' she said. 'Who will give it to him?'

Mum began striking at the point where the ice coffin joined the edge of the crevasse. Bright glassy chips of ice flew through the air. After a bit she stopped and handed the bar to my sister Agnes, the Tea Lady. Agnes paused and then took it in her wrinkled hand. She began to chip at the ice.

Each member of the family stepped forward in turn. Some were sad. Some were not sure. But all of them took the bar and chipped at the point where the ice coffin touched the cliff. Finally it was held by only a thin wedge of ice.

My mother took the bar and handed it to me. I stared at the ice bridge that had saved our lives. 'Amy told me how your father saved you in the Cool Room,' she said. 'And on the river when you floated on his body. Now you can repay him by giving him the peace he deserves.'

I struggled with my feelings. Anger fought with pity and gratitude. When he was alive he'd gone and died on me. Left me in Pooper Scooper's terrible hands. But then, when he was dead he'd saved me several times. Once, right there, at that very ravine when I'd almost fallen to my death.

Mum was right. Father deserved his rest. He'd been dragged halfway across the state for the sake of a deadly secret. He was not coming back to life. That's the way it's always been. And always should be. You only get one go.

I struck the ice coffin once and it began to tremble.

Matchbox was whimpering. He was a very old dog now. And his master was about to leave him. The faithful dog gave one yap and leapt onto the coffin.

With an icy screech the block of ice fell into the chasm. Tumbling and turning it plunged towards its last resting place. The chasm was so deep that not a single sound escaped.

'Goodbye, dear husband,' said my mother.

'Farewell, Father and Matchbox,' I said quietly. 'And thanks.'

We turned and began to walk back up to the hut.

I was sad that my father and Matchbox had gone. And I knew deep down that my mother did not have long to live. I wondered what lay ahead.

Who would be there with me through all the long years to come? Through good times and bad. I looked up the hill and what I saw made my spirits rise.

It was a girl. Sharpening a Swiss Army knife on a stone.

She was chattering away happily to her mother.

And raving on about someone called Julie Spiros.

TEN

An hour later, Mum and Dad and I stood outside Mrs Sampson's cabin, enjoying the warmth coming through the open door and trying not to eavesdrop on Sprocket and his family who were sitting round the fire talking in low voices.

Mum, Dad and I had all agreed that family reunions should be private.

Theirs and ours.

I stared at the distant valley slopes shimmering white in the spring sun, and hoped that Con Rod and Purple Cloud were making good progress on their trek back to the train. Armed with Dad's spare

423

wheel-chains, they'd gone to fetch the mobile home to ferry Sprocket's family back to civilisation.

I felt Mum's hand on my cheek.

'Amy,' she said softly. 'Mrs Sampson was right. What's going to happen to these old folk isn't your fault.'

'I know,' I said, and I did.

'Keeping people alive for ever just isn't a good idea,' said Dad. 'Not for them or the planet or the op-shop industry. I wish I hadn't taken so long to realise that. I wish I'd thought it through before I spent five years of my life trying to germinate that plant. Thing was, when Sprocket's family first came to me and told me I was the only one who could keep them alive, I didn't know how to say no. Even though it meant deceiving the two people I love.'

I squeezed his hand to let him know that any dad who tries to keep people alive is OK with me.

'I was convinced you were having an affair,' said Mum. 'I wish you'd trusted us enough to tell us what you were doing.'

For a few awful seconds I thought they were going to have one of their arguments. But instead, Mum gave a thoughtful smile. Her eyes, still free of all stress lines, danced mischievously.

'Then again,' she said, 'I'm sort of glad you didn't.'

Dad, who'd been bracing himself for a fight, looked surprised, then relieved. Then, when Mum gave his hand a squeeze, surprised again.

But happy as well.

Later still, after Con Rod and Purple Cloud got back, and Mum and Dad were helping them and Sprocket cook up Purple Cloud's special stir-fried brown rice and dried seaweed for seventeen people, I quietly asked Mrs Sampson if I could have a private word.

I'd been putting off doing it for hours, because I was terrified.

But I couldn't put it off any longer.

'Mrs Sampson,' I said once we were outside in the afternoon sun, the golden snow crunching under our feet, 'there's something I need to ask you about the tea.'

'What is it, dear?' she said.

A spasm of fear went through my guts and I turned away and pretended to be staring up at the mountain slopes. They were glowing in the sunlight, except for one shadowy area which looked like a mouth open in anguish.

'When a person drinks too much tea at once,' I said in a shaky voice, 'and then it wears off and the person goes back to their right age, what happens then? Do they carry on getting old fast, or at the normal rate?'

Mrs Sampson was staring up at the shadowy area too.

'When I first came back here,' she said quietly, 'and stopped taking the tea, I didn't know.'

She sighed a long sad sigh, and I hoped she was thinking about her dead Germinator husband and about all the things that had happened since they first came to this valley eighty-two years ago. I hoped she wasn't thinking about how the answer to my question was 'they carry on getting old fast'.

She turned to me and put her hands on my shoulders.

'For my sake and the sake of your poor mother,' she said, smiling, 'I'm pleased to say the answer is at the normal rate.'

After we'd eaten, we packed up and headed down from the valley. Sprocket and his mother and the old folk travelled in the mobile home with Con Rod and Purple Cloud. I went in Dad's four-wheel-drive with Dad and Mum.

It was dark when we finally got to the deserted station where we'd first boarded the train.

We piled out of the vehicles, stretching and groaning, and the old folk hobbled off into the undergrowth to do wees.

Sprocket came over to me and Con Rod and Purple Cloud, his face serious in the moonlight.

'I've been thinking,' he said quietly, and I heard the emotion in his voice. 'I've decided to stay with my mother.'

I'd been dreading him saying that and yet I'd known he would and part of me was glad for him.

I told myself not to be selfish and gave him a big sad smile so he could see everything I was feeling.

'Sprocket's going to do correspondence school so he can help me with the old folk,' said Mrs Sampson, coming over. 'There's still enough skin-cream money for them to spend their last days somewhere warm and comfortable.'

'Surfers,' said Con Rod. 'You can't beat Surfers.'

Sprocket gave Purple Cloud a long hug. 'Sorry,' he said, his voice thick with feeling.

'Don't be,' whispered Purple Cloud. 'You're doing the right thing.'

'Thank you,' said Sprocket.

'Any time, my darling Sprocket,' said Purple Cloud tearfully. 'Any time.'

'You just say the word,' said Con Rod as he hugged Sprocket, 'and we'll be in Surfers the next day. Quicker if Weasel Dixon comes through with that turbo unit I've ordered.'

Mum and Dad came over, and Mum put her arms round Sprocket and gave him the longest hug of all.

'I enjoyed our time together, young man,' she said.

'M-me too,' stammered Sprocket.

I could see Dad was looking puzzled and a bit alarmed.

'I'll explain later,' I whispered to him.

Then it was time for me and Sprocket to say goodbye.

Before we could start saying anything, Sprocket's

mum took Con Rod and Purple Cloud over to check the oil in the antique Ford Falcons, and Mum and Dad wandered off.

I cleared my throat.

'I've never had a friend like you,' I said.

'Me neither,' said Sprocket.

We both knew that was all we needed to say, apart from a bit of stuff about keeping in touch.

We looked at each other for a long time. Then I realised Sprocket's face was moving closer to mine. I felt my veins start to pulse with little jabs of heat in the cool night air and I wished with every molecule of my body that I was two years older.

Out of the corner of my eye I saw two figures silhouetted against the full moon. They were in each other's arms, kissing.

For a second I thought I was seeing into the future.

Then I realised it wasn't me and Sprocket kissing, it was Mum and Dad.

. . . . .

Two years later . . .

SPROCKET

So, here we are, standing on the side of a beautiful mountain in early spring. Far off a kooka-burra is calling. And near by a koala slumbers in the fork of a gum tree. The sound of cicadas rubbing their wings in unison fills the air with a friendly buzz. A river snakes through the valley below.

Con Rod is here.

Purple Cloud is here.

And Barnabus, still wearing a beanie on his ancient head.

And Hilda, who even now, flicks her tongue like a reptile.

And Stanley, wearing a sad smile instead of a scowl.

My mother is here. And my mother is not here.

We are gathered around her open grave with the rest of my brothers and sisters.

It is just a small gathering of friends and

family. Agnes sniffles and wipes away a tear. She is very old but still her bossy Tea Lady self. 'Stand up straight,' she barks at Stanley, Barnabus and Hilda. Barnabus gives his nervous smile and tries to stiffen his bent and feeble back.

Stanley waves his walking-stick at her. 'Give us a break, you old battle-axe,' he says. 'This is a funeral, not a military parade.'

I can't help smiling to myself. My brothers and sisters seem grumpy. But they have good hearts. I have become very fond of them in the last two years. Barnabus in particular. I can talk him into anything – especially after I give his gnarled old feet a massage. He is like an easy-going old uncle to me.

Hilda wets her lips with her wrinkled, flicking tongue and stares at the Hummer which we had used to bring the wooden coffin to this remote and lonely hillside. She drove it here through rivers and tangled forests. She hasn't lost her touch despite her arthritis.

Purple Cloud hands everyone a small incense stick. Her hair is still decorated with little silver moons and stars. 'Lavender to give her wings,' she says.

Hubert steps forward. His hairy chest has long gone grey. He stands by the grave. He is the oldest and is entitled to speak first. 'She was a wonderful woman,' he says, choking back the tears. 'She gave birth to eleven children.'

'But she wouldn't let us have children,' says Stanley.

'Yes, she would,' says Barnabus. 'But only if we

gave up the tea. She said that if you refused to die you didn't have the right to bring new people into the world. There wouldn't be enough room if no one died. Remember?'

Hubert frowns at his younger brothers and strokes his long white beard. 'She grew wise,' he says. 'Unlike some I could mention.' He takes a deep breath. I can see he is trying not to break down.

Barnabus steps forward to say his bit. He gives Agnes a quick glance. Even now, he's still a nervous person. 'Mum never yelled at us,' he says. 'And never smacked us. Even when I put a frog in some cold tea and it went back to being a tadpole.'

He moves back to let three or four of the others speak. Finally it is my turn.

I stare down into the grave and speak to Mum as if she can hear me. I read a little speech that I have written especially for this occasion.

'You were a wonderful mother. OK, you were one hundred and three when I met you. But what a woman. I will never forget our two years together. Remember the time we went bungy jumping in New Zealand. And your false teeth fell into the river. And I dived in to get them and found thirteen pairs down there – none of them yours. Jeez, we laughed about that. And what about that time you went sky diving and every person in the plane was too scared to jump except you?

'Way to go, Mum. Way to go.

'You really tried to make it up to me for all the lonely times I had in foster homes. Taking me sailing. Going with me to movies. Teaching me mountain climbing. You were gentle and patient. An older parent is a terrific parent. You were wise, kind and loving. And you cared about people. And nature.

'When I hear a bird sing I will think of your free spirit. When I hear a stream burble I will remember your laugh. When I feel the wind in my hair I will feel your touch on my skin.

'And when I am old I will try to be like you.

'Who knew that eternal youth is really eternal death.

'But . . .

'A life well lived leaves a mark for ever.'

I lean over and throw my incense stick into the grave. The others silently do the same. Con Rod runs a hand over his shaved head and starts to sing an old Elvis number called 'Jailhouse Rock'.

'To symbolise her freedom from earthly chains,' explains Purple Cloud. I wonder if she is remembering the loss of her own son.

We walk slowly and quietly down the hillside.

My mother is gone. Two years has not been long. But when it comes to losing your mother is there ever a right time for her to leave?

I have to face it and move on.

'Where are ya going to live now, mate?' says Con Rod.

434

I look at his new mobile home floating on the river below. It has an enormous guitar welded onto the top. 'I'd like to live in there,' I say. 'With the two most wonderful people in the world.'

I put my arm around Purple Cloud's shoulders. She starts to smile and cry at the same time. It reminds me of the sun shining through a shower. The promise of good things to come.

I am upset that Amy and her parents have not showed up. No one knows where they are.

'Somewhere in New Guinea,' says Con Rod. 'Looking for rare plants. I sent 'em an email but no response. No computers in the jungle, I guess.'

'Amy would have come if she could,' I say.

Con Rod jumps aboard and starts up the motor with pride. 'Small block Chevy,' he says. 'Powerful and light.' He slips the motor home into gear and starts to move off.

'Wait,' I yell. 'Stop.'

I jump ashore. There is someone standing under a tree at the edge of the small clearing where we buried Mum. Someone I recognise.

'Mrs Tunks-Livingstone,' I gasp.

It is, too. Just standing there. Still sweet sixteen like before. Wearing green lipstick and a tank top. She even has the diamond in her navel. My head starts to spin. Has she found a secret supply of tea? Has she made herself young again? Just for me?

The guilty desires suddenly return. I am hopelessly

435

confused. She is a married woman even if she does look sixteen.

Jeez, she is beautiful. Perhaps even more beautiful than the last time I saw her. Those soft lips. Oh, man. What can I do? How can I resist her?

I start to run towards her, my heart pounding even louder than my feet.

'Mrs Tunks-Livingstone,' I cry.

AMY

It's hard to stay in touch for two long years, specially when you've got a dad who drags you through half the jungles in South-East Asia.

The things a girl does to stay out of boarding school.

But just because you lose touch with someone, doesn't mean you don't think of them.

I've thought of Sprocket heaps. I think of him when I'm doing correspondence school assignments and I have to write an essay about loyalty or bravery or compassion or people who do blue farts.

I think of him when Mum tells Dad stories of her happy childhood, the one she had with me. I think of him when something exciting or unusual happens, like the time at one of Mum's archeological sites when Dad discovered an exotic new plant that looked a bit like the tea plant.

Most of all, though, I thought of him last week when the email arrived from Purple Cloud telling me his mother had died.

I showed the email to Mum and Dad. Mum got a funny faraway look on her face. For a while I wondered what was going on. Then Mum explained she was trying to work out if we had enough money for an air ticket back to Australia for the funeral.

We did.

More and more these days, when I think of Sprocket, I think about kissing him. I might do it soon, if he stops gawking at me with that dopey confused expression.

What's the matter, hasn't he ever seen a girl waiting for him at a funeral in her mum's old clothes?

About the authors

MORRIS GLEITZMAN grew up in England and came to
Australia when he was sixteen. He was a frozen-chicken
thawer, sugar-mill rolling-stock unhooker, fashion-industry
trainee, student, department-store Santa, TV producer,
newspaper columnist and screenwriter. Then he wrote a
novel for young people. Now he's one of Australia's most
popular children's authors.

Visit Morris at his website
www.morrisgleitzman.com

PAUL JENNINGS is a phenomenon in the world of children's
books. His spooky, funny, naughty stories always have a
surprise ending, and are devoured by readers of all ages.
He has written over one hundred stories, and sales of his
books exceed 6.5 million copies. For his services to
children's literature, Paul was awarded the Dromkeen
Medal and made a Member of the Order of Australia.

Visit Paul at his website
www.pauljennings.com.au